THE LEGEND OF
BLACK JACK

A. R. WITHAM

Nepenthe House

Cover & Completed Art by Ryan Wing
Illustrations by James Turner Mohan
Map & Minor Illustrations by A. R. Witham

Printed by Kindle Direct Publishing
First Printing Edition 2022 in United States

arwitham.com

For Gloria,
Who Believes.

And Will,
Who Loves.

TABLE OF CONTENTS

The Wastelands
Werrun Fell
Benjamin's Map
(Amended by Jack Swift)
The Jutts
The Elder
Broken Pass
Paladine Arch
Tucumcari
Citadel Akkadian
Deuce Lake
Glyn Aker
Jaden Fields
Highyon Garde
Caer Tajiki
The Breechline
The Madrigal Verde
Highway of the Nomads
Eynrys Plains
Ruk Al-Satyr Wall
Pipen Gulf
Tower Yongshi
Falikos
Llykowen Swamps
The Irridin
Rimmy's Cull

They say he was an outsider. A man with no home, no family, no friend to call his own. The man with nothing left to love. The empty man.

You have heard his name. The face behind the mask is familiar, and you know his blue eyes.

He smells like sand and water and blood.

They say he traveled between worlds. They say he talked to animals. They say he killed a god, and they might be right. He prowled the border between light and dark. He beat the devil himself with a walking stick. He healed a thousand people in a day and killed a dragon that midnight.

Some old men still believe that story. Some old men were there.

Poor folk love him most. No one remembers how many he fed, protected, and kept alive during the Black Accord, but they will never forget his name in Glyn Aker. They remember he saved their children from starving to death. They remember he smuggled in blankets and coats and food. Some remember his real name.

They say there was a woman. They say he died for her. No one knows the truth.

All songs fade in time, but for a thousand years, this one, the simplest one, remained:

> *Ol' Black Jack, the man with the knack*
> *Stole the people their money back.*
> *One quick flick of his walking stick*
> *He fed the poor and healed the sick.*
>
> *Black devils fear his cunning spear*
> *He'll cut them down and disappear.*
> *So play us fair or just beware:*
> *There's nothing ol' Jack wouldn't dare.*

Those are the legends about him.

If you want to know the truth, I will tell you.

THE STRANGE MEMORY OF JACK SWIFT

*It takes courage to grow up and become
who you really are.*

E. E. Cummings

A boy is best seen through his father's eyes. He is beautiful, and seven.

Sun-kissed hair lashes in the wind, crazy freckles splay across that baby nose, skinny legs pound across the desert like the whole world is an obstacle course created just for him. That's what Dr. Alex Swift sees as he comes up over the ridge: his son.

Unaware his father watches, the boy skids into a hiding place behind a dead tree, his skin red from the sand and sun of the blazing Badlands. He wears his Chicago Bears T-shirt (a favorite this summer) and carries a stick that has more uses than a Swiss Army knife: bow, rifle, sword, and spear.

Near the hiding place, three big rocks are stacked atop each other like a stone snowman. At the peak sits a rubber bouncy ball, a blocky RAWLINGS logo on one side. On the other side is drawn the leering face of a mustachioed bandito.

The boy readies his weapon.

Dr. Alex Swift smiles. This is not truly his son. This is Chief Raging Bull, buffalo killer, and terror of the high plains. The bouncy-ball man is Dirty Bill Cody, murderer of exactly three gazillion fellow Sioux. They are mortal enemies.

The boy leaps into action, shooting, stabbing, and punching a dozen invisible assassins. "Your time has come, Dirty Bill!" shouts Chief Raging Bull, his voice higher than one might imagine. He stares down the stone snowman, an unblinking nemesis. "Dead or alive, you're coming with me."

Dirty Bill does not speak. His crimson head bobbles uncertainly in the breeze, his painted-on mustache locked in a dismissive sneer.

Raging Bull grips his shirt between his thumb and forefinger, revealing his US marshal's badge. (At least Dr. Swift assumes it is a badge. It is, in fact, a little plastic button that says, I GOT IT HOT AT THE CIRCLE B! over a cartoon of a winking pig with an apple in its mouth.) "Your choice, Bill," growls the high voice. "You can go back to Rapid City peaceful-like…or I can chop your head off." The very useful stick has become a tomahawk. "Which is it gonna be?"

It can only be assumed Dirty Bill begins firing. The Indian chief, too fast for mere bullets, dodges them all and leaps up on a rock, crying, "Say goodbye, Bill!" and jumps down hard.

Dr. Swift notices the wooden plank—the kind they use to keep their weight off the archeological dig—waiting below. The boy's sneakers strike the far end of the seesaw, and Dirty Bill's head pops clean off.

The boy hurls the tomahawk. The shot misses, whirling by just beneath the villain, clattering to the Badlands dirt. Bill's rubber head strikes the ground, bounces at a crazy angle, then *pang-a-pang-pangs* against two rocks with a rubbery enthusiasm.

"Wait, let me do it again," says the chief to absolutely no one, sprinting for the tomahawk. Dr. Swift checks the horizon. The sky has gone yellow purple, as it does when the desert is ready to abandon the day.

"Jack?"

The boy's head pops up from behind a rock. "Yeah?"

"Six o'clock."

"Yeah!" Jack runs back to Bill's body, carrying the head.

"Let's go."

"I have to chop off his head and hit it."

Dr. Alex Swift stretches, clasps his hands together, and raises them over his head, arching his back. It's been a long day down at the dig. "Are you an Indian chief or a US marshal?"

"Both."

"Ah."

Jack Swift glances up and sees his dad standing on the ridge above him.

A father is best seen through the eyes of his boy.

It's a good face, a rugged face, the face of a man who has spent his life in the sun, wrinkled and cracked in all the right places. The desert wind is kicking up, and Dad's lean frame is made leaner by the clothes blown tight to his skin. His red hair is cut bristle short—that's new—and Jack can just make out the white of the scar above Dad's eye.

It is an old scar. The family had been climbing Mount Katahdin in Maine. Jack's father had gone out too far on a ledge to shoot a picture of the sunset against the pines. The rock beneath him crumbled suddenly, and he fell, snapping the picture as he went. He whacked into the upper boughs of a pine tree, caught a limb, and bashed his forehead into the tree. It ripped a bloody cut above Dr. Swift's eye, an arcing scar that would never fully disappear. He had climbed down the rest of the tree, reassuring his wife and five-year-old son—thirty feet above—that he was all right. Later they found he had broken his arm and simply had too much adrenaline pumping through his system to notice. The photograph came out in a dazzling spectacle of orange, red, and yellow that looked as if the sun were sprinting through the trees. Dad displayed the shot framed in the living room. Every time someone would ask about it, he would shrug and say, "Just shows what you can do with a good camera."

It was an old scar. From back when Mom was alive.

Jack sets the trap again, knowing Dad will let him finish.

Dad pulls his phone from his pocket. "While you're chopping off his head, do you want dinner?"

"Can we get fried pork tenderloin sandwiches?"

"From Stearns?"

"Yes?"

"They're slow."

"Please?"

Dad shrugs, stretching his back again. "Number?"

"802-775-1141."

Dad dials in the dinner order from the middle of the Badlands. Jack picks up the stick—the tomahawk—and prepares to spring the lever trap again. He hears Dad say, "Hi, there. I'd like to place an order for delivery. Dr. Swift. Yes. We're out at the site."

Jack stomps on the big plank, rocketing the rubber ball

straight up into the sky. This time, the Indian chief's aim is true. Stick and ball collide with a surprisingly unsatisfying *thwonk* and separate at crazy angles. Jack hears the loud bounce as the ball ricochets down the rocks until it is gone, gone, gone. Gone, too, is Chief Raging Bull.

The boy sighs. For the rest of the day, he's not a hero, not a warrior, not an Indian chief or a US marshal. For the rest of the day, he's just Jack.

"Pork tenderloin sandwich and a club sandwich," says Dad. "No chips. Water. Yep, that's all. Mastercard." He waits a second. "Again?" Jack breaks the stick over his knee. Dad covers the mouth of the phone. "Register's out again."

"You want me to do the thing?" Dad tosses him the phone; Jack puts it to his ear. "Hi? Yeah. It's $21.42." Jack climbs up the sandstone embankment toward his dad. "Well, it's $6.75 for the pork tenderloin plus $5.75 for the club, a buck each for the waters, which is $14.50 plus 4.5% South Dakota sales tax, which is 65 cents plus a 15% tip, which is 2.27 plus four dollars delivery fee." He takes a breath. "$21.42." He listens. "Yeah, you can get a piece of paper."

Dad extends his hand and pulls him up. They smile, father and son. It's an old game for them. For most people, compound math is the most confounding thing when they hear it coming from the mouth of a seven-year-old kid…it's like watching a dog talk.

"Mastercard," says Jack, then recites the number.

Dad squints at him. "You memorized my credit card?"

"Isn't that how you want to pay?"

"Yes. Just be careful with that, Jack."

The boy nods, his big blue eyes innocent.

They walk. The wind kicks up, the sun moves down. Two silhouettes stride together toward the setting shimmer. The father and the boy move side by side in the Badlands wind. Storm's coming in. Lightning strikes somewhere out over the desert. No thunder. Not close.

Not yet.

They are nearing the end of their time in South Dakota. The dig has gone well, they've gotten their Indian artifacts and Cretaceous dinosaur skeletons, the interns are energized, and the Gruengartner Museum seems satisfied with the investment. They are not far from the Stronghold Table of the Oglala Sioux, and Dr. Swift has found a few additional late-seventeenth-century Indian artifacts that no doubt will add to his standing in the archaeological community, but that is nothing new.

Alex Swift is a digger, and a good one. His knack for finding hidden treasures borders on the supernatural. He always knows where to look, where to dig, where to find. Once, he told Jack it was simply a matter of following the lay of the land, of getting inside the era he was researching, to follow it along the slope of a hill, through the run of a riverbed, along the outskirts of a forest. The only problem was that the hill, the river, and the forest had disappeared into the memory of another age. But Alex Swift can sense their affect hundreds, even thousands, of years later. To Jack, it seems his father follows an invisible map only he can see.

Dad speaks. Jack replies. Another game.

"Eleven."

"Sodium."

"Twenty-five."

"Manganese."

"Forty-two."

"Molybdenum."

"A hundred and eighteen."

"Oganesson."

"Seriously?"

"Yes."

"There's an element called oganesson?"

"You didn't know that?"

"No. After manganese, I was just saying numbers."

Jack laughs. "It only goes to one eighteen. After that, it's all theoretical."

"What?"

"No one knows what comes after a hundred eighteen. The missing element."

Jack was thirteen months old by the time he knew all his numbers, fifteen for all his letters, and just before his second birthday, he recited Beatrix Potter's *Peter Rabbit* aloud, verbatim. Shortly after, he was reading three- and four-letter words, and after that, it was just an all-you-can-eat buffet of what-can-you-teach-me-next. The kid devoured information like the cat that found the cream. Jack's strange memory had never been an actual problem—not really—but it had been the source of several hushed conversations between Dr. and Mrs. Swift in the early days. The doctors assured them it was fine—not normal, mind you—but fine. Doctors called him eidetic. Most people said Jack had a photographic memory, but that was a misnomer. (When you think of your mother, you don't just picture her face; you remember a million little things about her, the way she moves her shoulders, the touch of her fingers, a favorite shirt and the way it smells. Not just images but thoughts.) Jack's memories weren't photographs, they were just thoughts that stuck. Mrs. Swift had made games of it, using flash cards, pictures, anything she could to see how far it could go. At one point, she hid an entire pack of Bicycle playing cards all over the house, let Jack find them during the day (in the cupboard, in the dresser, under the sink) and took them back as he found them. At dinner, she asked which cards were missing. Of course he knew: the black jacks.

"The missing element." Dr. Swift smiles. "Maybe you'll discover that one."

The boy rubs his arms inside his Bears T-shirt. The storm is still away, but not what Mom used to call *way-away.* "I'm cold. How long 'til sunset?"

"You can see on your hands." Off the boy's puzzled look, the father leans in and places Jack's hand palm toward the sun, blocking out the Badlands horizon. "Start at the horizon. Go up one hour per palm until you reach the sun, see? One..." He moves Jack's hand up little by little until it touches the sun. "About two palms high. Call it ninety minutes. Your hands are small."

"That's cool."

"Where's your ball?"

Jack stops.

"I...I forgot it."

He winces. Even a photographic memory is no match for a seven-year-old's capacity to forget his toys. Jack knows what's coming next. He's heard it enough times.

"What do we say to the in—"

Before Dad can complete the word *interns*, Jack blurts out: "Take only photographs, leave only memories. I know, I'm sorry, can we get it later, I want dinner please, I'm sorry."

Even as Jack's voice rises into a whine, he finds himself being led by the hand back toward the scene of the crime, back toward Dirty Bill's decapitated body.

They climb down into the rocks, searching. Jack doesn't look too hard; his dad will find it. He always does.

Jack wanders.

There are some cool rocks over to the right, down this little edge and down this little jump, and there is a little overhang here that would be cool to climb under and this little gulley that looks like it goes into the side of the mountain, and right at the bottom, there it is: the little rubber ball, the sneering face of Dirty Bill and something else.

"Hey?"

"Hey?" comes his dad's echo, somewhere up and left.

"There's a hole down here."

Dr. Swift lowers himself down into the stone crack beside his son, chimneying down from above with his back against one rock, his feet on the other. "Put the ball in your pack." Jack obliges as Dad pops the mini Maglite between his teeth and shoves himself headfirst into the hole like a mongoose plunging into a cobra den. His shoulders and arms disappear first, then his chest, then his legs.

Jack waits, digging in his pocket for a half-eaten stick of Slim Jim.

"Hey?" comes Dad's voice.

"Hey?" says Jack.

"It opens up. Come on in."

Jack sighs. He doesn't like dirt as much as his dad. "Okay," he says, and crawls into the dark.

The Maglite's LED is cold and blue. It takes Jack a moment to get used to the new light after the dying-sun-yellow sandstone of the Badlands. Dad is already at the next crack, working his way through. "Do you see down there, where the gully was? And the way the rock has come together here? This wasn't always filled in." Jack shrugs. Dad disappears again, this time jamming his body under a rock into a space that would make a spelunker hesitate. His boots kick at the sand until he makes it through.

"You coming?"

Jack looks wistfully back toward the sunlight, thinking of pork tenderloin sandwiches. "Can we just go?"

"Jack, come see this."

It is a hallway. Not a crevice or a narrow, not a natural formation, but a hallway. Smooth rock at right angles. As Jack climbs through the hole, he can just make out what look like Paleolithic markings, something like the Chumash cave drawings, but they are a thousand miles on the wrong side of America for Chumash. This is Sioux territory. This is something new.

Dr. Swift has done it again.

Dad's Zippo flares up. He lights one of the camper candles he keeps in some pocket and sets it near the hole they just entered. A marker. Dad has that grin on his face, the one he gets just before everything goes crazy. Just before he did things that got him a scar on his face. "Watcha say, Chief? Wanna go look?"

Seven-year-old Jack Swift worries about getting trapped beyond the light. Chief Raging Bull wants to see what is in the dark. And it is better to be a Sioux brave. He offers his hand.

They move through half-buried halls, Dad scanning the stone with his light. There are two-century-old wooden torches in the walls; some of them look rickety enough to crumble at a touch. Jack stays in his father's footsteps. He knows the rules on digs, even though he has never been part of an actual discovery before. No touching.

Not yet.

They come around a corner. Dad stops. He sniffs the air, turns to face the wall. His fingers dust the stone, feeling it, rough hands searching for something. "Step back, son."

Chief Raging Bull draws back against the wall. Dad heaves his shoulder against the stone. There is a creak, a crack, and a shower of dust as the dim outlines of rectangular shapes appear in the rock. Quickly, carefully, Dad dislodges the bricks, pulling them out and setting them to the side. He gestures for his son to come. Holding his hands tight to his chest, Jack comes.

There is a black hole leading into the dark. "What do you think's in there, Chief?"

"Big heap trouble," Chief Raging Bull replies gruffly. "Great Spirit say bad juju in there."

"Well, I guess I better go first and protect the chief. Stay here." Dad ruffles Jack's hair for the last time and steps into the tunnel. The boy watches his father's silhouette disappear into the unknown, moving farther and farther away. Dad reaches a corner, turns, and is gone.

The great chief waits, anticipating his scout's return, but his heart takes less than no time at all to turn restless. The smell down here is strange. It doesn't smell like rock, or not just rock.

There's something else, like sandalwood and leather. And it's dry—dry like a hundred years of sand. He doesn't like being down here, he tells himself, but that's a lie. What he doesn't like is being told to stay. He wants to follow. The curiosity at what Dad has found wends its way into Jack's mind.

He steps forward into the dark.

There are weapons. Spears, war clubs, tomahawks (*real ones!*), ancient bows, some still bent on dusty strings, all right here, decaying on an ancient wooden table to his right. There are shields too—tough buffalo-skin circles made of wood and strapped leather with intricate designs painted on the front. Jack looks at them with naked envy. He knows the first rule. Even the chipped and battered clay pots are extremely valuable, and Jack can only imagine what this unexpected trove of artifacts is worth. It was the first rule. *They're not yours.*

Chief Raging Bull does not care. The weapons belong to him, to his people, and he will take what he wants.

Jack's little fingers reach out for the shaft of a Sioux tomahawk. He grips it. The dust feels gritty and hard in his hands, like fine silt from the dark bottom of a pond taken out into the sunlight to bake dry. He lifts it from the table, feeling that heady thrill of excitement that comes with a real weapon.

Then he sees the snake.

It is completely white. A frosty pale color runs the entire length of the seven-foot albino as if the thing has been dipped in the wicked milk of some salty shaman's poison to bring it back from the dead. Pink pitiless eyes stare up at him as it coils silently into an aggressive posture, displaying the inside of its pink mouth, baring needle teeth.

Jack's seven-year-old mind screams panic. His left brain, the logical half, the smart half that keeps all the facts and figures like so many organized folios in a library, coolly notes that the bull snake isn't poisonous and can't possibly do him any real harm. His right brain trumpets: *Monster! I'm going to die! It's going to kill me! Run! Kill it, run, smash it kill it kill it KILL IT!*

There is a moment, a very short moment, when things can change, when Jack can bring his fear under control, when he can calm himself, stop himself from what he is about to do. But he is seven, and there are lessons even a good father cannot teach.

Jack strikes hard and fast with the tomahawk, missing the snake entirely. The table smashes in half, breaking the cave's silence with an earsplitting crack. The wood breaks; the weapons clatter to the earth in a cacophony of metal, wood, and rock; and everything begins to happen very, very quickly.

Ahead, where his father had gone, there is a shout and the sudden crack of stone. The rumble that follows is terrifying and fills the world. The ground comes to life. Dust falls from the ceiling like a cloud. Bits of stone clatter around his feet. Something big jerks sideways.

Jack drops the tomahawk, horrified at what he has done.

"Dad?" he shouts into the tunnel. There is no response from his father, but another crack, this one like the sharp bark of an animal, and the entire cave bends sideways before his eyes. One of the stones above him falls; a literal ton of rock collapses not five feet ahead. He scrambles backward away from the weapons, away from the snake, away from his dad. Jack thinks he hears something then, from down in the dark, something that sounds like his father's voice.

"Daddy?"

The cave-in happens all at once. If Jack were slower, he would be caught beneath it, crushed under the black earth of the Badlands, but his legs kick out at the final, terrible crushing sound, and throw his body back into the hall as a hundred thousand tons of rock flood the tunnel, obliterating everything beneath it in a tidal wave of stone.

Jack cries out for his father, attacking the rocks, yelling for his daddy, trying to reach him, trying to bring him back, sobbing hot tears and screaming.

That is how they find him, seventeen hours later, his fingers scratched and bloody, still trying to reach the place his father has gone.

13

We know what we are, but not what
we may be.

William Shakespeare

Alfred Pitankin, curator of the Gruengartner Museum, performed the eulogy. There was no one else to do it—there was no family. Pitankin, a narrow, precise buttoned-up little man, delivered the script with short, clipped sentences in the manner of an accountant. He used words like *honor*, *dignity*, and *service*, but the words felt less like a funeral and more like a boss bidding goodbye to a faithful worker who had elected to retire.

There was no body, of course. It would forever remain interred in South Dakota—the tomb of Dr. Alex Swift—and it made no sense to drag the few museum personnel out there, not with the expense of airline tickets and hotel rooms. More than a hundred of the museum staff were in attendance, along with several interns from the Badlands dig who traveled to Chicago on their own dime. Pitankin adjusted his glasses as he spoke, clearing his throat regularly.

Dozens of flowers covered the coffin. Atop it sat a picture of a man, but to Jack, it wasn't his father. The photograph was taken before the trip to Maine, and there was no scar. Jack sat in the front row in his little black suit, his hair combed by some matron, staring at his father's coffin.

A few of Dr. Swift's friends spoke, speaking of his kindness and dedication. Alfred Pitankin closed the ceremony by announcing a plaque would be erected to Dr. Swift on the site of the tragedy and requested donations for his young son, Jack Swift, "the survivor of the horrible incident." Then it was over. The audience—it was too kind to call all of them mourners— filed out of the auditorium. They looked at Jack with an expression that he had never seen before but soon recognized as pity.

The interns from the dig and attendants from the museum reassured the seven-year-old boy in cooing tones that he had been incredibly brave, that it wasn't his fault, never his fault

(of course it wasn't, of course it wasn't)

while dropping money into a Lucite box. They raised several

hundred dollars, telling themselves that money would be enough. Only Jack and Pitankin stayed to watch the empty coffin escorted from the room, and, with it, went the Indian chief who had, three days before, been his son.

That night, Jack woke up screaming

(of course it was, of course it was)

for his father.

Arrangements were made for Jack's care. A professor at the university offered his home, then backed out. A kindly spinster did the same, forgetting her niece was coming home that summer. Pitankin, ostensibly in charge of the boy, kept Jack in a well-furnished guest room of his stately home, but Pitankin was a confirmed bachelor, and wanted no part of a child. There was a second drive for money, but most patrons had just given to the "Gruengreen" fundraising event, and the results were less than adequate. Pitankin searched for more family. There was a distant cousin Swift in Ireland, but the woman was seventy-three and institutionalized. The buttoned-up little man grew restless, never quite unkind exactly, but his naturally terse manner became altogether brusque.

Jack hid himself in books. There were plenty in Pitankin's house. There was an actual *Encyclopedia Britannica* (Jack had never seen a four-foot-long book before), and he lost himself reading. The boy was left alone; school was not in session, and Pitankin only joined him at breakfast and dinner.

Soon enough, Jack was reading sixteen hours a day.

The encyclopedia took three weeks. He was on to the *World Atlas* when Pitankin said Jack was going to be placed into foster care at the end of the month. Jack covered the works of Robert Louis Stevenson, a compendium of N. C. Wyeth illustrations, and a text on advanced arithmetic by the Thursday they came to pick him up.

His first foster parent was Fritz Silag, a short man with a bum hip. Over the first few months, Jack got the idea that one of the old biddies at the Grunegartner had talked Fritz into the job. Retired, he had been an engineer by trade and had two hobbies: collecting *National Geographics* and restoring old motorcycle engines. Fritz tried to interest the boy with the engines. Jack read the source material on internal combustion and electronics but had no interest in the actual machine, or in Fritz. After their third trip to the repair shop, Jack closed the door of his room and went to work on the *National Geographics*.

It was during this time that Fritz's neighbor, Dr. Richards, discovered Jack. Richards was a thoracic surgeon at Rush University Medical Center and met Jack when the boy wandered over to his house looking to borrow some bread for a sandwich. When Jack spotted a medical journal lying beside the kitchen sink, he told Richards he had read one of the articles. Richards laughed. Then, through a mouthful of peanut butter, the boy asked, "Does the ulnar nerve serve any other muscles than the flexor carpi ulnaris and the flexor digitorum profundus?"

Richards took Jack under his wing. By the boy's eighth birthday, the two had become…well, not friends, but an affable mentor and student. Soon enough, Jack's frequent requests to watch the surgeon operate were granted, and Jack was allowed to sit in on his first procedure. Worried the boy would become faint at the sight of blood, Richards told Jack that surgery was just like carpentry: once the patient was asleep, cutting into them was no more painful than cutting into a block of wood. At the moment the initial incision was made, Jack nearly fell off the stool (it was *invasive* to cut into someone like that) but forced himself to remain upright for the chance to see a surgeon at work. Jack Swift discovered his first and only love: medicine.

Fascinated by the physiological makeup of God's greatest creation, Jack memorized every part of the human body, its location, appearance, and function. He poured through biology textbooks. The school advanced him a grade. When he was nine, he attended a junior-high biology class and got to dissect a fetal pig. While most of the girls (and some of the tougher guys) cringed at the "disgusting" idea of dissecting a pickled piglet, Jack requested not to have a lab partner so he could examine the body by himself. Most of his classmates considered his obsession with dead bodies revolting, or to use Kitty Keller's phrase: "just plain icky." Jack didn't mind the revulsion.

He was, in fact, delighted they thought of him at all.

Dr. Richards had no wife or children. Mr. Silag never married. There were no other kids in the neighborhood. And so the typical soccer matches and touch-football games of youth were replaced with *The Decline and Fall of the Roman Empire* and Homer's *Iliad*. Jack read *Pocket Medicine: The Massachusetts General Hospital Handbook of Internal Medicine* and the Brothers Grimm. By the time he was ten years old, Jack spent his time so interchangeably between Mr. Silag's and Dr. Richards's houses that neither man ever knew exactly where the boy was at any given moment. Once he realized this, Jack spent most of his time at the library. He stuffed his brain with information, jamming it down into his endless memory's gullet as if he were trying to choke it, flood it, break it. He just kept piling new memories on top of the old one

(the one waaay down there, the one where you kill your father)

but the nightmare always played out the same way.

It never changed, every detail, every design, every crack on every stone in blazing Technicolor. The rocks cracked. Then barked. Then fell. Jack had seen the scene so many times, he knew the design on the third deerskin drum, the pattern on the rug under the weapons table, the number of scales on the snake.

He read, throwing more dirt on the grave.

By the time he was twelve years old, Jack was a freshman in high school. If he took an extra course load each summer, Dr. Richards predicted Jack would enter college by the time he was fourteen and make his first year of med school by his eighteenth birthday.

If only Mr. Silag had stayed.

There was a cousin in Arkansas. She had broken her hip (an apparently fatal flaw in the Silag family), and Fritz was on his way to assist with her convalescence. Jack coming was out of the question—the cousin would not abide a child during her recovery, which was expected to be lengthy. Fritz promised Jack he would come back within the year, but that never happened. Jack was moved on to another foster home, and never saw Fritz or Dr. Richards ever again.

His second foster parent was a very pretty television reporter from the Chicago Fox station who liked the notion of raising a kid. The notion lasted five months before she realized she had been completely and utterly wrong. Jack was passed on.

The homes became kind of a blur after that, averaging one every three months, each one a temporary solution. Jack remembered every face, every name, but they all felt like the same person. He thought of them more as subjects based on the books in their houses: the computer manual place, the history of sports statistics, the plethora of cowboy novels, and so on. Finally, he landed a permanent home in an apartment building on the south side of Chicago with a woman named Rose Haig.

Jack realized how far he had fallen.

Rose Haig had fourteen foster children on loan from the state of Illinois. She collected them in the third-story ghetto down where the city became a sketchy blend of gangs and low-grade drug dealers. The smack wasn't on every street corner, but the power lines between buildings were a maze of hanging shoes indicating territory and trade locations. The apartment had four rooms, one for Rose, three for the fourteen children. No inspector ever came inquiring about the 4.3 children per room. For her troubles, Rose Haig received monthly from the state of Illinois between $408 and $613 per head, not one penny of which, Jack discovered, was spent on the children.

She ate. Burgers, pizza, Chinese egg rolls, Buffalo wings—if it was golden brown or covered in sauce, she gobbled it down. The healthiest thing she consumed was the precooked roasted chicken from the supermercado, but she would eat three of them.

Her belly spilled out on both sides of her waistband. Fat bulged below, between, and above her bra straps. It was incredible what she packed away, and how much of it came wrapped in plastic. The rest came in aluminum cans marked MILLER HIGH LIFE.

So many cans.

Like the rest of the children, Jack spent most of his time gone. His refuge of choice was (of course) the school library, which, while less well equipped than the public library seventeen blocks away, smelled less pungently of urine. One of the teachers at the school noticed Jack looked a bit young to be in his class and found out the boy's age. Jack was moved back to the seventh grade when the polyester-clad principal decided she didn't want the liability of a younger boy mixing with older ones. None of the teachers took much of an interest in him. They had learned not to get too attached to the foster food-stamp kids that floated in and out of their doors. The best the teachers could do was to keep the kids off the street from 7:25 to 3:10 every weekday. After that, the little snot-weasels were on their own.

During the first summer, Jack scrubbed trash cans at Carozelli's Deli and dug the garbage out from between the dumpsters every day for a few dollars and a meal (half a sandwich on good days...on bad ones, a pickle). Every weekend, Jack walked as far as necessary to every used bookstore, library sidewalk sale, or scholastic supply clearance he could find, carefully counting his dollars and looking over each book like a lifelong investment.

On July 1, Jack set about on a construction project. Carozelli let him take home two cinder blocks and a plank of wood. Jack found matching foot-wide spindles in the alley behind the electrical supply shop. He got the final plank from a guy at the Home Depot in trade for one of Carozelli's sandwiches. By Independence Day, Jack Swift had constructed the only thing he really needed: a bookshelf.

The top two rows were stacked with periodicals with names like *Annals of Internal Medicine*, the *American Journal of*

Respiratory and Critical Care Medicine, and *Clinical Infectious Diseases.* There were dozens of them, most beyond the comprehension of an average undergrad. All were well used; most were missing their covers. Every aspect of the human body and its workings were accounted for, down to the smallest tendon.

Noticeably missing from his medical menagerie was any hint of literature on psychology. Jack Swift had no interest in why the human brain thought as it did, but in how. To most, the difference was insignificant, but to Jack, it was as clear as the separation between sensible architecture and the myth of a haunted house. Jack Swift had no use for psychology or ghosts. He had enough monsters of his own.

The third shelf was stacked with hardbacks, the real sum and substance of the medical world: Braunwald's *Atlas of Internal Medicine, The Merck Manual,* and the Mecca of medicine, the *Physicians' Desk Reference.* The top two shelves would have collapsed under the weight of these many books; these were essentially on the floor, with a strip of plywood between them and the dingy carpet. Jack read each page a dozen times, devouring the words and pictures that were already tattooed on the inside of his skull. If Kitty Keller had known this, her opinion of the boy would have gone from icky to insane.

As Jack Swift went through books, Rose Haig went through men. They called him *sport* or *kid,* and one gentleman in possession of only eight of his fingers called all the boys *sluggo.* Regular as clockwork, Jack would come home to another daddy, usually propped up in the kitchen with a lit cigarette and a beer. Over time, the men became worse. Loudmouths became drunks. Drunks became addicts. They neglected him in the beginning, beat him in the middle, and in the end, they beat her.

The kids began leaving, moved to other foster homes. Jack petitioned his social worker to be transferred anywhere, but there was trouble with his case number. In the end, he was the only one left. Six were fostered out, the other seven just disappeared for good. The men were gone. So was the money.

And Rose Haig set about the steady business of drinking herself to death.

Wood struck flesh and bone in a thunderclap of sound that ran the length of the kitchen. "Do the dishes now, ya skinny runt, and the floor when yer done wit' that!"

Gripping the back of his head in pain, Jack kept his mouth shut. He had learned that trick long ago. He moved to collect the mop, and her foot slammed into his back. "The dishes first!" She towered above him like some angry pagan god, wielding the rolling pin in one heavy ham hand.

Jack went to the sink in a half crouch. There was blood on the back of his head. He silently wiped it away. Tepid water pulsed from the rusty faucet, whisking his blood down the drain in a whirlpool of gore. He gingerly reached for a cracked and stained dish—one of their better ones—and scrubbed, not daring to look around.

A missile of glass exploded beside him as a bottle struck the cabinet. Jack closed his eyes, expecting another blow. It didn't come. Behind him, he heard the low scrape of another liquor bottle dragged across the makeshift table, then the crunching of her slippered feet on shards of broken glass, moving toward her bedroom.

Jack finished the final dish, scraping with a dull knife the grime that had hardened there over the last few days. As he dunked it into the murky water, a hollow thud sounded from the bedroom, followed by the loud snort that customarily preceded her snoring. Jack walked inside and righted the discarded bottle. She lay unconscious on the bed with both arms stretched wide, ready to embrace the next drink. Two enormous pig legs splayed over the side of the cheap mattress at a cockeyed angle, revealing varicose veins spidering their way up pasty thighs. Jack took the wadded patchwork of cloth that served as a blanket and threw it over her sleeping bulk. Maybe it was a little too early in the fall to have a blanket over a sweatsuit, but dear Rose got the shakes at night and sometimes shook until the secondhand bed was ready to collapse. *Besides,* Jack thought, *better she throws it off in her sleep than wake up screaming for it.* He stepped from the room, doing his best to close the door, as it only had one hinge.

He finished the cups in the sink, swept the bits of glass from the floor into a rag, and dumped them into the plastic beach pail that served as a garbage can.

Put the cups away, finish your homework, and go to bed, he thought. *Tomorrow will be better.*

The cabinet door violently shoved itself open, and a furry, squeaking body plummeted to the floor.

Rat!

Jack brought his heel down on the animal's head, crushing it. He quickly withdrew his sneaker, grimacing at the sound of snapping bones, and wiped his foot on the linoleum. He waited until the body finished twitching its death throes and kneeled to examine the furry corpse.

Broken neck, excessive damage to the skull, his mind rattled off automatically. *Left eye cataract, swollen right cheek, profuse bleeding from nasal fossa.* With his foot, he flipped the creature over on its back and continued: *Progressed distention in the lower abdomen, probable result of malnourishment. Likely cause of death: my foot.*

His analysis complete, Jack picked up the rat by its tail and flung it through the open window above the sink. After the brief moment of a three-story drop, Jack heard it hit the pavement with a satisfying smack.

The boy scrubbed his hands and forearms with a lump of soap no bigger than a stick of gum and went to bed.

With the rest of the kids gone, Jack had the room to himself. There had been a time when as many as seven had lived in three bunk beds plus a loser's spot on the floor. On the long wall was his little bookshelf. The other kids had stolen many things, including his underwear, but never one of his books (not out of respect, mind you, but lack of interest).

Jack sat on his metal folding chair and dug into his backpack. The twenty-seven-problem calculus assignment was finished in eight minutes. In another six, his history homework joined it. Four minutes later, Spanish was done. He picked up his English text. *Gulliver's Travels*—the complete book, including the giant Brobdingnags, the flying island of Laputa, and the talking horses. Jack was actually related to the author (a great-great-great-uncle or something), but he tossed the book aside without opening it.

Much like psychology, there were few things in life less useful than fiction.

Jack Swift took up the last book, the only one that mattered. *Biology: A Complete Study.* Jack opened the well-used cover and flipped to chapter twelve. The class, an AP course Jack was sneaking into after school, had reached chapter five.

Jack was on chapter fifteen.

The boy scratched the upper part of his nose and began to read. Words rushed over him as he sped through one chapter, then the next, reviewing terms and definitions he knew by heart.

"Isotope: one of a series of chemical elements that have nearly identical—" Jack flipped forward a few pages, reciting the rest of the definition from memory: —*chemical properties, but differ in their atomic weights and electric charges. When a sample contains two or more isotopes, the following equation is applied:*

$$M_r = \frac{M_r(1) * \%abundance + M_r(2) * \%abundance}{100}$$

Easy, Jack thought, flipping through the book for something he hadn't memorized. *Give me something hard.*

There wasn't anything harder. Not unless he made it into college. And that was years away. Years.

He stood at his window, staring out on the yellow sodium vapor streetlamps of the South Chicago slums. The reflection in the window peered back at him, small for its age, and whisper thin. Thunder crackled somewhere deep over the city, and the first pats of rain tapped against the building. The cold October wind keened through the cracks, forty-year-old caulking no match for a late-autumn storm off Lake Michigan. He'd have to sleep in his jacket tonight, and his canvas Chuck Taylor shoes. A flash of lightning lit up the night, followed by a thunderclap. The storm wasn't way-away anymore—it was here.

Jack closed his eyes and let his palm rest against the glass.

He tried to shut out the storm, the cold, the sirens, the yelling upstairs. He tried.

He let the numbers slip across his mind, soothing, orderly, and purposeful. They made sense, they had order. The numbers were his way out.

If he could just be patient, if he were smart enough, he might earn a medical scholarship. And if not, then he'd find a way to pay for it, somehow.

Somehow.

A police siren wailed by outside, reality threatening to break him, but Jack's mind held on to the thought, as he held on to it all day, every day.

Dr. Swift.

That's how you get out of here. That's how you get back to the time when things were good. You still remember it, right? Back when they were alive? Hold on to that.

Hold on to that.

Because I can't go on like this forever.

I can't.

You can get out of here.

Just hang on.

It will get better.

Jack lay down on his mattress, reached to his dresser, and picked up the picture. The three of them—the family—in Maine. His dad grinning under that mess of red hair. His mom laughing, vibrant. And between them, a five-year-old kid smiled, bright-eyed and hopeful.

It will get better. Jack shut his eyes, praying it might be true.

He was long asleep by midnight and missed the moment he turned fourteen.

JUST A NIGHTMARE

> The most beautiful thing we can experience
> is the mysterious. It is the source of
> all true art and science.
>
> **Albert Einstein**

W hen Jack woke up, there was a rhinoceros in his room.

He blinked. It was still dark—the clock on the bedside table said 3:33—and the thing at the end of his bed was just a big shadow. But it was definitely a rhinoceros.

And it was standing on two legs.

Huh, Jack thought. *Wonder how I came up with that.*

The rhino was huge, bigger than an upended minivan. It stood hunched, but still, its massive shoulders brushed against the ceiling. There were two horns on its nose, one long and pointed, the other short and thick. The thing's massive chest was bare, but for some reason, Jack's imagination had dressed it in a set of brown tweed pants. A round potbelly stuck out over a golden belt buckle shaped like a leering face. On its feet were gigantic leather boots, each roughly the size of an old pay phone.

But what fascinated Jack most about the rhino were its hands.

They were huge. The boy imagined dipping his own hands into a huge vat of clay, letting them dry, then repeating the process again and again until all that was left were three humongous fingers thick as bread loaves and a fat crooked thumb.

"Wake up, *dok,*" it said. "We've got to go."

A *talking* rhinoceros. Even better.

It took a step toward him. The floor groaned under its weight—tiles beneath its booted feet cracked like gunshots.

"*Hmph.* You've got a big house here," it grumbled in a deep voice, the kind opera singers called a basso profundo, the kind of voice so deep it rattled your rib cage. "But it's rotten."

Its boot came forward, tested the weight, and the colossus took one step closer. "You're smaller than you look in the portrait," it said. "Did you shave your beard?"

Jack just stared, his jaw hanging slack.

It took another step. "What are you doing, living in a hole like this? I thought you were ric—" The huge shadow stopped. "You *are* Jack Swift, aren't you?"

The boy's mouth continued to hang wide. "Uh-huh."

"Good. Off we go."

Giant hands reached out to grab him.

Jack didn't like this anymore. As the enormous thing loomed over him like a black nightmare, Jack reached out for his bedside lamp and clicked on the light.

The nightmare didn't go away.

It was a monster. Its teeth were yellow and cracked. Its breath stunk. Its skin was wrong—rhinos were supposed to be grey—this thing was golden brown like a leather bomber jacket. Its armor-thick hide was cracked in a million different places. Its eyes were brown as acorns—eyes that suddenly flashed wide.

The rhinoceros reared back. Its head jerked up. Its horn punched a hole through the ceiling. Drywall shattered and fell in chunks around its shoulders as one giant foot fell backward with a thundering boom that shook the tenement building. It yanked its horn from the ceiling, staring at Jack through the falling dust.

It looked terrified.

"You're—you're a *kid!*"

Jack suddenly couldn't think of anything but rabbits. Hazel and Fiver and Dandelion—the rabbits of *Watership Down*. The author of the book

(*Richard Adams,* his brain spat out automatically)

said that, when faced with the oncoming headlights of a car, the rabbits would simply freeze and stare at their doom, bewildered. This was called *going tharn.*

Jack Swift had gone very, very tharn.

"Dammit!" said the rhino, thumping a fist against the wall. "I knew something was wrong!"

A furious pounding suddenly shuddered the floor beneath Jack's bed, the sound of a broom handle. "Knock it off up there!" yelled Mr. Nairt, the junkie who lived below.

Mrs. Abernathy's voice shrilled from above: "What did you do to my *floor?* "

Confused, the monster's eyes darted wildly as the tenement

building came alive in a furious shouting match. As the cacophony rose in volume and temper, the rhino's mouth opened and shut uselessly, thick fingers grasping its head, utterly flummoxed.

"O, bloody hell," it said, and picked the boy up in one hand like a doll.

Only then did Jack start screaming.

The colossus ran for the open window. *Open?* Jack thought crazily. *I shut it; how did it get open? There's no way that thing could fit through tha*— The monster's booted feet crushed tile as it barreled for the window like a charging tank. The arm holding him yanked back and—

It threw Jack through the window.

Mouth open in a wide O of terror, the boy shot into the cold night sky, three stories up.

Jack fell, twisting in midair, screaming. In a half second of incredulity, Jack saw what was (and to be honest, this was a difficult moment to achieve) the strangest thing he witnessed all night: there was a small brown lizard clinging to the shoelace of one of his Chuck Taylors. It winked. Then, a *whuff* of sound and the thing exploded outward, its skin stretching and swelling. Huge boots appeared on its feet, a leering belt gold belt buckle blossomed on its fat belly, and two thick horns grew from its nose. Falling, the rhinoceros grabbed Jack, clutched the boy to its broad chest, and spun in midair.

They hit the pavement with an earsplitting *crack.*

For a moment, everything was still. Lying on the unmoving creature's chest, Jack breathed, staring blankly up at the twinkling stars. An alley cat yowled and bounded out of the darkness, snuffing at the monster as it went.

The rhino had broken Jack's fall with its body. Jack looked down and saw the split and shattered remains of what had once been a paved alley; their landing had punched a crater in the earth. Broken stone spiraled out in every direction, a disjointed web woven by a mad spider.

"You okay, *dok?*" The rhinoceros sat up.

Dumbstruck, Jack blinked.
No. He was not.

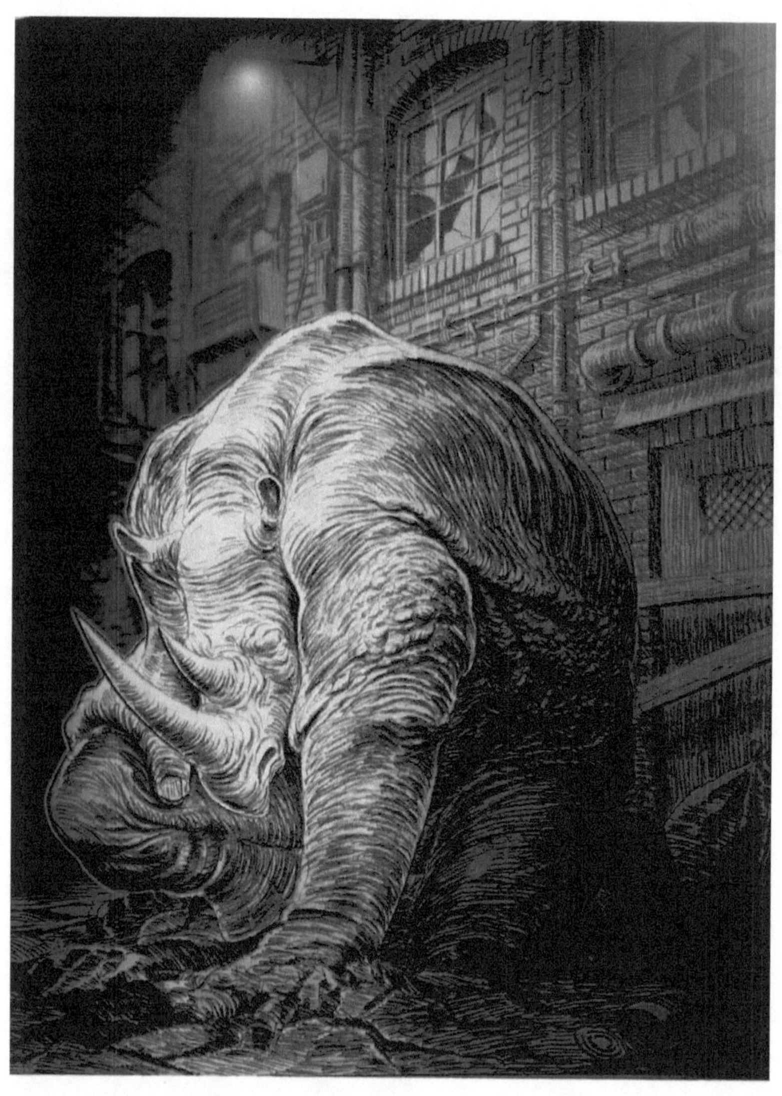

Lights snapped on all across the tenement building. Loud fights were common enough in the apartments, but this was something different—a bomb had dropped outside in the street. Heads began popping from windows as bad neighbors shouted and yelled at each other. More lights winked on.

The colossus grabbed a chunk of pavement and flung it at the streetlamp. The sodium vapor light shattered as the lamp's head was taken off and the street went dark.

The monster fled into the shadows.

Jack sat in the crater with a stupefied expression on his face, watching the lights come on in the surrounding buildings. Somewhere in the distance, a police siren wailed. *Just a nightmare,* he thought. *It's just a nightmare.*

The thing came back.

Over its mammoth shoulder was slung an impossibly huge satchel bulging with…something. As the beast slid its arm into the shoulder strap, it glanced up to the tenements—the noise was growing louder by the second. The monster turned to Jack, staring at him with those acorn eyes.

"I'm sorry, boyo," it said. "But you're the only hope he's got."

It scooped Jack up in one enormous hand—strangely, Jack felt no urge to resist.

He had entered a state of fixed fascination with his kidnapper. The thing had come out of a nightmare, chucked him out the window like a bag of garbage, changed into a lizard (and back again before his very eyes), protected him from a fall that should have killed him, and come out of it all without a scratch. The monster, Jack thought, was miraculous.

Taking the boy, it fled like a guilty thing into the night.

The rhino ran through the streets of South Chicago with the boy tucked under its arm like a football. It ducked through alleyways and back lots, keeping clear of any and all human contact. Running dead out, the thing was not even breathing heavily, its face a fixed mask of resolve, determined furrows etched in the earthy lines around its eyes.

Jack felt the cold air whipping past his cheeks; his hair flew back. Houses, buildings, and streets he knew sped by with astonishing quickness. Jack stared up at his captor and wondered absently where the thing was taking him.

Sirens grew louder, coming closer and closer until a CPD cruiser whooped around the corner right in front of them.

Rubber skidded against asphalt, bubble lights blazing blue and red. Jack had half a second to panic and jam his eyes shut before the cruiser smashed straight into the rhino.

The steel bumper caved in like a paper bag. The car's hood crumpled and bent with a horrific squeal. The car's rear tires lifted two feet in the air, then came back down with a clattering bang. Dying a horrible death, the Detroit-made engine block encasing a 250-horsepower motor gave up the ghost in a wheeze of steam.

With its free hand, the colossus smacked the police car's nose out of its way.

Before the cops could guess what hit them, the thing was gone.

As the monster sprinted around a corner, Jack saw the Calumet River laid out before him—an inky-black ribbon that separated the rich from the poor. Never pausing, the thing clutched Jack close and burst out onto the yellow-lit streets, heading directly for the Stearns Bridge.

Built before the Great Chicago Fire, the bridge was made entirely of stone, carved with cryptic designs that gave it mythical flair. Gargoyles clung to the outer edges like savage beasts looking down into the water, waiting for something tasty to come by so they could swoop down to catch it. The bridge crossed the narrowest part of the river and was only a few feet broad—a walkway for sightseers of another age.

The colossus, seemingly in its element among the other monsters, dashed for the center of the bridge like a thing pursued by all the demons of hell. Reaching the apex, it finally stopped, panting. Jack could feel its elephantine heart thundering against his own feeble chest as the creature peered into the blackness below.

"Hold on," it said, then shifted Jack under its arm and backed away from the edge of the bridge.

Suddenly realizing what the thing intended to do, Jack lost whatever sense of comfort he felt and began to shout at the top of his lungs. The words didn't make any sense, but they all amounted to: No! *No! No!* Pounding and shoving and punching at the beast, Jack tried to twist himself free like a frenzied cat, but the unyielding hand only gripped him tighter.

The rhinoceros muttered incognizable words in its impossibly deep voice and, with a sudden lurch, threw itself off the side of the Stearns Bridge.

Below, the water lay waiting to embrace them with icy fingers.

Still screaming, Jack stopped trying to shove the giant away and clutched the thing's chest, hoping against hope that it would save him from this fall, as it had done at the tenement. Plummeting toward the water, Jack stared down with terrified eyes as he saw his end approaching.

The Calumet River split beneath their feet, opening like a mouth.

There was no splash, no sound, no wet—they tunneled *through* the water, touching nothing but air.

Awestruck, Jack looked up and saw the opening above them close in a rush of liquid. The river chased them down through the tunnel as if it suddenly realized it had been denied its prey. It bore down, closing in, rushing at them in a maddening chase.

Looking down, Jack saw the dark, wet muck of the filthy river bottom speeding up toward him in a spiraling, twisting carnival ride that nauseated him nearly to the point of blacking out.

Realizing he was about to be crushed by the combined impact of the ground and the water, Jack Swift closed his eyes and mouthed a silent prayer.

Our Father, who art in heaven….

The tunnel of air, the riverbed earth, and the water chasing them all collided at the same moment in a huge underwater explosion of silt and debris that rocked the banks of the Calumet River and made the water boil for a hundred yards in every direction from the epicenter.

After a few minutes, the dust drifted to the bottom, and everything settled back down into its familiar place as if the event had never occurred. As the carnage cleared, it revealed no trace of the clutching pair.

And the water rolled, over and over, and silently covered what once was.

Chapter 3

THE TALE OF THE

FELL PRINCE

Draw your chair up close to the edge of the
precipice and I'll tell you a story.

F. Scott Fitzgerald

J ack pulled the covers back over his head.

What a weird dream, his slow-moving mind thought. That thing…the rhinoceros. That was strange. Kind of scary. But weirdly nice too. He turned over, gripping the smooth goose-down comforter between in his fingers.

(your blanket isn't goose down)

It's just a dream, I don't

(a blanket isn't a dream, and it's not yours)

My blanket is—he felt it with his fingers, touching the puffy fabric—this one is just fine.

The bed was softer too. Bigger. There was a warm crackling in the fireplace

(when did you get a fireplace?)

Shut up.

He smelled oil lamps, candles, and something else—something earthy and soft and good, the thick greenhouse smell of the shop Dad used to take him every year to buy their Christmas poinsettias. That rich, hearty dirt smell. Voices too.

"You thought this child was a full-grown man?" asked a steady voice. "He can't be a dozen years old."

Fourteen, Jack replied in his sleep. *I'm fourteen today.*

"Look," replied a familiar basso profundo. "It was dark. If I knew how those Toshan eklektrick bulbs worked, I'd have turned one on and checked. All I could see was he didn't have a *beard* like in the portrait."

I don't shave yet.

"I'm not positive you have the wrong man," the steady voice mused. "His aura is the same, yes?"

"That's how I found him."

"And you are alive."

"Yeah. One of those fast carriages gave me a bruise, but it'll heal."

"Then I'm glad to have you back safe. *Dok* or no."

Dok. The talking rhino had called him that.

(*it's* still *calling you that*)

Jack's eyes flashed open.

This was definitely not his room.

This room was strange. Everything was made of wood and paper. Thin, curved posts and lintels, all polished to a high sheen, framed the room in dark beams. Every inch of lumber was elegantly arched—there wasn't a single ninety-degree angle to be found. The only thing that came close was a shoji-screen door that looked like it led outside. *What is this place, some kind of Japanese cabin?*

The talking rhino from his dream

(not a dream)

was towering above

(not anymore)

and took a step toward him.

Jack sprang backward in the bed, smashing his skin against the rough wood of his headboard, gripping the covers.

They are *goose down,* his mind spat out uselessly.

A strong hand reached out to stop the monster.

"You should wait outside. You're panicking him."

The rhinoceros suddenly looked like a rebuked child. "Aw, he's not scared of me. Just give him a few—" It moved toward Jack again. The boy crammed himself farther into the corner.

"Go outside."

The brown rhino shuffled toward the door, disappointment on its snaggle-toothed face, and disappeared in a puff of smoke. As a lizard's tail disappeared under the door, Jack heard it mutter "—usually good with kids."

Jack was left alone with the man.

Salt-and-pepper hair. A trim beard. A hawkish nose. Tall. Big chest. He was in that strange age between forty and sixty, when it is difficult to tell just how old someone is. His grey eyes looked dangerous; his body looked weathered and unbreakable, like old steel. To many, the grey man was famous as a warrior, but those few who knew him well understood his purpose was much more difficult and more terrible. "I am Valerian Tsai, first of the Border Knights," the man said. "And you"—his sharp eyes studied the boy—"are no *doktar.*"

The man stood. From his belt hung a great sword, its leather-bound grip rubbed smooth with ancient sweat. Jack retreated farther into the corner. "My apologies." The swordsman raised his hands. "We thought you were someone else. A great healer named *doktar* Jack Swift."

Before he could stop himself, the boy said, "I'm Jack—" then found he had no choice but to continue. "I'm Jack Swift, but…but I'm no doctor."

"No," Valerian Tsai said. "You're younger than he would be, little more than a boy. I do not know at what age your people learn science, but can you heal sick men?"

Jack's eyes narrowed; the grey man said *science* like it was a foreign word. "Look," Jack said suddenly, "I don't know who you are or where this is, but I'm not the man you're looking for, so you kidnapped the wrong guy, okay? I'm not a doctor."

Valerian cocked his head, amused by the outburst. "Perhaps not," he said as a piece of paper appeared between his fingers like a sharp card trick. "Or perhaps not yet."

Warily, Jack took the paper. A newspaper clipping. There was no date on the page, but it featured an article about a respected doctor receiving an award from the American Medical Association. The man in the photograph was in his late thirties, with a short blond beard, accepting a plaque with a smile on his handsome face.

My face.

His first thought was not how impossible it was.

His first thought was not to marvel that he could be staring at his older self in a photograph, nor was it to question how Valerian had got the newspaper, or even to wonder if the entire experience was some kind of elaborate hoax. There was only one thought ringing through his head:

I'm going to be a doctor.

He had never expected to succeed—not really—not since his father died. Despite his intelligence, despite his teachers, despite his endless reading, Jack had always been convinced that, at some point, poverty would stand in the way, that he would have to drop out and give up.

I'm going to make it out!

The boy looked up with shining eyes. "Where am I?"

The swordsman smiled. "Perhaps it would be better if I showed you."

There were two moons.

It was hard not to notice the second one.

The first looked very similar to Jack's moon, all white and grey. The other was also very similar to Jack's moon but twice as big and only as it appeared at the autumnal equinox: orange and gold and brilliant and fat. Double moonlight lit their way as the boy and the knight walked a grassy path up the side of a hill. As they ascended, Jack saw a small encampment of buildings tucked away in a low valley, hidden in flickering firelight, some kind of camp. Trees dotted the path, cherry blossom and bamboo. Silent fog drifted through the branches, separating moonlight into moving shafts that drifted, merged, and separated. Fireflies danced in the still air. As they came up the hill, Jack saw hundred-mile tracks of moonlight riffling over the ocean—this was an island on the sea.

Jack breathed. "Where are we?"

"You're a man of reason, Jack," said the swordsman. "Use logic. What do you know so far?"

"I know there was a talking rhinoceros in my room. I know it turned into a lizard—twice. I know I fell off a bridge into a tunnel made of water. And I know none of those things are possible. So I'm dreaming."

"Very likely," said the knight. "Let's wake you up." Valerian pinched Jack's arm—hard.

The boy jerked away from the sting. *Ow!*

The swordsman nodded. "Not dreaming, then. What else?"

"Then I'm going insane."

"You don't look insane to me, but we'll keep it as an option. What else?"

Jack found himself thinking of the words of Sir Arthur Conan Doyle: *When you have eliminated the impossible, whatever remains, however improbable, must be the truth.* But all Jack had was the impossible, and he didn't like the way the truth was shaping out. "It's…it's—"

One of the fireflies zipped by too close to his face, and the boy realized the creature was a miniature woman. The tiny girl with dragonfly wings was half dressed in gauzy, transparent scarves that wrapped around her torso and legs. She winked at him, then darted toward the trees and disappeared into the multitude of dancing lights.

"—magic."

"Majik," agreed the knight. "But you forgot this question: How did you *get* here?"

"That…" Jack cleared his throat. "That thing jumped. Into the river. How did I—"

"Look up."

Jack looked. In the trees above his head was a white circle of light, woven of wood and vines. Each limb was blooming with leaves and white flowers, each branch circled and twisted around the other in perfect geometric artistry formed from the living boughs, a symmetrical ring. Tree frogs and fireflies gathered around the circle, as if it were a magnet for them. The thing was alive.

Above it, in the very center of the ring, Jack could just make out the swirling waters of the Calumet River.

"The young people call it a jaunt gate," said the knight, "although I will always know it by its old name, Elaña. It is a doorway. I sent Memphis through that doorway…to find you."

"The rhinoceros thing?"

"O, you should not call him a rhinoceros to his face."

"Its name is *Memphis?* Like the city?"

"Not the one in your American Tennessee, the one in your African Egypt, and that city is actually named after *him*, but yes."

Jack's mind couldn't process that one. "And your Memphis got the wrong man."

"No," said the swordsman. "He got the right man...at the wrong time."

That statement didn't process either. "I don't understand."

"Time is a fickle thing, Jack. It is difficult to control, and moves differently in different places."

Relativity, Jack thought, glad to have something familiar to hold on to. Einstein was right—maybe more than he knew. Jack pointed up. "That's a doorway through time."

"And other things."

"And your pet monster missed the *right* me by a quarter of a century."

Valerian's grey eyes turned steely. "His name is Memphis Kubiak, and he bent time and space in a way that would leave most wizards burning and broken in an agony that you could never fully comprehend, and he did it to save the life of man to whom he owes *nothing*." The swordsman rested his hand on the pommel of his sword. "It would do you dishonor to speak ill of him."

Jack swallowed.

Valerian Tsai continued. "If you are here, now, it is not a mistake but the will of the *wikk*. Come. There is something I must show you, and there is very little time left."

The big man strode up the path.

Jack followed.

The sea surrounded them in all directions, a great mystery in the dark. Along their path, they passed several statues of warriors and wizards and monsters that looked as if they had been carved centuries ago. Several arms were missing from the statues, most of the faces were gone, and the rest was decaying into ruin as the island took back what man (or beast) had created.

They reached the top of the hill. At its pinnacle, on a flat rise, stood a small structure that looked something like an ancient Chinese pagoda. It was made of thick oak beams, exposed to the open air, topped with an elegantly curved roof. Inside the pagoda hung a massive bell. It was huge, poured from several tons of bronze. Etched into the bell's exterior were interlaced carvings, designs that bore no resemblance to any art Jack had ever seen, even on his father's archeological digs.

It was beautiful.

"This is the Agrat-ban-Nakane," said Valerian Tsai, touching the metal softly. "The Great Bell of the West. In the days of my youth, the Island of Falikos was dedicated to her service. The Nakane, and all the Great Bells, were once the greatest majiks in all of Keymark."

"Keymark," said Jack. "Is that where we are?"

"Sit," said the knight. "And I will tell you part of its story."

Jack sat, and listened.

"Once upon a time," the story began (as all good stories used to), "there was a country strong and bold and great, where adventurers and pilgrims from all over the world came to consult with the wise, learn from the great, and challenge the brave. There were wonders then, things you cannot imagine: cities built of light, songs that gave life to stone, and creatures wondrous and cruel. It was a time of glory and majesty, and the *wikk* ran through it all—deep and strong and filled with hope—*that* was Keymark.

"In the old days, we had great majiks. There were many deep powers created in those times. You are sitting beneath one of the few that remain. The old Elven Fremest, wizards to you, created the Great Bells, ten of them, to be a place of healing. To hear them ring is to have every wound closed, every poison turned, every ill cured. In the spring, thousands of pilgrims would gather here in the valley—the crippled, the leprous, the blind—and the bell would heal them all.

"But this is the way of the world, Jack: Nobility becomes pride. Strength becomes arrogance. And power becomes greed. Our rulers lost their path. It is the way with all men, given enough time. The great wonders faded, our powers left us, and the best of what we once were slipped through our fingers forever. And once our kings had torn themselves apart from within, the barbarians came for the remains.

"Little by little, all the royal blood of Keymark was chipped away until there was only one heir left—the prince of Werrun Fell, the last son of the High Kings. In him remained the one piece of greatness left to us. The prince sought out the old secrets, the ancient majiks, and drew the *wikk* to him like a moth to a flame. He attracted great men to his side, marched his armies across Keymark, and took back the land. The scavenging nomads fell before him like paper kings, and they fled.

"But all men, Jack, are a shadow of their fathers. The strength of the High Kings burned brightly in the Fell Prince, as did the corruption that destroyed them. He learned the joy of power in his march across Keymark and, with it, the thrill of cruelty. He did not spare the weak or the sick or the dying. Farmers were killed with the warriors, women and children slaughtered alongside the men. He massacred everything that stood in his way and became not a ruler but a butcher.

"And so *this* is how the Fell Prince succeeded in delivering the unity he cherished: so great was his cruelty, Keymark united against him.

"There was a terrible war, and it ended a century ago, at the Battle of the Jaden Fields. A century ago, the last prince was struck a fatal blow, and it was a century ago he should have died.

"The *wikk* is life, Jack. Every breath we take gives to and takes away from it, and we are only allowed to possess so much of it. But the Fell Prince had learned the old majiks, the cursed majiks, and with his last living breath, he called upon a forbidden power that was blacker than death—it was damnation. He took the healing *wikk* all to himself, and in that moment, he ceased to be a man. He became the undead, the Necrórceror.

"The sky went black. Thunder ripped the air apart. The earth cracked. And to this day, the great river Breechline is torn in two at the spot where the Fell Prince spoke his last living word. To save himself, he took every drop of life the *wikk* had to give.

"And that, my boy, is where the tale leads to you."

"Me?" Jack's eyes flashed wide. "What do I have to do with it?"

Valerian Tsai gripped the massive mallet hung from chains beside the Great Bell and heaved it back. Jack realized what the man intended to do and clapped his hands over his ears. They were virtually underneath the thing; both of them would be struck deaf. Valerian Tsai hurled the giant clapper with all his might at the Agrat-ban-Nakane—and five tons of metal and wood clashed.

Not a whisper.

Impossible, Jack thought as he took his hands away from his head. There was nothing, not even a vibration to indicate the bell had even been struck, as if every bit of physics had been sucked into a vacuum.

"That, Jack Swift, is the Black Accord." Valerian let the hammer go. "The Fell Prince made a deal with the devil, and robbed Keymark of its healing majik."

Jack stared at the useless thing, realizing the point: "*That's* why you needed a doctor," he said. "You can't heal yourselves and you needed me to save someone."

Valerian nodded. "I still do."

"Can't you get another doctor? A real one?"

"The majik has been spent. It will be days before Memphis can make the jaunt again, and by that time, my man will be dead."

Jack ran his fingers through his hair. It could be nothing. If these Keymark people depended on *bells* to heal themselves, didn't it stand to reason that their medical skills were limited at best? The man Valerian wanted Jack to heal might only need stitches, or maybe treatment for shock. It might be easy.

"This man—" Jack began.

"Xiang-lo," Valerian said.

"Xiang-lo. Is he cut? From a sword or something like that?"

Valerian smiled. "We may be crude by your measure, but in the century since the Accord, we have learned to stitch a cut. This is a pain from *inside* the man." Jack's hopes for an easy fix disappeared. "His stomach hurts, and his skin burns."

Jack sighed. *Upset stomach and a fever.* The symptoms were too broad. It could be anything from internal bleeding to a bad side of beef. "I need to talk to him."

"You can't, unless you can speak in dreams," Valerian said. "He fell asleep almost two days ago. We have not been able to wake him, and his heart is growing weak."

Unconscious, thready pulse—not good. *And taking a history is impossible...* Jack raised his chin. "Then tell me everything. From the beginning, and don't leave anything out."

Valerian closed his eyes. "It began six days ago, with a low pain throughout his body. He did not feel well. He stopped eating. The fever set in three days ago, and then this area"— Valerian prodded himself in what Jack registered as the lower right quadrant, known in the medical journals as McBurney's point—"began to hurt so badly that he could not get out of bed. What food he took he could not keep down. The pain grew worse until he blacked out. The fever has gotten worse. I—" Jack saw frustration on the grey man's face. "I can tell you no more, Jack Swift."

Fever, vomiting, generalized pain, moving to the lower right. If these people risked their lives trying to save this man, then Xiang-lo was important, and judging by the knight's eyes, a friend. *Generalized pain, moving to the lower right.* Something sounded familiar about that, but he couldn't quite—

"We have some of your healing books, if that might help."

Jack blinked. Medical books? Was that possible? "How did—?"

"We…borrowed some things from your office during Memphis's first jaunt to your time." Valerian smiled. "I apologize for the theft."

"My offi—" Dr. Jack Swift, the *older* him, had an office. So, in reality, the books *belonged* to Jack…just not yet. His head spun with that thought.

Books. Medical books. That was something he could work with. Now, maybe, just maybe, something could be done.

"Where are they?"

"Back in the cabin where you woke. There were—" Valerian's great sword ripped from its sheath, gleaming brilliantly as the man spun. Jack had never seen anyone—ever—move so fast. "Show yourself," the knight's voice rung out, dangerous.

A figure stepped out of the shadows, hands upraised. "Your ears are excellent, Captain. Peace be on you." The man stepped into the moonlight. He was tall and blond; his shape was lean and powerful, like a bullfighter's; and he carried himself with the same cocksure pride. On his hip, Jack noticed, the man wore an elegant great sword identical to Valerian's, save the intricate designs were tinged with red instead of silver.

Valerian sheathed his blade with a snap. "Jack, this is Campion Rei, Border Knight, my second-in-command, and one of the best men you'll meet."

"*Sakai,*" Campion said in greeting, flashing perfect teeth. "You are the one here to save Xiang-lo. Well met." The swordsman bowed but did not offer his hand. He turned to Valerian.

"We have pressing business, Captain. If the boy is to work his science, it must be tonight."

"The young *doktar* is…not ready." Valerian glanced at Jack. "There may be nothing he can do."

"Nothing?" said Campion. "Xiang-lo will die before sunrise." He turned his blue eyes on Jack. "Do we have the wrong man?"

"No." Valerian's face was thoughtful as he looked at the boy. "We have the right man." The knight nodded. "Just give him a moment."

Those grey eyes looked into him. As he looked back, Jack found himself saying: "I'll take a look at the books and…see what I can find."

A slow smile crossed Valerian's salt-and-pepper beard. "Well done. I must go with Campion. You can find your way back?"

Jack balked, frightened of being left alone here on this bizarre little island. "I don't—"

A strong hand fell on Jack's shoulder. "Jack. I am Valerian Tsai, first of the Border Knights, and *nothing* on this island will harm you tonight. I swear it." The grey man disappeared into the forest with Campion and was gone.

Alone in the dark, Jack cast one look over his shoulder at the Great Bell of the West, then made his way down the hill.

Inside the cabin, Jack found the books in the huge leather satchel the rhino had carried. As he pulled them out by the handful, Jack was awed at the thing's strength. *There must be five hundred pounds of books in here.* Not just books either: medicines, vials, syringes, scalpels, forceps, IV bags, and a vast array of medical equipment. It was everything that a field surgeon could need…except experience. As Jack rifled through the bag's contents, his eyes lingered on a notepad that read: FROM THE OFFICE OF DR. JACK SWIFT.

He began looking for answers, steadily moving through pages and pages of information—information he was familiar with but never thought he would have to use so soon. The more he looked, the more Jack realized there was little or no chance Xiang-lo's condition would go away without serious medical treatment. *Generalized pain, moving to the lower right*—he checked the indexes, trying to narrow it down, but without Dr. Richard's help, it was almost impossible. *Surgery is just like carpentry,* Dr. Richards had said. Except that Jack wouldn't be working on a block of wood. He'd be working on a person. And if he screwed it up, he would kill him.

(just like Dad.)

He read for a long time. Jack wasn't sure how long (he never could keep track of time while he was reading), but long enough for the fire to dwindle to blue flames and red coals.

When Valerian Tsai returned, Jack barely noticed. The swordsman sat quietly on a chair, folded his hands, and waited. Jack knew he was there but couldn't stop reading. He had referenced and cross-referenced everything, running down the series of symptoms the knight had described, but he just couldn't stop until he was certain.

"Appendicitis." Jack snapped the book closed between two fingers.

"And what does that word mean?" asked the swordsman.

Jack rubbed his bottom lip between his thumb and forefinger—a habit that accompanied his thinking. "There's a…a piece inside his body, near his stomach, about the size of your little finger. It doesn't *do* anything, it never has, it's a vestigial organ. But right now, it's filling with poison. And if it doesn't stop, it's going to rupture; the poison will go into his body and—" Jack stopped there.

Valerian nodded, then asked the inevitable question: "Can you heal him?"

Jack's eyes closed. He had almost grown hopeful in the beginning, thrilled that he was actually diagnosing a case. But appendicitis meant surgery. And surgery meant the unthinkable.

His voice croaked, "No."

Dammit, his brain shouted, *I'm only a kid!*

"It's complicated, he'd need anesthetic, and if I give him the wrong dose, I'd kill him, and—" He stopped, gritting his teeth. "I'd…I'd have to cut him open, Valerian. I'd have to slice his belly open and cut a piece of him out. I—" The boy looked up, fear and tears clouding his vision. "I might kill him."

The knight's eyes flashed. "If you do nothing, he will die."

"Not necessarily," Jack had to defend himself. "If…*when* it ruptures, his body might wall off the poison, and he would be fine. It's been known to happen."

He was grasping at straws, and both of them knew it.

The knight's head lowered, his shoulders fell, and for the first time since Jack met him, Valerian looked like a tired old man. The grey man clasped his hands together, his face tight. "I see." The knight stood. "You must be tired. The bed is yours. I apologize for expecting too much of you at too young an age, please forgive my mistake. We will have you home as quickly as possible."

Jack could feel the distance in the grey man's voice. "Valerian—" He didn't know what to say. "I can't do it, sir. I can't cut him open and dig my hands through his guts. I just—" Near tears, Jack clutched his fists. "I can't live, knowing I killed a man."

If Jack were a warrior—if he were Chief Raging Bull…if he were *Valerian Tsai*, he could do it. But he was just Jack Swift, a frightened kid who only wanted to go home.

A strong hand settled on his shoulder. Jack looked up into those steel eyes. "There are few things in the world more frightening than first blood, Jack. One day, you will be ready for it." The grey man didn't smile, didn't nod, he just looked Jack in the eye. "You tried your best."

A moment, then the grey man was gone.

Jack Swift sat alone in the cabin, staring into the void. And in that instant, he knew the truth: Valerian was wrong.

He hadn't tried his best.

He hadn't tried at all.

As he pulled the covers over his chin for the second time on his fourteenth birthday, Jack felt more alone than he ever had in his life.

Alone in Keymark.

Alone with his conscience.

His father is falling from a cliff, reaching out to him.

Daddy screams as the earth gives way, screaming something, something Jack can't understand, something terribly familiar but unthinkable.

In the impossible slowness of dreams, Jack leaps forward, his outstretched fingers just brushing his father's many-pocketed shirt. He can feel it, feel the brush of the cloth against his fingertips, just as when Dad was alive, as real as daylight.

When Jack hits the ground, he is a thousand yards away, a million miles, a galaxy too far. But still, he can see his father in every detail. The red shock of hair, the scar above his eye, every crease in his skin, and those eyes—those Alex Swift eyes that love him and fear him and condemn him.

His dad disappears below the lip of the chasm, his face open and helpless, and is gone forever. His heart stabbing his chest, the seven-year-old boy sprints across the universe, across the miles, across the bare inches that separate him from the edge of the cliff, hoping to catch his dad, hoping to save him, praying for one last chance.

At the bottom of an eternal drop, there is nothing but the yellow rock of the Badlands. A hawk screams overhead. And far, far below, a white bull snake slithers into the rocks.

Valerian's eyes snapped open. He slept—as he always did—seated, both hands gripped to the pommel of his knightsblade, meditating more than sleeping, his mind churning through the myriad of burdens that weighed on his broad shoulders.

Memphis was there. Behind him stood the child.

The boy's hair was ruffled, his clothes were disheveled, his face was pale, but something was different. There was a determination in his eyes, the kind of fresh steel that accompanies a warrior onto the field of battle, a face Valerian Tsai had seen a thousand times, and he knew what it meant.

The boy named Jack Swift stepped forward.

"I'll do it."

4

BLOOD

Primum non nocere. *First, do no harm.*

Hippocrates

The operating room was anything but sterile. The floor was pounded-down dirt, the walls were splintered wood that collected dust by the handful, and the smoking fire in the corner exhaled nearly as much soot into the room as up the chimney. It was dark, it was dirty, and it put the odds against Jack Swift before he even began.

Jack had two concerns, other than the obvious: that Xiang-lo would die the moment he touched him. The first worry was the anesthesia. Dr. Richards had told him repeatedly that in almost any surgery, the drugs used to put the patient to sleep were by far the most dangerous part of a procedure; more men had been killed by a tiny slip in the amount of medication used than from any mistake a surgeon made. The gas passers, as Richards called them, were the background heroes of the operating room, and kept their patients walking the thin line between sleep and death.

Jack had made the calculations for the correct amount of anesthesia, but in the end, it proved unnecessary. Memphis would keep Xiang-lo asleep. Such majik was well within the monster's mastery, said Valerian, and keeping Xiang-lo out of consciousness and out of pain would be the rhino's task during the procedure.

The second concern was more personal.

"I don't want to see his face."

Valerian nodded as if he had been expecting the request. "That has been arranged."

Good. So the knight understood. "Not just his face," continued Jack. "I don't want to see any part of him other than his belly on the right side. There are medical sheets in Memphis's bag; cover him with those. His chest, his legs, but especially his face. I don't want to see it."

Surgery was just like carpentry. Jack had to remember that. But the only way to treat a man like a block of wood was to remove his face, remove his personality, remove any trace of humanity from him…and even then, he would still be a Pinocchio.

If everything went well, Jack would love to hear about Xiang-lo, about who he was, what his dreams were, and how he'd lived his life. But right now, all Jack wanted to know, all he could know, was where to cut.

Besides, some darker part of his mind chided. *You don't want another face haunting your dreams when you kill him.*

They had followed his instructions perfectly. The patient

(always the patient, never a person)

was laid out on a table, every inch of him covered in thin green medical sheeting, save for his white belly, which shone like a spotlight in the darkened room. Memphis stood at the man's

(no)

patient's head, his massive hands on either side of the bump under the sheet, murmuring strange words softly in the dark. There were other people there, hidden by the surgical masks that Jack, through Valerian, had ordered them to wear. They were silent, standing like statues, waiting. The grey man himself stood aside as Jack entered the room. The knight's worn face was eerily calm.

Jack walked to the patient. There were the tools, laid out on a wooden stool near the operating table, still in their sterile plastic containers, just waiting to be used. The scalpels, the forceps, the clamps. Cold steel ready to plunge into the man's warm belly.

The belly. Soft and fatty and pale, vulnerable as a newborn baby.

The boy put on the thin latex surgical gloves, feeling them snap over his wrists, then donned the mask.

Jack swallowed.

Memphis had been thorough if nothing else. Every kind of surgical tool he could possibly need was readily available, from clamps and forceps to ointments and swabs to needles and syringes of every kind. Dr. Swift's office must have been completely bare by the time the thieving rhinoceros was done.

The first step was the intravenous drip. Valerian's assistant, Kenyan, had been meticulous in following Jack's instructions for preparing the room, but this was something Kenyan could not manage herself. The most extensive experience Jack had known with the art of phlebotomy was sticking a needle into the skin of an orange. That was practice. This was different.

He extended the metal stand, screwed it in place, took the plastic intravenous bag from the table, and hung it from the hook. Jack removed the sheet from the patient's arm, thanked God the patient had good veins, and took hold of the butterfly needle at the end of the IV tube.

He told himself it was no different from an orange. In the end, it wasn't. The needle pierced the vein and found a home, easing healthy fluid into the man's—*patient's* circulatory system.

And now there was nothing left to do but surgery.

Jack found the bottle of Betadine, the worldwide standard in surgical antiseptic, resting by the tools. He opened the bottle, poured the orange liquid onto a sterile cloth, and quickly swabbed the open space between the green surgical sheets. The skin turned darkish orange as he cleaned it, and suddenly the skin didn't belong to a man—it belonged to Jack.

He found the container of latex sheathing and tore the package open with a rip that, in the silent room, sounded like a roar. He removed the adhesive strips, settled the transparent latex window over the area where the incision would be made, and stuck it firmly to the patient's skin. It was under that window, that minuscule six square inches of the universe, that would be the sole focus of his entire being for the next several minutes.

Or the rest of his life.

Those six inches of skin, and the one tiny little freckle that lay within them.

Jack found himself staring at the freckle. There was something about it that unnerved him. In a perfect world, there would be no freckle. It should be just a sheet of plain white patient skin masked in Betadine. But there was something about the imperfection, about the tiny, little dark spot, that made it impossible for those six inches of flesh to belong to anything other than a man.

He stepped back.

"I…I can't do this." He shook his head, flexing his fingers desperately. "There isn't…there isn't enough light," Jack continued. "In an operating room, this should be lit up with very, very bright lights. I can't—I'm not going to be able to see inside—"

His desperate sentence was cut off as Memphis raised one hand from the bump under the sheet and changed his tone. A tiny globe of white light appeared over Xiang-lo's belly. It started small, no bigger than a bulb on a Christmas tree, but slowly grew to the size of a golf ball, blazing like a Hollywood klieg light. It rotated, and the area facing Jack darkened like the hood over a lamp, giving him room to work without being blinded.

The boy swallowed, his mind racing, his fingers twitching. In the harsh light, motes of dust and soot danced in the air, falling from the ceiling, changing their course with every breath, each one shining bright in the rays of the blazing, hovering orb.

The newly revealed threat gave him another reason to pause. "There's too much dirt in the air. An operating theater needs to be sterile. If I cut him open, the wound will go septic and he'll die."

The rhino's brow furrowed; more arcane words poured quietly from his mouth as he shifted two fingers of his free hand. The light dimmed slightly, but Jack watched in amazement as the free flotsam of the air suddenly stopped moving. The room was still, in a state of suspended animation, the motes of dust hovering in the air like fixed stars.

"Is there anything else?" came the grey voice behind him.

Jack Swift was out of excuses.

He picked up the scalpel. It was cold in his hands. Just one inch of a stainless-steel blade would do the work. He gripped the instrument and moved the tip toward the patient's skin. The freckle stared at him like an accusing eye. Slowly, Jack pressed the blade against the skin, just north of the freckle. His lips closed tight against each other.

The blade trembled. Jack felt it start in his fingertips, then move up through the bones of his fingers, to his wrist, up his arm. The scalpel twitched back and forth, unsteady and unsure. Jack bore down on his own muscles, forcing them to remain still, but they rebelled. His fingers shuddered in a crazed dance. He gritted his teeth, trying harder, but the palsy had taken over his entire body.

Expelling a breath, Jack took a step back.

Air shot through his nose. He gripped the scalpel wrist with his free hand, trying to control the shaking, but every muscle was rejecting the idea of cutting into that skin. Unable to control his own body—

His father was there.

Right beside him, in a million different memories. That red shock of hair, the scar above his eye.

Dad had repeated one piece of advice throughout Jack's childhood, and his warm, steady words echoed inside Jack's head now: *Do it with your whole heart,* his calm voice said. *Sometimes you'll succeed and sometimes you'll fail. But never let anyone say you didn't give it your best.*

The boy stopped shaking. He swallowed once. He stepped forward.

And he cut.

Jack's hands did not betray. The scalpel split a thin line down the skin and it was over. Dr. Richards had been right: the initial cut was terrifying, but once it had been made, there was no choice but to move forward. The door had been opened, and there was no shutting it now—not until the deed was done.

There was surprisingly little blood. Part of him had expected a torrent of it, despite having seen Richards do surgery half a dozen times. He had not struck a vein or an artery, and there was no massive hemorrhaging like he had feared. The path was open.

"Forceps," he said to no one in particular, and reached for them himself. He pulled the incision open and clamped it back with the surgical tool. There was a soft *click* as they locked into place, and Jack found himself staring down into the hole he had just made in Xiang-lo's body. Now there was blood, but not an overwhelming amount, and most of it stayed right where it should be—on the inside.

He dabbed the area with a surgical sponge and took a closer look. There were the organs, laid out like a puzzle made of meat. They pulsated mildly as the heart continued on its course, and Jack could identify the large intestine, part of the small intestine, and the cecum. They looked different than they did in the books, where they were all laid out in their neat, separate colors, but he had watched Dr. Richards's surgeries closely in the mirror suspended above the patient, and the organs' location, shape, and size gave them away.

But there was no appendix.

Jack reached out and grabbed the golf ball of light, moving it in closer to the patient. Part of his mind registered how odd it was that he could touch the ball, and it actually had weight in his hands. He moved it down for a better look, and for the first time, dug his fingers inside a living body.

The fear, which had disappeared since the incision, came back into his mind. *What if I misdiagnosed it? What if it isn't appendicitis? What if it's something else? What will I do then? If I blew it on the diagnosis, there wouldn't be—*

There.

The vestigial sac of the appendix was supposed to be finger size and pinkish red. It wasn't. The organ, now filled with septic bile, had swollen to the size of a sausage, and was yellowish black. Necrosis, the death of the tissue, had spread throughout most of the organ, turning healthy flesh into blackened garbage. Judging from the size of the swelling, it was a wonder the thing hadn't burst already. There was absolutely no chance that the patient's body would be able to wall off that much poison. If the sac burst now, the patient would be dead in minutes.

The trick was to keep it from rupturing. Flexing his fingers, Jack murmured, "Clamp," and plucked it from the tray. This was the tricky part. The object was to shut off the appendix from the rest of the body, tie it off, and remove it. His fingers tried to shake again. He stopped them and went in.

He moved the clamp to the base of the finger shape, where the appendix jutted off from the large intestine. Muttering a silent prayer, Jack closed down with the clamp, watching the flesh bulge against the pressure, hoping the force wouldn't burst the ballooning sac of poison. He heard the metal connect with a soft *snap*, and the clamp held.

Breathing a sigh of relief, Jack pulled back. He watched the appendix twitch and spasm inside the cavity, straining against the force of the clamp. If only Kitty Keller could see *this. Icky* was the word she would have used, and for most people, she'd be dead right. But to Jack, *this* was better than majik.

Sutures. He picked up the needle and surgical thread, forgetting to request them out loud, and went to work stitching the base of the throbbing sac. This part was harder than it looked. There was a reason young doctors spent months practicing sutures on everything they could get their hands on. It was delicate work, and inside the body cavity, there was very little room to maneuver. Jack managed as best he could, slipping the needle back and forth through the base near the clamp. For the first time since the surgery began, he felt lost. Simply watching someone do this wasn't enough. It required practice, and the boy suddenly wished he had spent some time sewing before he began.

After twenty-three minutes and several readjustments of the light globe, Jack managed to tie off the stitch and pull it tight against itself. He wasn't sure he had done it right, but it was the best he could manage, and he feared that any more sutures would force a rupture. The only question was whether it would hold.

He took the scalpel in hand again. Now was the moment of truth. He gritted his teeth and went in for the final cut.

At first, things went smoothly. Carefully, he slit down through the base of the appendix, severing it from the main. The organ cut easily, much more so than the outer skin had, and in moments, the appendix was free.

And then everything went wrong.

A jet of yellowish fluid suddenly burst into the cavity, exploding like a punctured water balloon.

Now there was blood. There was a lot of it.

Panicked, Jack grabbed the severed appendix, snatched the poisonous sac out of the patient's body, and thrust it down on the tray next to his surgical tools with unexpected force. The instruments clattered loudly and spilled to the dirt floor. His heart racing, Jack stared into the void, realizing what had happened.

The sutures were bad. All he had done was create a series of perforations for the septic slime to pour through. He had screwed it up. And now the abdominal cavity was filling with poison, just as if the appendix had burst on its own—only now, Jack was responsible.

He froze. Bile coursed through the open wound, killing Xiang-lo by the second.

"Suction!" he screamed, knowing his patient's only chance was to draw out the poison before it spread. For a moment, Jack half expected a nurse to arrive with the suction tube and clean up his mess. But when he turned around, all he saw were blank and frightened faces.

There was no suction. Memphis had been thorough, but not so much as to bring a gasoline-powered generator with him. Jack needed a vacuum, and the closest one was a world away.

"Suction," Jack repeated desperately. "I need…the poison is spreading in his gut; I need to suck it out. Memphis, *do* something!"

The rhino was sweating, his eyes closed with the effort of maintaining several enchantments at the same time. "I can't," he said. "I don't…I don't have a spell like that, I've never—"

Jack spun on Valerian Tsai. *"Do something!"*

The knight's face was hard. "There is nothing I *can* do, Jack. He's in your hands."

Terrified, Jack turned back to Xiang-lo. The bile was running everywhere. In a few minutes, he would be dead. Without some kind of suction or a vacuum, he—

Jack stopped, staring at the fire. Air. He needed *air.* He bolted suddenly, darting across the room toward the flames. Startled watchers quickly moved out of his way as Jack leapt to the fireplace, looking for—

Bellows. The same as the ones in his world: two slats of wood with a nozzle in front, connected by an accordion-like bag to blow air into a dying fire. Push them together, air was forced out; pull them apart, air was drawn in. A medieval vacuum.

Jack picked it up, pushed past one of the men, and grabbed a length of rubber surgical tubing. He snatched his scalpel from the floor, cut the tubing, and jammed it over the bellows nozzle. Seizing one of the candles from the mantle, Jack quickly poured melting wax over the connection, forming what he hoped would make an air-tight seal.

As he dumped the wax, Valerian stepped toward him. "Jack—"

"Hold this!" He jammed the bellows into Valerian's hands. "Start pumping!"

Valerian didn't question him. The swordsman expanded and compressed the bellows in a strong, steady rhythm. Soot vomited out of the tube. As Valerian drew in, Jack pressed his finger against the tube's opening and felt his skin pull tight. *Suction.*

"Stop! Push them together!" Valerian did. Jack poured a bottle of hydrogen peroxide into an empty coffee cup, plunged the tube into it, and swabbed the end clean, sterilizing it as best he could. He glanced at Xiang-lo. Yellow bile was collecting in his wound, forming wicked pools of sepsis.

Jack stuck the tube into Xiang-lo's gut. "Pull!" Valerian did. A shot-glass-size gulp of bile sucked up through the tube and into the bellows. "Stop!" Jack removed the tube and aimed it at the floor. "Push!" The swordsman did, and Jack felt a surge of relief as blackened poison spewed out on the ground.

He had suction.

"Okay," Jack said. "We go again, but don't push until I say so, or we're going to turn his guts into the bottom of a campfire. Ready?"

They both were.

An hour later, Jack was finally convinced that all the poison was gone. He set down the surgical tubing and checked his sutures. It was an ugly job, but they would hold. More importantly, they were actually clean.

He closed his patient up with a new needle and a fresh pack of surgical thread, trying to keep his stitches small so the scar wouldn't be too gruesome. He finished the last stitch, tied it off, and cut the thread.

He stared at the six square inches of his patient's skin, now closed and whole. The tiny brown freckle was right where it should be, and the man it belonged to was still alive.

He released a sigh of relief. He looked up to see Valerian, Memphis, and the rest of the room staring at him in silent awe.

Jack Swift tried to say something, but his mouth didn't work. He looked at his gloved fingers, covered in blood, and it was then—and only then—he finally fainted.

ISLAND OF DREAMS

We may live without poetry, music and art;
We may live without conscience, and live without heart;
We may live without friends, we may live without books;
But civilized man cannot live without cooks.

Edward, Earl of Lytton

Home.

He flexed his toes in the long, cool grass, enjoying the smooth caress of natural green. He didn't like encasing his feet in leather, but anything was preferable to the foreign touch of Toshan blacktop—it felt dark and oily and dead. If he never put on a pair of boots again, it would be too soon.

Memphis Kubiak stretched, outspread his massive arms, and yawned as wide as an open atlas. The journey through the jaunt gate was always draining. The trouble was he had to do it *twice* on his short trips—once out, once back. Add to that the Toshan surgery (three spells, thank you), and Memphis felt like a tree drained of all its sap. He slept six long hours (a thing unheard of for a Juttlander trol unless they were hibernating) and woke in his own beloved Keymark.

As he walked through the compound at the base of the island, Memphis was hailed by men and masters alike. He was well liked in camp, especially among the cadets. The trol was different from the other masters—not because of his race, size, or abilities, but because he was always willing to show the young Watchmen a trick they weren't supposed to learn. Once the cadets got past the trol's intimidating size, they came to regard his visits as a rare and special treat.

A delicious aroma filled Memphis's huge nostrils—he suddenly realized he was as hungry as a bony dog. There were a great many good things that could be said about home, but the best was the food.

Memphis ran across the compound, followed his nose to the kitchen, bounded up the stairs, and crammed his bulk into the doorway. The savory fragrance inside hit him harder than the cop car had; he staggered under an assault of fragrances, peppers, seasonings, and simmering meat.

"Give me everything!" Memphis shouted. "Just stuff it in a barrel and hand me a shovel!"

"Get out of my kitchen, you barebacked bag of snot!" came the response. "I'll serve your ribs for *lunch*!"

Wellam, the cook, was shorter than five feet tall but weighed well over two hundred pounds, much of it in his belly and cheeks (both sets). Sweating buckets from the heat of his several stoves, his plump face was lobster red. Wellam had turned cooking into his own particular brand of majik; he could transform a spitted lamb into a savory delight that tickled the senses, or convert a basket of fruit into a king's feast. He worked ceaselessly to fill the bellies of three thousand young and hungry Watchmen (who ate as only young men could), and he did it three times a day. Wellam never failed to keep up with a legion of voracious appetites, or to delight the camp with each new banquet. Valerian Tsai had hired him personally to feed the training Watchmen; the cook's food was the single greatest boost to morale on the entire island.

Overseeing his own small army of roasters, bakers, sauciers, and sous-chefs, Wellam's kitchen was a madhouse clogged with dozens of men darting this way and that, trying to keep up with the frantic pace their master set. The cook himself stood over a simmering cauldron that brimmed with a sweet aroma that made Memphis salivate. Wellam threw in a fistful of some mysterious ingredient, snatched one of the tin seasoning canisters that hung about his chest like ammunition, whacked it three times on the edge of the pot's lip, and scuttled on to the next concoction. Memphis was amazed, as always, at how fast the little fat man could move.

"But I'm *starving!*" cried Memphis, making his voice as annoying as possible.

"Inside, then, idiot! The wind will ruin my birds!"

Memphis jammed himself through the door, pulled it shut, and took a long, deep breath of heaven. The air was rich with spices. Pulling on his long, thin mustache, Wellam scurried down a long slab-stove lined with three dozen turkeys, each simmering in a bed of its own sauces. The cook darted to a bird that caught his eye and sniffed it. His eyes went wide, and he suddenly ripped the turkey from the stove by one leg and hurled it across the room, eyes blazing. *"Who's the clap-headed boob who fouled my bird with jellispice?"* He got no answer from his staff, who had learned long since to keep their mouths shut. Wellam regarded cooking as an art and had an artist's temper. "Feed that slop to the dogs!" One of the sous-chefs snatched up the discarded bird and fled past Memphis. The trol had to stop himself from stealing a bite of the delicious-smelling thing as it passed right under his nose.

"Wellam—"

"*Fine*, you great gob of guts! I'll waste my precious time to serve you myself!" Wellam stormed to a rack of twenty roasting hogs turning over a massive fire. With his bare hands, the cook grabbed a roasting spit and pulled it from the fire, his calloused fingers completely unaffected by the piping-hot metal. He whipped a butcher's knife from the strap around his ample belly and, in one slice, cut away a ham leg. He tossed the spit (caught by a quick chef before it hit the ground), threw the ham over his shoulder, and stormed toward Memphis. Halfway across the room, Wellam suddenly halted at another huge, boiling pot and scowled at it. Memphis tried to learn patience as the cook produced a tiny taster's spoon, dipped it in the stew, and placed it on his tongue. "More garlic. No. Herrykin." A few shakes went in the pot, he tasted it again, and his red face relaxed. "Very nice, Ritsuki. You're coming along." One of the lesser chefs beamed at the rare compliment. "Do the main stew for tonight. Now I want you to be sure to put an extra quarter of griffin's milk in the—"

"Wellam!" Memphis couldn't take it anymore; the roast ham called to him like a long-lost lover.

"All *right*, you great slab of beef!" The cook snatched five potatoes from the boiling pot, his face puffing redder and redder as if he were about to explode. "You don't want to *wait*, you don't get the *glaze!*" Less than a third of the trol's size, Wellam came like a thunderstorm, shoved the roast ham and potatoes into Memphis's hands, and shot out a threatening finger. "And *don't* come back asking for dessert! I've got a rice pudding flambé that would send you to the moons, and you're not getting any!"

"Thanks!" Memphis escaped through the door, stealing several large boiled eggs from a basket as he went. The temperamental cook yelled, "Put it on a *plate*, you barbarian dolt!" and slammed the kitchen door.

Memphis found a shield near the armory to use as a plate. He took half a moment to give thanks for the meal and tucked in. The ham was delectable (even without the glaze), and between bites, he gobbled the potatoes and eggs like popcorn. He finished them all. The trol's stomach bulged like a balloon, and he let the extra air free with a terrific belch. As he eyed the naked hambone, Memphis found himself wondering how long he should wait before he asked Wellam for seconds. He wanted pudding.

The trol leaned back in the grass and let his belly hang out. He closed his eyes and smiled, content. Valerian had ordered him to take care of the Toshan boy, but at this moment, Memphis wanted nothing more than to bask in the Keymark sun and doze happily. One lazy eye opened; he spied a familiar young Watch cadet coming his way—the perfect solution to his problem.

Jack was dead asleep when the door banged open like a shotgun.

He leaped to his feet, standing on the bed, poised to strike. Jack was fed up with being scared out of his sleep and had had quite enough surprises.

Standing in his room was a young woman. She was lean as a whip, dressed in tan pants and a tight green shirt cinched at her waist. Short red hair—red like the coals of a fire—topped a tanned and freckled face that spent most of its days in the sun, out-of-doors, and on the move. She had almond-shaped green eyes and smelled like cherry blossoms.

"Are you going to attack me with that?"

Jack glanced at the pillow he had cocked over his shoulder like a club and lowered his weapon. The girl *(woman, maybe— she might be eighteen)* kicked the door shut with one foot and looked Jack over with a critical eye. "For someone who's supposed to know all the secrets of the universe, I'd say you're a little young. Soup?"

A puzzled look froze on Jack's face until he realized she was carrying a steaming wooden bowl. "You Toshans know what soup is, don't you?" the woman-girl continued. "It's food. You eat it. Or you can drink it. It's good either way." She paused. "Are you mute?"

Jack blinked. "Uh…thank you." The aroma of the soup danced under his nose, and Jack realized he was famished. As the redhead set the bowl down on the table, he smelled warm potatoes and cream, along with a few vegetables he didn't recognize but smelled delicious.

"The Grey Knight will see you when he can," said the girl, "but for now, you belong to Memphis. He says get dressed and come find him down by the kitchen. Unless you're planning on walking around camp in *that.*"

For the first time, Jack realized he was wearing nothing but Fruit of the Loom underwear. His face went beet red; he grabbed a blanket from the bed and covered himself. The girl grinned, and in that moment, she reminded Jack of a better-looking version of Kitty Keller—appealing but wicked.

She put a hand over her slim hip. "Anything else you need?"

Jack couldn't manage a response, trapped between looking at the beautiful girl, covering his shame, and the intoxicating smell of the soup. He stuttered, tried to get something out, almost formed a sentence, and gave up. "No."

"Right." And she was out the door. Jack raised a hand to stop her, without a single idea of what he intended to say. She stuck her head back in. "I've never met someone like you before," she said. "I thought someone so smart would have more to say." She shut the door on him.

Jack felt like he'd just been in the center of a whirlwind. He breathed, and when he inhaled, the smell of the soup took over. At first, he ate. But after a few mouthfuls, he drank.

She was right: it was good either way.

The island of Falikos was beautiful. The night before, the world had been shrouded in darkness and mystery; now it came to life, vibrant and warm—sunlight (only one sun, at least, so far) and a baby-blue sky above Jack. Lush grass beneath his feet. Everything was in the full bloom of spring, and cherry blossoms were everywhere. The entire island was populated with wild bamboo, green and tall, towering over truncated little black-olive trees ready to be plucked by anyone who passed by. Jack passed lush patches of flowers; some he knew, like the night-blooming jasmine and the bougainvillea, but most were strange and wilder things that did not grow on his earth. The sea breeze felt wonderful as it rippled through Jack's shirt, tickling the hair on his arms. Something was unusual about the ocean wind, but he couldn't quite put his finger on it. It played with his hair, and he smiled. Jack Swift was far from home, and it felt wonderful.

The encampment was made of several buildings: bunkhouses, barracks, cabins, huts, tents, several stables, at least three barns, working metal smithies, a stone watermill that sat by the creek, and something huge that looked like a beer hall. Some of the buildings were brand new, while others seemed very, very old.

The people were impressive. Most were young (only a handful looked older than twenty), slightly shorter than the Midwesterners he was used to, but lean muscled and fit. The green-and-tan colors the woman-girl had been wearing seemed ubiquitous—he saw no jeans or T-shirts—and everyone, *everyone* was armed. Swords, spears, knives, maces, and longbows were standard gear, and it made the boy a bit nervous as he walked among them. The foreigners gave Jack strange and interested looks; most tried to hide their curiosity as he passed, but some smiled readily, and a few even waved. Ducking his head, Jack waved back. He frequently caught hushed phrases containing the same three words: *Valerian, Xiang-lo,* and *Toshan.*

Jack stopped cold when he saw the crocodile-men. They were coming straight for him, salamander-smooth skin glistening in the sunlight. Small eyes topped reptilian faces bristling with crooked, sharp-looking teeth. Thick, muscular tails (that looked strong enough to knock a man down) trailed just above the grass behind them. Jack stepped back, his eyes wide. The crocs passed by him, giving him a cursory nod, and one of them winked a blue eye.

There were other creatures too. Catlike men, covered entirely in short fur, competing in wind sprints up and down a long stretch of grass. Near the smithy, several squat, heavily muscled women drank from a tin pot of coffee. Not one was taller than three feet, their purple-black skin dusky and hairless. On an open field, more crocs played a game that looked strikingly like football. Jack hurried on, avoiding eye contact.

He had never thought the rhino could be a welcome sight, but Jack breathed a sigh of relief when he found Memphis. The huge beast was lying with his back against a tree, drinking from a great oaken mug and picking flowers. The boy couldn't help but smile as he approached—the thing looked like Ferdinand the Bull, sniffing the daisies.

The trol's lazy eyes drifted over to Jack, and it raised a hand in greeting. "'Lo there, boyo. How do you feel?"

Jack stopped a few paces away, out of arm's reach. "I'm all right," he answered. "Slept pretty well, although I don't really remember going to bed."

"Yep." The thing took a drink from its mug. "Valerian took care of you after you passed out."

"Passed out?" Jack didn't remember anything after sewing the last stitch on Xiang-lo, but he was positive he had never fainted in his life.

"Your patient's better." The trol took a drink and set its mug down on the grass. "Last I saw him, he was asking for milk."

Jack's heart thrilled. The question had been creeping around in the back of his mind from the moment he woke up. "Then Xiang-lo is—"

"Better." The rhino grinned a warm smile. "Better. He's got some pain, a'course, and Kenyan had to replace a few stitches, but he's awake and fine as sand as far as Kenyan's concerned. She ran us all out of there early this morning—said we were getting in the way."

My patient is alive, Jack thought, glowing, *and asking for milk.* "I should see him. Check his vitals, see if—"

"Wait, wait, wait." The rhino waved him off. "You did what you came to do. Kenyan's giving him those little anabodic—"

"Antibiotic."

"Anti-*bitotic* pills you gave Valerian, and if something goes wrong, she'll find us."

"Still, I should make sure she's giving him the right dosage—"

"Did you tell Valerian the right dosage?"

"Yes, but—"

"Then let her follow your instructions. Relax, Jack." The trol winked and drank again. "We may not have science here, but that doesn't mean we're all idiots. Besides"—it toasted the boy with the mug—"you're a hero today. Enjoy it while it lasts." Memphis offered Jack a plate with a large chunk of meat wedged between two massive hunks of dark bread and a few purple berries on the side. "Now eat."

Jack took the plate. The soup had been a good appetizer, but a trol sandwich was a genuine meal. He dug in and found himself wolfing it down. Memphis grinned and took another gulp from the mug.

"I don't know how you did that last night. I've seen majik in my day, great majik done by the best in Keymark, including the High Elves Fremest, a long time ago. But what you did, that was something *special.* To me, a man's guts have always been just a bloody glob of ropes. The only time I'd seen them was when they were spilling out in a heap." Jack stopped eating in midbite and glared at the trol. "Sorry. But you, *you* turned it into a puzzle or something. You knew where each of the pieces were, and what they were doing there. You knew which one was causing the trouble, that appengix-thing, and took it out. Easy as pie."

Jack didn't bother to correct the creature. There was a delicious sauce on the mutton that was both sweet and tart at once, and it demanded his full attention. He reached for the trol's mug, the size of a small barrel in his tiny human hand, and took a sip. Fire shot down his throat, exploding into his guts.

"Pphwaagh!" Jack expelled the stuff in a violent spasm.

Memphis turned, startled. *"What? What?"*

The boy coughed and shook his head to clear it. "What *is* this stuff? *Gasoline?"*

The trol looked at the mug and laughed. *"Gronk!"* It smiled. "That's *my* drink, boyo, not for little ones like you. Hell, most full-grown men can't stomach it." Memphis held the mug aloft. "The drink of the mighty Juttlander trols; it makes us strong and brave." It took an elaborate swallow of the stuff. "But mostly"— it winked—"it's the only thing strong enough to get us drunk."

Jack laughed despite himself. The trol grinned. It presented its massive hand, and Jack took it. Memphis pulled him to his feet, and they were left standing eye to eye. The trol's fingers felt calloused and leathery and warm—comforting around Jack's own. Without thinking, Jack said, "Nice to meet you."

The trol smiled and raised an eyebrow. "Not spooked of me anymore?"

"Not anymore."

Memphis tapped thick fingers against his secondary horn. "Good. Then we're friends, Jack."

"Good. Now, can I get something else to drink? That *gronk* is about to melt my face off."

"Follow me." The trol turned and walked. It

(*no, not it. He*)

He set a pace that was tough for human legs to keep, and Jack jogged to catch up.

The two of them disappeared down the hill together.

"Boyo?"

"Yep?"

"What's *gasoline?*"

The Irridin Sea stretched out before them like an infinite blue silk handkerchief dropped by God. The ocean breeze sent Jack's hair flying back from his head and pressed the shirt flat against his chest. Wispy clouds moved slowly on the vast horizon, and seabirds much larger than seagulls dotted the vista. The sandy white beach beneath their toes would have given Cancun a run for its money, and the gentle waves were the perfect shade of Caribbean blue green.

"Here you are," said the Juttlander, spreading his arms.

"It's beautiful"—Jack nodded—"but I need a drink, remember?"

"What, you need more than an ocean?" Jack looked at the trol, confused. Suddenly, Memphis slapped his head. "*Salt* water! I forgot! Heh, strange thing about your sphere. No, boyo, the Keymark sea is as it should be: fresh."

That's what was wrong with the sea air, thought Jack, *no salt. Weird.* (*Not* that *weird,* said the voice in his head. *The Black Sea in Asia Minor is fresh water, and that's in your sphere, boyo.*) *But it can't be clean. Do they drink from it?*

Memphis strode into the water, lowered his massive hands like twin shovels, scooped up gallons of the Irridin, and drank it down. Jack peered at the water, hesitating. "Are you sure it's safe to drink? I mean, what about pollution?"

Memphis looked up curiously. "Pollution?" The word was completely foreign to the trol.

In that instant, Jack decided he loved Keymark.

The boy kicked off his Chuck Taylors, scooped up a double handful of seawater, and drank. Perfect, cool, and fresh. "Good?" asked Memphis. Jack nodded, drinking, drowning the taste of trol liquor from his mouth. "Not afraid of the water, are you, boyo?"

Jack took another gulp. "No. Why?"

"Because you need a *bath.*" And with that, the trol hooked Jack under the armpits and flung him twenty feet into the sea.

Jack screamed in surprise, exhilarated by the sudden flight. His arms pinwheeled as he splashed down, backside first. A good swimmer, Jack kicked up and surfaced, whipping the hair from his eyes.

The trol was doubled over, laughing. "*Ahhahah*ha! The look on your face…*ahah*…oh, oh, *heh,* O, I'm sorry, Jack, but I just couldn't resist. You okay?"

Jack was laughing. The reek of sweat and blood and fear from the night before was washing away. "Fine as sand!"

Memphis produced a square hunk of soap from his satchel and tossed it out to the boy—the soap was huge, the size of a good novel. "Take your time," said the trol. "You smell like you need it." He pulled out a big leather-bound book, flipped it open, and began to read.

Jack dragged off his clothes and threw them on the shore. The soap was harsher than he was used to and grated against his skin like a pumice stone, but the water felt good. As he washed, the same thought kept racing through his mind, over and over.

My patient is alive. He's alive.

Jack threw the soap on shore and darted into the water. He lost track of time, playing in the waves, bodysurfing like a dolphin, and when he checked the shoreline again, Memphis was gone. Jack stood up and looked around, walking toward his clothes. Beyond the beach, the bushes rustled with movement and Jack called out, "Memphi—"

Three girls appeared, each carrying a small tin pail and a towel. All three were well muscled, with long legs and short hair. The girl in front was unlacing her shirt, chatting to the others.

"—when he woke up, he didn't seem like much, really." *Dammit! The redhead with the soup!* "I just felt sorry for the poor thing, hiding behind the sheets. He looked like a rabbit in a trap."

"But he healed Xiang-lo, didn't he?" another girl interrupted. "The whole camp's heard about it. He must possess great majik—"

"*Science,*" the redhead corrected. "The Toshans call it *science* where he's fro—"She stopped short. "And here he is! Hi, Jahk!"

Jack stood frozen before the three girls buck naked.

He covered himself with the big bar of soap and backed down into the water, hoping it wasn't as crystal clear as it looked. The redhead stood with her hands on her hips, making no move to turn away or do up her own blouse. One of the girls behind her whispered something, and the other girl giggled. The redhead narrowed her green eyes. "You Toshans aren't much for wearing *pants.*"

Jack flushed crimson.

"Is that *really* the Toshan?" asked one of the girls.

"He must be," said the other. "Look how skinny he is. And pale!" She turned to him. "Will you do some science for us, Mr. Jahk?" Curious, the trio moved down the beach toward him.

Jack considered swimming for it—into the open sea. He wasn't sure how far he would get, but staying here was no longer an option. His certain death by drowning was only prevented by the sudden reappearance of the trol.

"Hey! You girls! Get away from him!" The Juttlander made a beeline for the trio, his huge feet pounding the sand.

"I tried to get them away," the redhead lied sweetly, "but they wanted him to do some science." She glanced at the boy in the water. "He *is* awfully cute, Uncle Mem. Maybe he could d—"

"No! Absolutely not!" said the trol. "He's not going to perform science for you like some kind of carnival monkey!" Memphis was loud, but Jack was a little annoyed that the Juttlander looked like he was trying not to laugh. "Now *scat!*"

The girls scurried down the beach, clutching their buckets and giggling. The almond-eyed redhead lagged behind, walking backward, her hair rippling in the breeze. Jack saw her lips move and heard: "Lucky for that bar of soap." She grinned like an imp and was gone.

Red as a spanked baby's bottom, Jack stormed out of the water. Memphis tossed him a towel. "Don't get yourself in a twist, Jack," said the trol. "Those girls have been in training for a year; to them, a body is just a tool, not something to be ashamed of."

"They. Were. *Giggling!*" Jack said. He tried to force his wet jeans back onto his legs and stumbled in the sand.

"Wait, wait," said Memphis. He reached into his satchel and removed a pair of tan cotton trousers. "I borrowed these from Keiko, they should fit about right."

Jack snatched the pants out of the trol's hands and put them on, lacing up the front tightly, murmuring, "Skinny...*pale...* 'Do some science for us, Jahk!' Who *is* that redhead anyway?"

"Leah? O, she's harmless. She can shoot your eye out from fifty paces but, other than that, completely harmless."

Jack slicked back his hair. "Did she say I was cute?"

Memphis looked at Jack like he had just turned into a four-headed cat. "Don't even think about it, boyo. Leah's off-limits."

"Thank God."

Memphis offered him a pair of boots, but they didn't fit, so Jack kept his Chuck Taylors. The black canvas shoes looked ridiculous with the rest of his Japanese-peasant getup, but they felt like home. "Here." Memphis handed him a leather knife belt. Jack pulled the weapon from its sheath; the hawkbill blade was the size of a Bowie knife, its tip sharpened to a wicked point. It was heavy, the grip felt good in his hands.

Jack looked up at the trol's leathery face. "Am I going to need this for something?"

Memphis shrugged. "Armed company is polite company."

Jack cinched the belt to his waist and tied the leather strap around his thigh; it hung low, like a gunslinger's rig. It was comforting to know his hosts trusted him with a weapon (not that it would do much good against the trol's tough hide, or Valerian Tsai), but it proved he was no prisoner.

"Very sharp," said Memphis, eyeing him. "You're just Keiko's size."

"Keiko," Jack repeated. "That sounds like a girl's name."

"Don't ask. You up for some exercise?"

"Um…sure." Jack rarely pursued anything more physical than carrying his books home from school, but it seemed rude to say no. "What kind of exercise?"

Memphis grinned. "O, just the standard kind around here."

When Jack met Abrahim Qin for the first time, the old man was fending off two swordsmen who were both trying to slaughter him dead.

"So, you're the healer we've all heard about, eh?" Abrahim said, dodging the blade of an attacker. "I'm Abrahim Qin"—he cracked his knee into the man's gut—"swordsmaster of the Watch"—he smashed the man in the head with a fist—"Border Knight"—and spun to block the oncoming thrust of the next man—"and anyone who can fix somebody who looked as bad as Xiang-lo"—he kicked the man's knee and punched him in the face—"is welcome to work under *me*."

Abrahim slid under his opponent's swing like a runner stealing second; his sword flicked up the man's inner thigh, halting just below the crotch.

"Yield," he said, "or lose 'em."

The man dropped his sword.

Lying in the dirt, Abrahim tapped the flat of his blade against the man's thigh with a condescending pat. "We don't heal people here," he said, getting to his feet. "Just the opposite. I'm training these whippersnappers to fight." Abrahim stood relaxed. "Join up, sit in, or just watch, but don't get in my way or I'll stick ya."

He sheathed his sword with a snap and turned to his students: twenty of them—humans, lizard-men, and cat-things—kneeling in a fifty-foot-wide half circle around the knight. "Benjamin here did poorly," the old man said. "Balance on his back foot, his swing was wide, slow on the *riposte,* and that's how I got under his guard—if you can call that a guard." He turned to Benjamin. "Thirty minutes with Holt. Every time your shoulders go beyond his mark, you get fifty. Go." The young man bowed and ran to the edge of the ring.

Abrahim picked up the less fortunate cadet he had cracked in the skull. "Shake it off, boy. You'll be fine." The cadet stood on wobbly legs while Abrahim gave his appraisal: "Teng was slow. Stupid. Weak. How many times have I got to tell you your blade isn't your only weapon in a fight? I left myself open three times for a quick kick, and you didn't even see it. Horrible, Teng." His tone became dismissive. "Recover for an hour, but don't come back here until you've got your open-hand work down. Go." Teng half bowed and stumbled to the outer ring.

Abrahim slapped his hands. "Anna. Wil. You're up. Don't hold back; I won't. If I get cut, it's my own damned fault." Two new students stepped into the ring and drew their blades. The old man grinned like a wolf.

Jack turned to Memphis. "This is your idea of *exercise?*"

The trol shrugged. "Abrahim's okay, he's just…crotchety." He eyed the cadets. "I've got a class, so you're going to stay here. This group is a little more advanced than I realized, so don't join in unless you want a nasty scar."

Before the boy could protest, Memphis was gone.

Jack watched twenty cadets go through the punishing task of earning their stripes from Abrahim Qin. It was insane. The old man smacked them down by twos, shouting at them all the while, leaving them battered and beaten. Not one of the students left the ring without a bruise or a bleeding cut. And with every defeat, they bowed and thanked the crusty swordsmaster for the lesson.

The old man was quicker than a cat and just as lithe. Only his face was wrinkled; his body was tight as a drum. Thin, short, and wiry, Abrahim was marked with his profession: a crooked scar ran across his shoulder, another slashed across his ribs, and one eye refused to open fully. As he outpaced his young students for two straight hours, the old man reminded Jack of a human walnut.

The last two students left the ring, one limping badly. The old man barked, "Jack," and the boy froze.

Abrahim's eyes grew hard. "Don't make me ask twice."

Swallowing, Jack walked through the cadets into the circle. The old knight sized him up, frowning. "*Hmmph.* Not much to work with. Know any open-handed work?"

Jack didn't bother mentioning that he didn't *want* to fight; Abrahim wouldn't care. "No, sir."

Abrahim sighed. "Fine. Off with your shirt, and we'll start." Jack reluctantly removed his shirt, his skin feeling pale and soft. Humiliated that his body was weaker than a man six times his age, Jack crossed his arms over his thin chest. "Lord," said Qin. "I'm glad you're not on the Watch. All right. We begin."

The next few minutes went by in a frenzied rush as Abrahim showed him punches, blocks, and kicks. The old walnut got behind him, taking Jack's sweaty wrists in his gnarled hands, dictating the movement of the boy's body like a puppet master. He never stopped talking.

"Without a weapon, go for the nose. Hurts like hell, gives you a few seconds before they can react. Forget the eyes—too much time, too easy to dodge. Never go for the mouth, it's a weapon. A good smack to the ear will send them spinning, but never try it with a helmet—you'll break your hand." He kept Jack punching all through this, the old man's body a forceful ghost behind Jack's own.

"Snap the punch straight, never roundhouse, takes too much time. *Pop* when you throw a punch. Throw with the weight with your shoulder, not your hand, there's no weight there. *Shoulder,* boy! That's it. Never slow it down. Straight punch, *straight!* Forget the chest, it's a wall of bone, and usually armored anyway. *Shoulder, boy!* If you get a clean shot at the throat, take it, if not, don't. You'll hit half bone and half air, if you hit anything at all. Go for the gut if you've got time, but quick-snap back to defensive when you do. *Snap, boy!* Hit low, two inches under the rib cage. Never punch the crotch—wrong angle. Hit where?"

Concentrating on throwing his shoulder into the punch, Jack didn't understand the question. He turned to ask Abrahim to elaborate when an explosion of pain shot through his lower back; the old man had jabbed him in the kidney—*hard.* As Jack turned, Abrahim grabbed him and spun him back around. "Don't stop until I say so! *Punch.* Keep going." Jack fumed in pain and humiliation but turned to jab at the air. Pain stabbed him every time he shot out with his right.

"*Shoulder, boy!* Hit where?" the old man repeated.

"Nose, never the eyes, never the mouth, never the chest, ears with no helmet, throat if open, gut two inches low." Jack felt the old man's body stiffen in surprise at his quick answer, then Jack's legs shot out from beneath him and he fell to the ground in a heap.

"Fine. Sweeps. Get them from behind, force them back quick, they'll go down." He grabbed Jack's hand and yanked him to his feet. "Kicks. Knees first—break the kneecap. Kick me there."

"What?" This was going too fast for Jack.

Abrahim's foot smashed the back of Jack's knee like a hammer. He went down, arms flailing. "Forgot," said Abrahim, "that's the other sweep. Must be getting old. Kick me there."

Jack jumped back, out of Abrahim's range. He was getting angry, and Jack was going to hurt the old man if he tried to knock him down again. "Sweep or knee kick?"

"Surprise me." Abrahim walked quickly forward. Jack stumbled back in indecision, then stood his ground, fed up. He opted for a knee kick; his foot lunged out, was caught by the old man's gnarled hand and yanked to the sky. Jack hit the ground a third time.

"Chose right. Can't do a walking sweep. Kick was wrong, though. Ball of your foot isn't solid, ankle bends with the blow. Hit with the heel. Concentrates the force, and nothing gives but the other guy's knee. Next kick: to the groin."

Time slowed as the old man's foot came up. Jack cried out, trying to stop it, prepared for blinding agony. The foot struck sharply against his inner thigh—not higher. The old walnut held his foot there, leg fully extended, perfectly balanced, and smiled a toothy grin. "Won't do that to you. Not the first session. Population's low enough as it is."

The foot pulled back, snapped forward, and smashed Jack's chest. Wind shot out of him as he toppled backward. Still shocked from the threat to his manhood, Jack somehow managed to keep his feet.

"Only try *that* when they're distracted or weak. If they stay up, it gives 'em an open shot at you. What are you waiting for? *Punch me!*"

Jack was getting the hang of following Abrahim's orders as soon as they were given and shot a fist at his face. It felt good to take a swing at the old man, and a part of Jack hoped he actually tagged him.

He never stood a chance. Abrahim knocked the blow aside with his left forearm and punched with his right, stopping the blow inches away from Jack's face. "Blocking. That's first. Again."

Forearm stinging, Jack threw his fist again, faster. Abrahim's crossed arms caught Jack's hand in a wedge. The old man's foot cracked Jack in the knee, sending him sprawling. Through sheer ferocity alone, the boy managed to stay up. "That's the second. *Again.*"

Jack rubbed his throbbing knee and came again. This time, the old man spun toward him, caught Jack's punch with his left hand, and cocked his right elbow, ready to break Jack's nose. "And third, which brings us"—Jack suddenly swept Abrahim's ankles, smashing the old man back with the flat of his palm; Abrahim grinned as he let the force push him over, rolled in a backward somersault, and pounced up—"to tumbling."

He strode toward Jack. The boy kicked out, using his heel this time. Abrahim caught his ankle and held him there; Jack hopped to keep his balance. "*This* is a position you don't want to be in." Panicking, Jack swung with his right fist, immediately caught by Abrahim's left. "Puts you in a nasty spot." The old man shoved his right shoulder under the boy's legs. "Lets me do *this.*" The old man hoisted the boy like a sack of grain and sent him flying. Jack smashed to the ground in a cloud of dust.

Abrahim Qin hunkered down, peering at the boy. "Forgot to tumble. You should have been able to roll out of that—I didn't do it hard."

Jack's bruises screamed otherwise. His entire body was shattered in little pieces all over the clearing, he was sure of it. For an instant, he thought he was paralyzed, then realized the pain was pulsing all over his body in great thumping wads—paralysis would be better.

Abrahim turned to the class. "Not terrible for a beginner. A good mind, but no strength. See you tomorrow." He pulled his shirt on and threw his sword—his *real* sword, a knightsblade etched in blue—over his shoulder. The knight walked to the boy, bent at the knees, and looked Jack directly in the eye. "Good sweep at the end there. But I said that kick was only for the distracted and the weak. I'm neither." His walnut face grinned. "Get some rest, you look beat." He turned and was gone.

Jack tried to roll over and found it too painful to bother. He had been having a good morning, a nice morning, and then he got beat up by an octogenarian Genghis Khan. Blood tasted salty in his mouth; he was a mass of bruises—all without the old man landing a punch.

Someone pressed a nozzle to his lips; water poured into his mouth, washing out the blood and dirt. Jack tried to swallow but gagged.

"Easy, take it easy," said a voice to his left. Jack opened his eyes and found himself looking at a tall black-haired cadet, the one he had seen facing off with Abrahim at the beginning. "That's Abrahim's Famous First," the cadet said. "No shame. When he finished with me the first time, I was in a pond swimming for my life. Everyone's been trounced at least once. Just makes you want to get him next time."

"Why"—Jack swallowed—"why would you go through that a *second* time?" The cadet grinned and offered his hand. Jack took it; the tall boy pulled him to his feet. "Thanks," Jack said through his dirt-clogged nose.

"Benjamin Halfpenny," said the cadet.

"Yeah." Jack nodded. "I saw you go up against him. I thought he was killing you, but after what I just went through, you must be *incredible* to stay up that long."

"Thanks. I'm getting better. But the rule says we don't graduate until we beat him."

"Which means we're all going to be here until the old bugger dies," came a voice. Leah, the little firecracker, stood right behind Benjamin. "Got your bell rung pretty good, Toshan."

Jack reddened. "Hey"—Benjamin turned to face her—"the Azure Knight just said he had a good mind, which is a bigger compliment than I ever got. And I remember what he said after *your* Famous First."

"He told me I fought like a retarded duck," said the girl, "but I'm getting better."

Benjamin smiled. "Jack, Leah Archer."

"We've met," said Jack. *At least, this time, I'm wearing clothes.*

"Well!" came a familiar voice as Memphis ambled out of the woods. "Three of my favorite people, all together at once. Now, this *is* nice." He put a big hand on Jack's shoulder. "Did you have a good time?"

Jack scowled at the trol.

"Mmph. Well. Come along with me, boyo. My majik lesson is taking longer than I thought and—"

"*We* can take care of him, Memphis," suggested Leah, suddenly all sugar. "Maybe he'd like to spend some time with people his own age."

"Yeah," Benjamin chimed in. "Come with us, Jack!"

"Well, I—"Jack paused. Watching Memphis do majik was tempting, but spending some time looking at the infuriating redhead wouldn't be half bad either. "Sure. I wouldn't mind."

Memphis rubbed his minor horn, considering. "All right. But we'll have a few rules." The trol raised a finger. "First: No talking about your Toshan science. These two will ask. So will others. We *had* intended on keeping you a secret, Jack, but *that* didn't last long. There are some who wouldn't like the idea of what you are, and I wouldn't want you encouraging them to do something about it." Jack narrowed his eyes—he didn't like the sound of that. "Second: And this is for you two." Memphis eyed

Benjamin and Leah. "Don't let him out of your sight. He's your responsibility. That means no swordplay, no knife fighting, and no majik!"

"Of course, Uncle Mem!" Leah nodded, glancing at Benjamin. "But you *do* realize this means we'll have to be excused from drills for the rest of the day…" She blinked her big almond eyes.

The trol screwed up his lips, stopping a smile. "Tricky, you two. All right. Excused. Third rule—"

Before he could finish, the two cadets had Jack by the arms, running.

"Don't worry!" shouted Leah.

"We'll take good care of him!" yelled Benjamin, and they disappeared into the woods.

Jack ran with them, exhilarated. The two cadets were delighted to have the afternoon off (they trained nine out of every ten days—or *tendays*—which Jack figured was the Keymark equivalent of a week), but instead of relaxing, they tore across the island with reckless abandon. Sprinting to the backside of the Black Rock (the big hill Valerian had led Jack up last night), they scrabbled up the cliff face like monkeys. The colossal rock seemed out of place on the island; it looked as if it had been hurled there by some tremendous sea giant (which, for all Jack knew, it had). He learned the Island of Falikos took its name from the rock: *fal,* elvish for *black,* and *kos,* which meant *rock* in something called the Hero's Tongue. As they shouted and hollered to each other, dangling from the rock, Jack realized Leah was right: it was nice to be with people his own age.

There is nothing in the world so appealing as youth.

Jack pulled himself over the lip at the top of the cliff, trying to catch his breath. The cadets weren't even winded; both were in terrific shape. Benjamin lounged under the pagoda of the Great Bell, weaving a whistle out of tall grasses while Leah experimented with a majiked globe she created out of thin air—the thing blew everything out of proportion when you looked through it, like a crazed magnifying glass. The three of them giggled and laughed, lounging idly in the sun.

Benjamin Halfpenny was a good sort, a spear fighter from the Eynrys Plains (wherever those were), and pleased as punch to have been accepted into the Border Watch. Leah Archer, despite first impressions, was incredibly friendly once Jack learned (from Benjamin's example) to take her sharp tongue with a grain of salt. Unlike her counterpart, Leah considered her admission into the Watch as a matter of privilege.

"What about Memphis?"

"What about him?" Benjamin said.

"How did he get here?" asked Jack. "I saw plenty of men and women and…cats and lizards and a few charcoal-colored dwarfs, but Memphis is the only trol."

"Oh, that." Leah nodded. "Valerian rescued him when he was a baby." Jack smiled at the absurd thought of an infant trol. "His parents abandoned him."

"Abandoned him?" Jack said, startled. "Why?"

Leah shrugged. "He's a runt."

A runt? If Memphis were a runt, full-size trols must be gargantuan. "His parents just left him out to die?"

"Wasn't worth feeding him." Leah shrugged. "Valerian found him, took him in, discovered he had a knack for majik, and now he's one of us."

"The Border Watch."

"Well"—Leah glanced at Benjamin—"Memphis is a Watchman—we're only trainees."

"Trainees training for what?"

"To defend the elves—" Benjamin shouted suddenly.

"The Kern—" Leah joined the refrain.

"And the Paladine Arch!" both of them finished together, a familiar battle cry.

Jack grinned. "Defend them from who?"

"The bloody Necrórceror." Benjamin spat the name like poison. "The Fell Prince was—"

"The Fell Prince *is*," came a low voice. The trio turned to find Campion Rei, Valerian's handsome second-in-command, standing near the Great Bell. "Not *was*. It would be best if you remembered that, Halfpenny." He locked eyes with the cadets. "What are you two doing away from your training?"

The cadets snapped to attention. "Looking after the Toshan until Master Memphis is done with his students, *jai*," said Leah. "He gave us the day off."

"He would." Campion smiled. The blond knight looked at Jack. "I should congratulate you, *doktar*. What you did last night was truly inspiring. I had hoped to speak with you"—he glanced at the cadets—"privately."

Leah and Benjamin took the hint; they said quick goodbyes and disappeared down the Black Rock. Jack looked at his feet; there was something intimidating about the Border Knight—of all the physical specimens on the island, Campion was by far the finest.

"You brought hope back to Keymark last night," said the swordsman, "and back to me. When I saw what you did for Xiang-lo, I thought it was possible you might work your science again."

As the knight drew his arms from beneath his greatcoat, Jack understood why Campion had not shaken hands when they first met. His left arm was strong, thick with muscle. His right was amputated below the elbow.

"It is an old wound," said Campion, eyeing his stump. "I have made allowances for it, but I am not the man I once was. And a swordsman without a good right arm is—*well.*" His blue eyes came to rest on Jack. "Would you heal me?"

Jack's heart stopped.

His mouth moved, but nothing came out. There was nothing he could say—not even the best surgeon in the world could give Campion Rei back his right hand.

"I…" Jack gritted his teeth. "No. I can't. I can't heal that."

The knight's blue eyes fell. "Ah." He swallowed. "Science is not the marvel I had hoped. I understand." He riffled the great-coat and hid his truncated stump. "I apologize, *doktar*. I should have thought better before asking you."

A deep, loud gong sounded over the island. For a moment, Jack thought it was the Great Bell, then realized that was as impossible as healing Campion's arm. "Dinner," said the knight. "You should go. I will join you shortly. *Sakai.*" Campion bowed and walked away, his steps measured and slow.

Jack took one last look at the knight and ran down the hill.

The Great Hall Barrelmount was one of the old buildings, constructed for the first Border Watch more than a hundred years earlier. The other venerable structures on Falikos were crumbling to vines and ruin, but the Barrelmount, built with an ancient and sturdy grace, remained.

Inside, the age-old hall pounded with new life. Cadets and masters, three thousand of them, laughed and joked and bellowed and banged, jubilant in their camaraderie, ravenous for their meal. The round tables, twenty men to each, were stacked high with food: sizzling beefsteaks, steaming hams, golden-brown turkeys, roast pork, simmering stews, baked apples, cold pears, melting cheeses, warm breads, a riot of colored vegetables, and a delicious-looking rice pudding flambé. Jack could not find Leah or Benjamin but seated himself between a coal-skinned dwarf he had seen working near the smithy and a toothy crocodile-man. Jack nervously introduced himself and asked the croc's name.

"Bill," it said, and went back to dishing ladles of steaming lamb stew into its bowl. Across the room, everyone was filling their plates, but not one of them ate.

Campion Rei and Abrahim Qin entered the Barrelmount and, to a man, the Watch stood. The Border Knights took their places at the head of the hall, standing on either side of an empty seat—Valerian Tsai was not in attendance—and Campion's strong voice broke over the Barrelmount. "Today has been a great day for Falikos, and for the Watch. I am pleased to announce that which so many of you already seem to know—that Xiang-lo has been *healed!*" A great cry rose inside the hall, and a huge round of applause, cheering, and table thumping blasted the air. After a full minute (during which Jack could barely hear himself think), Campion continued. "We owe this great moment to the man who worked the miracle—*doktar* Jack Swift!"

The room exploded. Jack found himself reeling as the entire Watch hailed him in full voice, everyone pounding him on the back and shouting his name. It was the kind of praise you dream about from the time you are very small, the cheer of a thousand voices, all for you.

"Men of the Watch!" Campion announced triumphantly, "This day, *this day*, marks a turning point in our battle against the dark majik of the Fell Prince, and the beginning of the end for the Black Accord!" The largest cheer of all buckled the walls of the Barrelmount.

Then they ate—like starving men, cadets gobbled down their food as fast as they could get it, calling for more of everything. Jack saw a fat little man with a long white mustache running from table to table, barking orders at the multitude of chefs that followed him like ducklings, appearing with tray after tray of something new and delectable that begged to be tasted.

As the meal was devoured, several of the Border Watch cadets burst into song; the young men and women banged the tables in rhythm:

He'll bring on the ham and the lamb and the steak
He'll bring us more chicken, more duck and more cake
We'll finish off more than he thinks we can take!

He's Wellam the Cook!

Bring more suckling pig and one more roasted boar
We'll shuck it right down 'til we're all on the floor
We'll drag ourselves up and we'll beg him for more!

He's Wellam the Cook!

We'll finish the pudding, the pies, and the bread
We'll gobble it down 'til our bellies all spread
If we're going to battle, at least we're well fed!

Hail Wellam, Wellam the Cook!

Yelling along in full throat, Jack felt his head go light. The clamoring throng, his bursting belly, and the pale beer he had mistaken for water all collaborated to spin his head. Woozy, he snuck out the door.

Jack stepped into the crisp night air and took a deep breath. The ocean breeze felt good against his face. Pixies flitted in the sky overhead, winking in the double moonlight. Following them, Jack walked up the hill, hands in his pockets, alone.

Soon enough, he found himself standing beneath the jaunt gate, looking up. He watched the pixies dance around the shimmering ring of white boughs, and the twinkling stars above it. Somewhere up there, through that ring, far, far beyond it, lay the bottom of the Calumet River.

"Thinking about home?" came a steady voice.

Jack turned, startled. Valerian Tsai stood like a statue, his eyes closed, the tip of his knightsblade buried in the earth between his feet. Jack could not imagine how he had not seen the knight before—Valerian stood only a few feet away.

Home.

Jack realized the truth: the pull of home had led him here—not the pixies, not the moonlight—*home* had been tugging at his mind all day. He didn't really miss it, not quite yet, but he had come here just to make sure the door was still open.

"When will I go back?" Jack asked.

"Three days." Valerian did not open his eyes. "Memphis should have his strength back by then."

"Can't you take me back?"

"I cannot quicken the Elaña, Jack. I am no wizard, just a swordsman. Memphis will do it. Xiang-lo's surgery took more effort than he expected."

A pixie darted through the trees close to Jack's nose. On impulse, he reached out to catch it. As he did, the bruises in his arm stung sharply, and Jack released a painful breath.

Valerian's eyes flashed open. "Are you hurt?"

"No, I—well. Abrahim gave me a beating."

"Mm. I saw." Jack glanced at the knight. The grey man smiled. "You put in a good first effort against him."

"*Hmpf.*" Jack shrugged. "My dad always said if you're going to do something, you do it with your whole heart."

Valerian nodded. "Your father is a wise man."

"He's dead."

Valerian cocked an eyebrow. "That does not make him less wise."

Jack looked up at the sky, silent.

The knight unbuckled something from his arm. "Here," he said, and tossed it lightly to Jack. It was a thick bracer—an armband made of boiled leather, carved with swirling designs, strapped with twin brass buckles. It looked old and tough. "That is what the young people call a skidshield," said the knight. "My generation knew it as an *aërling*. I have worn it for—O, more years than I can count. It is a very rare thing. Go ahead." Jack strapped the bracer to his left arm, clamping the buckles tight. It felt good against his skin. Valerian smiled. "Go ahead, touch it."

Jack tried and couldn't. His hand skidded away. Something blocked him, something just above the bracer—but there wasn't anything *there*. He traced his finger around the invisible field and found a flat skid of resistance just a bit bigger than a license plate. He flicked his finger against it. The skidshield flashed bright, and his entire hand shot away from it, too fast, like a bullet's ricochet. *Ow!*

"That bit of armor has saved my life more than once," Valerian said. "It should save you a thumping from Abrahim."

"Th-thank you," Jack said. He liked the weight of the skidshield on his arm—it felt safe, like a piece of the knight protecting him against the unknown.

"You are welcome."

"Valerian? What are you doing up here?"

The swordsman's eyes closed again. "I am guarding a doorway, Jack Swift."

"Guarding it from what?"

"The jaunt gate is awake now. And there are other things that may have woken with it. I am a Border Knight—this is one of the borders I must defend."

Jack leaned back against one of the big trees, looking up at the white vines. Under the twin moons, he glanced over at Valerian Tsai, and there was something, the shape of his silhouette, the way the knight stood, that reminded Jack—just a little—of his dad.

"Do you mind if I stay with you for a little while?" the boy asked.

There was a long silence. "I would like that."

The boy sat. The man stood. And together, they watched the stars.

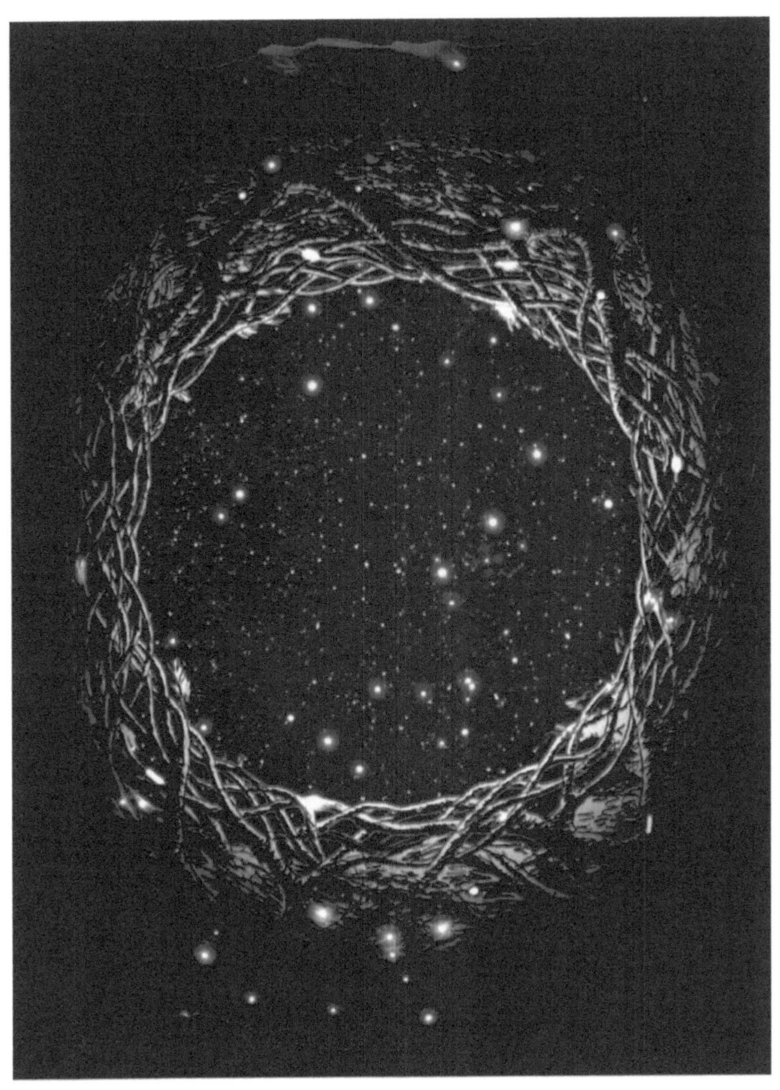

THE
LAST DAY

*If an injury has to be done to a man, it should
be so severe that his vengeance need not be feared.*

Machiavelli

I t is all very well and good to romanticize a medieval lifestyle: the lack of pollution, the absence of machines, a natural world unmolested by man—these are all wonderful notions, no doubt—but by his last day on Falikos, Jack would have gladly traded them all for a working toilet.

The island had no running water, which meant no showers, and his baths were always taken at whatever temperature suited the Irridin on that particular day. Memphis's pumice soap was as far as personal hygiene went, and Jack longed for a bottle of actual shampoo. The toothpaste (or tooth *powder* they used here) tasted exactly like Glidden's Dijon Mustard, and after brushing, Jack always felt like his teeth had gone yellow. Mirrors were hard to come by; deodorant was nonexistent. His only set of clothes was the one on his back, and after three days, Jack found himself looking for a washing machine. For whatever reason, be it majik or something different in their body chemistry, the cadets all smelled just fine (Leah, infuriatingly, still smelled like she had just stepped out of a cherry orchard), but Jack found himself regularly sniffing his funky armpits.

Abrahim Qin worked Jack like a rented mule. The Hollywood actors made it look so simple—thrusting and dancing with their tin swords. But a real sword is long, thick, and heavy, and Jack could not block a forceful strike with both hands. He was utterly useless with a blade, and Abrahim said so. The old knight switched him to a pike, and when Jack proved equally inept with that, Abrahim finally thrust a bo staff into his hands. "Useless weapon in a war, but we need to do *something* with you," the old walnut snorted. "If you can't manage this, I'll teach you to fight with a bloody toothpick." Valerian's skidshield fended off the worst of Abrahim's blows, but by the end of the day, Jack's knuckles were rapped raw.

He felt useless and stupid, and to make matters worse, the only thing Jack *was* good for—science—was taken away from him. Kenyan (whoever *she* was) was tending to Xiang-lo's wounds, keeping his stitches closed, and Jack's assistance was not needed. The boy grew increasingly frustrated; he wanted to see his patient, to check on him—if for no other reason than to look the man in the eye and say, I *did that. I fixed you.* But Valerian Tsai would not allow him even that.

But the worst ignominy of all did not come from Jack's vanished patient, his bruised knuckles, or his ripe armpits.

Worst was the kiss.

Last night, outside the Barrelmount, Jack had gone to find Leah. So far, he had been unable to impress the little firecracker, and he found the challenge occupied his mind more and more. He caught himself daydreaming about Leah, wild fantasies of showing her the wonders of his world. *What would she think of a car? Or better yet, an* airplane?

He saw Leah's shadow against a tree, walked toward her, and found her locked in Benjamin's arms. He kissed her neck. She giggled. Benjamin planted one right on her lips. She didn't seem to mind.

Jack's heart died a little.

He snuck away like a thief, guilty, embarrassed, and angry.

As he crept back to his cabin, he found his hands balled in fists. *You never had a chance,* his mind chided. *You never do.* Jack squeezed his eyes shut, trying to push away the humiliation. *You should have known, the way they looked at each other—she never thought of you once. Why would she?*

That night, he tried to sleep, but his guts coiled in knots like snakes.

You're so smart, aren't you?

And so, Jack Swift's last day began in bitterness, rose to open conflict, and ended in murder.

If he had known what was to come, if he could have foreseen the events of that day, perhaps he would have behaved differently.

But it must be remembered that Jack's heart was sick, and there are few creatures in the world less acquainted with wisdom than a fourteen-year-old boy. Lesser men have been forgiven worse. And no one (not even the elves) can see the future—not until it has arrived to leer at us from the dark, and by then, it is too late.

The trouble began with the map.

Benjamin Halfpenny brought it to Jack as a going-away present: a map of Keymark, drawn in Benjamin's own hand, inked on thick vellum parchment. He rolled it open proudly, showing Jack the Eynrys Plains that he called home.

"I don't *care* about your home," Jack shot at Benjamin, hating him. "Where's Falikos?"

Benjamin gave him an odd look. "Here, see?" He drew an arrow pointing out the island on the southern tip of the map.

Jack scrutinized the parchment. "You got it wrong," he stated flatly. "The sun comes up over there, which, according to this, is west."

Benjamin's dark eyes narrowed. "Yes…"

"The sun rises in the *east*," Jack growled. "Or didn't they teach you that in whatever you pinheads have that passes for a school?"

Benjamin shook his head, confused. "Sun's up in the west, time to get dressed. Sun's down in the east, time for the feast," he said. "Maybe it's different in your home."

Jack struggled for a retort *(Rises in the west? What kind of backward place is this?)*, but he saw Leah approaching. His blood grew hotter. "Well, why didn't you at least write down the *names* of anything?" he said loud enough for Leah to hear. "What kind of a stupid map *is* this?"

Leah came, curious at their raised voices. "What's going on?"

Jack answered first: "Benjamin gave me a map with no names on it."

"Yes, there are!" Benjamin protested. "See, there's an arrow drawing to it right there: *Falikos.*"

"That's just a bunch of squiggles. Can't you write?"

Fed up, Benjamin jabbed his finger at the chicken scratches by the island. "It says Falikos! Right there!"

"What, are you kidding me?" Jack said. "That isn't English!"

Benjamin stared at him blankly. "What the hell is *English*?"

Jack stopped cold. *What—*

Leah chuckled. "Looks like our brilliant young *doktar* can't read."

It was one embarrassment too many. Jack snatched the map out of Benjamin's hands and ran. Both cadets called after him, but it was too late—Jack Swift had reached his boiling point.

He had been able to read from the time he was two years old *(if you count* Peter Rabbit, *and I do!)*, but now, something about this screwed-up world had robbed him of even that. *Illiterate!* his mind screamed. For the first time in his life, Jack felt…dumb.

Dumb bunny, dumb bunny, dumb bunny, screeched the kindergarten chorus in his mind, mocking him as he walked. *Dumb bunny, dumb bunny—*

The chorus still sang when he found Memphis. Jack snatched the trol by the arm and thrust out the map. "How I can understand *you,* but I can't understand *this!*"

Memphis stared at him. "Good morning!"

"I can't *read!*"

"Why would you be able to read?" The trol raised an eyebrow. "You and I understand each other because of the *wikk.* There are lots of different languages, like Elvish or the Trader's Dialect or the Hero's Tongue and whatever the Nomads speak, but here, if you *want* to be understood, you are. Writing's different—ink doesn't have a will." The trol scratched his head. "What, did you think we were all speaking English? The British Empire didn't get this far, boyo."

"But I can't *read!*" the boy repeated.

"Why do you *care?*" The trol scowled. "You're going home tonight. You don't need to."

"Of course, I need to!" Jack said stupidly. It was a ridiculous conceit; Jack didn't speak French, Russian, or Chinese either, but that didn't matter—what mattered was Leah had *giggled.*

"You Toshans are all the same." Memphis smiled. "You think you need to know everything in th—"

Jack's temper soared. He needed to prove he was smarter than everyone else, and he needed to do it right now. "You want to see what I know? I'll show you what I know!" Jack had only heard the levitation spell once, when Memphis used it to move a pallet of wine barrels, but he'd memorized the words, the phrasing, and the inflection perfectly. If Memphis wanted to make fun of him, he'd flip the big trol rump upward. Jack shouted: "*Udarik ip bradåstaka!*"

Nothing happened.

Jack blinked and spoke the incantation even more loudly. Still nothing. The trol's stumpy toes wiggled in the grass, still planted firmly on the ground. "Are you done?"

Fuming, Jack threw his hands down. "I did it right! I know I did!"

"Actually, you did—it was perfect. But you can't do majik, Jack."

"But I did it *right!*"

"You said the *words* right, but there's more to it than that."

"But everyone here can do at least a little majik! I should be able to!"

"But you can't. And you never will."

Jack's blood boiled. He couldn't read, he couldn't do majik, he couldn't get Leah—and he had made a fool of himself proving he was useless. "Fine," he shouted, not liking the whine growing in his voice. "I'll do something I *can* do! And you *can't!*"

He stormed off. Memphis tried to put a hand on his shoulder, but Jack shoved it away. He felt guilty, weak and stupid

(dumb bunny, dumb bunny)

and the last thing he wanted was anyone trying to help.

By the time he reached Valerian Tsai, Jack was in a steaming rage. The knight was involved in a quiet conversation with Kenji Tuk, the archery master. Jack barged between them like a spoiled child.

"I want to see Xiang-lo—*now!*"

The grey man turned slowly. "Control yourself, *doktar.*" His steely eyes flashed a warning. "And gather your wisdom before you speak again."

Jack knew he was wrong; it didn't stop him. He needed to prove himself, and he needed to do it now. "You're putting his life at risk! What's the point dragging me all the way to this backward, ignorant hole if you're just going to let him *die?*"

Kenji's hand darted to the hilt of his sword; Valerian stopped him and took one step forward, towering over the boy. "Rein your tongue, Jack Swift. I will *not* tell you a third time."

Jack's rage flamed out in the shadow of the knight. Valerian Tsai had been nothing but kind, tolerant, and gracious, and here Jack stood, answering friendship with fury.

Shame flooded him. Jack dropped his head and bit his lip, feeling Benjamin's fine map crumpled in his hands. "I…I should at least make sure he's all right before I go. I don't know why I can't see him."

"It is not for you to understand why," came the knight's sharp voice. "There are a great *many* things you do not understand, Toshan. If you knew the nature of the ma—"

War horns ripped the air.

The trumpets came from atop the Black Rock, high, loud, wicked, and long—a furious bray that tore across the island. It was a terrifying sound, the sound of blood, the sound of war, the sound of murder and death; it echoed over the camp like black thunder.

Jack had not thought Valerian Tsai capable of fear, but when he looked in the swordsman's flinty eyes, he saw it. The Border Knight set his jaw. "They have come."

The terrible trumpet sounded again, this time joined by a chorus of full-throated brothers. Valerian ripped the knightsblade from his sheath. "Kenji. With me." He charged up the Black Rock. Kenji Tuk raced after the knight, unslinging the bow from his back.

Jack was left frozen in place, terrified.

Another trumpet blast rocked the island. Shouts came from the hill, and something much, much louder than war horns roared—something alive.

Jack broke and ran like a rabbit.

The camp was in an uproar. Cadets and masters ran through the compound, gathering weapons and shouting. Booted feet pounded everywhere—Jack was almost knocked down several times trying to make his way through the tumult. He found Benjamin Halfpenny crossing the yard with his pike, the young man's eyes white and wide.

"What's going on?" shouted Jack.

"I don't know! *Have you seen Leah?*"

"No, I—"

"*Watchmen!* To me!" Abrahim Qin yelled at the top of his lungs. The old walnut's practice blade was gone—his fist gripped his gleaming blue knightsblade. *"Men and women of the Watch! Rally to me!"* Cadets gathered around the old knight, gripping their weapons, faces nervous and frightened. Barking orders, Abrahim shoved men into place, one eye on the Black Rock. "Ranks! Form *ranks!*" Benjamin Halfpenny fell into line, a man of the Watch, and the boy named Jack stood with him.

Abrahim strode the line, shouting commands as the Watch faced the Black Rock. It had grown darker, the spaces between the trees filled with a roiling black mass that poured down the hill like oil. And there was something else up there too—something huge and black and boiling with fire.

Screams came from the hill, and Jack suddenly thought of Valerian Tsai—the Border Knight had launched himself straight into that tide. Jack clutched at his staff, wishing he had tried harder with the sword.

Cadets poured out of the woods, bloodied and shouting, trying to reach Abrahim's line. A cloud of black arrows fell from above. Fleeing men were cut down from behind as the enemy emerged from the trees.

The things were nothing close to human. Black creatures ran crouched, long claws swaying above the ground like razors, fangs bared and dripping yellow ichor. The smallest were no more than two feet long, the large ones nearly dog size. Some had bows, but most had nothing but claws. Tendrils sprouted from the monsters' forearms, wiggling like a thick pack of half-buried worms. Armored in dark exoskeletons, chitinous insects, the monsters reminded Jack of massive two-legged cockroaches.

"Versläng," cursed Benjamin, and the things had a name.

"Hold the line!" Abrahim's voice rang out, steady as a rock. "Remember your training! Men and women of the Border Watch! Hold the line!" The young soldiers stiffened, gathering their courage, and held their weapons ready.

From the trees, a tall shadow emerged, towering over the versläng. A dark samurai wreathed in blood-red armor. His wicked blade shone with an unearthly light, lit with crimson flames. The versläng chittered and twitched at his armored feet, gathering around him by the hundreds, by the thousands, awaiting his command. The red devil raised his fist. The war horns sounded, and the roaches came like a black flood.

Jack paled. Nothing stood between him and the oncoming tide.

"I'm sorry I yelled at you," Jack found himself saying to Benjamin. "It's a beautiful map."

Benjamin met Jack's eye. He said nothing but nodded. Together, they turned to face the charge.

Abrahim's knightsblade suddenly leapt to life in a searing blaze of gaslight blue—the sword thrummed with the power of the *wikk.* He trumpeted: "If you die today, *die well!*" He leapt into the flood.

The two forces collided with a crash—the battle was joined. Swords flashed; arrows loosed. Jack found himself unable to move as the Border Watch rushed past him, screaming into the fray. Straining bodies pushed and shoved and fought for their lives. Lost in the confusion, Jack saw Abrahim Qin tear into enemy after enemy, his blazing blue blade ripping through the versläng like cardboard. The Watch gained courage from his valor and hacked their way through the tide.

The scarlet samurai strode through the battling figures, his flaming sword destroying everything that stood in his way. He marched with a single purpose—flinging aside men and versläng alike—forging a trail straight for the old knight. Abrahim Qin charged, a shout on his lips. Their swords locked; sparks flew like fireworks. The old walnut parried, ducked under the return stroke, and dove through the red devil's legs. Abrahim sprang up behind him and drove his blazing blue blade into the dark samurai's armored back.

The crimson warrior bellowed in pain, spun—and took Abrahim's head.

Jack screamed.

The boy was smashed in the chest by one of the versläng and fell as the roach ripped and tore at his shirt, pinning him to the ground. Yellow fangs dripped vile fluid on his cheek. Jack cracked his staff across the thing's head, knocking it back. With spidery speed, it reared, launching itself at the boy again.

A pike stabbed down, pinning the screeching thing to the dirt. Benjamin gripped Jack's arm, yanking him to his feet.

"Get out!" he yelled. "Find Leah!" One of the versläng was suddenly on Benjamin's back, biting him. Jack swung his staff, batting it off; six more took its place.

"*Run!*" yelled the young cadet, then Benjamin Halfpenny was buried in a sea of black claws.

Jack ran.

The woods were littered with fleeing cadets, the screams from behind lent speed to their feet. Jack pounded his way through the woods, his heart trip-hammering against his ribs, fear clutching his chest.

He grabbed a tree, panting for breath. *I want to go home.* Tears bathed his face. *I want to go hom—*

His thought was arrested by a sudden, wicked crackle. Jack turned and looked up at Black Rock.

The jaunt gate was on fire.

Flames leaped through the branches as the ancient trees burned, embers scattered in the wind like flaming confetti. Black Rock blazed like a humongous bonfire. Amid the flames, burning, a huge creature ripped a tree from its roots and roared.

"*No!*" Jack screamed and was answered by a hiss. He spun—

Half a dozen black roaches crouched in a semicircle around him. Jack swallowed, and in that moment, he knew he had no hope of getting away, no hope of going home, and no hope of surviving. He gritted his teeth. His eyes lit with the fire of a cornered animal.

If you die today, then die well.

Jack Swift launched himself at the monsters.

He clubbed the first across the face, smashed the second's arm, then punched his staff through the armored chest of the third—its shell cracked with a satisfying crunch. The rest attacked him. The staff was ripped from his hands. He reached for his knife, but a versläng grabbed his wrist—the tentacles of its forearms flicked against his skin, slick and wet. Something stabbed him in the leg. A knife lunged through the bodies, grazing his neck, drawing blood. Jack swung, kicked, and shouted as he was dragged to the earth.

A heavy blow smashed down, crushing two roaches beneath a brown foot the size of an old pay phone. Jack was yanked six feet into the air as the remaining versläng erupted in an explosion of emerald fire.

Steam curled from thick, leathery fingertips. Bloody, Jack cried out, "Memphis!"

The trol was smoking and burned, cut in a dozen places; there was a slash on his forehead, and most of the skin on his left ear was gone. For the first time since they met, the rhino looked like a monster again. Jack was hoping for a smile, that reassuring grin that said everything would be all right, but it didn't come.

"Did they bite you?"

"No, I—"

More versläng poured out of the trees. Memphis flicked his fingers, and a raging globe of light burst like a thousand fireworks, blinding them as they shrieked.

"Get to the docks. Get a boat. I will find you. And if I can't…find Valerian. *Find him, Jack.* He'll get you home."

Jack began to protest, but the trol hurled him fifteen feet backward as the versläng attacked. Jack took one look behind him, watching as Memphis torched the first group of roaches in a blaze of emerald majik, then hammered the creatures into jelly, their shells cracking under his mighty fists. Then they were on him, and Jack saw no more.

Very few people would have been able to remember the path under the circumstances (the western docks were overrun, and Jack had been to the southern docks only once with Leah and Benjamin), and most would have become hopelessly lost, but Jack Swift's uncanny mind remembered everything, and it saved his life.

He broke through the trees and saw the boats, some docked, some pulled up on the shore. Holding his neck where he had been stabbed, Jack sprinted for the boats, hoping he was finally safe.

The versläng made it there first. A group of them burst from the woods on the near side. They spotted him, calling to each other in gibbering cries, and he was cut off.

Arrows launched at him, barely missing his head. Jack plunged back into the trees, looking for an escape, but another pack of roaches darted at him from the woods. He turned right, sprinted away from them, and found himself at the end of Falikos, standing above a twenty-foot cliff overlooking the Irridin. Cornered, Jack spun, saw the versläng closing in on him from all directions, and was left with no choice.

He jumped.

Jack hit the water feet pointed, arms clasped to his side, and shot straight down like a torpedo. The arrows that followed him pulled up short and drifted, but he knew the moment he surfaced, they would come again.

His memory barked: *Tree! Get to the tree!*

It was during the hike that Benjamin

(dead, Benjamin's dead!)

pointed out the tree—it had fallen into the water and leaned up the cliff like a gangplank. The only reason it had been remarkable was the group of foxes that occupied its hollow trunk.

Jack came up for a breath, gulping as much air as he could. As arrows split the water around him, he spotted the tree, not twenty yards away. He shot back under. *Twenty yards.* Jack had once swum the length of Dr. Richards's pool underwater, but that had been three years ago, when he hadn't been hurt, bleeding, and hunted.

He swam.

One piece of luck saved him: the attack on Falikos had been joined by a storm raging offshore, and the normally clear water of the Irridin was cloudy with silt. The murky water made it hard to find his way but protected him from searching eyes above. As he swam, Jack realized his last breath would be the only one he would get—coming up for air now would tell the roaches exactly where he was going.

He swam faster.

Jack found the tree under the water, but there his luck ended. It was hollow, but there was no way to get inside. He needed air. Jack straddled the trunk from underneath, gripped it with his legs, and began stabbing the tree's belly. The knife chopped through the waterlogged wood, punching a small hole. His lungs ached for oxygen, but Jack forced himself to resist the growing need to break to the surface. He gripped the edge of the wood and pried it down. Nothing happened. Squeezing his eyes shut, Jack forced everything he had into one last desperate yank.

The wood ripped away. Jack squeezed his shoulders through the hole, forcing his shoulders and body to follow. Still underwater, crammed inside the trunk, Jack wormed his way toward the waterline—stars danced before his eyes as he began to pass out.

His head broke through, and he sucked in sweet air. The sound was deafening inside the claustrophobic space, but at that moment, Jack didn't care if the versläng heard him or not.

A few quick breaths of dank, moldy air, and he forced himself to stop breathing. He wiggled his way up the trunk toward a tiny hole of light. He edged his eye up near the hole, and it was then he heard the footstep.

He froze. The versläng was above him. Its chitinous feet clicked against the bark. It gibbered something, calling to its companions. Jack jammed his eyes shut and prayed.

The giant roach hurled something down into the water. It croaked; the others on the shore did the same. Just above Jack's head, something smashed into the tree. The boy tried to bring up the knife, but it was pinned against his side. Something *whacked* into the tree, and he watched helplessly as the versläng's claws began to shred through the wood, just inches from his face.

There was a shout from the shore, and the versläng above him suddenly disappeared. Jack wormed his way to the tiny hole and peered through. A group of cadets had fled for the docks like Jack, only to be met by the gang of cockroaches. There was a cry as both groups attacked, but soon, the Watchmen were driven back, retreating into the woods. The roaches went after them.

As Jack watched, a versläng hovered over one of its slain brethren, licked its chops, and suddenly ate the corpse. It gobbled down the body whole. Sickened, Jack watched in horror as the roach swallowed the last bite, then suddenly *grew* right before Jack's eyes—just a few inches—its armored shell expanded, turning from black to a deep indigo. It *yarked*, then ran into the woods to join the hunt.

Jack swallowed—now was his chance. He wiggled into the water and swam for the docks. He slipped inside one of the smaller boats, not much larger than a canoe, and pushed off. His paddle raked against the water furiously. The boat sped out toward the storm.

An insectile cry rang out. Versläng thundered toward the beach. Pulling with everything he had, Jack fled to open water. Arrows chased him. The first hit the hull of the boat, but the rest sank into the water, and soon, he was out of range.

Jack looked over his shoulder to see the scarlet samurai striding to the shoreline. The roaches chirruped to him, pointing at the boat, the tentacles on their forearms flickering excitedly. Jack kept paddling. When he dared look back again, the samurai held a small wooden box in his armored hands. Not wanting to know what was inside, unable to look away, Jack saw the red devil open the box.

Three big insects crawled out from under the lid. An armored finger pointed at Jack, and the things leapt into the air. A trio of winged shapes sped for the boat with a deep, thrumming buzz. As they drew closer, Jack saw they were dragonflies—huge, monstrous, mutated versions of the ones he knew, each with the tail of a scorpion.

They fell on him, stinging his flesh. The boy shouted, flailing his arms as they darted between his hands. The skidshield on Jack's wrist flashed—one of the dragonflies rebounded against the force field like a racquetball. Jack grabbed the paddle and swung, smashing the bug like an overripe peach. The other two darted away, then returned to sting again. In desperation, Jack batted at them with the oar, shouting, but the dragonflies stung him again and again. Enraged, Jack dropped the paddle and snatched a dragonfly out of the air, crushing it in his hands.

The stings burned like fire. He could feel the poison etching its way under his skin. The last dragonfly circled, then dove; Jack brought up his forearm—the skidshield flashed, repelling the dragonfly, but its tail stabbed deep into his wrist. Jack reeled. The boat suddenly went wobbly. He fell, cracking his head against the keel.

He was passing out, the poison creeping through him. The lone dragonfly came in a nosedive, tail raised to strike. Half mad with fury and pain, Jack ripped his knife from its sheath and hurled it at the thing. The blade somehow caught the insect head-on, skewering it in midair. Pinned to his blade, the twitching dragonfly hit the Irridin and sank like a rock.

Groggy, Jack looked back. The versläng were boarding the remaining boats, coming for him. Jack sank against the rail, his head throbbing. There was nothing he could do. His staff was gone, his paddle was gone, his knife was gone. He couldn't feel his fingers anymore.

Losing consciousness, Jack finally gave up. He watched the dock with bleary eyes—shapes and colors blurred and twisted. Nothing was real. When the boats coming for him suddenly exploded into blossoms of emerald fire, it seemed like just another delusion. The flames looked beautiful against the water; the heat felt good against his wet skin.

Pretty—he thought—*it's so pretty.* And then passed out.

The tiny boat drifted for a time, then was caught up in the current and journeyed out into the darkening sea.

Chapter 7

VENTURE BRIGAND

Where there is a sea, there are pirates.

Spanish Proverb

R ain shot from the sky like bullets.

Heaving waves tossed the little boat to and fro as it plunged into the very heart of the storm, into endless fields of rolling water and black sky. For the next several hours, the boy was insensible, blind to the storm, his arm throbbing with a dull pulse that matched the rhythm of the waves pounding against the side of the boat—the tiny shell that lay between him and an infinite depth of blue and black. The storm passed by overhead, but Jack was not awake to see it. The next time he opened his eyes, the water was calm and smooth. From the swampy bottom of the boat, he pulled himself up to a sitting position and stared at the vast expanse of blue around him. There was no land—the Irridin was the entire world.

Dragonfly venom stung his veins.

His wrist was beet red, dotted with two white puckers where the things had got him the worst. Jack tore the sleeve from his shirt and tied the strip tight around the joint below his elbow. The effort was likely too late to do any good, but it was his best bet of slowing down the poison.

As Jack stared out at the endless ocean, his mind spewed up a helpful hint: *When lost at sea, most people die of thirst after three days or starvation after five.* Jack made a bet with himself that poison would beat them both to the punch.

Something ticked inside his mind: *You're not adrift in the Atlantic, idiot. This is the Irridin.*

He cupped his hands in the ocean, brought the water to his lips, and drank. The seawater was fresh.

Perfect. Now all you have to worry about is starvation. And poison.

Fish were everywhere: small red swimmers that looked like fiery bass; large bloated white puffers edged with deadly-looking spines; silvery fan-tailed racers that flashed by in massive schools; and light-green-and-yellow stripers that shadowed his boat, huddling under it for protection. Jack made several attempts to snatch them from the water, but without a hook, bait, or net, the fish eluded him—they swam tantalizingly close, always out of reach.

As evening fell, huge sharks arrived. Jack brought his hands back inside the boat.

White-tipped fins broke the waves as sharks devoured the stripers. A massive leviathan passed below and swallowed one of the sharks.

By his third day at sea, Jack would have gladly traded his hand for some food—he didn't want the hand anymore.

His wrist had gone from an angry red to a swollen purplish color; the white pinpricks were now yellowish, decaying tissue. The pain was unbearable. His mind fled reality, hallucinating. The sky twisted and bent according to no rules of physics. Clouds raced by with dizzying speed; a second sun was born from the first, glowing and throbbing in wild, expanding fiery coronas of yellow, green, and silver, beating on him mercilessly from its high golden throne.

At dusk, Jack was sneaking a handful of water, watching for sharks, when a white figure appeared in the depths beneath the boat. The pale, ghostly form looked just like another fish until its eyes snapped open. Jack stared down at his father—the dead face pale as a blank piece of paper, his empty eyes two holes punched through reality into the obsidian blackness of death. Dad's mouth opened as if he were trying to speak, trying to say something important, but nothing came. Nothing ever would.

Jack's first impulse was to dive down, down into the forever blue, to touch his dad, to rescue him, to pull him back into the world of the living. But, despite the delirium coursing through his veins, Jack forced himself to remain inside the boat. No matter how far the little vessel traveled, washed by the waves and wind, Dad remained exactly fifteen feet below the surface, staring up at him. Jack couldn't tear his eyes away, afraid to blink, afraid to lose his dad again. Eventually, the blistering sun faded below the horizon. Jack tried to hold on to the vision of his father, but slowly, light and time took him away.

He drifted through the night, never quite sleeping, never quite awake, the stars wandering above. He knew he was crying, but whether for his dad, Benjamin, Abrahim, Memphis, the slaughtered Border Watch, or just for himself, he couldn't remember.

When he next became fully conscious, a single sun was high in the air and the hallucinations had stopped.

His arm was much worse.

The purple color engulfed his arm up to the elbow and was now lined with dark threads that crept out of the punctures in a black web. The venom was taking over his body, and soon, it would spread to his heart.

Jack spent a long time trying to ignore the pain, ignore the wounds, ignore the venom creeping through his veins. He tried to pretend his head was clear enough to do the thing he had to do. Eventually, he mustered his courage and tore the other sleeve from his shirt. As he ripped it down the middle, he heard a chilling voice he did not recognize:

How are you going to be a surgeon with only one arm?

Ignoring the voice, Jack inserted his knife sheath into the loop of cloth below his elbow and turned. The tourniquet drew tight. His bloated arm screamed fiery pain. He gritted his teeth and twisted again. White-hot agony shot up his fingers through his entire body, right down to his toes.

His head went light, bright flashbulbs popped behind his eyes. He gasped for air, crying.

One more twist of the tourniquet, and he would lose his arm below the elbow.

Jack flexed his fingers for the last time.

Uttering a prayer, he dug down deep and found the strength to turn the handle again.

The black ship parted the fog like a ghost. Blood-red sails fluttered in the dying sun; light rippled on the deck in a carnival spectacle that made the wood seem alive, twisting with the souls that had been unleashed beneath her mast over so many years at sea. Long black runners—thin triangular flags—ruffled into the air from the pinnacles of all three masts, slender fingers reaching out toward their prey.

The crowsman had been at the watch for hours, dozing lightly in his open wooden perch. The fog had lulled him into a state of tranquility despite the fact that he was the ship's only line of defense against the unknown.

By the time the crowsman saw the boat, it was too late, and Kaymen Creed cursed his luck that God favored the helpless.

He did not cry out to alert the crew but descended the rope ladder quickly, stumbling as his poor footing refused to match the speed of his intent. If the captain found out he was sleeping in the perch, that the ship had come out of the fogbank unprotected and blind…well, the captain was not known for giving second chances.

Shoeless, calloused feet hit the deck with a thud. Kaymen knew his only chance was to kick away the cockle and its cargo before the captain or any of the crew could discover his mistake. Whoever was aboard would perish in the open sea, but as Kaymen's father had always said: *Your own life is worth a dozen others.* The irony that his father had been murdered by twelve of his closest friends never crossed the crowsman's mind.

Kaymen snatched a dock pole and snuck to the bow. Luckily, the fog was creeping in again, and his black deed would be hidden in the white mist.

The little cockle boat had only one passenger: a young boy no more than twelve. Blond hair was plastered over his face, his skin burned red by the sun. His arm was purple black, nearly dead below the elbow. A cloth was cinched tight around the arm, a knife sheath tangled up in the knots. Kaymen couldn't figure it—the boy had apparently done that to himself. *Well, then,* he thought, *if it's suicide he wants, I'll help him on his way.* Kaymen lowered the dock pole and pushed the cockle back out to sea.

"Good fishin', Kaymen?"

A lean, rangy figure appeared out of the fog, grinning like the cat that caught the canary. Kaymen cursed under his breath —*the pilot.*

"Caught a *big* one," said the pilot, eyeing the cockle boat. "Dinnae look like good eatin', though. Reckon that's why ya threw it back?"

Kaymen's shifty eyes glanced up and down the deck—the pilot was alone. The crowsman's hand slipped to the knife behind his back, his mind bent on murder. "Nar lissen, Pilot. I waz jest fishin' this li'l cockle outta d'water an misst 'er by a titch. Yer giv' me a hand 'ere an' we divvy th' treasure thar twix ye an me, and no one th' wiser."

"Treasure?"

All pirates have a weak spot for treasure, but none more so than the pilot of the black ship *Venture Brigand.* The lean man bent over the railing, taking a closer look at the cockle, and Kaymen raised his knife high to strike the killing blow.

Whatever strange angel watched over the pilot must have whispered in his ear at the last moment. As Kaymen's knife came down, the pilot dodged by a hair's breadth, yanked his own knife, and punched it through Kaymen's hand, pinning it to the ship's rail like an insect on display.

Kaymen dropped to his knees, screaming, "Ya pig-ey'd rat-fac'd black-soul'd son of a *whore!*" The pilot admired his handiwork with a scoundrel's grin. "I'll do murder on ya and yer 'ntire bast'rd family, ya yella cuss—"

"What th' devil's beard is goin' on here?" A loud voice boomed out, and nine swords, well-used weapons all, were at the pilot's throat.

The man grinned. "Kaymen's found a drift, Cap'n."

Captain Dagan Saltz, the Black Buccaneer of the South Irridin Sea, folded his arms over his muscled chest, scowling. Pirate legend had it that Saltz killed his first man on his eighth birthday and commandeered his fist ship at twelve. Four decades had seen him terrorize the southern world, bringing fire and death to every port, peninsula, and palace that had the bad luck to cross his path. Feared for his unique method of plunder, Saltz secretly shadowed brother pirates, lay in wait as the gang of rival robbers boarded and pillaged a passing vessel, then—after they had exhausted themselves—Saltz would kill every remaining man and seize the loot of both vessels at once. The Pirate King commanded a crew of fifty hardened villains, and the bodies of the men who crossed him littered the ocean floor.

His heavy chest was half dressed in a bright-crimson topcoat decorated with medals, insignias, and badges stolen from the men he had brought to their knees; his leather boots had been pried from the amputated legs of the last man who had challenged him. His brown head was bald as a stone, but a black braided beard spilled over his chest—two tips of the whiskered dreadlocks burned with an eternal flame, a half-failed curse from a dying sea witch—and his face was continually surrounded by black smoke, his eyes bloodshot from the fumes.

"Cap'n, please," stammered Kaymen, "I din't do nuthin' 'gainst yer—"

Saltz cuffed him across the face and spat a wad of tobacco on the man's dirty shirt. "Yer on *crow's* t'day Kaymen-man, yaright?"

"Cap'n, I—"

Saltz belted him hard enough to make the assembled crew wince. "Aye or nay, Kaymen-man?"

"Aye, Cap'n," Kaymen sniveled.

"Yer on crow's, me ship's eyes and ears, whilst we split the thick white wind, and ya let a cockle baby like this'un come striking-far from me ship, me crew and me own self 'thout so much as a hail and holler. An' compound the grievance *double,* do ya, by slippin' the crow, leavin' me blind whilst ya heave to what bounty the sea brings, sending to the blue what right belongs a-mine?"

"Nar, Cap'n!" sputtered Kaymen. "I's tryin' to pull her to when th' bloody pilot jumps me hindwise ta rob the loot what's yers!"

"Mine?" Saltz's calloused hands gripped the crowsman's shirt, pulling him close to his flaming beard. Kaymen squealed as his hand pulled taut against the pilot's knife. "I'll tell ya what's *mine!"* bellowed Saltz. "Every meal ya take, every sun ya see, every heartbeat in yer chest, and every breath ya *suck* is *mine.* But *yer* no longer part o' me or mine, Kaymen-man—ya belong to th' sea." His singing saber whickered through the air. Kaymen stood for a moment longer, staring dumbly at his captain, then his severed head fell into the sea with a plop.

No man aboard spoke a word.

The Black Buccaneer chopped Kaymen's arm off and kicked the rest of him overboard. He left the severed hand pinned to the rail. "Crew drop sail a'half."

Pirates jumped to the order, every man bolting to his task. Only the pilot did not move. "My knife? She's a good pig-sticker, that one."

Saltz sheathed his simmering saber with a snap. "The hand stays."

The pilot shrugged and shouted over his shoulder, "Long-boatmen, lower away to retrieve the drift!"

The Pirate King's thick eyebrows knotted together. "Ya giv'n orders t'me ship now, are ya, Pilot-man?"

"Yer ship, yer knife, yer drift, Cap'n. If ya want to let the cockle slip to the blue, it's yer pleasure." The pilot leaned against the rail, relaxed. "Should I call them back?"

The Black Buccaneer set his jaw. "Heave it to, an' pinch th' youngling to the truth. And, Pilot"—the bloody pirate leaned in close—"ya put an order t'me crew once more 'thout my say, and yer head will follow *his*." Saltz turned on his heel and disappeared into the mist.

Leaning against the rail, the pilot of the *Venture Brigand* hooked a calloused thumb in his belt and eyed the little cockle, wondering if this might be just the lucky penny he was looking for.

Jack woke to find he was hallucinating again: he was no longer surrounded by an ocean but a sea of treasure.

Sumptuous piles of gold coins in all shapes and sizes spilled out like a carpet all around him, splitting the seams of canvas bags and overflowing wooden chests. Some pieces were tiny and thin, hammered flat like the Roman coins he had seen on his father's archaeological digs. Some were wheels, delicately crafted into jewelry-quality designs. Others were ugly, fat slabs the size of saucers with no discernable design other than the dents the smithy's hammer had smashed in their sides. There were jewels too: rubies, diamonds, emeralds, huge strands of pearls, and a dozen different orange, purple, and aqua stones he had never seen before in his life. Stunning works of art, decorated fabrics, musical instruments, and extravagant furnishings littered the expanse of expense. The boy got the impression he had just missed a vast orgy where the owners had bathed and rolled in their opulent fortune, then suddenly disappeared. Jack laughed—he really was going insane.

He looked down at his wrist, wondering blandly if he had lost his arm.

There were leeches.

Glistening, fat brown-and-yellow-striped parasites wiggled and fed, their puckered mouths sucking greedily at his arm, some of them half a foot long, bloated and heavy with his blood. Jack screamed, swatting at the things, panicked and repulsed. The leeches fell away, excreting gobs of viscous yellow slime and blood as they splattered to the floor. Terrified, Jack looked at his arm, certain there would be nothing left but bloody bone.

The poison was gone. The puncture wound was still red and inflamed, but the spidery black veins had disappeared completely. Most of his arm was pink, and the worst damage he could find was a bad sunburn.

Jack was still trying to figure out what had happened when a blue webbed hand placed itself on his chest and pushed him down.

The thing was not human. Its face had the sloping, delicate bone structure of a gecko, but its scales were dry and pebbly like an iguana. Its blue skin was awash with intricate gold curlicues that swooped down the length of its body, ending at the long, webbed tree-frog fingers.

It picked up the leeches and placed them back on Jack's forearm. As the squirming things attached to the wound once more, Jack immediately felt a heady, dreamlike sensation seep into his mind. The blue gecko appraised him with big round yellow eyes, nodding.

A booted foot smashed into the gecko's side, sending it sprawling across the room with a *squawk.* Dreamily, Jack looked up to see a goliath of a man towering over him—huge knots of orange hair grew in random patches from the man's skin, several bound in greased pigtails. A meaty hand gripped Jack's wounded forearm, twisted it roughly, and examined it like a side of beef.

"Der junkleeches got der pisson outta 'im, Pilot. 'E's up." The hair-patch man glanced over his shoulder. "Time ta go to work on 'im?"

Several hard-faced raiders turned to the man in charge. The pilot lounged in a throne-like chair, his feet up on a long table, flicking golden coins over slim fingers. In the candlelight, Jack caught a glimpse of the man's face—his swarthy skin was olive toned. Long black hair spilled from his head like oil. He watched Jack with silky eyes.

At his nod, the hair-patch goliath turned to Jack with a broken-toothed grin: "Watcher doin' out ta sea all by yer lonesome, boy?"

Despite the soporific effect of the junkleeches, Jack's mind told him not to answer. Memphis had warned him to keep his secrets even from the Watch cadets; these men were something worse than Watchmen. And Jack had a feeling he knew what they would do if they discovered Falikos was overrun and unprotected. He clamped his mouth shut.

Bartolimon, the hair-patch man, grinned. He always enjoyed this game, especially at the beginning when they still had hope. The greatest pleasure in his short and brutal life was to see a man broken. He cracked a fist across the boy's jaw, then drove a second into his gut. The wind *wooshed* from his captive's lungs. The boy fell over, coughing—Bartolimon kicked him down. *"Watcher story, boy?"* He grabbed the prisoner's blond hair and ripped his head back. "Where'd ye come from?"

Jack gasped violently, trying to catch his breath. Bartolimon's fists pummeled Jack's gut in a rapid tattoo. The boy gripped his stomach, crying out in pain, trying not to vomit. Bartolimon cracked his knuckles. "Use yer mouth ta speek, young'un, while ye've still gotta tongue an' teeth t' tell th' tale."

In Jack's mind, he saw the Watch fall, saw his friends die, saw Abrahim beheaded, saw Benjamin buried in black fangs— they all went down fighting.

He spat in the goliath's face.

Bartolimon stared, stunned. The kid attacked, kicking and screaming like a demon. Fists and feet flew, hitting his eyes, his nose, his groin—anywhere they could reach. The helpless runt became a rabid wolverine. Bartolimon snapped his hand around the boy's throat and jerked him four feet in the air. Still, the boy struggled—Bartolimon was crushing his windpipe, but the little terror refused to quit. "Zheng! *Rope!*" A man lashed the boy's hands in a series of knots only a seaman could decipher and threw the rope over a beam. He yanked, pulling the boy into the air by his wrists. As Bartolimon shoved the frenzied prisoner away, the boy kicked out with one of those strange black shoes and belted him square in the eye.

Cruel laughter erupted from the assembled men; they slapped their thighs, delighted to see such a little thing take a lick out of the giant. A thin smile crept over the pilot's lips.

"That one's got some fight to 'im, Barty!" shouted one.

"Kick 'im again, little *bit!*" exclaimed another.

A new man came through the door, drawn by the laughter. "Wot's the rumpus?"

"Th' runt just cleared Barty's crow's nest!"

Frustrated by his stinging eye, humiliated by his mates, Bartolimon's face went scarlet. He ripped the boatknife from his belt and charged toward Jack, ready to gut him stem to stern. Jack's eyes went wide.

Metal struck metal with a clang, and the knife spun across the room. The pilot stood before Bartolimon, his cutlass already back in its sheath. "Ya kill *him*, Cap'n kills *you.* More food for the fish." The pilot flashed a grin. "Might take a whale to eat you, Barty, but it'll get done."

Bartolimon barked in the pilot's face: "'E's gonna pay fer that, Pilot!"

"Aye, he will, Barty." The pilot hefted a mallet in his right hand. "He will."

The club was huge. Thick metal flanges ringed the cudgel's massive head; the chipped and rusted iron had seen a dozen years of battle and crushed a hundred bones. The pilot slapped the thick end into his open palm and eyed his prisoner. "This is gonna *hurt.*"

Hanging from the rope, Jack gave up—his fight was finished. He had already been shot, stabbed, poisoned, and shanghaied, but he didn't want to get beaten to death.

"My name is Jack Swift; I came from the isl—"

"*O, no,* boychick," the pilot cut him off. "You're not gettin' out of *this.*" He cocked the huge mace back over his shoulder. The other men leaned in, awaiting the awesome moment of collision. Jack gritted his teeth as the pilot swung the weapon with all his strength.

The mace split Bartolimon's skull.

The hair-patch man hit the ground like a lead weight. The mallet whirled, smashed the chins of two raiders, and knocked them cold. Other men scrambled for their weapons—the pilot leapt at them, a shout on his lips. In a matter of moments, the entire gang lay beaten at his feet.

Bartolimon reared up like a wounded bear. The pilot swung underhanded and buried the mallet in the big man's crotch. Barty dropped to his knees. The pilot cocked the mallet over his shoulder and, with a swing that would have knocked a baseball out of Wrigley Field, cracked it across the giant's jaw.

Silence. The pilot dropped the mace and spun on Jack. "Couldn't hold out for *five* more seconds, could ya, kid? For jest a moment there, I thought ya were tough."

Jack stammered: "Y-you saved me—?"

The lean man cocked an eyebrow. "Who said anythin' about *saving* you?"

A crash, the door burst open, the pilot spun, ripping his cutlass free. Three pirates raced into the room, ready for a fight. The pilot breathed a sigh of relief and lowered his blade. "Little late, Punch."

One of the pirates, a short black scrapper, grinned widely. "Seems ye've got 'er under control, Pilot."

The pilot stepped into them, his oily voice quiet. "Tie and gag these, get Needles and the others up on deck, and dispatch the mates."

Punch shook his head. "We're gonna have trouble with Carnadale—"

"Poisoned his coffee half an hour ago. Ya couldn't wake him with a ten-man band. Bind these, then get him…and do it *quietly.*"

Punch and the others quickly tied the unconscious pirates. Jack dangled from the rope, afraid to say anything, fearing it would do him more harm than good.

The pilot tied his raven-black hair into a quick ponytail. His thumb popped the cork from a bottle, and he took a stiff drink.

"Jest a bit o' fortune—"He picked up a stray coin, flipped it up, and snatched it from the air. "Arright, boys, let's see what we're made of."

Punch and the others went through the door, ready for blood. As they did, Jack found his voice. "Good luck."

The pilot glanced over his shoulder at Jack and disappeared through the door.

Jack hung by his wrists, captive in a room of senseless men.

Gecko-things emerged from the shadows. As they crept over the pirates, Jack had the sickening thought they were going to eat the men alive. A creaking sound came from above; he glanced up. The blue-and-yellow gecko was crawling down the rope toward him. Jack swallowed. It stopped, wrapped its tail around the rope, and peered at him with big yellow eyes. Jack realized the thing was covered in brown splotches—bruises from multiple encounters with the pirates. The freshest one, where Bartolimon had kicked it, was oozing blood.

It waited for him to do something.

Swallowing his fear, Jack forced a smile. "Hello, there," he said, using the same voice he would use for a small child or a nervous dog. The gecko drew away. "It's okay, it's okay. I won't hurt you."

Booted feet suddenly pounded on the deck above. Jack could make out muffled shouts, then a scream. Urgently, Jack looked to the gecko. "Untie me."

Big yellow eyes blinked. "Please," Jack repeated. "Untie me...*please.*" The thing hesitated, then climbed down, tightened its tail around the rope, and began to work on the knot. Tree-frog fingers deciphered the elaborate tangle with surprising speed, pulling the complicated braid apart like a child's toy. The knot broke free, and Jack dropped to the floor in a heap.

Geckos scattered, fleeing. The blue one scurried up the rope to hide in the rafters, peering down at him. Jack's fingers tingled as blood flowed back into his arms. The poison was gone, but his forearm felt like it had been run over by a car. Jack unclamped the skidshield—the pirates had not taken it, mistaking the thing for common leather—and moved it over his bad wrist; it would serve well enough as a cast.

Jack spied a long quarterstaff leaning against the wall and took it. Made of a dark wood, maybe teak, each tip was capped in pure silver. It was beautiful, but Abrahim was right—a staff was a useless weapon in a real fight. *The trick,* Jack thought, *is to avoid the fight.*

Ignoring his own advice, he went through the door.

The *Venture Brigand* was unlike anything Jack had ever seen: the ship did not float *in* the water but *above* it. Huge arches descended from either side of her hull like wings, bowing gracefully down to the slender pontoons that supported her high above the water like a colossal catamaran. The speed of the ship was incredible; with its belly airborne, only the two outriggers skimmed the surface of the waves like twin surfboards. The vessel defied every oceanic law of physics, but the ship was not science —she was art.

Her deck was in chaos. A multitude of pirates, some human, most not, battled with a fury bordering on insanity, raging up and down the decks with cutlasses, axes, and knives. The howl was thunderous.

Jack wedged himself behind a wine barrel, praying he wouldn't be noticed. He spotted the pilot—teeth bared, screaming at the top of his lungs, fighting with reckless bravado—as he beat down his opponent and sprang forward, fiery eyes searching for the next challenger.

A heavy boot crunched into the stair beside Jack's head.

"Wha' in th' hail an' hammer is hap'nin 'board me ship?"

The battle stopped instantly. Jack peered up to see a brown barrel-chested man standing on the stairs above him. His beard was bound in dreadlock braids—two long whiskers burned like twin torches—and black smoke trickled evilly about the man's bald head.

The pilot stepped forward. "Men want a new captain, Cap'n."

Bloodshot eyes flared as the Pirate King scowled. "An' I s'pose ye'd be the man ta tell 'em so, Pilot-man."

"Aye."

Saltz's eye twitched, his body trembled in fury. "*Mutiny!* Ya men be blasted an' baked in the fires of hell isself!" He towered to his full height. "Which one of ya treacherous dogs stand wi' th' cursed, lyin', pissonous pilot?"

A shout rose from half the men. Others joined their voices until nearly the entire crew bellowed favor for the younger man. The pilot said nothing, an elbow cocked against the railing, fingering his sword hilt.

Saltz was livid—even the fires of his beard burned hotter. "Mutiny! *Mutiny!* I'll see the lot of ya sunk to the deep!" He turned to the pilot, scowling. "If ya want t'take me ship, ya must take *me.*"

"Reckon I will."

The Pirate King walked three steps and stood nose to nose with the young man, his bulk of banded muscle against the pilot's lean frame. He spoke in a raspy whisper that only the pilot— and Jack—could hear. "This nay be me first mutiny, Pilot-man. I've bested twenny better'n you. When I'm done with ya, I'll tear yer limbs from their sockets, crack yer bones, and suck the marrow before I stuff yer skull onna pike 'bove me prow and use yer black hollow eyes ta spy fer sharks." He raised his voice, shouting: "It's the pirate's duel!"

A blast of cheers roared from the crew, their hearts ready for blood. Men cleared a path, making a ring as the Black Buccaneer ripped off his topcoat, revealing his tanned and tattooed chest. The dark pilot cricked his neck and flexed; sinewy muscles rippled beneath his shirt.

Slowly, the Pirate King drew the singing saber from its sheath. The *wikk* hummed through the blade, swelling the air like a deep note struck on a grand piano. The sound reverberated endlessly…instead of fading, it grew louder as the air around the sorcerous sword simmered.

The pilot drew the knife and the cutlass he used so well, but Jack realized for the first time that, against the Black Buccaneer and the majik of the singing saber, the pilot stood the same chance as a fox fighting a bear.

Saltz lunged—the pilot parried with both blades and launched the attack. His speed was too much for the bigger man;

the Pirate King was driven back. The pilot nicked the captain's ear with his dagger, drawing first blood. Saltz shoved his boot into the pilot's chest and kicked him away.

The captain turned, masking his free hand (only Jack saw it flash into his pocket), and when Saltz spun again, a black steel-tipped dart flew straight at the pilot's chest. The younger man dodged—narrowly escaping the needle—and it struck the man behind him. The pirate fell to the deck, stone dead.

Saltz's singing saber blistered the air. The pilot was forced back against the railing as the captain pounded at him, the saber singing an opera of blood. The dagger in the pilot's hand shattered into a million pieces. One of the shards of metal spun through the air and cut the pilot's brow. Blood poured into his eyes. Half blind, the pilot staggered back. He gripped the cutlass in both fists as Saltz smashed him with a hailstorm of blows. The pilot's knees buckled. The singing saber cut a deep slash across his chest. Another swing came straight for his neck. Jerking back, the pilot lost his footing and plummeted over the side of the ship.

The crew rushed to the edge, hoping to see the splash as the pilot disappeared into the Irridin.

The man hung from the narrow arch that suspended the *Venture Brigand*, dangling over the waves by one hand. His other hand still gripped his sword. He clamped the blade between his teeth and grabbed at the slippery, wet wood. Above, Dagan Saltz laughed. "Cummon ye, Pilot-man, drop yer carcass to the sharks!"

Muscles straining, the pilot pulled himself up, planted his feet on the narrow beam of the arch, and stood, balancing precariously above the roaring sea. Hands outstretched, barely keeping his feet on the waxy wood, he made his way toward the ship like an acrobat on a balance beam. Saltz reached for another poisoned dart.

Jack found himself running. His staff smacked the Pirate King's hand; the dart *thwonked* into the deck rail. Saltz's fist shot out, cuffed Jack across the jaw, and spun to strike at the pilot—too late. The lean man reached the rail, vaulted over Saltz's swing, and landed on the deck behind him.

Saltz snarled, glaring at Jack. "Yer little monkey-boy dies ri' after ye, Pilot-man."

The bloody pilot grasped a ship's rope for support. "Then he'll be alive awhile yet."

The Pirate King lunged once more. The pilot cut one end of the rope. Clutching to the other, the man was jerked into the air. Captain Dagan Saltz, the Black Buccaneer of the South Irridin Sea, looked up…and was crushed beneath the falling cargo crate the pilot had unleashed.

The crew broke into a tumultuous cheer as the pilot landed on the upper deck. "Away the cockle!" he shouted.

Four men seized hold of the little boat Jack had occupied for four days and hurled it overboard. The pilot dragged the semiconscious Pirate King from beneath the wreckage and ripped the singing saber from his hand. "Dagan Saltz"—he grinned—"get off my boat." He kicked Saltz in the chest. Arms spinning, the Black Buccaneer toppled over the rail and dropped thirty feet into the cockle boat with a *smack.*

Dazed and defeated, Dagan Saltz shot a baleful eye upward as the cockle rocked madly beneath him. One flame on his beard had gone out; the other was lighting the rest of his hair afire. He was too furious to notice, screaming up at the ship. "I'll take yer head, Pilot-man! I'll take *all* yer heads! Give me my sword! Give me my ship!"

The pilot plucked a rusty blade from the man beside him. "A new sword for a new ship!" he said and hurled it like a spear. The blade whistled down and punched a hole through the bottom of the cockle. Taking on water, the tiny boat dropped away behind the *Venture Brigand,* leaving the dreaded Pirate King bellowing in vengeful rage, fully in command of an empty, sinking ship.

One of the crew shouted, "Hey-ho, the pilot Rooker *Flynn!*"

The crew burst into cheers.

The lean pirate grinned.

"*Captain* Flynn."

When Jack was brought to the captain's stateroom, he found the former pilot and several raiders (including Punch and the other men who had started what would later be remembered as the Cockleshell Mutiny) huddled around a tilting pile of maps, bickering and shouting at each other.

"We're carryin' the secon' biggest haul I ever seen," Punch was yelling, "an' you wanna go looking for trouble!"

"We're not lookin' for trouble, we *are* trouble," answered Rooker Flynn. "The Cull is not an hour to, and the biggest plum on the peninsula!"

"'Tis a fool's errand 'thout we first stow our swag at the Bladed Caves!"

Argument resumed in earnest—maps and bits of treasure were hurled across the room as each man made his point. One of the gecko-things crawled too close to the melee and was flung past Jack's head and out the porthole. "The *Brigand*'s packed to the gills with loot!" barked Punch. "There's nar point in pillaging the coast! I say we head for the caves!"

Rooker Flynn dropped one hand to his blade. "And yer *captain* says we make for Rimmy's Cull. Unless you're looking to mutiny twice in one day." The men swallowed, eyeing each other. None of them were prepared to go up against the pilot's speed now that he had the singing saber.

Flynn looked up to see Jack. "Ahh—my lucky penny!" He grinned broadly, slapping Jack on the back with a calloused hand. "Ya jest about saved my bacon there, kid. Have an apple." He shoved an entire bowl full of fruit into the boy's arms, gripped Jack's shoulders, and shook him back and forth like a rag doll. "I owe ya my life, mebbe. If there's anythin' I can do for ya, *ever,* ya jest let me know an', like *that*"—he snapped his slim fingers—"it's *done.*"

"Well, actually—"Jack began.

"Later. Punch!" Flynn strode across the room and grabbed Punch's shoulders. "Yer promoted. First mate. Tell the men we're headed for Rimmy's Cull and get these blood-damned lizards outta my cabin!" Rooker barged through the men and out the door.

Jack looked down at the bowl of fruit in his hands and realized he had not eaten in days. He crunched his teeth into a fat red apple and felt the sweet juice drip down his chin. As he took another bite, he spied the blue-and-gold gecko—the one that had untied him—hiding atop a bookcase. Jack tossed an apple to the thing. It didn't react at all; it simply caught the apple in one tree-frog hand. It started at Jack, blinked, and disappeared through a porthole with the fruit.

Half an hour later, Jack found the new captain standing atop the forecastle of the *Venture Brigand,* one leg cocked up on the railing. He had a small gold ring in each hand, one close to his eye and one extended toward shore. As Jack approached, he caught a glance through the nearer ring, and the waves looked impossibly huge in that small space. It was as if the two empty rings made an impossible spyglass, a magical gadget.

Jack cleared his throat. The captain opened one eye, then closed it again. "Get enough to eat?"

"Yes, thank you."

"Good…good…" the captain said without interest. "Go have some more."

"I want to ask for that favor now."

Flynn slipped the spyglass rings back onto his middle finger and glared at him. "I'm on the verge of making fortune-hunting history, boychick. I ain't got time for sidetracks."

"I—"Jack forced himself to stop stammering. "I need to find a man."

Rooker shrugged. "Ship's full of 'em, take yer pick."

Jack gritted his teeth. "I need to find Valerian *Tsai.*"

Flynn's face changed. A strange shadow passed over it, a mix of surprise, puzzlement, and fear. For the first time, the pilot looked human…almost boyish. In that moment, Jack realized the mutineer couldn't be more than twenty years old. "Valerian Tsai? He's jest a *legend,* kid. Nothing more. The Grey Knight's a tale people tell their babies at bedtime."

Jack cocked his head. "I was with him four days ago."

Rooker Flynn's eyes widened, then narrowed sharply. "Jest who the hell *are* you?"

A loud voice suddenly cried out from the crow's nest: "Land ho! *Land ho!* Rimmy's Cull dead ahead!"

Slowly, Jack began to realize that not all the fog that surrounded them was the product of nature—an acrid smell ebbed its way into the white wind, and the fog became smoke. From somewhere out in the void, Jack heard the terrified screams of thousands of people. Red light flickered ahead, and suddenly the *Venture Brigand* broke through.

Rimmy's Cull was on fire.

Chapter 8

VICE & VENOM

> *To keep you is no benefit,*
> *to destory you is no loss.*
> **Khmer Rouge**

Sam Rimmy found the cove, sheltered on the east and west by large, sloping limestone jetties that reached out into the ocean like the encompassing arms of a loving mother. He built the first structure from the blinding white rock that made the cliffs gleam and started a modest sea outpost. Located at the tip of the Masthead Peninsula, the anchorage occupied the perfect port for passing vessels looking to sell their goods, and Sam's trade flourished. Over the centuries, his single shop grew to a city of gleaming white stone, a broker's bazaar of imported fruits, foreign garments, strange spices, exotic liquors, majik potions, and strange animals bought and bartered by every race and culture on the globe. As the bold blue-and-white diamond insignia flag of the Cull became a symbol of trade throughout the world, the white city took its place at the center of the hub, the crossroads for every commodity, cargo, consignment, and saleable sundry on the continent, a premiere destination for the gold mines of Ali Mifune in the west, the spice traders of Cull Laverlock in the north, and the mercenary rumrunners from Javernis Twist in the deep-blue south. The Cull that still bore Sam Rimmy's name was a wild, untamable, magnificent place, and a hundred thousand souls called it home.

It burned gloriously.

Smoke and haze enveloped the doomed port like a death shroud. Shouts of panic burst through the burning fumes as unseen men, women, and children fled like ghosts in the haze.

The pirate ship *Venture Brigand* entered the harbor as a shark smelling blood.

Captain Rooker Flynn turned to face the crew. Most of his men were nervous, but their eyes sparkled at the thought of easy plunder. "Arright, boys," he said, "we hit 'em hard an' fast an' we're gone afore they knew we were here. Cut a swath down the dock an' take no truck from man or beast. Anything shiny goes in the swag fast as fish, and any man not back on the *Brigand* in an hour gets to swim back to the Bladed Caves. Yaright?" The men bellowed their assent; their new captain was no fool. "Each man to it, then!"

As the crew sped to gather their gear, Flynn snatched Jack's shoulder. "Don't think I've forgot about ya, boychick. You're sticking right by my side. Kaito!"

"Yessir?"

"How long's Jannisan been dead?"

"Three days, sir!"

"Good. Bring me his clothes." Rooker turned to Jack. "If you're gonna play pirate, boy, ya'd best look the part."

Jack swallowed. "You're giving me a dead man's clothes?"

"Until you kill one yerself."

The pants fit, but the shirt was too big for Jack's skinny frame. Every item of clothing was pure black—apparently Jannisan had little imagination. Rooker eyeballed Jack up and down. "Ya look about as dangerous as my little sister. An' that staff's a pretty little stick. Ya want a sword."

"I'm better with this."

"Kaito!" Flynn shouted. "Gimme that greatcloak, an' yer scarf—quick now!" Rooker wrapped the cloak over Jack's shoulders and looped the gauzy black scarf around Jack's face like an Arabian Bedouin. Rooker took a step back, surveying his handiwork. "Ya look less a girl, but I'll never buy a pirate without a blade." Flynn pulled his old cutlass belt from the deckwheel and slung it over Jack's shoulder. "Perfect! Two weapons an' no face! Terror from the high seas!"

The *Venture Brigand* came to rest straddling Swordfisher's Dock. A hatch popped open, and raiders plunged from the belly of the *Brigand*, weapons brandished and ready for blood.

Captain Flynn glanced at the boy in black. "What's yer name, boychick?"

"Jack."

"Well, stick to my hip like a child to its mother, Jack, or I'll stuff my blade in your neck. *Ho!*" He snatched Jack and dragged him overboard.

Rimmy's Cull was all one angle—up. Cobbled streets of fat white stones twisted crazily uphill from the docks, making the pirates' charge a mad dash against gravity. Into the smoke they plunged, weapons at the ready, but they met with not a flicker of resistance as citizens threw themselves out of the way of the robber gang. As they charged up the hill, the buccaneers gained confidence, realizing the captain's plan was a masterful one: if they worked quickly, they could be away without shedding a drop of blood.

Booted feet smashed open the door of a jewelry house at the top of the rise. Piles of loot disappeared from the showroom as pirates stuffed gems in their sweaty shirts by the hairy handful. Outside, two citizens fought back when a pirate ripped a necklace from a woman's bodice, but the pair was quickly kicked down the street by half a dozen cutthroats.

Rooker Flynn's silky eyes scanned the crazy city streets around him, ignoring the glee of his compatriots. "Punch! Take six an' eyeball what's ahead!" He grabbed Punch's collar and whispered, "This blaze is a piece of good luck, but it ain't an accident. Whoever started it is somewhere out there. Keep yer tip up." Punch nodded and led his team down a wide courtyard into the smoke.

Jack watched as flames engulfed the city. "Why isn't anyone fighting the fire? Aren't they going to form a bucket brigade or something?"

"What's a bucket brigade?" asked Captain Flynn. "The town magicians'll snuff it like a candle. Shoulda had it out afore it spread this far. Probably drunk. Speakin' of—grab me a bottle from the saloon."

Jack turned the way Flynn indicated, then stopped. He realized that the ornate designs above the shops weren't just artful embellishments—the lines and squiggles were *signs*. To Jack, they were utterly incomprehensible.

"Which one's the saloon?"

"What are ye, kid? Some kind of feeblemind? The one that says *saloon*!"

Jack gritted his teeth. "I can't read."

The captain stared at him, then laughed a loud, braying cackle. "Ya cannae *read*? Where'd ya come from, boychick, the idiot house?"

Jack's blood burned with humiliation. He wanted to sock the pirate in the face. Rooker Flynn cocked his head, curious. "Ya dinnae *look* like a dolt. Not with those canny eyes." He brought his face even with Jack's. "Jest where *are* ya from, boychick?"

Before Jack could answer, there was a shout. Through the fog and smoke staggered Punch, bleeding from his shoulder, limping. *"Back!"* he croaked. "Back to the shi—"Something behind him split the smoke, swirling contrails of vapor. Punch's eyes grew wide, and he fell, a black arrow jutting from his back.

Jack felt a nightmare grip his chest. He stumbled backward, grabbing Rooker's shirt in white knuckles. He couldn't breathe. His heart fluttered in his chest, a desperate bird caught within his ribs. He heard hoofbeats ring against the white stone like the hammer stroke of death. A tall rider emerged from the smoke, silhouetted against the fire, a burning sword in his hands—Jack's nightmare come to life.

The scarlet samurai came on horseback, flanked by a horde of gibbering, twitching versläng. They poured from the bridge tunnel, a dark plague spreading over white cobblestones—a black cloud surrounding a flaming eye. The red devil raised one armored fist, outstretched one hooked finger, and breathed one word: *"Kill."*

Versläng charged, screeching for blood. Jack turned, but the captain was already gone, running like a rabbit. The boy's foot caught in his oversized cloak, and he stumbled, his head cracking against the white stone. He scuttled backward like a crab, but the versläng were almost on top of him.

A cry rang out from his left as a huge mob of men appeared from an alley, screaming an attack. Brandishing old swords, hatchets, and pitchforks, the riot plunged into the side of the versläng, punching a hole through the middle of the group. Weapons rang, shouts were raised, and the battle was joined.

As Jack scrabbled to his feet, a second horseman pounded into the courtyard. The man's hair flew madly as he leapt from the saddle and joined the fray. There was something familiar about the way he fought, the way he moved, the way his red hair flashed in the sun—then the figure turned, and Jack realized why.

Leah.

She fought like an Amazon queen, pounding at the enemy, a blade gripped in each hand, felling the versläng as she rallied the Cullans to her call. "Stand your ground!" she shouted. "Push them back! *Back!*" Leah Archer led the untrained men like a battle-seasoned commander, driving them to valiant attack.

Jack spun to see the pirate taking advantage of the distraction, barking orders to his men to pack up and move out, slapping the ones who moved too slowly, glancing nervously over his shoulder at the battle behind them. Jack caught up to Flynn as the lean man heaved a large wooden chest over his shoulder.

"Captain! You've got to help them!"

Flynn kicked one of the pirates, sending him racing for the dock. "They dinnae need my help, boychick, they're dying plenty well on their own."

The captain turned down the hill. Jack's hand flashed out and gripped his sleeve. "Rooker!" Jack shouted. "*Please.* You said you owe me your life."

"I did, boy. And I'll be happy to repay the debt if I ever see you again." Rooker Flynn disappeared into the shadows, fleeing to the *Venture Brigand.*

Jack cursed him and ran back toward the courtyard.

Leah knocked the scarlet samurai from his mount. As he fell, she smashed her blades against the plate mail protecting his legs, arms, and chest. Had he not been so heavily armored, she might have beaten him. The samurai's right hand snapped out, gripped her throat, and yanked her off her feet. Leah dropped her swords as metal fingers choked the wind out of her.

Jack plunged forward and smashed his staff against the red devil's helmet. The samurai reared back, brought his sword up, batted the stick from Jack's hands, and kicked him to the ground. Jack looked up just in time to see the flaming sword coming right for his head.

He threw up his hands and something *ptanged*—the sword ricocheted away as the skidshield flashed bright. The red samurai roared, threw Leah twenty feet across the courtyard, and gripped his flaming sword with both hands to strike again.

Before the blow could fall, a group of Cullans smashed into the samurai's side, pounding at him with a dozen homemade weapons. As the dark warrior was pushed away, Jack snatched his staff and bolted to Leah's side.

She lay limp in the street. Jack grabbed her under the arms and dragged her backward, looking for a place to hide. He spotted a narrow stone stairway, its half wall facing the courtyard, and dragged Leah up the incline into the shadows. As her weight settled against him, he realized she was breathing. *Thank God.*

A single versläng appeared at the bottom of the stair. Its claws scraped against the stone like knives. The tiny tentacles of its forearms flittered in excitement as it crawled up the stairs toward its prey.

Jack was trapped under Leah's body. As he fumbled for the cutlass slung over his back, the versläng pounced. Jack tore the sword free and batted the cockroach aside. It hit the wall, hissed, and climbed again. Unable to move, Jack hurled the sword at the creature. The black thing leapt over him and landed in a crouch atop the stair. Razor teeth grinned as the versläng twitched on its haunches like a cat preparing to pounce. Jack yanked at the staff, but it was trapped beneath the girl. Desperately, he shouted, *"Leah!"*

She jolted awake. The versläng hurled itself at them, all teeth and claws. As Leah sat up, Jack planted the butt of the staff against the stone, and the flying versläng impaled itself right on its silver tip. Skewered, the cockroach fell in an inelegant arc and landed with a sickening crunch at the base of the stairs.

A knife pressed to Jack's throat. Leah's green eyes blazed as she held the blade firmly to his neck. *"Who are you?"*

Jack's mind froze. Leah was about to kill him, but wh— *The mask!* He ripped off the black scarf, revealing his face. "Hi."

Leah jerked back in shock. "The *doktar!*"

She flung her arms around him, her powerful body pressing him as close as she could.

The sounds of battle faded away as the carnage moved onward. When Leah drew back, Jack saw a tear trickle down the side of her slim nose. "Abrahim would be proud of you, Jahk."

"And you," Jack said. "You were incredible."

Her eyes met his. "Were you with him? Abrahim? Is he…"

Jack dropped his eyes. "He's dead."

She shook her head, exhaling a breath. "I didn't think a Border Knight could die. Are you sure?"

Jack nodded.

"What about Campion? Or Memphis?"

"I don't know."

Leah gritted her teeth. "Valerian?"

"I was standing right next to him when the horns sounded," Jack said hopefully. "He ran right into the thick of them. I…I don't know what happened after that."

Leah took a breath. "Benjamin?"

Jack tried to turn away but couldn't leave her eyes. Slowly, he shook his head. A lost and desperate expression crept across Leah's face as her silent hope came to an end.

"How"—she cleared her throat—"how did you get out?"

"Memphis got me to the southern docks. You?"

"We were unloading a shipment of supplies on the north shore when the horns blew. We tried to get through, but there were too many. We held the docks as long as we could, but no one ever made it." She let out a breath. "We trailed the red devil here. I thought he was going to kill you, Jahk. How did you turn his blade? Abrahim didn't teach you *that* well."

Jack felt the armor on his wrist. "Valerian saved my life."

Puzzled, Leah held up Jack's arm. "The skidshield!" she said, shocked. "This is old majik, Toshan. He *gave* that to you?"

Jack nodded and pulled his sleeve down—he somehow got the feeling Leah envied the gift. "How did the versläng get on the island?" he asked. "Through the jaunt gate?"

Her face turned grim. "Someone let them through."

"*Let* them through?" Jack balked. *"Why?"*

"You don't have traitors in your sphere, Jahk?"

Something tore at Jack's heart. The idea that someone could have opened the jaunt gate and let in that massacre was unthinkable.

"Xiang-lo," Leah said suddenly. "He was the key."

"Xiang-lo?" Jack balked. "My patient? What about him?"

"Valerian didn't tell you?" she said, surprised. "If Xiang-lo belongs to Necrórceror, there—"

She was cut off by a cry of pain. It came from the courtyard, a low, keening wail. Jack and Leah stood. The battle had moved on, but the carnage it had left was littered in the forms of the dead and dying.

Jack and Leah found the wounded man who had cried out. His belly had been slashed open by one of the versläng, the edges of the wound tattered and bloody. Others, the scattered survivors of the battle, soon joined his cry. Leah barked a command to the two that could still walk. "You! Get these men inside! There—at the carpenter's! Now!"

She turned to Jack, her eyes burning with a purpose. "Time to work your majik, *doktar.*"

The boy stopped short. "No. Leah. No, I can't…it's not just some…some *spell* I can cast to make them better…I'm not qualified to—"

"And who *is* qualified, Jahk?" she said suddenly. "Answer me that. There is no one, not in Rimmy's Cull, not in all of Keymark, that can help them save *you.*"

Jack looked around at the wounded men. He was suddenly angry at Leah, angry at this girl who was ordering him to perform a task far beyond his abilities, beyond anything he had ever done. Anger became panic as he realized what she was demanding of him, and what was at stake.

She saw his despair and pulled him close, her voice hard. "The Border Watch is dead, but these can be saved. You have the power to save them, *doktar.* If you do nothing, their deaths will haunt you."

"Leah. I can't…"

She straightened, her fiery eyes burning into him. "You can, Jahk. And you *will.*"

The carpenter's shop was dusty, dry, and dark—only two crooked windows and a heavily shielded fire lent their weak light. Oil lamps were lit quickly, revealing a sprawling series of rooms containing dozens of half-finished tables, stools, chairs, and chests that filled the shop with the thick, heady aroma of fresh timber.

Jack's first patient was the most badly wounded: a blonde woman whose fine silk clothing was now muddy and burnt, a woman who had charged into the battle armed with nothing but a pitchfork and a handful of courage. She was cut in several places and had been bitten through the thigh. Leah brought several needles and a dozen spools of thread from the tailor's shop while the other battered Cullans brought scrap cloth for bandages. Jack's shaking hands made several attempts before he managed to thread the first needle, but as he prepared to suture the wound, Leah touched his arm.

"No. Stitching can be done by any housewife, Jahk. We need you to stop the poison with your science."

Jack turned. "What poison?"

Leah frowned, realizing exactly how limited Jack's knowledge was. "The versläng were created by the Necrórceror," she said. "From the mud, slime, and shell of the Shadow Swamps. He built them to throw at his enemy like a plague, infested with disease. Before the Black Accord, the *wikk* would have been able to heal the poison—to turn it and kill it—but the Fell Prince's bargain stole that majik. The versläng were created for just that weakness, Jahk—the slime of their fangs is a venom. It does not kill quickly, but even the slightest bite from a versläng is a sentence of slow death."

Jack felt sick to his stomach that anyone could create something so horrible. Suddenly, his mind clicked. "Junkleeches! Junkleeches can get the poison out!"

Leah shook her head. "That has been tried. No versläng bite has ever been cured by the leeches, not once in the hundred years since the Accord."

Jack slammed the tailor's tools down on the bench. "Then there's nothing I can do! I can't just yank the poison out of them! This isn't majik, Leah! It's science! There are limits to what I can do!"

Leah stared him down. "If you do not find a way, these people will die."

"Then they're going to die!" Jack kicked a wooden stool out of his way and stormed out of the shop. The Cullans, who had briefly sparked with hope, now fell to black thoughts. They had seen the venom of the versläng work its course before, and they knew the agony waiting in their very near futures.

Outside, Jack plunged his head into a water trough to cool off. He jerked his head back, letting his waterlogged hair rush a stream down his face. Leah's faith in him was absolute, and absolutely misplaced. He had nothing to give these people.

His head pounded. *Why don't the junkleeches work?* He had seen the leeches in action, seen them suck the dragonfly venom out of his arm like a hiker would to a rattlesnake bite. Even in Medieval Europe, primitive surgeons had used leeches to remove evil humors from the body in the hope of casting out the spirits of disease and infection. But if the junkleeches didn't work, then the versläng were infected with a sorcerous poison that could not be cured by man or majik. *But it doesn't make sense!* A poison in the bloodstream should be sucked out unless—

It's not poison.

He stopped. They were good people, but they were primitive. They had no scientific method, not even stupid medieval mistakes to fall back on. They had always depended on the *wikk* to heal them, and only a century to learn to survive without it. *What if they call it a poison simply because they didn't know any better? The versläng were created from a swamp. The poison takes a long time to kill. The slime of their fangs is a venom—*

There were monsters in Jack's world too. Deadly ones. Jack had first heard of the dragons when he was eight years old. He had run to his father and asked if the dragons were real, expecting the comforting reassurance that a parent so often gave: *Monsters don't exist.* But these monsters were real, his father told him, alive and well on the remote islands of the South Pacific.

Komodo dragons.

Huge lizards—some over eight feet long—attacked goats, boar, water buffalo, and were known to gobble monkeys whole. But the truly interesting thing about the Komodo dragon was its bite. The dragons, big as they were, would not battle their victims. They bit once, then retreated to wait, sometimes as long as a week, for their prey to drop dead. There was no poison in the Komodo dragon's fangs. But their teeth teemed with microscopic pathogens, riddled with disease. *Bacteria.*

And from salmonella to streptococcus, Jack Swift knew how to kill bacteria.

"Soap."

Leah stared at him blankly. She had expected the *doktar* would be back as soon as his temper wore off, but she hadn't expected such a bizarre return. Her frustration lashed with sudden force: "They're dying of poison, Jahk, not dying of dirt! Is your plan to make them *smell* better for the funeral?"

The boy simply grinned. "I know you primitive pinheads can make soap. Memphis gave me a huge hunk of it for a bath when I first got here."

"Jahk, I don't underst—"

"I don't expect you to. It's Toshan majik. Now get me a bar of Ivory."

Confused, Leah exited the carpenter's shop, looking for the simple thing that would eventually save more lives than she could imagine.

Jack took over, barking orders like Abrahim Qin. The carpenter's shop became an operating theater; Cullans converted every bar, bench, and board into makeshift surgical tables while Leah organized the rooms into a jerry-rigged triage for the wounded. Without answering any questions, Jack instructed them to wash the wounds inflicted by the versläng with soap until it lathered. When the wounded complained of the pain—and the seeming uselessness of the treatment—he scrubbed harder. Soon, Jack passed the duty of cleaning the wounds off to the others and focused on stitching the bites and gashes. The injured woman with the bitten leg was first, and Jack finished sewing her wound shut before he realized that he had just sutured a massive trauma without hesitating.

When the two Cullans washing the wounds began coughing, the boy ordered them to cover their mouths with makeshift surgical masks from their sleeves. *Who knows what kinds of diseases these people might carry?* Jack covered his mouth with Kaito's black scarf. Motes of sawdust floated in the air like mosquitoes, and Jack realized he was working in a place where infection was literally falling from the sky. He told his team to get buckets of water and wet down every inch of the floor. Used to taking strange orders by now, the Cullans doused the carpentry, and soon enough, the floating dust was nearly gone. Nearly.

Finishing a series of stitches, Jack saw several wounded dulling their pain by drinking some sort of clear liquor from a green bottle. Quickly, Jack ordered himself a shot. When the woman delivered it, Jack touched a burning candle to the glass, and the booze caught fire immediately, burning like Kentucky moonshine. Grinning, Jack told the Cullans to get every bottle of the stuff they could get their hands on and pour it on the wounds before they used the soap; 151-proof alcohol made a fine antiseptic, and the Cullans were only too happy to administer it liberally.

As Jack worked, his confidence grew. The versläng, he realized, were careless. They fought only to knock an opponent out of the fight, knowing their disease-ridden bites would finish the job for them, and their sloppiness was an unexpected boon. He left the simple stitching to his assistants and began operating on patients who were more seriously wounded.

Working among the wood and timber of the shop, Jack found himself thinking surgery had become more like carpentry than Dr. Richards had ever imagined.

Leah worked majik. Like Memphis, she knew the sleeping spells and used them on the patients in pain. They worked together, Jack cutting and stitching, Leah weaving her *wikk*. The pair was lit in the dancing red and yellow sparks of her majik—a mesmerizing display of midnight fireflies and softly falling fireworks.

Time began to fade and blur. With each patient, Jack became more of a surgeon. Things he would have never even dreamed of trying an hour ago were accomplished with careful precision as his miraculous mind flickered through the medical books in his head, finding the treatment for each injury. He wasn't perfect—not by any stretch of the imagination—but he lost his fear of making mistakes, and when he made one, he would adjust quickly and without self-rebuke, looking for another solution.

Eventually, Jack came up against an injury too grievous to heal. He knew that the older man didn't have much of a chance; he was gashed and battered, badly burned. When Jack felt the man's heart stop beating, the boy felt something in his soul crack. Beneath his mask, his chin quivered. Tears brimmed over his eyes. He shook his head, stepped back from the table, and set his carpenter scalpel down. Jack wanted to run, to tear off his mask and flee, but he couldn't let Leah see him like this. "I…I need a break." His voice trembled.

As Jack walked out into the hallway, he held his hand out for support against the wall, trying to stop the fluttering in his chest, the trembling under his skin. He heard noises and turned to find the main room of the carpentry was filled to the brim with wounded.

Rimmy's Cull was decimated by flame and fang, and there were none left who dared stand against the invulnerable scarlet samurai, the bringer of blood. Word passed quickly among the survivors of the attack that a man in black—a powerful spellweaver who had mastered the secret of the white *wikk*—had taken over Hebron Tanderneck's carpentry in the Craftsman's District. It was said that the black wizard could stop death itself, and so the wounded came. They came in wagons, in wheelbarrows, carried on planks, from all over the white city to find the one man who could give them hope.

They were lined up outside in a mob that stretched farther than Jack Swift could see.

He felt his head go light and fell against the wooden wall. Leah put out a hand to support him, but Jack found he couldn't even feel her fingers. She turned from the front room, looked over her shoulder, and found a small, crooked door that led to a back alley. "Come on."

Jack pulled off his mask and took the chilled waterskin Leah offered. He emptied half the water down his throat, swallowed, and took a breath. "How many?"

Leah's face was a mixture of concern, anxiety, and pride. "Hundreds."

Jack exhaled in one long, low breath that seemed to go on forever.

He hadn't realized it until now, but he was weary to the bone. Exhaustion had settled firmly on his shoulders, heavy and thick. His body was sapped of energy, but even worse, his brain felt like it had been replaced by a wet phone book. "I don't know if I can keep doing this."

"We've got a system going—the men up front have gotten a handle on treating the bites. You're only getting the ones we can't wash and stitch, the ones who won't live without you."

"Leah, I can't—"

"You said that before. But you did, Jahk. You did." Jack looked into her eyes and realized that Leah was as tired as he was. He couldn't even guess how difficult it had been for Leah to keep her sleeping spells going for...*how many hours has it been?* Behind the fatigue, however, Leah's eyes still burned with that fire he had seen in her from the beginning.

In the moment, he loved her for that.

"Leah, I—"

Stone clattered behind him. Jack spun. The knife at Leah's belt whisked out of its sheath as they laid eyes on the creature.

The blue-and-gold gecko from the *Venture Brigand* fell to the street. Its back leg was broken in three places, it had several fresh cuts, a blackened patch that looked like it had narrowly escaped a fire, and its tail had been cut off.

"Just a tam," Leah said dismissively, sheathing her knife. "Come on, let's get back inside."

"Wait. I know this one." Jack moved slowly, trying not to frighten it, but the gecko-thing was too feeble to run. It looked up at him with those big, frightened yellow eyes, and Jack knew it had resigned itself to death.

"Jahk. Leave it alone." Leah sighed. "Tams are just animals that know a few commands—like a dog nobody bothers to name. It's not a person. Let it go."

Jack touched the tam. It flinched but did not try to bite him. Its pebbly skin felt rough and smooth at the same time. Its wide eyes blinked, unsure if Jack intended to kill it, not caring if he did.

"It set me free," Jack said. "It untied me." Looking at the tam's wide eyes, Jack knew what he had to do. "Get me a piece of wood."

Leah didn't question; she picked up a thin strip of lumber resting against the alley wall and handed it to Jack. As he snapped the wood into a shorter piece, the tam jumped, startled. Jack took hold of the broken leg and looked the creature in the eyes. "Hold still. This will hurt."

He rebroke the bone quickly. The tam didn't move a muscle. With deft fingers, Jack placed the shaft of wood over the break and tied it to the leg with cloth strips. The splint was crude, but the bone would heal, given time. Jack looked the tam in the eyes. "I know you can understand me. Do not let that come off until your leg heals. Once you're able to use your leg again, you can untie the knots." Jack smiled. "I *know* you can do that."

The tam's face changed. It was impossible to be sure, but it looked like the thing was trying to mimic Jack's smile.

Jack stepped on a wooden box, lifted the tam up, and set it gently on the edge of the roof. "Stay hidden until you get better. And thanks." From the ledge, the tam blinked, then disappeared, the splint tapping against the tiles of the roof as it scuttled away.

Jack stepped down off the box to find Leah looking at him with a strange expression on her face. "What?"

Ever so slowly, a smile curled across her lips. "You are truly incredible, *doktar* Jahk. Truly—"She moved close to him, close enough that he could smell her. Even now, her skin still smelled like cherry blossoms. He felt her touch against his skin and an electric tingle ran through his entire body. "Incredible."

She disappeared through the doorway into the carpenter's shop.

Jack stood for a moment, letting the sensation wash over him. He could still feel her breath, still feel the tiny flutter of her soft flesh on his. His skin sparkled like the summer fireworks of her majik.

As he pulled the mask over his face and stepped through the doorway, Jack Swift felt like he could do anything.

Hours passed, but Jack's team worked without complaint. The scarlet samurai had done his wicked work well, but the men of Rimmy's Cull were determined to save as many of their people as they could. During those hours, Jack learned how much he could endure, and he was surprised at how deep the well inside him went.

Then came the *thump* on the roof.

It fell like a giant's fist—the building buckled from the sudden force. Hidden dust fell from the ceiling as a support beam cracked. A sudden shouting came from outside Hebron Tanderneck's carpentry. Jack looked up at the sound and caught several specks of dust in his eye. The shouts outside became screams.

"Leah? What's—"She was gone. Jack was startled to find one of the Cullans beside him in Leah's place. Had he done the entire operation without her?

A cold shiver jolted down Jack's spine.

He ran from the small room where he had been operating and pushed toward the front of the shop, fighting against the mob of people who were fleeing the other way. He broke through and stopped cold at the sight that met him.

Hebron Tanderneck's shop was on fire. The buildings across the way were ablaze. And there, silhouetted against the wicked flames, the gleaming crimson armor.

Leah stood in the doorway, gathering the remaining Cullans. "Rally!" she cried at the top of her lungs. "Rally to me! *To me!*" They gathered quickly, forming a wall in front of the shop. But many (too many) were terrified of the flaming devil and fled.

Black versläng clustered around their bloody master, eagerly awaiting the slaughter to come. The samurai raised one gauntleted fist and pointed directly at Leah. "I want the girl."

Leah drew the twin swords slung at her hips. "Come and get me."

Versläng charged, grinning knives. Jack snatched the silver staff and was out the door. The versläng punched into the Cullan wall like a fist—the ranks were broken, each man was on his own. Jack swung the staff, batting the versläng aside, cutting a path toward Leah. She charged directly for the scarlet samurai.

Her swords clashed against the flaming blade of the red devil, but the warrior was too strong, too fast. He toyed with her, letting the girl break her strength against him until, inevitably, she would fall.

As Jack plunged through the versläng, two men joined him—the stretcher-bearers who had helped move the wounded. They charged with him through the fray, a battle cry screaming from their lips: *"Black Jack! Black Jack!"*

They hit the red devil like a cannonball, weapons smashing his chest, arms, and head. Leah redoubled her attack, and together they let fly with a devastating barrage of blows that battered the armored figure in a rain of steel. Leah struck out and smashed the flaming sword out of the samurai's right hand, sending it clattering across the white stones.

In that moment, Jack had one second to think they could defeat the devil—

A stroke of thunder without sound.
A violent thump of wind. Time slows.
The Crimson Armor unleashes a single burst of power.
A silent shock wave rends the very air.
Dust pulses once, away, away.
Jack's clothes ripple, his hair flies back, his skin pushes back
from his bones, even the blood in his veins falls away, away

*from the Crimson Armor, away from the dark center, away
from the awesome concussion that hits him like a slow train.
Jack is water in a still pond,
the samurai is a comet.
In that instant, Jack glances sideways through the dust, to Leah.
That fiery hair. Those eyes. Those green eyes, those proud, perfect, frightened eyes. And Jack is shot away,
away from
the center of the sphere,
away from her*

—and hit the ground like a bag, skidding backward across white paving stones that cracked beneath the shock wave.

The versläng, the Cullans, *everything* in the path of the pulse, was thrust backward, scattered like dust, then Jack finally heard the noise that tore over the shattered courtyard—the low crawl of delayed thunder.

The red samurai held Leah like a trophy in one outstretched hand. Somehow, she found the strength to fight. Leah kicked out—her foot caught under his helmet, knocked it from his head, and revealed the monster's face.

Long blond hair flowed from his brow, lilting across high cheekbones and sapphire-blue eyes. An elegant face, a bold face, a handsome face.

The face of Campion Rei.

No! Jack's mind screamed. *That's impossible! She's in his* right hand. *Campion doesn't* have *a right ha—*

The armor. Jack suddenly knew it like he knew the color of his own skin. *The armor gave Campion his hand back.*

Leah's eyes became hate. *"Traitor!"*

"No, little girl." Campion Rei grinned with perfect teeth. "I am the *prince's* man. And I will teach you to think better of me." He gripped her throat tight.

Leah's green eyes fluttered shut.

Jack lunged forward. He didn't have a prayer against the Border Knight, but he would kill Campion or die trying.

A rough hand jerked him back. Jack spun, ready to kill, and suddenly recognized the face of the man who stopped him.

Rooker Flynn.

Blood trickled down the pirate's forehead; cut and nicked in a dozen places, the right side of his face was black with smoke. He gripped Jack's arm like a vise. "If ya want to live, keep *still*." The captain jerked his chin at the carpentry, and Jack realized what had caused the *thump.*

There was a dragon on the roof.

It crouched atop Hebron Tanderneck's shop, its long tail wrapped around the chimney. Deep-indigo scales shone dully in the firelight, its serpentine neck leading to a saurian head. Within the sunken holes of its skull lived peering eyes of purest black.

Campion dragged Leah's limp body into a wagon and threw her atop a pile of golden treasures that Jack's impossible memory immediately recognized from the hold of the *Venture Brigand.* Roaches surrounded her, collecting the edges of a huge sea net laid out beneath it all. The dragon leapt from the rooftop with a single beat of its leathery wings and landed all six legs atop the wagon. Campion turned to the thing. "Take the trophies to my Citadel Akkadian." Versläng hooked big brass rings to the dragon's talons, connecting the net. Campion patted the dragon's huge head like a dog and nodded at the building. "Burn that."

A jet of fire shot from the dragon's mouth and engulfed the carpentry in roiling flame. Jack felt his skin draw tight from the heat.

The dragon beat its wings, once, twice, three times, against the unimaginable weight of the treasure of the *Venture Brigand* and lifted it into the air. Leah's arm dangled limply from the net. The dragon bellowed once, a cacophonous screech that jarred Jack's bones, then leapt into the sky, disappearing into the smoke.

"Kill the rest," said Campion Rei as he replaced the red helmet, hiding his true face.

Versläng moved, seeking out anyone still living. As the screaming began again, the Crimson Knight walked into the smoke and flame of the burning corpse that had once been Rimmy's Cull.

Rooker Flynn gripped Jack's shirt and hauled him to his feet.

Together, they ran.

It is bad luck to be superstitious.
Andrew W. Mathis

Trees towered into the air like skyscrapers, dwarfing even the proudest of the colossal California redwoods.

Within and among the gargantuan trunks blossomed entire ecosystems; mosses, ferns, plants, and smaller trees sprouted between the mammoth cracks and fissures of the roots, each a small village of verdant fauna producing a riot of life. Tremendous stags, wild boar, giant marmots, spider monkeys, creeping martens, and dozens of creatures beyond description coursed their way through the weald, the greenery teeming with life both fanciful and deadly. Birds made their nests in the upper reaches of the trees, cawing, twittering, and cackling to each other in mating and warning calls that made the invisible heights of the forest seem even more alive than the earth below it. The forest continued for uncountable acres, miles, and leagues. The borderlands of Keymark had been war torn and ravaged for centuries; the land was blasted, scoured, and burnt to bare earth over and over again, but the Madrigal Verde survived.

Spanning the vast domain between the Irridin and the main artery of the Breechline River, reaching almost to the swampy Llykowen Delta, the Madrigal was home to no tribe or race that walked upright. In ages past, there had been attempts, by bold men who sought the shelter of the colossal trees, to tame it, to shape it, to carve their way into the bosom of the forest. The water was abundant, the hunting was spectacular, and the winters were a haven (snowfall never entered the Verde—each white flake disappeared instantly as it touched the first leaf of the green canopy). The forest spawned life so easily, so majestically, that it was too enticing a paradise to dismiss. But one after another, each settlement was obliterated by roving packs of animals, by mysterious fires, or simply swallowed whole by the forest caves where men entered but never returned. The Madrigal was a preserve to green plants, furred animals, winged birds, and no man.

Two men collapsed between the roots of a titanic tree. The smaller one fell on his back, gasping for air. He wanted to flee, but his exhausted muscles could go no further. "I…I have to rest," he panted. The bigger one said nothing; his eyes looked into the forest, not knowing it looked back.

"He took my ship!" spat the captain. "He took my treasure! I'll have his blood!" He ripped the singing saber from its scabbard and strode off into the trees.

"Where are you going?" Jack shouted.

"To get my *swag*!" Rooker stormed through a copse of shagbark hickory matted with kudzu, chopping branches and vines with the shimmering sword, cursing all the way. In a moment, he was gone, vanished into the vastness of the Verde.

Jack struggled to catch his breath. More than anything, he wanted to sleep—just drift off and let the world go away, lulled into slumber by the gentle chirruping of the forest around him, and the soft pad of pliant, thick moss that held his body like a mattress. He wanted to forget Keymark; he wanted to forget everything.

He settled back into the roots, letting his aching shoulders sink into the pillowy moss. He just needed to sleep. He could forget, just for a little while, just for a few moments, about home, about Campion, about Valerian, about Memphis, about—

Leah.

She was clutched in a monster's claws, borne through the air, captive of a creature. *If you don't do something to save her,* Jack realized, *no one will.* The Watch was dead, Memphis was gone, and Valerian was lost. *There's no one else left who even cares.*

His mind took a selfish thought: *There's no one else left who cares who* you *are, or if* you're *alive or dead.*

Jack came to his feet. The strange forest whirred and chirruped around him, but there was not the slightest human sound. Rooker had vanished into the bush as if the forest had swallowed him. Abruptly, Jack bolted into the woods, following the path the pirate had hacked through the trees.

He ran through the narrow trail, down a low rise, and managed his way over a four-foot root as thick as a VW bug. Pixies flittered in the trees. Insects were everywhere, some of them mothlike and beautiful, but the boy made certain to touch none of them; his experience with dragonflies, versläng, and junkleeches was more than enough to caution him from experimenting. Huge baobab trees with smooth, creamy trunks that belonged only in the jungles of Madagascar blocked his way. Jack shoved through massive plants—some with palm fronds larger than a car, others with vines that snaked down from the branches like dipping fingers. As Jack moved, he saw what looked like a huge Venus flytrap, green with yellowish vines, sitting plump and robust in the veldt. He couldn't be sure, but Jack thought he saw—exposed from the mouth of the plant—the twitching leg of a deer.

Rooker's trail ended. The ferns and plants were thick, and Jack could find no evidence of the pirate's passing. He scanned the forest, but there was no trace of the captain.

Now what are you going to do, genius? he chastised himself. *You're alone and everyone who helped you is gone.* Jack felt a rising panic clutch his throat, and suddenly, the forest seemed like a massive coffin, just a part of the colossal tomb that was Keymark.

Alone.

Through the trees, Jack spotted the edge of a vast ruin: an ancient castle overgrown with vines and roots. He remembered Benjamin's map tucked in his pocket and pulled it out. One of the destroyed Twelve Towers was located near Rimmy's Cull, and by appearances, the crumbling castle fit the bill. It was his only point of reference, and he decided to make for the ruined tower.

As he cut through the trees, he heard a whacking sound ahead, its source hidden by the foliage. Jack rushed toward the sound, plunging through the green. Branches whipped at his face, roots grabbed at his feet. Jack charged onward, his only thought that he was alone in the world, and if he lost Rooker Flynn, he might stay that way forever.

Jack came to a stop at the verge of a wide dirt crossroads in the shape of a Y that passed through the middle of the Madrigal. Wagon tracks cut deep in the bare earth, left by the thousand carts that traveled the highway to Rimmy's Cull.

Standing at the crossroads was a corpse.

It had once been human, but death, dirt, and time had transformed it into something else. Its skin—what remained of it—was greenish yellow, tinged with mold and rot. Exposed bone poked through its deteriorating flesh, revealing the dirty white of its ribs, shoulders, and calves through tattered and disintegrating clothing. Even from a distance, the thing smelled rank, filling the clearing with the sick rotting-orange stench of death.

Jack threw himself to the ground as the zombie turned toward him. The black sockets where its eyes had once been burned with two tiny shards of light, green pinpricks set deep in the recesses of its skull. Jack clamped his jaw shut, choking down the scream that wanted to escape his throat. He froze, knowing that if the dead thing came for him, he would be helpless, too terrified to fight or flee. The incandescent eyes of the ghoul stared dully at the spot where Jack had been, flickered, then dimmed as the versläng joined it on the road.

Jack heard the incomprehensible chittering of the roaches as they moved toward the corpse. Holding his breath, Jack peeked over the ferns. There were half a dozen versläng and two more shambling corpses. They came toward the object the ghoul had been hammering into the ground at the crossroad: a wooden post. Suddenly, the zombie raised its head to the sky and let forth a moaning wail—a horrific sound that forced Jack to cover his ears in terror. He felt the familiar tingle of the *wikk*, darker and more violent than anything he had felt previously, as birds and animals fled from the howl of death. The wailing zombie reached up and planted rotting fingers on either side of its head. In a sickening sound of tearing sinew and cracking bone, the thing ripped its own skull from its neck. It took one step forward and impaled its head on the wooden post. As the decapitated body dropped to its knees, another zombie drew a hammer and an iron spike from its belt and, with sudden violence, hammered the head to the crossroads post.

The skull hung at a cockeyed angle, facing the road, fixed in place like a grim warning. Watching.

The versläng and zombies turned and walked up the road. Jack heard the underbrush rustle around him and realized the forest was teeming with walking corpses, each one carrying a hammer and an iron spike. Frozen in place, Jack felt them moving past him, pushing slowly through the trees, quietly following the versläng along the highway.

Jack crouched like a frightened rabbit, his eyes fixed on the mounted skull at the crossroads post and the headless corpse kneeling before it like a dark reverent. Thick grey globs dripped from the cracks around the spike and—in the deep recesses of its eye sockets—Jack could see tiny green lights, still flickering and winking in the dark.

"Kekubi," croaked a voice in his ear. Jack spun to find the pirate crouched directly behind him, one eye squinting at the road. "Lovely."

"R—"

"Shut up," Flynn hissed. "That one's fairly fresh." He jerked his chin at the spiked skull. "I'll wager his ears still work. Come on." He vanished into the trees. Jack cast one look back at the severed head and followed.

Rooker paused at a stream, filling a leather waterskin. He splashed water over his face, scrubbed his gums with a dirty finger, and settled back against a mossy stump as Jack tried to collect his racing thoughts. "What did we just see?"

Rooker's grin was crooked. "Things are about to get interesting." He took a swig from the flask. "A *deadeye.* One of the Necrórceror's. That spell—that moan the kekubi made right before it tore its own head off—that spell put that rotten ol' boy right into the Fell Prince's head. Whatever it hears, the Necrórceror hears; whatever it sees, the Necrórceror sees. Puttin' 'em up and down the highways, I'll wager." He took another drink. "The Fell Prince is setting up watch."

"For what?"

"Maybe troops. Maybe somethin' more specific. Either way, the Fell Prince is coming back." He eyed Jack. "Yer pal Valerian Tsai's got a manly job of work ahead."

"I don't know if Valerian's still alive."

Rooker shot him a look. "Then tell me what you *do* know."

Jack hesitated for one moment, then told Rooker everything—about Falikos, the Border Knights, Valerian Tsai, the massacre, Campion's betrayal, the murder of Abrahim Qin—everything but the surgery and where Jack was from…that he kept to himself.

"So." Rooker nodded. "The Border Knights, eh? The Noble Seven. Heh." He picked up a rock and tossed it in the air. "The Azure Knight is dead, the Crimson's gone turncoat for the prince, and the Grey's gone missing. Whadaya know." He chucked a rock in the stream. "Well. War's good business for a pirate, anyway." He slapped his knees and got to his feet. "Good luck to ya, kid." Rooker made for the trees.

Startled, Jack turned after him. "What are you doing?"

"I told ya, boychick. War or no, I'll not see that kind of treasure again, and I aim to have it back."

Jack grabbed Rooker's arm. "Wait!"

The pirate gripped his sword hilt. "Take back yer hand or lose it."

Jack gripped the arm tighter. "I'm going with you."

Flynn laughed, yanking his arm free. "To what end? Rescue yer fair maiden? A noble notion, sure and true, but I dinnae think yer up to the task."

Jack stood his ground. "Look. That dragon took—"

"Dragon?" Rooker spat. "Ha! A dragon would swallow that titchy snake whole! That beastie's jest a little jabberwok."

"What's the difference?"

Rooker sighed. "Everyone knows there's three different kinds of wyrms, kid: wyverns—those are the little ones; jabberwoks (what ya saw); and dragons—them are the big ones, the *bull* wyrms."

"But it's not a worm," Jack couldn't help himself—science was the only thing he had to hold on to. "It had six legs. Six legs technically makes it an *insect.*"

Rooker cocked an eyebrow. "Kid, you sure think you know a *lot* about things you know nothing about."

"What?"

"What?"

Jack frowned. "Whatever it is, you can't take it alone."

Rooker slung the singing saber over his shoulder. "Don't need to take *it*, jest need to take the swag."

"Do you even know where it's going?"

"No, b—"

"I do." *The Citadel Akkadian*, Campion had called it. Where it was, Jack had no idea, but he hoped the pirate wouldn't know that.

"I reckon I can track a thirty-foot flying lizard hauling a sack full of loot an' a screaming girl, boychick. And I dinnae need a whelp suckin' on my teat while I do it." The captain strode for the trees.

Jack racked his brain, trying to think what would convince the captain. Even if he tailed the pirate, it was likely Flynn would ditch him eventually. The only trump card he had to play was—

"Lucky penny!"

Rooker Flynn stopped. He turned slowly. "What?"

Jack crossed his fingers. "I'm good luck. You said it yourself."

The captain snorted, but Jack could tell he had hit the right note. "That was once, kid. I dinnae expect it again."

"Think about it. I was with you when you took the *Brigand*." Jack moved closer. "But when you left me, you *lost* your ship, and everything on it."

The pirate eyed him, caught between greed and superstition. Rooker Flynn did not give a whit for piety, loyalty, or honor, but his heart was betrothed to Lady Luck.

Jack twisted the knife: "When you turned on me, luck turned on you."

The pirate growled. "I s'pose I could make use of a peon." Rooker suddenly thrust a finger in Jack's face. "But ya get nary a penny of my haul! If ya want the girl, ya can have her, aright, but the treasure belongs to me!"

Jack smiled, presenting his hand. "Not a penny."

"We have a bargain." They shook, the pirate's strong hand gripping Jack's. The captain spit on the ground and eyed the boy, waiting. "Spit." Jack spat. Rooker nodded. "Luck to us both, then."

Rooker Flynn strode into the Madrigal Verde, and Jack Swift followed.

The heavy taloned foot came down upon the gentle blue waters of the Irridin, and steam shot to the sky like a geyser, boiling from the terrible heat. The sea charred black beneath it, cracking and hardening like ice. Jets of steam vented from red cracks between the coal-black surface that had once been water, now a growing expanse of burning ash.

The dæmon towered on its black island, master of every living thing, hating all life.

It was born of no father or mother—it had willed itself out of nothingness, issuing forth from the void in a catastrophic birthing of blood and blackness, wholly formed and burning, given rise by the powerful hatred it personified, drawn into being by cruelty, lust, and rage that burned as a furnace in its black soul, the living embodiment of malevolence.

The Fell Prince, the only power in Keymark masterful enough (and fearless enough) to command the beast, had summoned it from the pit. The dæmon was neither living nor dead, and its name and sigil could only be claimed by those who existed in the shadowlands between the realms it bridged, powerful entities of the same ilk as the cold Necrórceror. The beast had roamed the spheres for a span of six ages, sometimes in the thrall of those who could command it, frequently serving no master but itself, but always with a single-minded hatred for the living. It came from fire, darkness, and death, and its sole purpose was to condemn all vital creatures to the burning pit it called home.

The dæmon's true name was unpronounceable to the limber tongues of the quick or the stone tongues of the dead. There were few in time's long history who escaped the bloody and relentless slaughter it carried with it like a blade, but those who lived to flee it had given the beast another name: the Crownéd Dæmon Chulurath.

Its claws were bloody with the remains of the little men on the little island—a battle unworthy of its strength—and the dæmon's appetite for blood had been left whetted, piqued, and unsatisfied.

It did not like bearing the thing called Xiang-lo—a living being it was not permitted to kill—and was pleased when the bird came to take it away. The carrion fowl dropped from the cloudless sky, a tremendous stygian vulture—what the men of the Fourth Age had called a rôk.

It plucked Xiang-lo from the dæmon's talons, coming closer than most living things dared, and bore the man away, to the north, to its master.

Thick diamond-shaped nostrils sucked the damp sea breeze, smelling wood, fish, and fire. The beast had followed the scent across the ocean. The spoor was not difficult to recognize; to the dæmon's senses, the scent stood out like a bright-red ribbon that coursed its way through the blue sea air. Its prey had drifted across the water, been taken aboard a ship, a vessel with no woman-flesh aboard, and (after ejecting one of their own) they had run to ground—to the burning white city that now blazed before the beast like the towering spires of its home world.

The Crownéd Dæmon Chulurath growled deep in its throat and walked toward the flame. With each blackened footprint it left behind, a hundred fish rose to the surface of the sea in a trail, their bellies bloated and white, their eyes blackened holes.

The dæmon hunted its prey, following the scent of the man-child called Jack Swift.

Jack and Rooker took the Bootlegger's Trail, an old smuggling path through the Madrigal Verde that the pirate knew well from past experience.

The rangy captain strode the winding green trail with relentless energy, his legs strong and bandied from years of fighting the constant roll of the sea, and Jack was hard-pressed to keep the pirate's pace.

Overall, Rooker Flynn made an excellent companion. He treated the boy as a partner, servant, and sidekick—what could best be described as a shipmate. Jack's job was to gather fruits, nuts, and mushrooms (they had no longbow, so meat was scarce on the menu) and to make camp each night while Rooker lounged by the fire mending his clothes with a fish-bone needle, telling tall tales and singing dirty songs. In the morning, Jack would roast the occasional chipmunk-size marmot that had fallen into one of pirate's clever snatch traps he placed near camp each evening, and the captain got the lion's share. Rooker Flynn's high spirit made each day more of an adventure than it already was, and Jack found he was almost enjoying himself in the majestic forest of the Verde.

Rooker's only complaint was that he had nothing to drink but water and daydreamed endlessly about the barrels of booze on the *Venture Brigand*. After a particularly hearty lunch, Rooker tromped merrily through the forest, singing the same song for the third time that day:

Oh,

Drink, boys, and take yer fill
Of whiskey, wine, and beer!
A gallon of cider to warm up yer blood
And never a man shall fear!
Why waste your time thinking?
The ship, she ain't sinking!
The beauties will see us and cheer!

So,

Drink, boys, a flagon or three
Will surely crack yer smile!
She's going a-roving into the sunset
Off into the Treasured Isles!
We're all going swimmin'
With bowlegged women
They're coming to us by the pile!

O,

Drink, boys, and guzzle it down
We never will kill our supply!
We'll knock the sauce back 'til we fill up our guts
And slosh it all down 'til we die!
Our bellies will strain
With the booze they contain
And rally our battle cry!

Yo!

Drink, boys, and take no heed
Of bashes and gashes and scars!
For no matter what the ill weather portends
We'll all hang together to the bitter end
And the lot of us sail to the stars!
Our legend will grow with the dangers we face
The ballads they'll sing of the women we chased
Our deeds will be told by the men we lay waste
'Til victory is ours!

As Rooker belted out the song, Jack chimed in, adding flourishes in a high counterpoint to Flynn's baritone, repeating the verses flawlessly. When they reached the finale, Rooker stopped and gave him an annoyed glare.

"Took me a tenday to learn that shanty, and ya pick it up in a trice." He crossed his arms over his chest. "That's a rare mind for a dunce who cannae read."

"I'm an auditory learner." Jack shrugged. "I hear something and I remember it."

"Auditory." Rooker scowled. "Another one of yer big canny words. Jest where do ya hail from, boychick?"

Jack swallowed. He had managed to avoid talking about himself (Rooker was only too happy to fill the empty space with stories of his own), but the hard part was restraining the billion puzzles in his head. If he had been with Memphis, the questions would have come out of him like a fountain: *What is that bird? Is it poisonous? How do these trees get so huge?* But the one question that kept him from asking all the rest was: *What do you do to Toshans here? Burn them like a Salem witch?*

"I wasn't born in Keymark, if that's what you mean." The boy was a bad liar and decided a half-truth was better than nothing.

"That I can see," Rooker snorted. "Yer accent's an odd one too. All clippy with yer hard *R*'s. I've been 'round the world twice an' never heard a tone like that. What's the name of your city?"

Again, Jack settled for the truth: "Chicago."

"Che-ga-go?" repeated the pirate. "Never heard of it. I'll warrant it's not much of a town. Where is it?"

Inspiration struck Jack. "If you've been everywhere, you should be able to figure it out."

Rooker played right into the game. The captain spent the next hour positing multiple theories on Jack's port of origin, naming dozens of different lands the boy had never heard of. Jack dodged questions with half answers, and, in the end, Rooker convinced himself the boy came from someplace called the Hyperion Mesa. That—claimed Flynn—explained Jack's clippy accent, his blond hair, and, somehow, his illiteracy. The boy simply shrugged, and the grinning pirate was cocksure he had hit the bull's-eye.

They walked on, each satisfied he had won the game.

They discovered the village on the evening of the third day, untouched, unburned, and uninhabited. Either versläng and kekubi had invaded it or the Madrigal Verde had taken back what it owned, but there was not a sign of a single living soul. A pot of stew lay in a cold hearth, burned black from a long-dead fire; gardens stood unattended; a discarded ax was buried in a partially chopped tree; a loom stood half strung with an intricate woven carpet waiting to be finished.

Rooker scavenged the cabins like a starving rat.

He ransacked inside every box, above every mantle, and underneath every rug. Disappointed with the meager take (just a few copper coins and a silver-rimmed vase that was too awkward to carry), the pirate stuffed his pack with endless bolts of silk from the loomer's cabin. They made light freight, Rooker claimed as he jammed them in his bag, and would turn a decent profit when they hit a real town. Jack guessed the pirate would have taken everything that wasn't nailed down if only he had been equipped with a wagon.

Eating the beef jerky Jack discovered hung in a cellar, the two men found a stream and filled their waterskins. Rooker put of a pot of coffee, took off his boots, and went to work on his calloused feet, shredding the dead skin off with a cheese grater. "Ahh," he sighed happily. "Ya want this when I'm done?"

"No. Disgusting. Thanks."

Jack eyed the sword slung across Rooker's back. The singing saber was not elegant like Valerian's blade—it was a brawler's weapon—but the sharkskin pommel was handsome.

"Can I take a look at your sword?"

"What, ol' Bessie?" Rooker smiled and drew the singing saber from its beaten scabbard—the silver blade hummed. "Be careful with her. She bites."

Rooker tossed the blade to Jack, and a searing jolt of *wikk* shot up the boy's arm.

At Theodore Roosevelt Junior High for about three weeks one winter, the vending machine in the cafeteria had a loose wire. The kids discovered it before the adults did, and (as kids do) challenged each other to a competition: put one hand on the vending machine, one hand on the Coke machine, and see how long you can hold on. The kids turned themselves into lightning rods, electric current jangling through them in a painful, sizzling loop. Steve Jarosinski got the record—eight seconds—same as a rodeo bull rider.

As in junior high, Jack cried out and let go instantly.

Rooker Flynn caught the saber before it struck the ground. "Stings, don't she?" He grinned. "But ya get used to it." He gripped the hilt tightly as if he enjoyed the burn. Jack never wanted to touch the thing again.

They ate, washed up, and prepared for the afternoon trek. As Jack was tying his shoes, one of the laces snapped. He quickly unlaced it, knotted the break, and threaded it back through. The sneakers were beaten and battered, but his Chuck Taylor All Stars were the only thing left of home.

Rooker rolled his eyes. "Ya should get boots. Those crazy moccasins don't match yer Black Jack getup."

Black Jack. The Cullans had yelled that when Jack attacked Campion. Leah always pronounced his name the other way, with the *ah* in the middle. "What's Black Jack?"

Rooker snorted. "Kid, ya really are from Che-ga-go if ya've never heard of *him.*"

"Who?"

Rooker thumped his fist on a log to the rhythm of the old song:

> *Ol' Black Jack, the man with the knack*
> *Stole the people their money back.*
> *One quick flick of his walking stick*
> *He fed the poor and healed the sick.*

Black devils fear his cunning spear
He'll cut them down and disappear.
So play us fair or jest beware:
There's nothing ol' Jack wouldn't dare.

Jack grinned. "So he was a hero."

"Hero, pirate, healer, priest—take yer pick." Rooker grinned. "Robbed the Three Princes blind, way back when. They say he gave it all to the beggars and the paupers and the ragaboys in the street, but—"

"Like Robin Hood."

"A robbin' hood? I *said* he was."

Jack laughed. "So why were they yelling his name, back in Rimmy's Cull?"

"Ahh, with that stupid stick and that raider getup, they probably thought y—"Rooker's eyes suddenly lit up. "They did! They thought you was *him*!" He leaned back laughing. "O, that's rich! Black Jack, you! A halfwit what cannae even *read*!" The pirate brayed like a mule. "Lord a Sea an' Sky! Never underestimate what desperate folk'll pin their hope to, kid. By the time they're done in Rimmy's Cull, they'll be tellin' people you was the first to heal the sick since the Black Accord!"

That's exactly what Jack had been doing, but the captain had been too busy trying to save his stolen gold to notice. Jack badly wanted to tell Rooker the truth—to rub the pirate's nose in it—but that would only lead to more questions. Rooker slapped his knees, giggling. "O, boychick, if only they knew the tru—"

He stopped cold. Jack froze, having learned to trust the captain's ears. The birds had gone silent; the woods were deathly still; even the sky above seemed to have fallen mute. The *wikk* washed over Jack—a different feeling from the ever-present tingle of the Verde—the new sensation was ugly, menacing, and malevolent.

Rooker tapped Jack's leg and whispered, "Move." Flynn stole silently into the green, quiet as a church mouse.

They went that way for half an hour, creeping under the silent trees. The feeling of the dark *wikk* grew stronger, heavier, until Jack was convinced he could smell it, thick and ripe like rotten meat. Rooker ducked down into a gulley, hiding in the rocks near an open cave mouth. They hid, not making a sound. Jack didn't know what the

(rath)

It entered his head, a voice without sound. It wasn't a word—it was a feeling, a memory, a warning buried somewhere back in the forgotten, primeval part of his brain. It was instinct. And it was telling him to

(run)

get away as fast as he could.

"Let's get inside the cave," Jack whispered and moved toward it. Rooker grabbed his arm and yanked him back.

"I'll face any man alive afore I go in there," Rooker hissed. "Them caves is bad business. Once ya go in, ya dinnae come out. Be still."

They waited, hiding. The smell of rotting meat grew stronger. The *wikk* sung like a dark choir in the boy's ears. A sudden crash, and a tree smashed to the ground. The low crackle of flame. The rotting smell became the stench of charcoal, sulfur, burning flesh.

Jack heard something sniff the air—a *whuffing* sound no more than a dozen yards away. Trembling, the boy looked at Rooker and thought

(run)

that the pirate looked as frightened as he felt. Neither spoke; neither could. The thing *whuffed* the air again. Jack heard a massive footstep crunch into the ground, shattering branches.

A buzzing sound rattled the air. Startled, the boy looked to find it was the singing saber. The blade recognized the power closing in on them—it rattled in its sheath, quivering in anticipation. Rooker gripped the pommel, but the sword buzzed like a hive of bees.

The thing growled low in its throat; it came for them. Heavy feet thundered the ground. Rooker cursed and ripped the singing saber from its sheath, the sword screaming, unleashed at last. Jack gripped his staff as the two of them

(run)

spun to face the nightmare together.

Jack got one glimpse of the thing before it shattered the boulder with one tremendous clawed hand. The beast was huge, horned, and dark as Mammoth Cave when the lights went out. It wasn't just black—it absorbed light.

Jack scrabbled from the rubble. A dark taloned foot bigger than his entire body smashed down beside him; the gully floor burst into flames, the creek billowed steam. Jack spun away and

(run!)

watched Rooker flee into the cave.

Jack sprinted for it. He heard a *whump* behind him. Screaming heat burned at his back. Something hit him from behind, and Jack was thrown through the air. He smashed into the rim of the cave, his ribs crushing against rock. He bounced and fell backward into the dark.

The creature hit the entrance with the shock of a cannon. Jack flung himself backward. The beast pounded at the cave entrance, too big to fit through after him.

It smashed the rock, tearing at the cave mouth and bellowing madness.

A tremendous crack, and the cave walls shattered.

The walls are caving in, the walls are caving in...

Stone collapsed by the ton as Jack crabbed backward away from the rampaging terror.

As he fled, Jack caught just one glimpse—through the haze of rock and dust—of the beast's burning yellow eye.

It stared directly at him.

The cave mouth collapsed, and everything went black.

Jack was deaf and blind. All he could hear was the dull echo of the beast's bellow inside his head, and he saw nothing at all. He fumbled through the dark, grasping and tripping and shouting for Rooker.

He fell through a hole in the rock. His shoulder banged against a stone, then he hit the bottom, his bruised ribs yelping pain. He got to his feet, stumbled, and knew he was hopelessly lost. As he walked (or rather crawled) over the stone floor, he felt a damp cold gathering on his skin. The temperature had taken a nosedive to freezing. He stumbled through the black, lost and shivering, until a flame sparked to life somewhere ahead.

It was snowing.

Jack couldn't see the top of the cave, but a flurry of white snowflakes spilled down from the blackness. Thick white powder covered the cavern floor in a long tunnel that seemed to stretch forever. The space was huge, an underground cathedral bathed in ice.

Jack held out his hand, letting the snow pile up in his palm.

I'm underground…and it's snowing.

He walked toward the light and found Rooker Flynn. The pirate held his thumb and two fingers together—a small yellow flame danced at the end of his fingertips like a Zippo lighter…except there was no lighter. As Jack drew nearer, Rooker pulled one of the silks from his pack, tied it around a stick, and lit it. As the torch flared, Rooker snapped his fingers—the tiny flame disappeared. Jack called out, but the captain didn't seem to notice. The boy touched Rooker's shoulder, and Flynn spun, nearly taking Jack's head off with the saber.

"It's me! It's me!" Jack cried.

"What?" Rooker yelled, his voice tinny and far away inside Jack's head.

"What *was* that thing?"

"I can't hear you!" shouted the pirate. *"What was that thing?"*

Jack gestured, *I don't know*, and pointed upward. Rooker looked up at the snow, squinting as it fell into his eyes. "Yeah! Guess we found where the winters go in the Verde!"

A hundred Decembers collected all around them. Snowdrifts taller than office buildings piled up against the sides of the cave. Jutting crags and outcroppings were masked under domes of white, hiding their true shapes, buried beneath an endless snowfall.

"We can't go out the way we came in," the boy shouted. "We'll have to find another way!"

Flynn slapped the side of his head, shaking it furiously. "Nope! I'm stone deaf! Can ya hear?" Jack nodded. "Then find us a hole!"

Jack swallowed and led them off into the dark.

They got a second torch going, and Jack moved over the white cavern floor, snow piling on his shoulders. Over the next several hours, he looked for light—any light at all—or even a change in the wind to mark an opening, but found nothing. Claustrophobia tickled at his mind; Jack felt like he was trapped inside a giant snow globe.

He tripped and fell in the deep powder. His hand hit something under the white blanket. He dug around, his fingers numb, and finally found what had tripped him. Bones. The cave floor was littered with them. Tibias, scapulas, femurs, and humeri of all different sizes.

Skulls. Lots of skulls.

Most were human; some were smaller, some were bigger, and some didn't belong to anything he knew, but they all had one thing in common: they were all very, very dead.

His hearing came back, and he wished it hadn't. What he had thought were cave winds were something else.

Howls.

They began low and dull, but as his hearing returned, they rose to a shrill peak and never stopped. Completely unnerved, Jack tried to see where the sounds were coming from; he caught shadows, vaporous shapes that disappeared the moment he spotted them, just beyond the torchlight. Jack picked up his pace, but it soon became clear they were being followed.

He didn't tell Rooker. The pirate had enough on his mind worrying whether he was going to be permanently deaf. Soon enough, though, the captain caught on. He watched Jack's eyes, and he knew. The pirate drew his saber. "Tell me if they come," was all he said.

The shadows had been gathering for a long time when Jack stumbled over the bodies.

More than a dozen corpses, gathered at the base of a huge incline, half buried in the snow, each one perfectly preserved. They were settlers, pioneers, common folk who had made the mistake of trying to tame the Verde. Their last act had been to form a human ring—as if to defend themselves—and in that ring, they had died. The men still gripped axes in their hands. The women held cleavers and clubs. Jack found himself staring at the frozen face of a little girl no older than seven. She held a corn-husk doll in her tiny hands and had a pretty red ribbon in her hair that had turned white with frost.

An eager howl came from the blackness, the sound of a thousand animals calling to each other.

"I heard *that*." Flynn's eyes flashed. "Look." He pointed, and Jack saw eyes—unblinking eyes, like cold and hungry cave fish swimming in the blackness beyond.

"Go, go," said Rooker. "Up the hill."

They fled the circle of bodies and ran up the embankment. The snow gripped their legs, holding them back as they slogged up the steep incline. The hill was bigger than Jack thought.

His breath rasped in his lungs, steaming the chill air. The taller man made quicker work of the slope, moving ahead. The boy tried to keep up, scrabbling, tripping over buried bones. He fell behind. Rooker's torch moved farther and farther away.

The howls grew closer.

The hill grew steeper.

Jack found himself struggling for handholds, dragging himself up the nearly vertical slope.

Something soft brushed against his leg, and he screamed.

Cold fingers grabbed at his ankles. Jack kicked them away. The fingers came back, joined by more. They seized him. Pulled him down.

A hand shot out and grabbed his arm, yanking him up the cliff. Rooker Flynn dragged him to his feet and hurled his torch into the darkness below.

Hundreds of them. Apparitions of men, phantasms of green and silver, arms, heads, hands, and eyes. Snow fell through them like a cold mirage.

Far below, a little girl with a corn-husk doll stared up at Jack, coming for him.

One of the shades pounced on the torch, snuffing it like a candle, and she was gone.

The two men fled to the crest of the hill only to find more bodies.

Armored warriors. In a last-ditch effort, the military men had hastily constructed a defense, a tipped-over wooden cart piled high with rocks and flat iron shields, but it had done them little good. They were frozen solid, decaying to armor and bone.

Jack gasped for air—he couldn't run anymore.

Rooker spun as the howling specters came up the peak. "Never thought I'd die with earth under my feet." He ripped his sword free. "Cummon ye, Jack. Let's make 'em work for their supper."

Rooker snapped his fingers, tossed his majik flame onto the wooden fortification, and the cart became a bonfire.

The peak of the hill lit up like a giant torch. Jack saw the entire cavern laid out below them in crimson shadows. And there, coming up the hill through the blizzard, were the legions of the dead. Not hundreds. *Thousands.* They moved as a swarm, a multitude of faces, arms, and legs gathered as a single body, clutching fingers outstretched to take the living men down into the dark.

At the head of the swarm, a pale little girl with a corn-husk doll reached out. The red ribbon in her hair trailed over eyes blazing with rabid hunger.

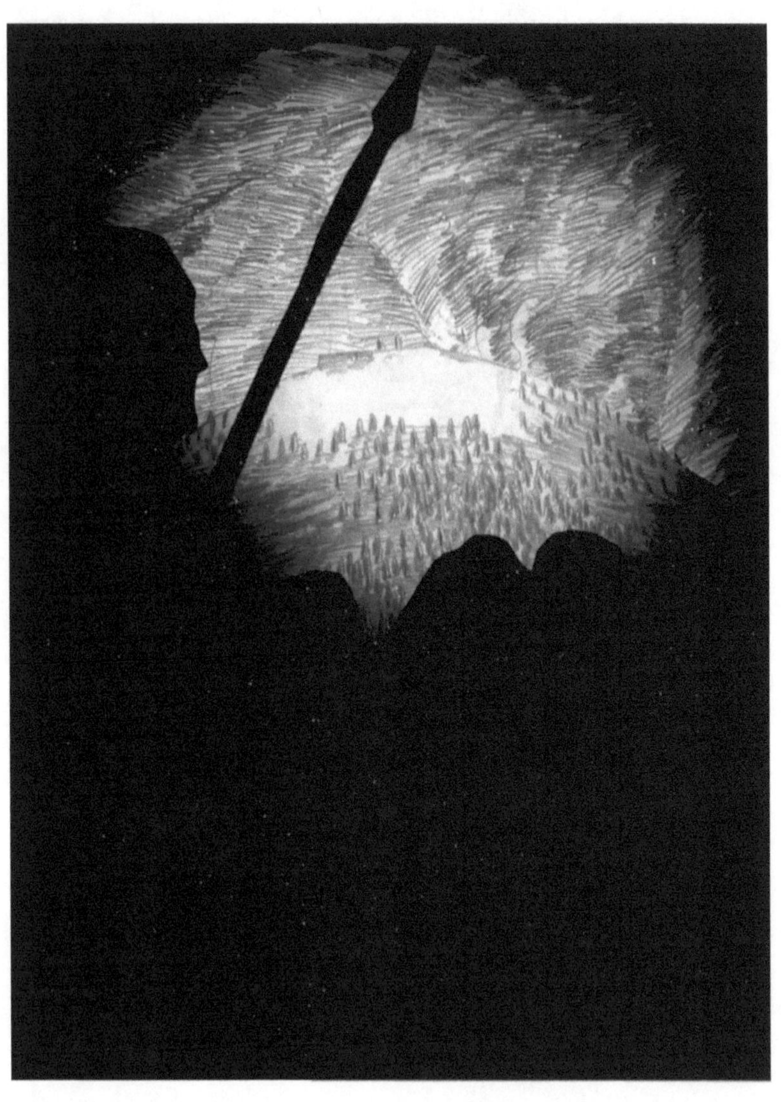

Jack couldn't move. All he could think was

(so cold)

it always hurts more when it's cold.

Colorado. *The trip to Snowmass. Mother had been beautiful then, wrapped in white. All the kids used the same sleds—those big aluminum discs that moved so fast, and when I hit the tree and lost my tooth, it hurt like hell because everything hurts more when it's cold—*

Jack suddenly bolted for the flaming cart.

"Jack? Jack!" yelled Rooker, but the boy didn't hear him.

Jack darted straight into the fire. He grabbed the warrior's metal shields—the heat seared his fingers, but he ripped them out of the blaze. Steam erupted as they hit the snow.

Rooker looked at him like he was insane. "That ain't gonna stop 'em, kid! We have to fight!"

Jack shoved a sizzling shield into the pirate's hands. "We're not fighting! We're *leaving!*" The boy ran at the far edge of the hill and threw himself over the side, landing flat on the big round metal sled.

Rooker Flynn stared, dumbfounded as the boy shot down the slope like a sea otter. He spun to find the swarm coming right at him and hurled himself over the ledge with a yell.

They skidded down the hill, curved metal shields hissing through the snow like twin snakes. As they picked up momentum, the shields began to skip, smacking against the bumps. Jack kicked out one leg, dragging his foot like a rudder. His sled caromed up an incline and popped over the top—his stomach went woggly as he got airborne. Somewhere behind him, Rooker screamed.

Out of control, Jack shot over a drop-off and dodged just in time to duck an overhang that should have taken his head off. He rocketed through a narrow tunnel, speeding walls closing in on either side, and then everything went bright.

He shot out the cave mouth like a bullet. He hit a rock, skipped, lost the shield, and crashed down rolling in the high, thick grass.

Grass.

Jack stared at it, stupefied. Warm sunlight streamed down on his cold face. He was outside, beneath the trees of the Madrigal Verde.

He heard a shout and spun to watch as Rooker Flynn was vomited from the tunnel with a *whoop.* He flew like a rock, smashed face-first into a tree, and crashed down into the bushes.

Jack leapt to his feet, limping toward the downed pirate. "Rooker!" He spotted Flynn's legs sticking up from a tangle of broken branches. Jack tore through the wreckage, worried the pirate was knocked out, or worse.

Rooker Flynn was laughing.

He lay on his back, holding his belly, giggling through a wide-open mouth. Jack stared at the pirate like he was nuts.

Rooker didn't stop—the laugh just kept getting bigger and louder. The pirate gasped for air, unable to breathe through his own roaring cackle.

It was contagious.

Jack snorted, then chuckled, then began giggling. He couldn't control it. He laughed until tears streamed from his eyes. His ribs hurt. His mouth ached from smiling so wide, and still, he couldn't stop. It was hysteria, and it built on itself until they were both braying like it would never end.

Jack let it go. The fear, the uncertainty, the worry—it all melted away like snow in grass.

They giggled in the forest, laughing together like the two greatest fools under the sun.

10

TALL TALES
&
WHITE LIES

*A lie can travel halfway around the world
while the truth is putting on its shoes.*
Mark Twain

The captain and his first mate tromped merrily through the woods, enjoying each other's company. Rooker's tales entertained Jack, but (now that the pirate allowed the boy to talk) Rooker enjoyed Jack's stories even more. The captain particularly delighted in the lyrics to one Toshan tune and turned "Great Green Gobs of Greasy Grimy Gopher Guts" into their marching song.

Flynn made a few brief attempts to teach Jack to read but soon moved on to a much more important endeavor: gambling. They had no dice or cards, so they made up contests, betting on how long it would take to find the next watering hole, which one of them could get more fruit, or who could go longest without taking a leak. The only currency they had was the gear on their backs, so they bet their cooking pot, their waterskins, their cups, their knives, spoons, and forks. Jack made use of the games he had learned at summer camp—from Twenty Questions to Red Triangle to the Murder-with-the-Icicle mystery. Frustrated, Rooker made the deadly mistake of challenging Jack to a memory game.

In twenty minutes, the boy won every scrap of the pirate's silk. Playing the game one step further, Jack allowed the pirate to win back several items, and the captain wound up hauling all the heavier gear like it was a privilege.

Neither of them discussed the giant black thing that had tried to kill them—it was an unspoken agreement, and they were content to leave it unspoken.

The following morning, just after sunup, they found an abandoned homestead, and this time, the pirate found something to raise his spirits: whiskey. With a bottle in his hand and a crate of the stuff over his shoulder, the captain whistled cheerfully until they made camp (much earlier than usual), and Rooker Flynn got down to the serious business of drinking.

He knocked the stuff back with bravado, and right quick the pirate was schnockered. He sang bawdy songs, chucking wood into the fire like bombs. Rooker demanded a story from Jack, and the boy decided on Aesop's fable of the goose that laid golden eggs. Rooker liked the part about the eggs, but when Jack told him the end—where the farmer cut open the goose and got nothing but a dead bird—Rooker was furious. It was a stupid ending, he demanded. It would be a much better story if the farmer got all the gold eggs, hid them, and ate the goose.

Jack laughed. He was stone sober, but the night was warm and soft, and the fire crackled merrily. "Your turn," said Jack. "Tell me one about the elves."

"Elves? Bah!" The pirate swallowed a shot. "Cowards, the lot of 'em."

Jack was taken aback. The Border Watch on Falikos held the elves in high regard—Valerian had described them as a great people. To hear them called cowards was a shocker. "Why do you say that?"

"They ran," Rooker spat. "Back in the Time of the Princes. They got some fat majik, them fair-haired boys do—some say they even made the *wikk*—but when Keymark went belly up, they ran. And up there in the Elder Wood, boychick, they cast their big spells—the stone shook and the rocks rumbled and up went the Kern. Made their own by-God mountains did the elves. Locked 'emselves behind 'em, and no one yet's made it over *that* wall. You see this?"

Rooker drunkenly ripped Bessie from her sheath and let her ring in the night air, firelight glinting on the simmering blade. "The elves made ol' Bessie, way back when. Five, mebbe six, centuries since she first saw daylight—but she's still sharp as a razor and sings like a troubadour. But Bessie's jes a trinket compared to other things they made." He nodded, looking at the blade. "The elves coulda done somethin'. They coulda stopped the Necrórceror an' the Black Accord. But they was all locked up tight in their little hidey-hole—or off lookin' for their precious White Lady—and mindin' their own precious hides."

Something about the story didn't feel right to Jack. "You

don't think they would have helped if they could?"

Rooker leaned in, conspiracy in his silky eyes. "Elves is immortal, kid. They live forever. *Forever.* Now. If you knew that ya could never die…unless someone stuck a knife in ya…what would you do?" Rooker chucked another log in the fire. "Elves dinnae fight—not even to save their own skins. They jes run off and find a trickier place to hide. Heh. They'd all be dead by now if it weren't for the Border Knights, and that's God's truth."

"So." Jack leaned forward. "Tell me about the Border Knights."

"Men," said Rooker suddenly. "Damn fine men. Best there ever was, I reckon."

Now there's *a surprise,* Jack thought. According to the pirate, the elves were cowards, the llystra—the crocodile-men—were thieves, the catlike jinx were murderers, and the dusky hammer-dwarves were all stupid as rocks. Captain Rooker Flynn had never said a kind word about any race or tribe in Keymark—until now.

"Men." Rooker swallowed another shot of rotgut. "Every last one of 'em. They could toss the world on its ear if it pleased 'em, and if I wore the Armor, you bet yer boots I would. Misguided—maybe. Too brave for their own good—probably. But men." He flicked the bottle with a dirty fingertip. "If I ever admired a man—and I ain't sayin' I do—but if I did, it'd be Valerian Tsai." Rooker toasted the air and downed another gulp.

"Lissen, Jack. There's *one* passage into the Elder Wood. One. And once upon a time, the Juttlander Horde got it inta their heads they'd find it, raid it, and steal every treasure the elves had. So them big horn-nosed trols came stompin' down outta the mountain lookin' for the Paladine Arch, bent on murder.

"That's when the Border Knights came. I don't know where from, some say from the Salt Barrens, some say outta the west, but they came. Seven men. Seven against seven hundred. The knights stood beneath the Paladine Arch and told the Horde no.

And them horn-noses—O, they laughed. They told the knights to get outta the way or they'd cook their hides for boot leather. But the Noble Seven dinnae blink. They jest told them big brown-bellies to turn tail and stomp on back to the Jutts, because they weren't stompin' through that Arch. So the trols stopped laughing. And then they came like hell.

"Now. They say there was seven hundred, and mebbe that's a lie. Mebbe the tale's got taller with time, as most do, but whatever the truth is, the Horde went at 'em fist, fang, and fire, but the Noble Seven held the Arch. They say there was enough trol bones left on the ground that day to build a bridge—and the boat to sail under it. When it was all over, them brown-bellies ran back to the Jutts with their whipped little tails tucked between their legs. And the Border Knights have held the Paladine Arch ever since."

Rooker downed the rest of the whiskey.

Jack stared into the fire. *Seven versus seven hundred—*

"S'pose them days is over now." Rooker clicked his tongue. "The Crimson Knight went traitor." He hurled his bottle into the fire, shattering it. "So much for noble." The pirate pulled two more from the crate. "Well, let's drink to the Border Knights, kid, and be done with 'em."

Jack eyed the bottle. "No, thanks."

"Cummon ye, Jack. One shot for each."

"No, thanks. My foster mom drank."

"What's a foster mom?" asked Rooker. "Some kinda wet nurse? Did your real parents hate you or something?"

Jack scowled.

Rooker grinned, sensing he'd found a sensitive spot. He took a shot. "Betcha they did. Betcha they left you a screaming whelp on an abbey's doorstep."

"No."

"What, then. Your real ma and pa too stupid to take care of you? Were they dumb? Too dumb to read, like you?"

Jack gritted his teeth. "Stop it."

"What, did yer da leave ya? Did he hate ya enough to leave?"

A cloud of red steam formed in Jack's brain. *Stop it.*

"Rooker—"

Rooker took another swig. "Bet he was the town drunk."

"No."

Another shot. "The village idiot."

"Stop it."

"Bet he was," Rooker sneered drunkenly. "Betcha yer da was biggest moron in Che-ga-go. Betcha they used to pin feathers to his backside an' tell him to chase his own tail."

From between gritted teeth: *"Stop talking about my dad."*

"Oooh, soft little boy for his dear da." Rooker cackled, spilling his drink. "Wha's'a matter, boychick, yer da not teach you how to take a belt? *Mine* did. Mine taught me to take both sides of a belt, one on the lips and one on the crack. Shoved a bottle down my neck, then beat me blue for drinking it. Made a man outta me afore he choked, and I was only seven. But not *yours.* Noo, not little Black Jack's dearest da, nossir. What'd he do for you? He didn't toughen you up. Not hardly. Bet he was soft too. Bet he had soft *hands.* Couldn't teach his boy to take a licking."

Blood sung between Jack's ears. "Stop."

"Couldn't teach his boy to be a man."

Jack attacked Rooker Flynn.

"Take it back!" Jack's balled fists beat the pirate, his knuckles smashing the captain in a berserker fury again and again. *"Take it back!"*

Rooker threw up his hands, trying to protect his face. Jack smacked him a good one in the eye. "Crikey!" Bam! "Uncle!" Bam! "Stop!" *Bam!*

Rooker yelped, but Jack didn't let up, hammering him. The pirate struck out his foot and toppled Jack to the ground.

"I take it back, dammit! *Aright?*"

Jack lay in the dirt, panting, unable to believe what he had just done. He had thought plenty of rotten thoughts about his dad over the years—but they were *his* thoughts. And it was *his* dad.

Rooker stared at him through one good eye. "I take it back, aright? I'm sorry."

Jack shot air through his nose. "Yeah. Me too."

Rooker leaned back on his elbow and grinned. "My ol' captain—the good one—he always said ya can't trust a man 'til ya throw up some dust with 'im." He wiped blood from his lip. "Little scrapper ain'tcha, kid?"

Despite himself, Jack chuckled. "Seven years in Illinois State foster care. I can take a punch. Make one too."

Rooker grinned. "Come on. One shot." He held up the bottle. "To *real* men. To the Noble Seven."

Jack eyed him, sighed, and snatched the bottle.

"The Noble Seven." They both took a swig.

"And to you an' me. To *mates*."

Jack squinted. "Mates." And drank.

"An one more for luck." Rooker clinked the bottle and took a pull. By the time they were done, they had toasted all seven Border Knights: the Azure, the Amber, the Indigo, the Titian, the Jade, the Grey, and one final spit for the Crimson.

Jack didn't remember much after that.

When Jack woke the next morning, there was a giant lizard on his chest. The blue-and-gold tam stared Jack in the face with those huge yellow eyes. Jack blinked; so did the tam.

It held out its hind leg. The bandages were ratty and looked like they had been dragged through a hundred miles of mud (which they had), but the splint still held.

Jack shook his head, trying to clear the cobwebs from the cracks in his brain. He undid the splint, tossed it aside, and reached out to feel the leg. The tam's bones were mending nicely, faster than a human's would. Its wounds and burns had been replaced by pearly-pink healing skin. Jack raised an eyebrow as he realized the thing's tail had grown back.

"Clean bill of health," grumbled the boy. "Now geddoff."

It did. Jack got up, found the waterskin, and drank it down. His mouth felt like a toilet; his tongue was thick and fuzzy, his gums burned, even his teeth hurt. *Why do people do this to themselves?*

He glanced over at the remains of the fire and saw Rooker Flynn splayed out where he had fallen, curled up with an empty bottle—one boot off, part of his blanket burnt and snoring like a fat lumberjack.

Uh. Never again.

Jack reached into his bag, pulled out an apple, and crunched into it. The tam squeaked and held out its hands, wiggling one finger.

Scraping his tongue against carpeted teeth, Jack tried to figure out what it was doing.

He looked down at the apple in his hands. Tossed it. The gecko caught it, squeaked, and devoured the fruit down to the core. It threw the remains aside and cupped its hands. The finger wiggled again.

Hand over another one, buddy.

Jack bit his apple, considering. The tam was intelligent…at least a bit. On the *Brigand*, the tams followed commands, used like servants, or—more to the point—slaves. They were treated with less respect than a dog, but they seemed to understand language.

And that gave Jack an idea.

Camp Happy Hollows was the worst summer of his life. The food was terrible, the counselors were potheads, and the kids were rotten, picking mercilessly on the pint-size little runt they called Jackie Slow. They pushed him around, made fun of him, and, on the third day of camp, Benny Brannigan took all of Jack's underwear. They had Jack's name in the back, but Benny wore them anyway.

The nights—some of them—were good. Sitting around the campfire, singing songs. One of the camp counselors taught them to sing "Michael Row the Boat Ashore" in sign language. Jack picked it up immediately, of course—and caught a beating for it, of course. The camp counselor felt sorry for Jack and gave him a book of American Sign Language as a weird kind of apology. It hadn't made him feel any better, but Jack memorized the book.

Looking at the tam, the boy lifted his fist to his jaw and twisted one knuckle at the side of his mouth. *Apple.*

The tam blinked. Jack held up the apple and repeated the gesture. Staring at him with those big yellow eyes, the tam mimicked the movement.

Jack repeated the process, using the pulling-apart gesture when he showed a pear, the face-scratching move for the peach. The tam repeated his movements each time.

Jack put the apple, the pear, and the peach in front of him, then spread out his hands and said, "What do you want?"

The tam blinked then responded in American Sign Language.

Apple.

Jack handed it over.

As the tam ate, possibilities poured into Jack's mind. Maybe it was the hangover talking, but if the thing was as smart as he thought, he might be able to teach it—

He looked up and saw the tam pulling at its mouth, looking at him seriously. The boy realized it was mimicking the unconscious lip-pull that Jack did when he got lost in thought.

Well. A miniature amphibian blue-and-gold Jack Swift who likes apples. Jack chuckled at the thought as he looked up—

The sound died in his throat.

A huge and horrible figure stood at the edge of the clearing.

The monster had the powerful body of a freak-show strongman, topped by the big black head of a bull. The horns jutting from either side of the monster's skull were bigger than a Texas longhorn's. Its gnarled hands held a massive war axe.

Two smaller shapes flanked it on either side: one a man-size crocodile who was missing an eye, the other a hungry-looking jinx-cat.

The tam disappeared.

Jack stood frozen in place. *"Rooker!"* he hissed.

The captain grunted, snored loudly, and turned over in his sleep.

The creatures closed the distance.

Jack almost made a dash for his quarterstaff, then remembered the speed of the sprinting cats on Falikos.

The jinx would rip him to shreds before he made it three steps.

Jack stayed put, facing them down bare-fisted.

Behind him, Jack heard Bessie's familiar song ring out.

The boy smiled.

Rooker was up.

Just out of axe-swinging range, the big bull stopped. It snorted; puffs of air jetted from huge nostrils. It lowered its head—Jack feared it meant to impale him on those huge horns. Instead, it spoke.

"We followed you from the Cull," it said in a deep voice as smooth as oil. "We mean to serve."

The huge thing lowered itself to one knee, bowing before Jack.

The croc and the cat knelt, lowering their heads.

Jack stared at them, dumbfounded.

"I saw you in the white city with my own eyes," said the bull. "You healed many men. You saved many lives. And you stood against the Traitor Knight." It raised its head, looking Jack straight in the eye. "Black Jack has returned to Keymark."

Oh, hell.

The trio waited, expecting Jack to say something.

Nothing came.

Jack wanted to blurt out that they had the wrong man—that they had made a mistake. But all of them were bruised, cut, and muddy; slashed and burned from the Battle of Rimmy's Cull; exhausted from the tenday slog through the Madrigal Verde trying to find the one man they believed could save them. They were beaten, they were battered, but they still had hope—hope in the man they thought was Black Jack.

Waiting, the feral cat's eyes grew restless. Beside him, the croc's big tail twitched. The bull raised its head. "You *are* the Black, aren't you?"

Jack made up his mind. *This is going to hurt.* "I—"

"*Aye*...he's Black Jack." Rooker Flynn stepped forward. "The legend in the flesh. And you can get off your knees." The pirate snapped Bessie back in her sheath. "The man's no King David."

Dumbstruck by the pirate's bald-faced lie, Jack watched the trio get to their feet. Relief washed over their tired faces.

"I'm the captain Rooker Flynn," the pirate continued, "the Black's second-in-command." Jack shot him a dark look, but Rooker's poker face was set. "An jest who are *you* three?"

"I am Django Barón," replied the huge longhorn, bowing low. "This is Li-Bao Sen of the llystra."

The crocodile-man nodded sharply. He was similar to the crocs Jack had met on Falikos—his skin slickery smooth as a salamander—but Li-Bao was thicker. Heavy-duty muscles rippled just below the surface, standing out like cordwood: huge biceps, rippled abs, iron thighs—Li-Bao looked like he should be breaking running-back records in the NFL. Two scimitars were strapped over his back, the sword belt riddled with stilettos. One eye was sapphire blue; the other was covered by a leather patch bolted to his skull with three metal studs.

"The feral tom travels under the name Chance," continued Django, "and claims kinship with the Cerulean Rajah."

"It is not a claim," interjected the cat. "I am twenty-fourth in the line of heirs to the Cerulean Throne—I am a rajah-in-waiting." Chance's face and body were similar to a rangy black-and-tan African serval cat, with large pointed ears over a slim, curious face. Ridiculously thin, he moved like a stack of coiled springs. He wore no clothing (in fact, he had nothing but a long cloth bag strapped over his furry shoulder) and had no weapons, but he carried himself with pride.

Chance was not unique among the feral toms in his claim to some noble house or another—most cats in the world regard themselves as royalty.

"My father's father told me tales of you from the time I was a mouser, Black." His tail flicked eagerly. "I will be pleased to kill your enemies."

Jack swallowed. "Um…thank you."

"We tracked you from the Cull," said Li-Bao. "The cat's nose trailed you to the cave—there he lost you."

"Not for long," interjected Chance.

Ignoring the cat, Li-Bao Sen's one blue eye stared at Jack. "You surely did not enter the caverns?"

Relieved to finally have something to say (something that was not a lie), Jack nodded. "We did."

"They say no man may enter the tunnels of the Madrigal Verde and live." The croc's eye narrowed. "You are brave."

Django nodded. "The tales say Black Jack spoke to the animals of the forest. When I saw you conversing with the tam, I knew we had found you." The sense of relief in the bull's voice was unmistakable. Django Barón was utterly convinced he had found the hero he was looking for and that, from now on, everything would be all right.

"Ya came at a good time," said Rooker. "We're headed to the Citadel Akkadian to take revenge on the Crimson Traitor…and to rescue Black Jack's mistress."

Jack glared at Rooker—his eyes furious—but the pirate didn't flinch. "We may allow you to join us. But first"—Rooker folded his arms over his chest—"we want meat."

The trio snapped to attention as if given an order. "Boar or deer?" asked Django Barón.

Rooker shrugged. "Both."

Before Jack could utter a word, the trio made for the trees.

"We'll have them for you in a trice," said Chance. "Or I'm not the greatest hunter alive." And as quickly as they had come, they disappeared into the Verde.

Jack spun. *"Mistress?"*

Rooker shrugged. "Wha'd ya want me to say? Doxie gal? Sweet little tootsie? Not quite the legend of Black Jack, is it?" Flynn ducked away before Jack could hit him. "Talk about good fortune…ya really *are* a lucky penny, boychick."

"You lied to them!" shouted Jack.

Rooker leaned against the case of whiskey and grabbed a fresh bottle. "I gave 'em what they wanted."

"Forget it." Jack thrust a finger at him. "When they get back, I'm telling them the truth."

"Ya could, sure and true," said Rooker, the words flowing easily. "But ya'd see more blood than ya'd like."

Jack turned. "What do you mean, blood?"

"Kid, do ya even *know* what that big bull was?"

"No." Jack had seen crocs and cats on Falikos, but no man-bulls.

"That's a minotaur," said Flynn, "and one of the last, I'll wager. I dinnae even know there was any left on this continent. And do ya know why?"

Jack cocked his neck and felt it pop. His upper spine was beginning to cramp up on him—an old trick his conscience had, a way of letting him know when he was starting to feel guilty.

He exhaled. "Why?"

"Honor," said the pirate, letting the word hang for a moment. "They're honorable beasties, minotaurs. Live for it. Honor for breakfast, lunch, and supper. Going after a fair maiden in distress is sweet ambrosia to them. But if ya insult one—or lie to one—honor must be upheld, and blood must be spilt." Rooker raised a finger. "Ya tell that black bull who ya really are now, boychick, and he's either got to kill ya, or kill himself. And that's why there's no minotaurs left." He popped the cork from of the jug. "That's where honor gets ya."

Flynn tossed back a shot.

"Besides. We need 'em. If ya think the pair of us is going to storm the Citadel Akkadian all by our pretty little lonesomes, yer too witless to read the writing on the wall." Rooker grinned. "But then, ya *are*, aren'tcha?"

Jack fought the urge to punch Rooker in the face again.

Lying to these people, dangling a thread of hope in front of them, was despicable—and calling Leah his mistress still stung like a wasp. But if Jack was to have a chance of rescuing her, the pirate was right: they needed help.

You already tricked Rooker by making him think you're good luck, he thought. *Is it really so different to use a dusty old legend to get these monsters to do the same?*

"As soon as we've got her, we tell them the truth."

"Soon as I get my treasure back, ya can do as ya please." Rooker shrugged. "But I hope yer luck can outrun a charging bull."

The blue-and-yellow tam reappeared atop a rock. It peered at Jack with a quizzical expression on its face.

Apple?

Jack Swift sighed. *Everybody wants something…*

He picked up his staff, slipped on his cloak, and pulled on the gauzy black mask of Black Jack.

…but the ethics are starting to get a little bit slippery, boychick.

Jack's spine was stiffening up tighter. He jammed his palm under his chin and popped his neck again.

AKKADIAN

*Being a hero is about the
shortest-lived profession on earth.*

Will Rogers

J ack breathed a sigh of relief as they escaped the Madrigal
Verde—he was not sorry to leave the forest behind. The low-
grade tremble of *wikk* that hummed constantly under the green
canopy dissipated at the verge of the trees; Jack had the sensation
that he had been released from the forest's grip.

They entered the chaparral country to the north—a series of
low, rolling foothills covered with tall tan grasses and man-high
brush. Tough scrub oaks, junipers, and manzanita trees peppered
the landscape. It reminded Jack of California wine country, and
sure enough, there were wild grapevines growing in rambling
patches along their path. The group picked them by the handful
as they traveled; they were purple, sweet, and good.

Water was scarce, but Li-Bao Sen had a knack for finding it
in the oddest places. It seemed the croc could sniff water, and
always came back with his skins full to the brim. The llystra
drank constantly, going through gallons at a time, but brought
more than enough to go around. The one-eyed lizard didn't
speak much; when he did, his statements were brief and to the
point. The croc carried himself with a kind of quiet dignity that
reminded Jack of a serpentine Spartan.

Chance was different. Grinning, joking, and purring all the
way, the cat would not shut up. During the day, he chattered
constantly—to the point that Jack had to move away from him
to get some quiet—but at night, the jinx changed.

His eyes lit up like mirrors, his tail began to flick, and a
toothsome grin spread over his face. As soon as the double moons
rose, Chance would disappear silently into the brush, invisible in
the tan grass. Jack never actually saw a kill, but the feral tom came
back each night with fresh deer, his whiskers dewy with blood.
Chance never ate with them—the cat preferred his venison raw.

The croc and the cat were not friends. They had been
thrown together by a common goal: to find the man called Black
Jack. If left to their own fortunes, they would have likely killed
each other.

Li-Bao sharpened his scimitars on a whetstone as Chance strolled up.

"Dull blades mean a dull mind," purred the cat.

The croc scowled. "Even the dullest blade is sharper than those little pinpricks of yours."

"Poor, dumb lizard doesn't un-der-stand." The cat smirked. "Cats are clever and cunning, so much more than crude brute force, but I don't expect you to grasp that idea."

"A pussy *would* mistake backstabbing for brains and cowardice for courage."

Chance leaned against a rock, grinning. "Who is the better warrior, Li-Bao? You need *two* swords to fight." Chance popped his claws. "I need *none.*"

"Go play with a ball of string."

Chance took a step forward. Li-Bao gripped his swords.

"Enough," came a voice. Django Barón. The minotaur towered above them. The croc and the cat backed down, but only just.

Jack popped his neck. "What's the matter with them?"

"The Pipen Gulf," said the minotaur. "The jinx and llystra have been at war for generations over that miserable beach." Django turned to Chance and Li-Bao. "But this is not the place for blood feuds. We all serve the Black here."

Jack eyed the croc and the cat. "What's so special about the Pipen Gulf?"

Both answered at once: "Good fish."

The minotaur sighed. Django Barón was unquestionably the leader of the Trio—that was how Jack thought of them: the Trio—but the bull had his hands full. As Li-Bao and Chance moved away, the minotaur said, "They bickered the entire way here. It is good to finally have someone noble to talk to."

Jack looked up at the bull. Django was thoughtful and well spoken, but the minotaur treated Jack—Black Jack—with a re-spect bordering on reverence, and it made the boy uncomfortable.

"I must ask a boon," said the bull.

"A what?"

"A favor." The bull held up a bowl full of red berries he had crushed into an inky paste. "I was hoping you would mark me."

Jack looked at him, confused. "What?"

"With your sigil. As a sign of my fealty."

Jack had no idea what the bull was talking about. Django took Jack's hesitation as a sign of anger.

He ducked his huge horned head. "I apologize. I did not mean to be so bold. But it would mean a great deal to me." He raised his eyes hopefully. "Perhaps you would allow me to make the mark myself."

Not knowing what to do, Jack said: "All right."

Bowing his head, the minotaur dipped one finger in the ink and carefully drew this on his bare chest:

Django Barón breathed a sigh of satisfied relief. "The emblem of the Black." He looked down at the boy and smiled. "Now the world knows I belong to *you.*"

Jack swallowed.

Rooker Flynn led the way toward the mountains, setting an eager pace for gold. The captain took great delight in giving orders again (despite having a much smaller crew) and settled comfortably into his place at the top of the totem pole. Jack kept his distance from the Trio—he was cautious around them, not wanting to give himself away—and was left in the company of the tam.

It disappeared frequently during the day, feeding on grapes and berries, but always came back by nightfall and took up permanent residence at Jack's side.

The gecko learned incredibly fast. Over the next few days, Jack taught it more words and phrases, building a specialized vocabulary between them. The Trio was impressed that Black Jack understood the odd gestures the tam used. Rooker kept his original opinion of the thing and kicked at it whenever it came too close.

Early on, Jack asked the gecko for its name.

Tam.

Jack signed: *You don't have a name?*

It blinked. *Not deserve name. Only tam.*

It slunk into the chaparral, looking for more grapes. As Jack watched it go, he felt pity for the little thing. Even dogs had names.

Grasslands gave way to rock; low hummocks grew steep. Rooker quickened his pace, smelling treasure. Under his command, they hiked long into the night over craggy terrain. The waning twin moons gave little light. Django stumbled in the dark; one huge horn cracked against the rock like a gunshot. He insisted he was all right, but Jack called off the march.

He woke the next morning to find the others staring into the horizon. Jack climbed the rise, and his eyes fell upon the Citadel Akkadian.

Most of the Twelve Towers had fallen with time, through war, treachery, and ruin. Of those that remained, Akkadian had survived only because of its impregnable perch among the red cliffs of the Bonespur Range. Nestled high in the mountains, it loomed like a giant eagle over the vast plains below. The tower had an otherworldly majesty—as if it belonged to another time and place—surrounded by cliffs that matched the face of Mars. Vast portions of the citadel had been assembled from tremendous stone blocks, constructed by the dwarves that called the Bonespur home, but the majority of the tower was carved into the heart of the red rock itself. Akkadian was not the largest of the Twelve, or the most elegant, but was easily the most defendable, and so she stood.

Jack looked up at the tower in wonder. There was nothing on Earth that compared to it. Montezuma Castle, the great Gila Cliff Dwellings of New Mexico, and the ancient Jordanian rock fortress of Petra were similar, but even these grand structures paled in comparison to Akkadian. It was awesome.

Rooker emitted a low whistle. "She's a biggun, ain't she?"

Django turned to his master. "What now?"

Jack realized he had absolutely no idea. The plan was to rescue Leah (and the treasure of the *Brigand*), but he had never imagined how. The boy turned to Rooker, who offered no help whatsoever.

The Trio watched Black Jack, waiting. *Time,* Jack thought, *I need time! Give me a minute to think…* His mind stalled and fell into a free fall. *If only I—*

Jack looked at the tam, who didn't expect anything from him beyond an occasional apple. "Reconnaissance!" the boy blurted out. "We need to find out, ah, more about the citadel before we do anything." Before anyone could ask a question, Jack kneeled in front of the tam and signed:

I want you to get a closer look at the tower. Can you do that?

The tam blinked. *Yes.*

Get as close as you can. See if you can find a way inside. Find out what's up there. And see if you can find Leah.

What is a Leah?

Leah is a very pretty girl with red hair.

Tam will find pretty Leah.

Be careful. Look out for the jabberwok.

What is jabberwok?

Jack paused, then made the signs for snake, bird, huge, and fire.

Tam saw snake-bird-huge-fire in the white city. Tam fears it.

Jack paused. *You don't have to go.*

Tam will go. For Apple Jack, it will go.

The gecko took off for the cliffs at a run. Jack leapt to his feet. "Wait!" The tam stopped, blinking curiously. *Be careful.*

The tam cocked its head, signed, *Yes,* and disappeared into the brush.

The tam wasn't back by nightfall.

Dinner came and went without it. Jack sunk into his bedroll, unable to sleep. At every sound, he sat up, expecting the tam to come stumbling out of the sagebrush, wounded and bleeding and chased by every monster in the book. Jack tossed and turned all night, horrified that he had sent the little thing into unknown danger, into the lair of a great wyrm with nothing more than *Be careful* as protection. People treated tams like dogs, but Jack was worse: he'd never send a dog alone into danger. And what good was the time he had bought? Jack didn't have the first idea of how to storm the tower. The Trio was waiting for him to hatch some brilliant plot, some Black Jack–worthy scheme to get them inside, and why? There was nothing in it for them—they were only here because they had made the mistake of trusting him. Jack was afraid

(you know why you're afraid)

that he was going to botch the job. Even if the tam returned, his plan would be bad and

(yes)

he would lead them up there and

(yes)

they would run into something horrible

(and)

and they would die because of him.

(just like)

Stop it.

(Just like Dad.)

When he slept, the old nightmare came looking for him.

In the morning, there was no tam. Jack needed to do something other than wait and declared he wanted to get a closer look at the citadel. Everyone (except Rooker) offered to come, but Jack wanted to be alone.

He kept low, ducking under the scrub brush, moving through red rock gullies toward the citadel. Jack edged as close as he dared—a football field away from the base of the cliff—and got a good look at the tower.

It had one entrance: a long road that led straight up the side of the mountain, steep as a runaway truck ramp. The path was utterly exposed, laid bare to the view of the tower. There was nowhere to hide. At the base of the ramp was a severed skull nailed to a post with an iron spike—a watchful deadeye. At the top, a huge iron-studded gate blocked the entry to the citadel itself. Above that, Akkadian continued upward, layer upon layer of arrow-slit windows craning toward the sky until, finally, at the very top, seven thousand feet above the valley floor, the tower reached its pinnacle, a jutting spire of red rock, a crimson finger pointing at God.

Jack couldn't siege the Citadel Akkadian with a tank.

I just want to go home. Jack considered leaving then, just disappearing into the brush and never coming back. The Trio would be better off, and Rooker certainly wouldn't shed any tears. But then what? Valerian was gone. Memphis was gone. The jaunt gate was destroyed. Home wasn't on the menu. Besides, Leah was up there.

A blast of flame shot from the very pinnacle of the spire—the familiar gout of red and yellow he'd seen in Rimmy's Cull. Jack squinted, trying to see seven thousand feet up.

"Man," Jack muttered, "what I wouldn't give for some binoculars."

"I will get them for you," came a voice beside him. Jack jumped out of his skin and found the jinx crouched six inches from his face. The cat grinned. "Where can I find *binkonkulars?*"

Jack snatched his breath back. He had not heard the feral tom at all, not even so close. Chance was silent as a... *Well, he should be, shouldn't he?*

"They're a long, long way away." Jack sighed. "I told you to stay back at camp."

"I have been keeping an eye on you, Black. If there are enemies about, better they slay me first." He peered up at the citadel. "Your jabberwok is a large one."

Jack turned. "You can see it?"

"Can't you? I—"Chance stopped himself. "I forget. You are only jaelin, after all." The cat's slitted pupils stared at the spire. "There is a long ledge at the top. It makes its nest there."

"Can you see Leah?"

"Your woman may be there, but I cannot see her. Even my eyes are not that good. I...wait." Chance's pupils grew huge and round. "It hunts."

From the pinnacle of the tower, a dark shadow fell into the air. It dove seven, eight, nine, hundred feet, dropping like a bomb toward the valley floor. Huge, leathery wings snapped open and the bomb became a glider. It arced up and over the mountain, making for the sea.

The feral tom let out a low whistle. "It is good you are with us." Chance slapped Jack on the back, grinning. "We would not stand long against *that.*"

Jack was saved from a response by the arrival of the tam.

It wasn't bleeding, it wasn't injured, and it certainly wasn't dead. Big yellow eyes stared simply at Jack as it bit into a handful of grapes. *Hello.*

Back at camp, Rooker and the Trio watched an incomprehensible flurry of silent gestures between Black Jack and his tam.

Tam found snake-bird-huge-fire. It lives at the top. It smells.
You saw it?
Apple Jack said look for snake-bird-huge-fire. Tam looked.
No, what Jack had said was look *out* for the jabberwok. *Good Lord, it went to the very top! *Is Leah there?*
Pretty red hair lives in knots with snake-bird-huge-fire.
Jack exhaled the breath he had been holding since Rimmy's Cull. *She's there—and she's alive. *Can we get her out without the jabberwok seeing us?*
Big room at top. Snake-bird-huge-fire will see.
What about Campio— Scratch that. *What about red metal man?*
No metal man. Just red hair small men.
Red hair small men? There must be something lost in the translation. He repeated the gestures, and the tam nodded yes. Jack signed that he didn't understand. The tam made clutching gestures at his jaw. Jack took a moment to decipher the meaning: "Red hair small men *beards?*"
"Red Dwarves," interjected Django. "They built the citadel, long ago, during the Time of the Princes. They serve the Traitor Knight, but the Bonespur belongs to them. What is the tam saying about them?"
Jack ignored the question. *How many?*
What is how many?
How many were there? In numbers.
What are numbers?
Jack sighed. *Can you count? One, two, three—*
The tam suddenly grinned. *Tam knows numbers good.*
It flashed open tree-frog fingers, four on each hand. The hands flashed once, twice, four times, six. It held up one last hand and a finger.
Fifty-three.
Could be worse, thought Jack. *They only outnumber us 10.6 to 1.* He sighed. *Did they see you?*

Yes. Red hair small men not care about tam. Kick tam. Tam hide. Find quiet way down.

Quiet way?

Tunnel in dark. Easy to hide.

Jack paused, not daring to hope. *Can we take the quiet way up?*

Yes.

Jack suddenly wanted to give the tam a whole bushel of apples.

"What the hell is it saying?" growled Rooker. "Ask it about the treasure!"

"Shut up," Jack said. *I want you to make a map. A picture. Can you do that?*

The little gecko smiled. *Tam likes pictures.*

Jack dug through his pack, searching through giant piles of silk, his cup, the fish-bone needles, miscellaneous items he had won from Rooker, and finally Benjamin's map. He flipped it over. Perfect for another map. "Does anyone have a penci—?"

The idea hit him like a thunderbolt. Jack shot to his feet, his eyes sparkling like diamonds. The others stepped back, startled.

No. No, no, nonono. It's a bad idea, a horrible idea, a sick, stupid, ridiculous idea. It'll never work, it's impossible, it's

(not impossible. You've got everything you need, it's)

insane, you'll kill yourself, you'll get her killed, you'll get everybody killed. Stop it. Try something else, try anything else. Just not that.

But like all great ideas, it wouldn't go away. And like all great ideas, it was terrifying.

Staring at the peak of the tower, Black Jack pulled at his bottom lip. "I think I know a way."

Under cover of darkness, they moved toward the citadel.

The tam led the way. It moved north, away from the narrow path that led to Akkadian and the deadeye that guarded it. They traveled silently, keeping to the shadows, flitting like ghosts through the dusty gullies.

Hiding, the tam pointed a finger toward a narrow fissure in the base of the mountain—the crack would have been impossible to spot had they not been led there. Jack nodded. The tam scurried across the open space and into the crack. Chance followed, a silent sprinter. Rooker was next; Li-Bao followed him. Django glanced at the boy. "You go. I am not quick." Jack glanced up at the watch fires of the Citadel Akkadian and launched himself across the open plain. He reached the crack, jammed himself through, and was engulfed in darkness. Up ahead, Rooker snapped a torch to life and gestured for him to come on. Jack looked back as the huge minotaur loped to the split in the rock and wedged himself into the opening. His broad shoulders and broader horns jammed in the narrow crack. Jack grabbed a meaty arm and pulled. Django twisted, strained, and was through. He silently nodded and they joined the others.

The tunnel was narrow and steep. They climbed the uneven path, scrabbled through low-ceilinged gaps, and jumped deep crevasses. And they went up—always up.

The citadel builders knew of the secret way, of course, and had used it for a multitude of dark purposes over the ages. It was once called the Jagged Rail, but few remembered who had first given it a name. In the days of the old princes, it was a highway for illegal goods, smuggled prisoners, and secret escapes. During the rule of Prince Hiroshi, his several mistresses had used the Rail with great regularity—and Hiroshi's corpse had traveled down it when his wife decided his murder was best left a mystery.

The door was a surprise. The tam had made no mention of it, but there it was: a thick, heavy ironbound barrier built centuries before any of them were born. It had been shut for the last time eighty years before, killing any fear that Akkadian's enemies might use the Rail.

Outside the door's frame was a small crack. The tiny tam slipped through it, leaving them behind. It poked its head out a moment later, confused they were not following.

The crack was barely big enough for a tam, much less a minotaur. "Perfect," Rooker hissed.

Django grabbed the thick handle of the door and pulled. Rust dust fell from the frame, but the door didn't budge. The others joined in, pulling with all their strength, but the thing was as solid as the rock surrounding it.

"My turn." Rooker Flynn stepped in front of them. The pirate pressed himself against the door, his fingers stroking the metal around the lock like a lover. He edged his fingers into the tiny crack between the door and the frame and grinned. "Ball-and-pin job. Nice work too." He flipped open a small leather case loaded with thin metal picks. "There's a bar on the other side, Jack. Get yer little mate to move it to the right. Not the left, or we're done. *Right.* Got me?"

Jack called the tam back. He explained the difference between left and right but was nervous as the gecko disappeared into the crack.

Beyond the door, there was a creak, a puff of rust, and something slid into place. Nothing happened.

"Good. We ain't dead." Rooker went to work on the lock. His picks rasped and clattered—something small *clicked* inside the door. He reached for the handle, then stopped himself. On an impulse, Rooker peered at the lock. He snapped his fingers, igniting his little majik flame, and pressed one eye to the keyhole. He smiled bitterly. "Deadbolt drop. O, these boys were *good.*"

He licked his fingertips and inserted two more picks, carefully tickling them into place. He slid one up, and something inside the door snapped loudly. "Ya might wanna step back." The group did. Rooker Flynn opened the door. A rush of air flooded the passage as fifty long red arrows hurtled from the blackness, shot through the spot where Jack had just been standing, and smashed into the rock. Vile green ooze dripped down the wall where the tips had struck.

The captain blew on his fingertips, utterly satisfied with himself. "There's a small lake of acid above that sluiceway." Rooker jerked his chin at three all-but-invisible pinpricks in the top of the doorframe. "The picks in the keyhole are holdin' it shut. Don't touch." The pirate winked and disappeared through the door.

Jack swallowed, glanced at the others, and followed, careful to get nowhere near the door.

The Jagged Rail became a rock staircase leading up into the dark. Rooker snapped his fingers, tossed his fire at the torches bolted to the wall, and lit their way. As they climbed the stair, one side of the wall fell away into shadow, and they were left circling the edge of a vast pit. Rooker pointed out several steps to avoid. He didn't explain why, but no one questioned him.

At the top of the Rail squatted a large metal portcullis—the gate to the citadel itself. The tam slipped easily through the bars and crouched beyond it, waving them forward. Rooker Flynn frowned, examined the blockade, and placed his hands on his hips. "No traps. Not even a lock. But I'll be cooked over coals if we're gonna lift this." He turned on Jack. "End of the line."

"No." Django Barón stepped forward. "My turn, Captain." The minotaur took hold of the gate's metal crossbar, lowered his head, and hooked his great horns under it. Setting his feet wide apart, Django lifted. Powerful muscles bulged in the great bull's upper back. His thick neck became a corded tree trunk. His entire body strained with the effort. The huge gate rose a few scant inches. Django grabbed the crossbar in his fists, quickly yanked his horns free, and—biceps straining to keep the gate aloft for a few precious seconds—jammed his horns under the gate. He went to his knees, flattened his hands against the ground, and *bucked*. The gate shot up three feet. Rooker darted under the door, flipped a lever on the other side, and locked the gate into place.

Django Barón snorted, jerked his head, and heard a satisfying *pop* in his great neck. "Now"—he nodded—"we find the lady."

Inside the citadel, it was pitch black—this section of the tower was long abandoned, its windows mortared over. But Jack could hear, far above, sounds of life. Stumbling in the dark would be difficult, but they did not dare light a torch now.

Chance motioned for them to wait and disappeared silently into the blackness at a dead run. It was eerie, the way the jinx moved. A moment later, his head popped out of the blackness right in front of Jack's nose. "More stairs," he whispered and held out a rope. "Pass it along." The group strung themselves together like mountaineers, and Chance led them into the dark.

Holding on to the rope, Jack waved his hand in front of his face but saw nothing—just the cat's eyes shining in the dark. Chance led them over what felt like a polished stone floor, then up a long flight of curved stairs in a long, silent game of Blind Man's Bluff. Jack couldn't hear the jinx, but every once in a while, an invisible furry hand reached out to guide him.

Then he heard the voices.

The rope tightened. Jack groped blindly in the dark, panicking. He felt a paw on his chest. It pushed him gently, and suddenly, Jack's back was against a wall. Lantern light bloomed out of the black. It grew brighter with the sound of voices. As Jack's pupils adjusted, he discovered Chance had maneuvered the group into an alcove behind a stone pillar—a perfect hiding spot. "Shh," said the cat.

Six men—Red Dwarves—entered with the lantern, talking in harsh and guttural tones. Short, broad-shouldered, and heavily muscled, the dwarves' skin was red—actually *red*—a deep, hearty scarlet color that made them seem in a perpetual state of rage. From the way they spoke to each other, the notion wasn't far wrong. One of them was shouting at his fellow, and the two men suddenly clashed, striking at each other mercilessly, barking like rabid dogs. The biggest dwarf, nearly four feet, cracked them across the jaw with a truncheon, dragged them to their feet, and kicked them on their way, the two scrappers grumbling as they went.

It dawned on Jack they were the first voices in Keymark he couldn't understand.

As the lantern light faded, Chance's reflective eyes peered at Jack. "Farther?" Jack exhaled, then nodded in the dark. "Then up we go," came the cat's voice, and up they went.

Another hour they went like that, Chance leading the lifeline up the forever stair. Three times, they came across Red Dwarves on patrol, and three times, the companions found themselves neatly tucked away when the light came. Jack realized if they had lit a torch, they would have been discovered half a dozen times by now. Had it not been for the cat, they would have never gotten to the top.

Finally—light. Huge open windows littered the peak of the tower; silver beams of two-moon light cut long shapes into the floor. Chance collected the rope as the others blinked their sight back.

Which way?

The tam gestured for them to follow. It led up one last spiraling climb around a deep pit, and the stairs were at an end. They had reached the top.

The chamber was broad and open. Fat pillars of red stone grew to massive arches—they built on each other in row after row, cresting in the dome that marked the spire's peak. To one side, a massive arch lay open like a giant mouth, flooding the dome with double moonlight.

The floor was a charred carpet of ash.

The tam pointed to the open arch, its eyes big as dinner plates. Jack gritted his teeth, edged quietly to the corner, and peeked outside.

A long rock ledge thrust from the edge of the spire, a broad precipice overlooking the valley below. In the Time of the Princes, the rulers of the Citadel Akkadian had walked this ramp, arms clasped behind their backs, looking over the valley, lords of all they surveyed. The view was staggering, a panoramic vista of the endless chaparral and the forests beyond—on a clear day, the princes could survey their entire domain in a single glance. But the princes were all dead—save one—and the Citadel Akkadian was ruled by the Traitor Knight and his great wyrm.

Moonlight glistened on the jabberwok's diamond-hard scales. Tremendous claws gripped the red rock—claws that had twice torn a horse in half. Its long tail curled around its sleek body, looped over leathery, batlike wings and under its powerful jaw. Its saurian head bristled with jagged ivory teeth; the tattered remains of a recent kill still dangled from its lips. Its eyes were closed, but whether it slept, Jack Swift did not know.

Sunrise broke over the horizon of the west, and there, silhouetted against the dawn, was Leah.

Tattered remains of her Watch uniform flickered in the breeze. She hung by her hands, her wrists and ankles bound to a seven-foot iron spike. Like the wyrm, Leah's eyes were shut.

Jack ducked back behind the corner. His heart pounded against his ribs. *Alive.*

"What now?" whispered Django. *What now?* Jack felt his backpack and made sure it still contained the thing they had made for this moment. If his luck held, he would never have to use it. If his luck held, the jabberwok was a creature of habit.

"We wait," Jack whispered back. "He'll go to feed soon. When he does, we get her out and get her down."

"*Wait?*" hissed Rooker. "With the Red Dwarves below and the great wyrm above? Not a—"

Rooker cut himself off. In the beams of the rising sun, something glistered below.

The captain was down the steps in a flash.

Along the stairwell wall, a thick wooden door stood open a crack. Beyond it, the pirate felt the familiar flicker of his only obsession: gold.

"*Rooker!*" Jack whispered, but the pirate didn't hear or didn't want to. Rooker peeked inside the door, and there, laid out before him, was the vast treasury of the citadel. The spoils of the *Venture Brigand* were a mere fraction of the riches that awaited him. Gold and silver and gems and jewels piled high upon each other, winking in the dawn light—the prizes of a hundred campaigns, the pillage of a thousand raids, and the plunder of the world's ultimate bandit: taxes.

His pirate's heart skipped a beat. In that moment, Rooker Flynn was—for the first time in his entire life—completely happy.

He stepped inside to find seven sets of beady eyes staring back at him.

Red Dwarves, only half awake, sleep still crusty in their sockets, jumped to their feet. Crying out, they snatched up their weapons. One jumped to a tin tube mounted in the wall and shouted into it, sounding the alarm to the dwarves below: *"Hazara ek-seider!"*

Rooker stumbled back, lost his balance, and fell onto the stair. An axe whickered down and smashed the stone next to his head. Four more lifted into the air, and Rooker knew he was dead.

God's plans are laid out one at a time, and each man serves his purpose. The pirate got them past the traps. Django got them through the gate. Chance led them through the dark.

Now it was Li-Bao's turn.

The crocodile launched from the top of the staircase, hurling himself at the dwarves, and took one's head as he came.

Li-Bao Sen hit like a thunderbolt—all the Reds could do was scream as the one-man onslaught tore them apart. Li-Bao snatched one by the face, threw him aside, kicked another back into the treasury, and ran a third through with twin scimitars. The last dwarf charged Li-Bao from behind. The one-eyed croc flicked his muscled tail and sent the Red flying off the stair into the abyss.

Chance tilted an ear toward the stairs. "More coming." He popped his claws and ran for the fight.

"Now"—nodded Django Barón—"I fight by your side, Black Jack." And charged into the fray.

Jack gripped his staff and ran with the bull.

A fierce yowl erupted from the cat's throat as he joined the fight. The feral tom hit one of the dwarves like a bladed tornado, claws striking faster than Jack could see. Side by side, the croc and the cat battled. By the time Jack and Django arrived, there were no dwarves left to fight. A single moment of relief, then the well of the tower roared.

Every dwarf in the citadel pounded up the stairs toward them. The Red Dwarves had climbed the tower stairs from the day they could walk and came two and three steps at a time. Black eyes glowed red as they charged, bellowing for blood.

Rooker Flynn finally regained his feet, gawking at the coming rush of Reds. The pirate gritted his teeth; Bessie sang in his hand. "Well, if we're going, let's go!" He threw himself at the enemy.

Steel met steel in violence. Django charged to the fore, taking the brunt of the onslaught; his mighty axe tore through the Red Dwarves. Beneath the bull's horns, Li-Bao whirled, felling the ones that still stood. As Jack joined the fight, he heard the loud voice of Abrahim Qin: *Hit them, boy! Hit them!*

Arrows sprang up from below. A second force of Reds had taken up position across the chasm on the downward side of the spiral. An arrow impaled Li-Bao's shoulder. The lizard didn't seem to notice, hacking furiously at the dwarves nearby. A second volley of crossbows *twanged.* Jack saw a bolt come right for him. Panicking, he threw up his arm, and the missile bounced aside as it struck the bright flash of Valerian's skidshield. Chance was hit and staggered. Another Red struck him. Jack smashed the thing across the face, but a third clubbed the jinx's chest with a heavy mace. The feral tom toppled backward toward the abyss. Jack grabbed for him, narrowly missed his furry hand, and Chance fell.

He flailed, grappling air. The jinx's tail spun, falling, his body twisting as only a cat's could. One paw snatched the rock ledge below. Chance *uumphed,* claws scrabbling at the edge, legs dangling over the abyss. Above him, the Red archers took aim on their new and helpless prey.

The one-eyed croc backed into the wall, his tail coiling against the stone. "Damn *cats*," spat Li-Bao, and launched himself into the air. He hurtled across the abyss—fully outstretched from the tip of his blade to the tip of his flickering tail. The Red archers screamed as the croc destroyed them.

Jack felt the skidshield ricochet into his body as a dwarf stabbed at him. He smacked his staff across its jaw, sent the red-eyed thing somersaulting down the stair, and turned to help Rooker. The pirate's singing saber warbled bloody delight, hacking the enemy down, thrumming with vengeful glee. Rooker himself blazed furious bravado, roaring with every strike. The pirate, the bull, and the boy smashed at the rising Reds—but step by step, they were driven back, retreating up the stair.

Django was hit and roared pain. Hurling his axe aside, he charged into the Reds, his head low, skewering two on his great horns. The minotaur jerked his head, flinging them into the pit, and struck again. Jack ran to him but was forced to leap away from the frenzy of the raging bull. Beyond caring who was friend or foe, Django Barón attacked in a bloody berserker rage, annihilating everything that stood before his blazing wrath.

A hand shot out and grabbed one horn. Django tried to shove it away, but the strong grip held fast, jerking the bull's head up. It was Li-Bao Sen. Chance stood behind him, cradling one arm. No dwarves remained between them.

Django tilted his head back and roared a tremendous bellow of victory.

Above them, another, louder roar split the air.

The jabberwok was awake.

Jack turned to find the great wyrm staring directly at him. A wicked eye narrowed to a slit, its great chest heaved once, and its lungs shot fire.

The boy grabbed someone (he never knew who) and threw himself into the treasury. Fire flooded after him, turning the door to ash, burning coins to molten slag.

Choking from the smoke, Jack ripped off his burning cloak and beat out the flames on the minotaur's furred head. Li-Bao lay crumpled on the floor, his salamander skin cracked and steaming. Chance was senseless, smoldering. Jack grabbed his staff, barked at Rooker: "Get them out!" and ran up the stair straight for the jabberwok.

Jack Swift wasn't thinking anymore. The fight had stripped him of fear. All he knew was Leah.

Surprised, the jabberwok reared back as the boy came. Jack hurled his waterskin at the thing's mouth. The great wyrm snapped at it, snatching the skin with razor teeth. As it burst, Jack darted sideways, sprinted through the great arch, and onto the precipice.

"Jahk!" shouted Leah, her eyes wide in shock. She had woken to the sound of battle and heard the roar, but the last person in the world she expected to see come through the arch was the *doktar.* Her eyes flashed. *"Left!"*

Jack dove left. He felt the blast roar past him, burning his feet as it rolled over the red rock like a river of flame. He spun and hurled his staff at the jabberwok like a spear. Not waiting to watch, he ran to Leah, yanked his knife from its sheath, and cut the ropes that bound her hands. *"Duck!"* she shouted. He did, and the jabberwok's huge head shot over his shoulder, teeth snapping the spot where his head had just been. Jack drew the cutlass from his back and jammed it into the great wyrm's neck. Diamond-hard scales bent the blade; it shot out of his hands, clattering across the rock. He gripped the knife, his last weapon, and slashed the last of Leah's ropes.

She came free. Weak as a kitten, she fell, holding Jack tight. The great wyrm loosed a great bellow. It moved its tremendous bulk sideways, blocking the arch entirely, trapping Jack and Leah on the ledge with nothing behind them but a seven-thousand-foot drop.

Jack backed away, dragging Leah with one hand; in the other, he held his tiny knife. The jabberwok inhaled, the incinerator in its lungs roared, and it ejected an inferno to roast them alive.

It screamed, twisting like a snake; its flame jet ripped the sky. Rooker Flynn's singing saber was embedded in the great wyrm's tail, the blade shrieking a single high, operatic note. Rooker yelled, *"Come o—"*

The jabberwok's tail struck Rooker full in the chest and sent him flying. It turned to face Jack and came for him.

Jack grabbed Leah and sprinted straight for the cliff, the great wyrm at his heels. Realizing what Jack meant to do, Leah screamed. Jack clutched her tight, lowered his head, and—seven thousand feet over the valley floor—he jumped.

It was a bad idea, a horrible idea, a sick, stupid, insane idea.

And it was all Galileo's fault.

The challenge at the Leaning Tower of Pisa was one of the first great scientific experiments in the history of the world. Aristotle—the great philosopher and mentor to Alexander the Great—stated the principle that heavier objects fell faster than lighter ones. An upstart Italian physicist set out to prove him wrong. Galileo Galilei climbed to the top of the Leaning Tower and, testing the theory, dropped two balls: one heavy metal, the other light wood. Both globes struck the ground in the same instant, and Aristotle's conceit was crushed. Scientific method was born of that moment, and over the centuries, Galileo's experiment evolved into the formula:

$$V_t = \sqrt{\frac{2mg}{\rho A C_d}}$$

Terminal Velocity, thought Jack as the jabberwok launched itself off the cliff after them. *You can't fall faster than we can— you can't catch us now.*

A fascinating scientific fact.

But it wouldn't help him much when they splattered all over the rock.

Science is made in fact. Magic is made in variables. Terminal Velocity's variable is the drag coefficient—more surface area, less velocity. If you want to slow down, all you have to do is increase your surface area. A lot. But even the great Leonardo da Vinci failed to cheat Galileo's gravitational fact. In the end, the French discovered the secret:

Silk.

Leah screamed like a banshee.

They rocketed through the sky; wind tore at their faces. Tears streaming from his eyes, Jack looked up and saw the great wyrm plummeting after them. "Hold on to me!" he yelled. "Hook your arms through my pack! *Now!*" Crying, Leah obeyed.

Sixteen hours to sew the silks. Rooker had grumbled and walked away, but the Trio had joined in, doing as Black Jack asked without question. The seams were triple- and quadruple-stitched, the ropes bound fast. The science was simple, the theory was sound. But like all science, there was a wide gulf between idea and execution.

It was a bad idea, a horrible idea, a sick, stupid, ridiculous idea.

And it was all Jack's fault.

They plummeted toward their death.

Not yet.

Leah was screaming.

Not yet.

The jabberwok roared down at them.

Not yet.

The ground sped up at them.

Now.

Jack threw the chute. The pilot line shot out behind him, rattled the air, and snapped open with a *whap.*

The lines jerked taut—the main chute yanked free. Jack and Leah were ripped backward, straps digging deep. He clutched Leah's belt, holding on tight as whistling air filled the silk, billowing wide in a huge multicolored bubble.

It worked.

The jabberwok screeched. It was forced to dodge the huge thing that sprang up toward it—a giant jellyfish in the sky. A rush of air buffeted Jack as the jabberwok sped past. It turned its head, hate shining in its wicked eyes, cheated of its prey.

The great wyrm opened its tremendous jaws to roast them out of the sky, shot up one jet of flame, and crunched headfirst into the rock.

Jubilee howled from Jack's throat. Leah stared up at the floating jellyfish above her in awe.

As they drifted downward, one burning ember of the dragon's last kiss floated up, caught inside the bubble, and lit the silk. Fire ate through the canopy. Air rushed through it. The ropes caught on fire. The parachute became the *Hindenburg*.

They fell. The ground came fast. They hit.

Jack's knee cracked into his chin.

Air shot out of his lungs.

He rolled, bounced over the rock, and tumbled to a stop.

Jack sucked in one great whooping breath.

Still alive.

Leah lay on top of him, breathing hard. Nose to nose, she stared at the boy. She pushed aside her mop of strawberry hair, panting.

"You… What…" Leah stammered, her eyes wide. "How did you *do* that?"

Catching his breath, Jack winked. "Toshan magic."

She kissed him. Full on the mouth. Hard.

A trumpet of pain roared. Jack's eyes darted sideways to see the jabberwok, shattered and crushed, crawling its way toward them on broken legs. Its head was caved in, one eye was gone, its jaw was shattered, and its teeth had been left on the rocks. But still, it came. Its chest wheezed a keening, bubbling rattle that counted down the moments to its death. But the great wyrm would not die—not before its prey.

A gurgle. Its lungs filled with fire. The jabberwok raised its head for one final blast.

Sizzling emerald flame shot into the wyrm. Fire hammered its body, struck its head, pierced its throat. The jabberwok collapsed—dead.

A giant silhouette emerged from the dawning sun. Its smoking fingertips were enormous, as if someone had dipped long-fingered hands into a huge vat of clay, let them dry, then repeated

the process again and again until—
Memphis.
A huge grin broke over the rhino's face.
"Boyo, I didn't know you could *fly*."

Festival of the Wyrm

Life may not be the party we hoped for,
but while we're here, we should dance.

Unknown

Every living thing has a soul. It is unique, and dwells within us from the moment of our birth to the instant of our death. Some say it is pure when it comes to us, light and white and good. Others claim it is wicked and black from the very beginning, and it is only through our thoughts and deeds that we can save it—and ourselves—from eternal corruption. The nature of God's gifts is always a matter of debate. Whatever the truth, it runs like a river through our entire lives, flowing and ebbing and changing as it runs. Without it, there is no delight, no despair, no pain, and no joy. The soul is a river, and it is alive.

In the language of the *wikk*, that river is *aura*: the color of one's heart.

Jack Swift's aura was light green—the exact same shade as the underside of an aspen leaf—and Memphis Kubiak knew it well.

The trol followed the pull of that color for sixteen days, never resting, never sleeping, moving on and on, remembering only the promise he had made to the boy:

I will find you.

There are few things in the world harder to kill than a Juttlander trol. Campion Rei nearly succeeded. Memphis survived the ambush on Falikos only by the slimmest of margins; in the end, he had escaped into the sea. Deep water terrified him, as it did all trols—their dense bodies sank like rocks with no hope of surfacing, and it took a long, long time for their great lungs to drown.

Memphis only managed to stay alive by becoming the little brown lizard that had once held on to a screaming boy's shoelace. He floated that way for five days, bobbing in the waves as helpless prey for sharks. When he finally washed ashore, crawling, beaten, and bloody, he forced his exhausted body to keep moving forward. *I will find you.*

He followed the pull of the boy's aura east, through the Llykowen Swamps, hoping to find allies there; instead, he found the Tower Yongshi crawling with the Necrórceror's vermin. Memphis fled through the muck, his huge feet sinking in the black mud as versläng came at him by the dozens. He fought them off, sapped of his majik, crushing their shells with his huge fists until he finally broke free to solid ground. *I will find you.*

Running north, he stumbled across the kekubi as they hammered their staring deadeyes into the dirt. They came for him, howling. They would not stop, relentless, and Memphis was hunted like an animal along the Ruk-al-Satyr Wall for four days and nights, haunted by their howls. Memphis ran, plunging forward into his twelfth night without sleep. *I will find you.*

Across the Breechline River, he came. Across the blasted cracks of the Jaden Fields, he came. To the Citadel Akkadian, he came, all the while following the shining heart of the boy, that color—the underside of an aspen leaf—that so closely matched his own.

And as Jack jumped into his arms, Memphis Kubiak felt his own soul finally breathe easy, and shine just a bit brighter.

The celebration was unrestrained. The last three surviving members of the massacre on Falikos could not come together closely enough, hugging and touching and grabbing each other with joyful abandon, pressing their bodies together in an effort to make sure the other was real. Words piled on each other like converging rivers, each talking over the other in an excited babble as the three of them embraced.

"Back together again." The trol smiled, hugging them both in his great arms. "Here I was, all worried about you." Memphis jerked his horns at the dead jabberwok. "And you two manage *that.*"

"*He's* the one that did it." Leah smiled at Jack and launched into an excited account of her amazing rescue. Jack couldn't ignore the sparkle in her eyes—the way she looked at him made him feel like a million bucks.

Both she and the trol wanted to know Jack's story, and he told them everything: the *Venture Brigand*, Rooker Flynn, Rimmy's Cull, the Madrigal Verde, the Winter Caverns, and the arrival of the Trio.

"They think you're Black Jack?" said Memphis, surprised.

"The Black? Really?" Leah grinned.

Jack nodded. "We would never have made it inside Akkadian without them. They rescued you as much as I did."

"And here they come now," said the trol. Jack looked up the ramp and saw the Trio coming down, still far away. "We'd better get moving," said Memphis, getting to his feet. "There's a deadeye down there, and I'd better blast that thing before the Fell Prince knows we're here."

Jack followed Memphis close. "What do I tell them? About Black Jack?"

"You say one of them's a minotaur?"

"Yes."

"Then I'd say you're tied to the tale you told, boyo." Memphis grinned. "Besides—you healed the sick, killed the beast, and rescued your lady fair. I'd say you fit the bill just fine."

"So"—Leah grinned—"it looks like I owe my life to the great Black Jahk." She took his arm and smiled. "My hero."

Jack couldn't keep the smile off his face.

The runner had traveled to many places and had seen a great many odd things. He had seen horrible wars, gruesome battles, and places of indescribable beauty. He had seen the marriages of the mighty; the first presentation of their infant scions; and their sad, solemn funerals when their lives came to an end. He had seen many odd things, yes—but never a giant flaming jellyfish in the sky.

Tucumcari was a small town, and insignificant. It boasted only three hundred souls, and most were poor farmers, scratching a living out of the dirt, coaxing life from the hardscrabble soil of the Bonespur foothills. They were a simple people; they paid their taxes to the tower, fought off the occasional raid by Red Dwarves, and made their way as best they could in a hard land, living under the ever-darkening shadow of the Citadel Akkadian and the great wyrm that nested there.

Hatch the Smith was chief among them not because he held any office of power (they had no such things in Tucumcari), or because he was wealthier than most (he was not), but because Hatch was the best man among them. And for that reason, the runner went to him first.

Farmers and stockmen gathered in a group, staring into the distance at the outline of the Red Tower, speaking in hushed, amazed tones, pointing and arguing over what they had just seen. Hatch Smith stood with them, silent, his huge hammer over his shoulder. The hammer and its master had made many things for the village of Tucumcari: picks, saws, hoes, trowels, adzes, axe-heads, and shovel blades, but never a weapon—he had given that up long ago. As the big, quiet man stared thoughtfully at the outline of the spire, the morning sun at his back, the runner came alongside him.

"Hatch—"the runner began.

"Find out what you can and get back quick." The big man's dark eyes never left the tower. "And Finnegan"—Hatch turned —"be safe."

The runner nodded, then bolted into the manzanita trees quick as a wink. More farmers gathered around the silent smith, talking softly, sharing what they had seen plummeting from the citadel's peak, trying to piece together what had happened. As speculation grew, questions rose to wild conjecture; stories of the burning bubble became the arrival of a great beast to challenge the jabberwok. Others claimed the thing was here to mate with the wyrm and give rise to some new terror. Some claimed the giant jellyfish heralded the arrival of the Fell Prince himself.

To all this, Hatch said nothing.

The great wyrm had haunted his village for three years now, looming over Tucumcari like a great shadow. And during that time, the Crimson Knight, who had once ruled the Bonespur with dignity and grace, had become distant and cruel. But Hatch the Smith counted only one thing: Campion Rei was a Border Knight, and so they owed him their loyalty and their lives.

Tucumcari was four miles from the base of the Bonsepurs, an eight-mile round trip. Finnegan was slower than usual—his return took almost fifteen minutes.

"The great wyrm is dead!" cried the runner jubilantly. A sudden shout broke out from the villagers, a trumpet of pure joy. The runner grinned. He was used to delivering news, but lately, most of it had been bad, news of battle, fire, and death. "And there is more!" Finnegan savored the moment, delighted to have every eye on him, anticipating the revelation. "Black Jack is *back*!"

One breath of stunned silence, then a great shout exploded from the throng. As one, the Tucumcaris darted into the scrub oak, making for the tower as fast as they could run, raring to see the great wyrm dead, and a legend come to life.

Hatch made no effort to stop them but took Finnegan by the arm. "Go on."

"Half a dozen of them." The runner grinned, barely able to contain his excitement, bouncing on his powerful legs. "And a motley crew if there ever was one: Juttlander, llystra, a feral tom, two young jaelin, and a minotaur."

"A minotaur?" repeated Hatch, showing surprise for the first time.

"Aye. He's the one what told me about the Black. You'd never know it to look at him, but the bull swore to me the boy is Black Jack himself. It was *him* what flew from the cliffs, inside some kind of great seed pod or a giant feather. I don't understand it, and neither do they, but he bested the wyrm. Bested the wyrm in the *sky*, Hatch!"

Hatch's face was unreadable. "If the wyrm is dead, it means nothing but good for us." He slung his great hammer over his shoulder and stared at the mountain, his eyes dark.

"Let's go and meet this Black Jack."

Celebrations were a rarity in Tucumcari, but when they came, they were seized with both hands. Villagers emptied the hamlet in minutes, and soon, every living soul was cheering at the base of the citadel. The dead jabberwok was the centerpiece of a tremendous festival; villagers danced around the vanquished monster with triumphant shouts of jubilee. Children took turns whacking the dead beast with sticks and ran away giggling. Musicians broke out their instruments: lutes, pipes, and harps jangled a steady rhythm of elation as the crowd became one tremendous party.

Butchers went to work. They peeled back the diamond-hard skin of the jabberwok with crowbars, cut away chops from the bone, and roasted huge slabs of sumptuous meat over a tremendous bonfire. Dragon steaks are a rarity in Keymark, prized beyond all other cuts of meat, reserved only for the richest of men.

As Jack Swift took his first taste of the ceremonial prime cut the villagers offered him, he understood why: dragon was *delicious.*

The instant he finished eating, Jack quickly pulled the black scarf over his face—for once, he was glad of the Black's mask. He had no idea how to deal with the Tucumcaris; they came to him in waves, each one thanking him for killing the great wyrm, heaping praises upon him, honoring him, telling him what a pleasure it was to meet the legendary Black Jack. Some brought gifts: a gold necklace worn by one woman's grandfather, several jeweled rings forged of platinum and silver, jars of expensive spices; one odd man even offered the mounted head of a gigantic stag that had been in his family for generations. Befuddled, Jack said as little as possible, nodding and shaking their hands as they pressed in close, and he was soon surrounded by presents.

Django Barón found himself the center of nearly as much attention as his master. The minotaur was a rare curiosity, and everyone wanted a look. Uncomfortable with so many eyes on him, Django joined in with the musicians, using an old cello like a guitar. The bull was a surprisingly good guitarist. Nimble fingers moved expertly over the strings, his deep voice matching the low thrum of the strings, singing merry tunes as fiddle players joined in the revelry.

Memphis was surrounded by children. This far north, the people were familiar with trols, but had rarely met one so friendly. He performed majik for the kids, sending up fireworks that burst into the sky above the jabberwok to cries of amazed delight. Memphis asked them riddles, told them tales, and even juggled a pair of giggling children six feet in the air until a group of horrified mothers put a quick stop to *that*, much to the disappointment of all involved.

Chance moved freely among the younger and more attractive women, seducing them with his suave golden eyes, purring in their ears, making sure each knew his part in the defeat of the jabberwok. Li-Bao Sen said little (as always), eating his steak and listening to the music. The croc's face remained stoic, but the tip of his tail tapped to the merry rhythm of Django's guitar.

Even the tam joined in the celebration, scuttling back and forth between the merrymakers, its head bobbing up and down. Jack leaned up against a wine barrel, watching the dancers as the tam curled up alongside him.

You flew. It gestured with its little tree-frog fingers.

Jack tossed an apple to the tam. *Yes.*

Better than snake-bird-huge-fire.

Yes.

The tam nodded, grinning. *Do it again.*

Jack laughed. *Not in a billion years.*

The tam bit into the apple and went back to bobbing its head to the music. Jack looked at the little gecko, smiling. If it had not been for the tam, he never would have found a way inside Akkadian, never rescued Leah, and tonight, the celebration, the praise, the festival, all of this would never have happened.

You did a great thing today.

It looked up at him curiously. *Tam did as tam was told. Not great. Only tam.*

Maybe. But even a tam deserves a name.

The gecko looked up at him, its face brightening. *Apple Jack can give tam name?*

Jack glanced down at the apple. It looked just like the kind Dad liked best—

"Fuji," he murmured under his breath.

Fuji, repeated the tam instantly, nodding. *Tam likes Fuji.*

So, that's your name.

The tam suddenly grinned ear to ear. It leapt into the air, chirruping gleefully like a bird. *Name! Tam has name!* It hugged Jack's leg, then abruptly disappeared into the dancers, unable to contain its joy, leaping with every step as if someone had just given it the best birthday present ever.

Jack smiled, standing alone until one of the girls grabbed his hand and he was pulled into the merriment.

He danced with the Tucumcaris, a spinning celebration around the fire. Jack had memorized the steps and claps without even thinking about it, and once he lost himself in the rhythm, he gave himself over to the celebration and let go. Django picked the huge guitar faster and faster. Chance grabbed Jack up in a fast whirligig that made everyone laugh. The air was heady with the smell of steak, fire, beer, pipe tobacco, and sweat. Fireworks lit the air. Drums pounded and strings hummed as they danced and sang and clapped. He grew dizzy, grinning wide, then spun around and suddenly found he was dancing with Leah.

Firelight flickered brightly against her hair. Her face was radiant, smiling, those green eyes shimmering as the shadows of the fire caressed the contours of her face. Her hands found Jack, pulled him close, and they moved together in time to the music. He felt her fingers against his skin, felt her breath on his lips, smelled the heady scent of cherry blossoms on her flesh. She laughed, moving closer, and at that moment, she was more than enough to break his heart.

He kissed her.

She let him, for half a moment, then pulled back and put up one finger between them. "Benjamin."

Jack took a step back. He hadn't even thought of his friend for days, and suddenly felt embarrassed at what he had done, at what he had thought.

"No," Leah said quickly, reading his eyes. "Don't. He's gone. But I loved him, Jahk. And I'll mourn him for a while longer."

Jack nodded, not sure how to feel, not sure what to say. After a moment, he simply put out his hand.

Leah took it.

And they danced.

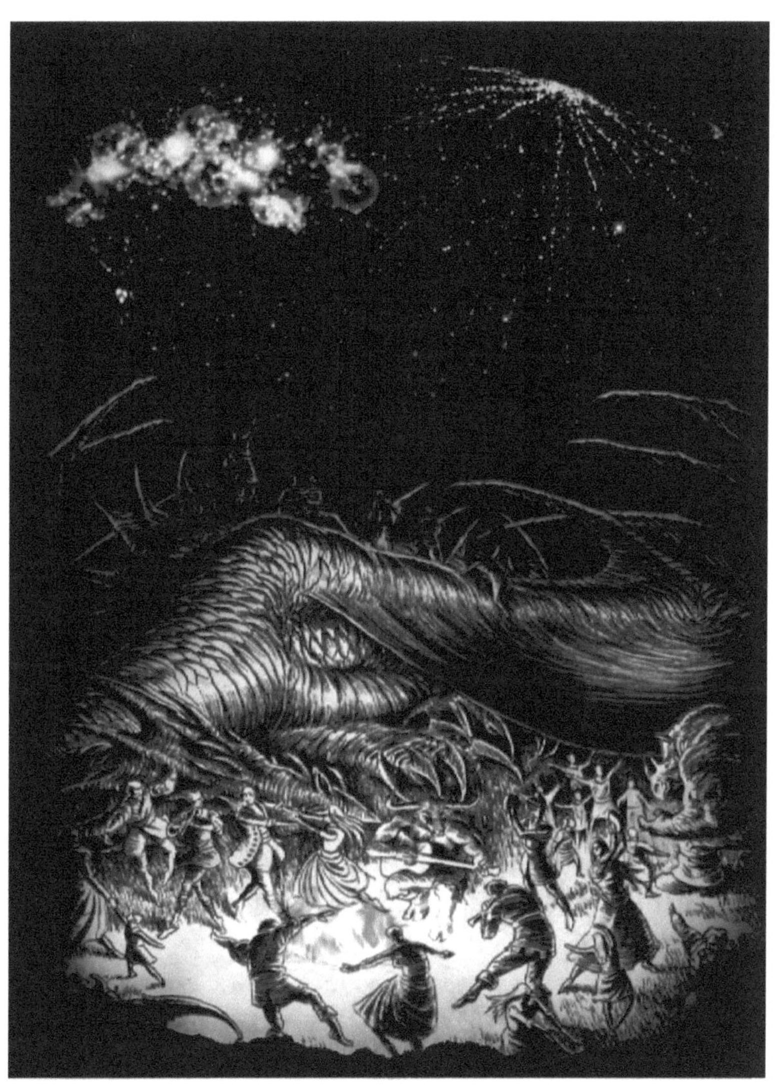

As the sun dropped below the peak of the Citadel Akkadian and faded away into the east, the jabberwok lay stripped half to the bone. The Tucumcaris, their bellies filled with steak, were mellowing with the evening as the lively music gave way to more melodic strains. Jack sat in a small group around one of the fires, looking at the stars. As Jack stared up at the two moons, he tried to find a constellation he knew: Orion the Hunter, Draco the Dragon, Cassiopeia, even the Big Dipper, but he could not find one of them.

Suddenly, he felt a long, long way from home.

He wondered idly where Rooker was. He hadn't seen the pirate since…well, since the battle with the jabberwok. Django had assured him Rooker was fine, but Jack hadn't seen him during the party. *Well, that's all right. He's probably off in the shadows with a jug of wine and one of the girls. Probably two of each.*

Memphis sat close by, chatting with the big Tucumcari named Hatch Smith. The quiet dark man was huge, packed with muscle, and utterly hairless—his scalp, forearms, and eyebrows had been burned clean by the fires he worked—his head looked like a bowling ball. Jack caught the big man staring at him several times. Something about the look made him uncomfortable, but Jack didn't think much of it; he was too busy staring at Finnegan.

The runner was a man, yes, but only from the waist up. His legs were massive, covered in short, soft hair, bent backward like a jackrabbit. Jack estimated if Finnegan stood at his full height, he would be taller than Memphis, but the runner preferred to hunker. He fidgeted ceaselessly, bouncing back and forth on his powerful legs. Jack guessed when Finnegan moved with a purpose, he could outrace an Olympian sprinter without breaking a sweat.

As Django finished a tune, Hatch the Smith suddenly called out: "Play us the song of the Paladine Knights."

Django's head lowered, and his thick fingers strummed the strings. His low, deep voice sang slowly:

Listen, my son, and learn every shade,
The Colors of Masters, the Knights of the Blade.
Come near me and sit you on one bended knee,
And I'll sing it to you as my dad sang it to me:

Amber for Dawning, Grace no man can earn;
Crimson for Midday, and Valor that burns;
Indigo for Dusk, promised Truth of return.

Titian for Moon, and for Faith come what may;
Azure for Sky, and all Wisdom survey;
Jade for the Living, 'til Death pass away.
All rise up as One, united by Grey.

Listen, my daughter, and learn every shade,
The Colors of Masters, the Knights of the Blade.

There was a moment of stillness around the campfire, then Hatch spoke: "Those days are gone now. The Noble Seven are broken."

Leah lowered an eyebrow, frowning. "We don't know that—"

"Our runner has been hearing the tale all over Keymark," said Hatch. "The Azure is dead and the Grey is gone." Hatch leaned forward. "Unless you know better."

Memphis's jaw drew tight. "We were with the Grey on Falikos, training a new Watch to guard the Paladine. The Crimson Knight—"

"*Your* knight," interjected Leah, her words sharp. Hatch did not react.

"—betrayed the Watch," Memphis said flatly. "He betrayed the Grey, betrayed us *all*, and let in the Necrórceror's vermin. If any man alive could survive that swarm, Valerian Tsai would be the one." The trol's words were bold, but his voice was without hope. "But part of your runner's tales *are* true. The Crimson murdered the Azure Knight, Abrahim Qin."

"So," said the smith. "Campion One-Handed has gone over to the Last Prince." He let out a long breath. "The other four Border Knights may stand for a time, Juttlander, but with their best gone to dust, without Valerian *Tsai*, they will be like a great lion whose head has been chopped off—they still have claws, but not long to use them." Hatch took another swig of his wine. "The Last Prince has returned. And without the Border Knights to stop him, David's Tower will fall. The elves will fall." He hurled his tankard into the fire. "And with them, Keymark."

"Not if we have anything to say about it," said Leah, her voice tight.

"We'll find the Jade Knight," Memphis said.

Jack's ears perked up—this was the first he had heard of this new twist.

"He protects the Jaden Fields, in Glyn Aker, and that's only three days from here." Memphis nodded. "We'll find him. He'll know what to do."

Hatch tapped his hammer with one blunted finger. "The Azure Knight is dead. Perhaps the Jade has already followed him down into the dark. Or worse, gone turncoat like the Crimson."

Memphis snorted disdain. "The Jade has not turned."

Hatch eyeballed the Juttlander. "A tenday ago, I would have said the same of our Crimson."

A nervous look passed over Memphis's face. "The Jade is loyal," he stated, as if saying the thing would make it true. "Campion is busy cutting off the southern ports and will have his hands full finishing off the llystra in Tower Yongshi." Li-Bao's one good eye narrowed at the mention of his home, and Jack heard a low growl in the croc's throat. "Unless the Fell Prince has emerged from his hole in the north, there are few terrors powerful enough to dispatch the Jade."

"There may be one," Finnegan suddenly piped up, his high voice nervous. "Since the deadeyes started going up, I'm not sure what to believe—when people are scared, they tend to make skeletons out of shadows. But there's one story I've heard too many times to be a lie: they say something dark roams the Breechline River. They say it is unstoppable, a devil made of blackness and flame."

Jack felt his heart go cold—he knew exactly what the runner was talking about: the shadow-thing that had tried to slaughter him and Rooker in the Madrigal Verde. "Tales grow tall in dark times," Finnegan continued, "but there are some that would call it a creature of the black sphere, an *ûzguk:* a dæmon."

No one spoke a word—the mere name of the thing had a dark power.

"They say it hunts," Hatch broke the silence. "For what, or *whom*, I do not know."

Memphis suddenly laughed, startling everyone out of their dark thoughts. "If the Fell Prince has summoned an *ûzguk*, Hatch Smith, there is little hope left for any of us." He spread his big hands. "But as you say, tales grow tall in dark times."

"Half the Border Knights are dead or turned," said Hatch. "Those are not *tales*, Juttlander. They are truth." He flicked sweat from his brow. "How fortunate we are that the moment some heroes pass away"—Hatch's eyes turned to Jack—"new ones come to take their place."

The man's words landed like a bullet to Jack's chest. The boy shifted in his seat and dropped his eyes, unable to meet the smith's stare.

Memphis slapped his thighs as he stood. "Then we make for the Breechline River tomorrow morning"—he smiled—"and we find the Jade."

Hatch rose with the trol. "Good luck to you," he said without warmth. He turned to Jack. "My people are at your service, Black." The word sounded hard in his mouth. "What would you have us do with your kill?"

Jack was blindsided by the question. *What would I want with a dead jabberwok?* "We'll take a few steaks, I guess, but the rest should go to the Tucumcaris."

"And what of the remains?"

Jack cocked his head. The question was straight out of left field, but Hatch seemed intent on an answer. "You can have them."

Someone from the back of the crowd gasped, and a low murmur came over the people who had gathered around. The smith's eyes narrowed. "It is your kill, Black. The wyrmscale will make many suits of armor, shields, and helms, all of them worthy of a prince." Jack glanced at the jabberwok—he had no idea the dead thing could be so priceless. "The teeth are unbreakable," continued the smith, "and will remain sharp forever. The fire in its lungs will not go out for a hundred years. These are weapons men would covet."

"*That's* where I know you from!" Memphis said suddenly, snapping his fingers. "You used to be the armorer at Highyon Garde! Hatch Hanjin! You built the armor for half the samurai in David's Tower. Your work is *extraordinary!*"

Hatch eyed the trol darkly; he did not seem to appreciate the admiration. "Once, Juttlander. That was a long time ago." The smith turned his focus back to Jack. "The jabberwok is a fortune undreamed of by simple people such as we, Black. Tell me what you would like done with it. I can build the armor and you can do with it as you please; I could even sell the pieces for you and give you the profit. But surely you would not give *away* so great a treasure."

Jack hesitated. He felt like he was being backed into a corner; the smith was looking for a specific answer, and Jack didn't know what it was. *It doesn't seem like he even* wants *the thing. Should I take it with me? How am I supposed to do* that? *I don't want it. Besides, I'm never coming back here…I just want to go home.* Jack spread his hands and made his decision: "The jabberwok is yours."

Shock appeared on the faces of the Tucumcaris who were listening. A great shout went up. Jack was suddenly pounded on the back by a hundred hands as a cavalcade of voices thanked him. Soon, the camp was in an uproar, and the celebration and music and dancing began with renewed vigor: every man, woman, and child in Tucumcari was now filthy rich.

Jack looked to find Hatch still watching him, half hidden in the firelight, his face an unreadable mask.

Jack moved to Memphis, who was packing up his big satchel. Jack whispered: "Why do I get the feeling he doesn't like me?"

"Because he doesn't like you." Memphis glanced into the shadows. "I think we'd better get moving."

"To the Jaden Fields?" Jack remembered the spot from Valerian's story about the Fell Prince—the site of the Black Accord.

"We're going to find the Jade Knight, boyo. Xiang-lo was there before he got sick so—"

"Xiang-lo?" Jack stopped short. "My patient?"

"Right. He was looking for a jaunt gate, a hidden one. If he found one, the Jade Knight will know about it."

The old question tickled at Jack's brain: "Memphis. Why wouldn't Valerian let me talk to Xiang-lo after the surgery?"

The trol didn't look up, his answer too quick: "I don't know."

Jack was certain he did. *Why will nobody give me a straight answer?*

"Memphis—"

"Aren't you listening, boyo? *A jaunt gate.* If the Jade knows where it is, that means you're going home."

Home.

The word pushed everything else out of his mind. *Home.* Chicago. Carozelli's sandwiches. Kitty Keller. Science class. His bed. His books. America. Even Rose Haig. She might be a mean drunk, but she had never tried to kill him. *Dammit,* Jack thought, *I miss being safe.*

Memphis grinned. "Get your kit packed, boyo. We're making an early start."

Jack moved through the throng, found his pack, and began stuffing clothes into it as quickly as he could. *Home,* he thought. *I'm going home!*

A rough hand reached out of the darkness, snatched him by the arm, and dragged him into the shadows. A voice whispered in his ear, "I do not know what you are, boy." Hatch Smith leaned in close. "But I know what you are *not.*"

Jack swallowed hard. The man with the bowling-ball head gripped Jack's shirt with iron fists. "I met Black Jack," said the smith. "When I was just a boy. And he was older *then* than you are *now.*" Hatch looked Jack up and down. "I never saw his face, but he had purpose in his walk. He had strength in his voice. You have neither." Hatch picked up Jack's silver-tipped staff. "And he had Nepenthe, his great spear. *This* is nothing but a stick." Hatch hurled the staff away. "You are *not* Black Jack."

Jack felt his neck tighten up. He wanted to run, but there was no escaping the smith's grip. Suddenly, he realized there was no use fighting it—he was found out. And deep down, a part of him was glad. "No," he said. "I'm not."

Hatch raised a hairless eyebrow. "You do not deny it?"

"No," the boy said. "My name's Jack, but that's about the only thing that's true." He confessed everything then, how the people in Rimmy's Cull had thought he was the Black, how the Trio had followed him through the Madrigal Verde, mistaking him for a hero. As he told the truth, Jack felt like a poison was draining from his system. "I only wanted to save Leah."

Hatch tightened his grip. "The girl knows. And the trol."

Jack said nothing. If this went badly, he didn't want Leah to suffer for it.

Hatch balled his thick fingers into a fist, clenching and un-clenching his fingers as if he couldn't make up his mind whether to kill Jack or not.

"I don't like liars."

"Neither do I. But I didn't lie to you, Hatch. When you asked who I was, I told you."

"Hiding the truth is the same as telling a lie, boy," snorted the smith. "The man that reared you should have taught you that."

Something inside Jack's head snapped. "Don't talk about my dad." Jack shoved Hatch forcefully with both fists, his blood burning red hot. "Don't."

Hatch took a step back, alarmed by the boy's fury.

"You tell them what you want to, Hatch." Jack's voice sounded sharp and cold in his own ears. "But I did what I had to do. I did my best. *That's* what my father taught me."

Hatch stared at the boy.

After a moment, the smith cocked his head. "So you do have some sense of honor after all."

The ringing in Jack's ears subsided. He felt the blood drain from his limbs, and he instantly felt weak, as if he had just pulled himself back from a cliff's edge by his fingertips. He wiped the hair away from his face. "Are you going to tell them or not?"

Hatch stared at him intently, rubbing his big hand over his mouth. "Black Jack was a hero of the people, boy. He fought for us, defended us, and asked nothing in return. You did just that. You could have kept the jabberwok for yourself, but you gave it away. Your friends fight for you, the people love you, and you do honor to your father." Hatch's shoulders straightened. "Whatever your name may be, you are a hero."

Jack lowered his eyes.

"These are bad times, boy, with worse to come," Hatch said. "The people need hope. I would not rob them of you."

Hatch the Smith slung his heavy hammer over his shoulder. "We owe you. *I* owe you. And if we can repay the debt, we will."

The big man took one last look at him and walked away. "Good fortune, Black Jack."

Rooker Flynn would not come down.

The pirate had spent the entire night barricading himself—and his treasure—inside the Citadel Akkadian.

Jack and the others stood locked outside the gates. In the pale dawn light, the boy found the tin speaking tube the Red Dwarves had used to call the alarm. He hollered into it for fifteen minutes until, from somewhere high above, the pirate captain answered.

"What?"

"What are you *doing*, Rooker? Come down here!"

"Sucks to *that!* Ya stuck me in the back, boychick! Ya gutted me like a *fish!*"

"What are you *talking* about?"

"Ya told 'em about the *treasure!*"

Jack opened his mouth, not knowing how to respond. "Rooker, I didn't tell them anyt—"

"I *seen* 'em! Last night, all dancin' around like fools! And now the party's over, yer come to steal my swag! Well, give it yer best shot, kid! I barred all the doors and reset all the traps on the secret passage, so if yer thinkin' about breaking in, be prepared to lose yer skin!"

Jack took a step back, flabbergasted. "Rooker! I promised you I wouldn't take any of your gold! We spat on it!"

"Spit on *you!*" came the retort. "I see through yer canny little trick, boychick! You won't take a penny, aye, sure, that's what ya swore. And mebbe yer jest man enough to keep yer word, but all those fools'll be happy to take some *for* ya, and more for themselves besides!"

Jack fumed. This was ridiculous. "Will you listen to me, Rooker! I don't want any of your damned gold!"

"And ye'll get none of it, neither!"

Leah shot a breath through her nose and jammed her hands to her hips. "This is some partner you've got yourself, Jahk."

Li-Bao Sen did not speak often, but when he did, his statements were short and to the point: "He's an ass."

"Right," said Chance. It was the only time the two of them had ever agreed on anything.

"What do you think you're going to do?" Jack yelled, trying to pound some sense into the invisible man high above. "There's more gold up there than you could ever carry out! And even if you could, you'd never be able to defend it on the road!"

A moment of silence came from the tower as the pirate considered this for the first time. After a moment: "Then mebbe I'll jest sit on it right here!"

"Don't be an idiot!"

A fusillade of foul language poured out the tin tube like sewage.

"He *curses* like a pirate," stated Memphis, rubbing his ears. "Come on, Jack. We don't have time for this."

Jack wanted to throttle the pirate, to grab Rooker with his bare hands and choke the stupidity right out of him, but he knew it was useless. Django Barón placed one big hand on the boy's shoulder. "Come, Black. He has the gold-lust on him, and no one can cure him of that—not even you."

Jack bit his lip. Rooker Flynn was greedy, reckless, and irritating—but for a time, he had been Jack's only friend.

"We're going to the Jaden Fields to find the Jade Knight!" Jack yelled. "Come with us!"

"Damn ya to the deep and be done with ya!"

Jack smashed the tin tube with his fist, leaving it dented and bent. He spun on his heel and stormed down the ramp, uttering a few choice curses of his own.

Behind him, Rooker's voice trailed on. "I can see ya! I see ya runnin' away! Go ahead! Go get all the help ya want, boychick! Ya ain't gettin' in! Not with an army, ya hear me, Jack? Jack?"

And so the pirate was left alone, rich and caged in his golden tower.

"Jack!"

FATHERS SONS & BROTHERS

Am I my brother's keeper?

Book of Genesis

H e treated his plants like children: with affection, care, and love.

When Farrior Han first came to David's Tower, the man asked for a room high in the pinnacle of the uppermost spire, not because of the security it afforded or the staggering view over the Banpai Range below, but because it offered the greatest amount of sunlight for his flowering children.

The little room was hot (almost unbearable in the summer), but a panoply of life blossomed within his little greenhouse—roses, jacaranda, calla lilies, hyacinth, night-blooming jasmine, mewslips, tropical jellysnappers—and the stone outside was thick with blossoming mauve bougainvillea that crawled right out the window and grew nearly to David's spire.

He had no children; few Border Knights did. It was not against their oath (they were not monks), and Valerian had actually encouraged his brothers-in-arms to marry and raise families. But Farrior Han, the Amber Knight, was content with the offspring he had, and knew their beauty would outlive him just as well as children would.

Sweating, he carried the heavy burlap sack up the stairs of the tower. Highyon Garde (called David's Tower for the Last High King who made his throne there) was the greatest of the Twelve—not so high as Akkadian or as stunning as Yongshi—but of the remaining towers, she was the most heavily defended, the Crown of Keymark. The generals and samurai who guarded the tower thought Farrior was insane to haul his massive bags of planting soil to the spire every tenday, or even to make his room there—the spire was meant for aesthetic beauty, not actual use—but the exercise kept Farrior in shape and helped clear the worries from his mind.

He had good reason to worry.

Runners kept arriving at the gates of Highyon Garde; none of their news was welcome. The Border Watch had been murdered, Tower Yongshi was overrun, and Rimmy's Cull was burning. A strange samurai in red plate mail led versläng through the south, kekubi were everywhere, deadeyes stood watch along the Highway of the Nomads, and something black and monstrous was wandering the Madrigal Verde.

Worst of all, however, was the *lack* of news: no one knew what had happened to Abrahim, Campion, and Valerian. The three knights had been training the Border Watch on Falikos, but there was no word if they had survived the massacre there. Farrior knew it was doubtful that anything could kill even one of the Noble Seven, but still, a dark sense of foreboding had settled deep in his heart.

Farrior wished for his Armor. If only he had the Amber helm, he would be able to see his brothers or at least *feel* them. The Armor had that majik, and so much more—Farrior longed for the power of the elven aegis. But Valerian Tsai forbade the knights to wear the Armor beyond the Paladine Arch. The first and most obvious reason was that the *wikk* of the Armor was tied to the Paladine and faded beyond it. But more importantly, the Armor was meant to defend the elves. Any other use of its majik was a lure to corruption, and Valerian knew it. And so, the Amber Armor, like all the Armor of the Knights, was fixed in its place at the Paladine Arch, and there it would stay.

Farrior Han could do nothing but wait, and the inactivity drove him to distraction.

He and Stahl Shian, the Titian Knight, had been tasked to watch over Highyon Garde until the Grey returned. The Jade was guarding Glyn Aker (as always), and the Indigo stood alone at the Paladine Arch. The Noble Seven were scattered all over Keymark just when the Necrórceror was making his move. Farrior dreaded that every moment he wasted here was costing them more and more.

He shifted the burlap bags on his shoulders and kept climbing. It would take more than one trip up the tower to clear his mind today. A plan had been forming in the back of his head, and it wouldn't stop pestering him. He wanted to find Valerian. Farrior could leave tonight, take his Amber knightsblade, and head south toward Falikos. Stahl could remain here; there was no pressing threat to David's Tower, and one Border Knight could lead the samurai as easily as two. But leaving Highyon Garde meant disobeying the Grey, and no Border Knight had ever dared risked that.

Farrior finally entered his room, dropped the sacks, and took a long look at the plants he loved so much. His hand rested on the doorknob, and he realized his decision had already been made. He continued up the last stairs to Stahl's room.

Stahl Shian did not like residing so high up in the tower but refused to live apart from his leaf-loving brother. When Farrior reached the top, he found the Titian Knight's door standing half open. Farrior paused. Stahl was the oldest of the knights (save Abrahim Qin, who was older than dirt) and wouldn't like the idea much, but Farrior was convinced it was the right thing to do—waiting could only harm them. Taking a breath, Farrior stepped inside.

"Stahl?"

The furniture was overturned and broken. Stahl's knightsblade lay naked on the floor. The tower walls were covered in blood.

"Stahl?" Farrior shoved the door open and saw Stahl Shian lying outstretched on the carpet, gasping for breath. His chest was a bloody swamp.

Instinctively, Farrior reached for his Amber blade. As he drew it free, something sharp and cold punched through his spine.

A single moment of bright pain, then everything went dead below his waist. Farrior collapsed to the ground, his legs useless rags.

His arms still worked. He brought up his sword, then the knife slashed across his throat. His knightsblade clattered to the ground.

The last thing Farrior Han saw through dying eyes was the face of his murderer—a man he had once called brother.

Campion Rei stood over the dead knights, the knife bloody

in his hand.

Stahl had put up more of a fight than he'd expected—the old man was still quick on the draw and suspicious as a cat. But in that single moment of disbelief, Campion had struck first. He had only been lucky with Farrior; the man had stopped below, probably to care for his ridiculous plants, and had given Campion time to slip behind the door.

Luck had nothing to do with it, Campion told himself. *I'm younger, stronger, and faster. I could have beaten them both in a fair fight. But why risk* that?

Getting inside David's Tower had been simple; he was Campion Rei, after all, Knight of the Paladine—not only did no one try to stop him, but nearly every man bowed as he passed. Getting out would be just as easy, if he moved quickly.

Campion reached into his shirt (he did not wear the Crimson Armor, not in Highyon Garde—here, they knew enough to suspect *that*) and plucked out the vial. Unstoppering the top, Campion flinched, still uncomfortable with the gift the Necrórceror had given him. The squirming blind larvae reeked of death.

He bent over and dropped the larvae in Farrior's mouth. They wiggled down his throat with a sick flicker. With Stahl, he simply dumped the squirming black mass into the open hole of the Titian Knight's chest.

Campion flicked his teeth, waiting. He had thousands of versläng and kekubi, the combined raiders of the Cull and Yongshi, waiting in the forests of the Banpai Range. It would take him days, if not tendays, to bring David's Tower down, but eliminating the Border Knights would cripple the enemy before the battle even began.

And now, he thought, *they will serve me.*

Farrior Han sat up. Beside him, Stahl rose. The eyes of the Border Knights were pale and waxen, dead. Farrior's legs somehow moved; he ignored his severed spine and got to his feet. The larvae had done their work well. Campion peered at them and saw the low green light flickering deep behind their eyes.

Kekubi.

Soon the bloodlust would come over them. Every man, woman, and child the knights butchered would spread the larvae, passing on the Necrórceror's undead epidemic. Two kekubi would become four, eight, sixteen, thirty-two, until David's Tower had a panic inside the gate.

And then Campion would hit them.

He discovered his skin was crawling with revulsion. He couldn't stand looking at Farrior. He and the Amber had been closest in age. Men in their prime. Friends. Brothers. But like that…Campion tore his eyes away; Farrior was horrific—unbearable.

He almost questioned his path then, but the stump stopped him. It always did. That low phantom tingle where his right arm once was. Campion had hidden his deformity inside the Armor, hidden it from others, hidden it from himself. Inside the Armor, he still had his hand. But here, he was naked, forced to look. He hated that stump. It was a reminder of everything he had lost— a memento of what Campion Rei *should* be—a good right arm.

Soon, he thought. *Soon.*

Farrior Han stared at him with dead eyes.

Campion fled down the stairs, unable to stand the sight of his brother any longer.

The washerwoman was surprised to find the Border Knight coming down from the spire. She bowed, almost kneeling. Campion waved her off, smiling through perfect teeth. "Please, go on up. The others want you."

He slipped past her, disappearing down the steps. As the woman climbed toward the spire, she couldn't help but think how beautiful he was.

Jack is in the Winter Caverns, his body cold and numb.

The little girl with the red ribbon in her hair is Benjamin Halfpenny. His eyes are frosted over, milky cataracts of ice. His blue fingers clutch a corn-husk doll.

Jack runs. Shadows come for him. But this time, he knows their faces. Abrahim Qin shambles after him, the Azure knightsblade clutched in one icy hand. Kenji Tuk appears through the snow, dragging his longbow, one eye a hollow hole. Watch cadets reach for him, arms outstretched and grasping.

Far behind them, a tremendous shadow bears a blazing brand of fire, hewing its way through the dead, cutting them down like wheat, its face hidden in bottomless cowl. And the sound of slaughter

(rath)

Jack climbs but goes nowhere, flailing. Something grabs his leg. He looks down.

His father's face stares up at him with frozen eyes, his body crushed and broken by a million tons of Badlands rock. An albino bull snake curls around his wrist. It strikes out. Fangs plunge into Jack's ankle.

The snake drags him down into his dead father's cold, cold arms.

Jack bolted awake, shivering.

The morning was cold; dew had collected on his blankets during the night, robbing him of warmth. The boy got to his feet and slapped his arms to get his blood moving, shaking off the nightmare.

Akkadian was far behind. They had come west, deep into the Jaden Fields, and here, Jack finally understood the Black Accord.

Benjamin had been right to put the cracks in his map around Glyn Aker; the entire country looked as if it had been hit by the earthquake that broke the Richter scale. Huge cracks crisscrossed the land. Great fissures ran deep; severe jagged rock ledges loomed up ten, twenty, thirty, feet high. The land was literally shattered. Over the century since the Black Accord, wild grasslands had grown up over the fractured fields, lending them an eerie sense of calm, the hissing green aftermath of the bomb.

The mighty Breechline River was heroic, bigger than the Mississippi, more powerful than the Amazon, but the Necrórceror's dark spell had destroyed even her. As the Fell Prince spoke his last word, the Breechline was split in two. She broke the banks of the age-old path that led her to Rimmy's Cull and smashed free in a crushing tide of foaming water. She obliterated fields, farms, and forests, gushing south over the Hideko Heath like a whitewater stampede until, finally, she flooded the vast Llykowen Swamps and shoved half of that country into the sea, forming a vast, wrecked delta of broken stone and buried men.

Even now, a century later, the people of Keymark refused to give the river two names—in a persistent act of stubbornness three generations old, the river remained the Breechline. In the south, the llystra simply called their part of the river the Bastard.

Every step brought Jack Swift closer to the epicenter of the Necrórceror's aberration. Every step brought him closer to Glyn Aker, closer to the Jade Knight, and then—*home.*

Fuji tugged at his sleeve, begging for another apple. The boy handed one over and got up to watch the rising sun. Only Li-Bao Sen was awake. Neither one of them said anything, watching the sunrise.

Soon, Memphis woke to cook breakfast: eggs again. Leah made bacon. Django grazed. The cat, as always, slept late.

Jack moved closer to Leah, helping her. It was good to be back with her and Memphis. Without them, it would have been a quiet trip.

The Trio (it seemed) was losing its faith in Black Jack.

The boy had killed the jabberwok, true, but it was impossible to ignore the fact that his fight with the Red Dwarves had not been particularly heroic. Rooker Flynn, the Black's right-hand man, had deserted him for a pile of gold. And the lady fair they rescued did not exactly swoon for their hero the way they thought she should. To the Trio, the legend of Black Jack seemed a great deal more appealing than the reality.

Even the unshakable Django Barón was beginning to question him.

The minotaur kept his comments polite, but Jack could tell the bull had sniffed something rotten. The time was coming when Django would challenge his master openly. When that time came, Jack was afraid of what might happen.

All through breakfast, Django kept glancing at Jack's staff. As the boy finished his eggs, the bull said suddenly: "That is *not* Nepenthe."

Jack was caught short. "What?"

"Nepenthe," said the bull. "The Black's quarterstaff. The whomping stick. Or was it a spear?" The bull cocked his great horns. "The legends never were clear on that."

"Yes," said Chance, turning over in his blanket. "Which *was* it?"

Jack glanced at Memphis. Leah spoke up. "A stave, clearly. Can't you see?"

"Yes," said Li-Bao. "I see very well. That stick is not Nepenthe."

There was a moment of awkward silence. The camp was split in two groups, and neither wanted to speak next.

"No," Jack said. "It's not Nepenthe." He wasn't going to lie to them anymore. The Trio would follow the Black into the gates of hell, but Jack was not him. He liked Chance, Li-Bao, and Django immensely, especially the bull; he didn't want them to die for him.

Jack walked away without another word. Secretly, he hoped the Trio would do the same and disappear back into the south, and safety. But Jack heard Django pick up his gear—the bull would follow him another day.

Jack came over the rise to find a pair of corpses.

Headless, the bodies were trapped inside tight iron cages, strung up on a great white pole along the road. Crows cawed and squawked, picking at it through the bars, bickering over the remains. Into the top of the pole was carved the head of a red-eyed snake; from its mouth hung a banner smeared with crimson stains that could only be dried blood. It bore an emblem: three paths drawn together with sigils between each path.

"The standard of the Fell Prince," whispered Leah, staring at the thing darkly. "Three sigils, for the Three Princes who murdered their father, drawn together as one." She pointed. "You see? There at the center, the two slashes? Those are for royal blood. The Fell Prince hasn't earned his sigil yet, but he means to take his place as king." Jack felt a chill looking that the banner; it belonged to the Necrórceror—the man who'd cracked the earth.

Memphis laughed, breaking the mood. "Well! Let's show the little prince what we think of his standard!" He flicked his fingers, and the flag erupted into emerald flames. Crows scattered as the banner burned to cinders and the snake's head became a burning torch. "Let's keep moving," said Memphis, walking. "The Jade Knight is close."

Jack took one last look at the flaming flag, wondering what chance they had of finding a Border Knight in a place like this, and what chance he had of ever getting home.

The last bridge before Glyn Aker—the Bridge of Ahmen—crossed the Bastard side of the Breechline. Wide and stone-paved, the bridge was masked in fog, arcing away into nothingness. Iron clouds hung low in the sky; the waters below were thick as soup with flotsam and debris.

Memphis led them toward it.

"Wait," Jack stopped. Something about the bridge gave him a sick feeling in the pit of his gut. *Fuji.*

Yes, signed the tam.

Want to scout it out?

What is scout it out?

Like you did with the tower.

Yes, it chirruped. *Fuji is scout it out.*

The tam disappeared over the edge before Jack could tell it to be careful. Clinging to the rock, it scuttled beneath the belly of the bridge and disappeared.

Somewhere beyond the mist, Jack could just barely make out the shape of a huge wall, shrouded in white. There was no sound coming from the city beyond it. Jack couldn't shake the sense of fear crawling through his head—something about this felt *wrong*.

Fuji returned. *Scout it out is two dead men, six bugs, and a head.*

"Two kekubi, half a dozen versläng, and a deadeye," Jack translated for the others. "Maybe we'd better find another way."

"This is the only way," said Li-Bao. The one-eyed croc suddenly moved to the edge and slung one leg over the bridge.

Jack grabbed Li-Bao's arm. "What are you doing?"

"I was *born* of water, Black. And I would not see you threatened." Jack read between the lines: Li-Bao didn't think Black Jack was much good in a fight. What was worse, he was right.

"Keep one eye out," said Chance.

Li-Bao glared at the cat and hurled himself over the bridge. His long reptilian body hit the Breechline with a quiet splash. In a moment, he resurfaced, gave a push with his powerful tail, and disappeared into the water, a crocodile on the hunt.

Shortly, there came a whistle from the far side. Chance sprinted across the bridge. Jack was close behind. At the far end, Li-Bao stood over two decapitated zombies and a pile of insects oozing slime from their cracked shells.

The cat eyed the carnage. "I could have done it faster."

Memphis's fingers flashed; the deadeye went up in flames. In the flickering emerald firelight of the burning skull, Jack saw the gates of Glyn Aker. The huge doors lay broken and crushed, hanging from their hinges as if a wrecking ball had split them. Beyond the gate, the city was utterly deserted.

Jack felt something then, the dark tingle of the *wikk,* malevolent, bloody, and cruel. Something icy crawled up his spine as a thundering *boom* shook the earth at his feet. Jack watched as one of the buildings shook; the weathervane at its peak toppled and fell.

"What was that?" asked Chance.

Jack heard a sharp cry from the city.

Then he saw them.

A man and a woman fled the city together, running toward the gate. The woman carried a bundle in her hands. The man limped behind her, his leg badly injured.

The chittering came first, then the swarm.

Versläng poured into the street behind the fleeing couple; hundreds of roaches flowed over the stones like a black tide.

The woman tripped and fell. Sprawling, the bundle she carried fell to the street. Something inside it screamed—

The cry of a baby.

Andy Ibis worked for a long time to afford the wedding ring.

The stone was sapphire, the band was silver, and the love behind it was true. He proposed to Lindsay on a sleigh ride during a cold winter day; she had leapt into his arms crying. They married and moved into a modest home he built for her on the banks of the Breechline. They had not questioned their fertility in the first year, or even the second; they had been wed at the Spring Festival, and that—as everyone knew—guaranteed many children. In the third year, they began to wonder why they did not have a child. The old wives gave advice aplenty, from eating mustard seeds to bathing in oil, and there were several embarrassing suggestions from Andy's friends. Nothing worked. In the old days, they would have gone to one of the Great Bells (the Agrat-ban-Quiridin was nearest), and their infertility would have been cured. But since the Black Accord, the bells had lost their power, and the couple was left with a score of useless suggestions that all amounted to the same thing: keep trying.

It had nearly destroyed their marriage. Andy wanted a son, Lindsey wanted a daughter; they got neither. Their home life grew more and more empty, the absence of a child felt more keenly with each passing year as they watched their friends and neighbors give rise to a legion of babies. Soon, those children were growing, and too fast. The day Jute Keelan's son came to work his first day at the tailor's shop, Andy came home to find Lindsey crying, and she couldn't stop. There were fights, there were arguments, there was yelling, always with the same thought that neither one would admit out loud: *It's your fault.*

Then, the miracle. Lindsey caught pregnant. Andy doted on her night and day, urging her to stay in bed, catering to her every need. She loved him for it. As the months passed, her belly grew fat and ripe, and their love grew with it. Andy had plans for his son, Lindsay had plans for her daughter, and neither one cared who was right. The baby was healthy, they could feel it, and both of them knew that God had finally been kind.

Three days ago, the baby was born. Andy's child came into the world with a cry paired with war horns. Glyn Aker was under attack. As men ran to the gates to combat the invaders, Andy was left alone with his wife screaming her labor pains. He delivered the baby himself: a son. Hidden inside the midwife's house, Lindsey cleaned the baby and gave it its first suck while Andy looked out the window and saw his people dying.

The Jade Knight was there to protect them—he always had been. Andy had even met the man once, at a banquet on Midwinter's Eve. He would never forget the knight the rest of his life: tall, strong, and well spoken, the perfect picture of a hero. The Jade Knight fought valiantly at the gates of Glyn Aker, but vermin broke through; versläng and kekubi thundered through the streets. And there was something else with them, something dark and burning that smelled of charred flesh. The city was overrun; the men kept fighting in ragged groups, but Andy had not heard the heroic ring of the Jade knightsblade since the sun fell.

Andy hid Lindsey and the baby in the root cellar. Over the long night, the sounds of battle faded away to nothingness. In the morning, there was no sound of anything living—just the moaning wails of kekubi. Andy finally mustered the courage to climb the stairs and sneak a peek outside. He saw nothing but monsters. Versläng were everywhere. Shambling zombies roamed the streets. From his tiny window, Andy saw Jute Keelan's boy walk past, stumbling like a drunk, his eyes blank and dead.

Andy Ibis turned away and went to hide with his wife and son.

At noon, their baby—who still did not have a name—would not stop screaming. He would not suckle; Lindsey could not get him to quiet. Knowing they would soon be discovered, Andy took his wife and child up the stairs to the ruins of the midwifery and waited for their chance to escape. None came.

Suddenly, there was a bellowing roar and a tremendous boom of stone. The baby shrieked. Outside, one of the wicked cockroaches raised its head. It chittered to the others, sensing prey.

Jute Keelan's son moaned.

Andy grabbed his wife and son and ran.

They never had a chance.

As he pushed his wife toward the gate, something bit the back of his leg: a black arrow. He ripped it out of his calf, stumbling to keep up with his wife, shouting for her to run. Behind him, Andy could hear the clicking of the versläng's claws on the street like a billion insects running him down.

Lindsey fell.

Their baby, their tiny son they had wished for so desperately for so long, fell into the street.

He wailed, crying out in pain. As Lindsay scrabbled to pick the baby up, Andy turned to defend his family, holding nothing but a broken chair leg he had found in the rubble.

The monsters came for him.

Andy Ibis faced the swarm, knowing he would give his life before he let one of them touch his son.

Jack Swift ran for them. His legs pounded as fast as they could, but he would never reach them in time. The man would die. The wife would be next.

And the baby…

A high scream split the air.

A horseman. His animal's hooves cracked against the cobblestones like gunshots.

Roaches shattered under the stallion's hooves. The rider's brilliant sword shattered versläng shells. He pounded through the pack, galloping straight for the family.

A group of kekubi hurled themselves at the horseman. Corpse-like hands reached out for his reins; the rider cut them off at the elbow. Roaches crawled up the side of his horse; the stallion bucked them away, stoving their heads in with polished hooves. But there were too many to fight; the horseman was a gazelle among hyenas.

As one of the versläng crawled up the stallion's flank, a white arrow punched through its black head.

An archer.

He came at a gallop astride a roan stallion. Another bolt followed, and another—some arrows killed one versläng, some killed two, none missed their mark.

The horseman resumed his plunge through the teeming mass.

Still running, Jack saw the husband fighting off the versläng with a short club. The wife froze, caught between saving her husband or her son. A roach grabbed the club and ripped it out of the man's hands. Defenseless, he fought them off with nothing but his fists. Versläng surrounded him.

One leapt for the baby.

The horseman's blade cut the roach in half. He leaned down and snatched the infant up. Dragging the woman into the saddle behind him, the rider grabbed the man by his shirt and threw him over the stallion's neck. He rode at a gallop through the gate.

The animal came to a halt inches from Jack's nose. Instantly, the rider was off his mount. He shoved the reins into the husband's hands. "Take it. Go."

Andy and Lindsey Ibis stared at their rescuer. In her arms, their newborn baby screamed. To man and wife, the sound was heaven. Andy stammered, but no words came out.

The horseman slapped the animal's flank—it carried them away at a gallop.

The rider pulled a longknife from his belt and hurled it back into the swarm. A versläng had crawled up the archer's horse; the flying dagger punched through its chest, knocking it away. The archer fled the throng and galloped through the gate.

A roar split the air. It was horr

(rath)

Fear seized Jack's heart. The stench hit him; the burned-flesh and sulfur smell of the dæmon.

It rose like a burning tower. Flames crackled around its

shoulders, burning beneath its charred black hide, sizzling through the cracks. It was terrible to behold, a malevolent mockery of all things living. Diamond-shaped nostrils sniffed the air once—and its eyes fell directly on Jack.

It came. Versläng and kekubi scattered before it; those who did not were crushed under its flaming talons.

"Go!" the horseman shouted. *"Back!"* Memphis and the others did not need further encouragement; they ran. But Jack was fixed to the spot, terrified.

The horseman looked up at his companion. "Keep her safe." The archer nodded and darted away. He pulled Leah up into the saddle, riding hard for the horizon.

Jack stared at the horseman. There was something about his voice—

"Do you have to be told everything *twice,* Jack Swift?" The rider peeked through his hood, revealing the grey face of Valerian Tsai.

Jack gaped, overcome with shock.

The grey man's eyes shone. "You have to go." He glanced at the approaching dæmon. "Now."

Unable to speak, unable to disobey, Jack ran. At the far side of the bridge, Memphis waited for him.

Valerian Tsai stood alone. The Crownéd Dæmon Chulurath strode to face him. As it approached, the beast slowed, feeling the power of its enemy—it knew the man well.

Chulurath's head rocked back and forth, its body swaying like a cobra. Valerian, the mongoose, backed away, gripping his Grey knightsblade in one fist.

The beast lowered its head. Flames licked its curled horns. "Your Order is finished, *drei Paladíne.*" Its voice was oiled leather and broken glass. "I took your brother-knight and crushed his bones inside his shell."

"I have his steel." Valerian drew a second sword from the scabbard at his back. The Jade knightsblade thrummed green *wikk*, radiating true power. "Come taste it again."

Chulurath snorted, eyeing the simmering swords.

Valerian Tsai backed away slowly; the beast matched him step for step. At the center of the bridge, Valerian thrust the Grey knightsblade into the stone at his feet.

It stood like a warning cross.

Valerian threw aside his cloak, drawing a third knightsblade—Abrahim's Azure. "Come, *ûzguk*. Come to me and face the steel of three true men."

Chulurath hesitated. "Give me the Prize"—the dæmon grinned wickedly—"and I will let you live until we meet again."

"He is not mine to give or yours to take."

Infuriated, the dæmon's flames became an inferno.

The bridge stones burned black beneath its feet.

It came.

Valerian's voice thundered in a bark that Jack couldn't comprehend, a sound inhuman, guttural, precise, and wicked:

Keurk-äl ve gredd ûzguk Chulurath kharat!

Valerian Tsai drove the knightsblades into the stone. A crack split the air; the bridge detonated in a shower of rock and dust as the knight's trap snapped shut.

As the dæmon lunged for the knight, the burning stone beneath its feet shattered and fell. The flaming beast hit the Breechline River with an explosion of steam that shot up like a geyser, and the thing was buried beneath rushing waters.

Valerian tore the knightsblades from the bridge and ran.

"Go!" he shouted as Chulurath resurfaced, pluming smoke and guttering fire. It roared, the force of the thundering Breechline crushing against it, but its flaming claws gripped the stone struts of the Bridge of Ahmen and pulled, dragging itself impossibly forward.

Valerian Tsai grabbed Jack, forcing him to run.

He never ran so fast, so far, in his life.

Valerian would not stop, his fist tight against the boy's back.

Memphis ran alongside as they escaped into the woods to the north, but the forest around them teemed with the Necrórceror's monsters. Versläng kept pace with their flight, hounding them like a pack of wolves; their chittering voices screeching like a swarm of locusts. A gang of kekubi appeared, their drunken, shambling footsteps gone with the chase, now sprinting in jerky, spasmodic lunges. Jack never saw Django, Chance, or Li-Bao at all; they had fled long before him.

Valerian suddenly drew his shining blade and darted straight into the pack.

Memphis, alone, grabbed the boy and kept running.

The bellow of the beast sounded behind them, too soon, too close. The footsteps of the dæmon grew louder, pounding the earth like falling trucks. Memphis turned, shouted for Jack to keep running, thrust his hands upward, and a pine tree exploded into green flames. The trol grabbed a chunk of rock and smashed it into the trunk, severing the tree halfway through. As the dæmon crashed through the woods behind them, Memphis shoved with all his might and toppled the flaming tree down on the beast like a bomb.

It exploded green fire; wood blew outward in splinters as the tree cracked in half against Chulurath's body. Roaring, the dæmon snatched the trunk and swung the tree like a club. It struck Memphis. The trol flew twenty feet through the air and disappeared beneath a shower of wood and flame.

The dæmon turned its sights on Jack.

Alone, the boy ran.

His sneakers pounded over the earth, his heart thudded in his chest, his veins sang with blood. He heard the thing behind him, closer, smacking branches out of its way—then Jack fell.

A great claw snatched him up. He beat against it with his staff, but the cracks between the thing's claws flamed hot; the silver-tipped wood crackled into flames and burnt to a black cinder.

"At last," came the cruel voice of the dæmon, "the *Prize.*" Its horrifying yellow eyes narrowed. "You belong to the prince now, Toshan."

Exploding in pain and terror, Jack shouted: *"What the hell does he want with me?"*

Chulurath tightened its grip. The skidshield held it back, but flames blossomed, and the boy burned. Jack's clothes caught on fire. He tried to beat them out, but the claws of the beast held him fast.

Burning, Jack screamed.

A pop of white light snapped the air like a giant flashbulb. Blinded, the dæmon roared in pain, dropping him. Jack hit the ground with a smack, his tattered clothes burning. There was a shout; something struck the air like a sonic boom. The whirring tingle of the *wikk* reverberated everywhere. The beast howled, charged toward the shout, and disappeared into the woods.

Blind and half naked, Jack felt his charred clothes smoking. He tried to get up, but his head went dizzy, and—staring blindly into nothing—he passed out.

Jack Swift lay that way for a long time.

As dusk fell, a shadow passed over him. A hand grabbed his blackened shirt and dragged him away into the dark.

RITE OF PASSAGE

*In this world a man must
be either anvil or hammer.*

H. W. Longfellow

W hen Jack woke, he was not alone.

His mind shook off the slow fog of sleep as the flickering orange and black colors around him solidified into fire and a cave. As his eyes adjusted, the pain settled in. His chest burned like he had been sleeping on a hot charcoal grill. He reached down (not yet wondering where his shirt had gone), touched his chest, and winced.

It hurt. Oh, God, it *hurt.*

Jack looked down. His skin burned crimson; most of his chest was a black-and-purple cloud of bruises. And in the center, right across his ribs, three white stripes ran from his gut to his armpit, each bubbling with weeping blisters: the flaming fingerprints of the dæmon.

Oh, God.

Gingerly, he felt his ribs, looking for the break. He couldn't find one, but every time he moved, he felt like his rib cage had been shattered. Had it not been for the skidshield, the beast would have crushed him to jelly.

Wincing, Jack tried to get to his feet, then saw the man.

Jack was amazed he hadn't seen him before—the figure could have reached out and touched him. The firelight seemed to break around the man, wrapping him in shadow. A strange conical straw hat sat on his head, the kind Chinese railroad workers wore in the Old West. He sat very close, still as a statue.

Jack grabbed up a rock in one shaking fist. *"Who are you?"*

The stranger did not respond. Jack swung the rock at the man's head. A pale hand flashed out, plucked the rock from Jack's fist, and tossed it into the fire. Sparks flew up, and the cloak of shadow disappeared, revealing the man's face.

The archer.

The man (but he was no man) was lean and tall, blessed with impossibly high cheekbones above a slim, aquiline nose. His skin was fair—almost white—each muscle in his face etched like a master craftsman had carved it from marble. The longbow on his back looked Japanese, the wood jointed bamboo, curved in a large semicircle at each end, and inlaid with fanciful figures in silver. The arrows in the leather quiver on his back were burnished white, fletched with trim blue-and-green peacock feathers. The bowstring was a slim golden thread. But the man's eyes struck Jack most: they were silver.

An elf.

Jack knew it instinctively, better than he knew his own name. Something old and deep and primal told him it was true. And in that moment, he was barely able to contain the sudden joy that bubbled up from that deep place, as if he had just met a long-lost friend.

Jack's heart stopped as he realized he had tried to smash its head with a rock.

"Oh, God, I'm sorry, I'm sorry, I didn't…I wouldn't—"

The man held up one hand as the tingle of the *wikk,* pure and good like water, washed over the boy. Suddenly, the burning in Jack's chest subsided—it still hurt, but it didn't seem to matter as much.

"W-who are you?" Jack stammered. The thin man looked at him with those incredible silver eyes but did not reply. Jack found he could not stop talking: "Where are we? Where's Valerian? What happened to the dæmon?" The elf said nothing. He simply stared at Jack, a light smile at the edge of his lips. Jack's brows narrowed, unable to understand why the man would not respond. "What's the matter? Why won't you talk to me?"

"You talk enough for two, *doktar.*" Jack spun at the sound of the voice. The knight stood at the entrance to the cave.

"Valerian!"

Ignoring the pain, Jack leapt to his feet and threw his arms around the big man, hugging him tight.

The Border Knight smiled. "It is good to see you up and moving."

"I thought you were dead!"

"I am not," said the grey man. "And neither are you, so that's a very good start."

"What about Leah? And Memphis and—"

The big man held up a hand. "They're fine. Memphis is attending to them. Sit down, Jack. You've had a very long day." Jack did as he was told. Valerian said a few words to the elf in a lyrical language Jack couldn't understand. The thin man nodded and walked out of the cave, throwing one last look over his shoulder at Jack.

"That's an *elf!*" Jack whispered when he was gone.

Valerian smiled. "I *know.*"

"Who is he?"

"Nightingale."

"Nightingale what?"

Valerian smiled. "Elves don't have surnames, Jack. They have no fathers and no sons. They are immortal. Each one is unique, each one special, and when they are gone, they cannot be replaced. The Fair Folk have been here since the beginning, and I pray they will be here at the end. He is Nightingale, and that is enough."

No fathers, no sons. Immortal. Incredible. "Why wouldn't he talk to me?"

"Only because he does not speak. Come," Valerian said, "let's have a look at you." The Grey Knight clasped Jack by the arms and appraised the boy's bloody scars with an unflinching eye. "Not as bad as I feared."

Jack suddenly realized he could barely feel the burns. "Did he heal me?"

"No, the healing *wikk* is gone, you know that. He made you forget the pain." Valerian looked him up and down, surprised. "The dæmon had you in his fist for a long time, Jack. I had thought you would be worse off by far."

The skidshield.

Jack thought of the leather on his arm and gripped it, reassuring himself it was still there. "Your skidshield—your *aërling*—it held it back."

"Then I am glad you have it."

"What happened?" Jack asked. "It grabbed me, then there was a white light—"

"Nightingale. And me too. We led it away from you. It was touch-and-go there for a while, but right now, the beast is following a wild-goose chase toward the Broken Pass. We should be safe for a while." Valerian took another look at Jack's chest. "I don't suppose you have any *doktar*-science to heal yourself?"

"No." If Jack had some Bactine or even petroleum jelly, he could smear it (gingerly) over the burn, but as it were, he could only be grateful for Nightingale's forgetting-majik.

"Then let's get you cleaned up." Valerian smiled. "Somewhere under all that grime, there's a boy I once knew—although it seems you have changed a bit since we last met."

It was true. Jack Swift had come a long way from Falikos, and further still from Chicago. Three days on Falikos, five at sea, twelve to Akkadian, and four more to Glyn Aker. His body had hardened, his hands were calloused, and his ragged Chuck Taylors had nearly two hundred miles under them. His legs were muscular, his face was tan, his arms were strong, and the skinny little kid he had once been was long since left behind. Jack washed in a small stream flowing through the cave, scouring off layer after layer of blood and dirt.

When the grey man produced a straight razor and handed it to the boy, Jack was surprised. He felt his chin and realized it was covered in light, patchy stubble. Jack couldn't believe it—he had half a beard going.

"Um, Valerian? I've never actually *shaved* before." He eyed the wicked-looking razor. "And never with one of these."

Valerian lathered up a shaving brush. "Long, smooth strokes," he said. "Start at the base of your neck and move up. Your beard is young—it won't scrape like you expect it to…and don't dig in."

Jack glanced at the razor, nervous.

"Just go easy, son." Valerian smiled. "You'll be fine." He handed over the brush.

Son. No one had called Jack that in a long, long time.

Jack scrubbed up a lather. He covered his chin in suds to a Santa Claus beard of foamy white. He pressed the blade to his neck, hesitated, then moved it up slowly from the base of his neck, the way his dad used to do it. "Do you have…um…"

"Slower. You only want to shave once."

Jack slowed down. "Do you have a family?" His Adam's apple bobbed. "Do…do Border Knights have…sons?"

"Yes, we can have sons. And daughters. And wives. As for me, God never granted us a son."

Jack eyed the knight. "Us. You have a wife?"

Valerian's face darkened. "She is gone. Watch your nose."

Jack realized his razor was going off course. He corrected.

"My brothers have always been the men who stood beside me," said Valerian, "and my sons have been those I've trained. That is how I was raised by my father, and that is what I pass on. Slower."

Jack slowed down. "What was your father like?"

"O, he was many things. Great and terrible. Like all fathers."

Jack ran the blade over his jugular. "I'm scared, Valerian."

"You are doing well."

"No. I'm scared I'm going to forget my dad."

Jack kept the blade moving, but the handle shook. "I remember *everything*. I remember a formula I read in a book ten years ago. I remember every single note of Beethoven's Fifth. I remember every ingredient of a Zagnut bar. I remember his face, what he said, how he moved…I remember everything about him, but I'm beginning to forget *him*."

Valerian stared. "None of us forgets our father. He brought you up. He taught you what he knew. He made you. If you want to see your father, look in a mirror. He still lives."

The blade bit Jack's neck.

Valerian pressed a cloth against his neck. It came away bloody.

Valerian handed the cloth to Jack, who wiped himself clean. "You and I are very similar, Jack Swift. Both of us will make a life wielding a blade. Mine a sword, yours a scalpel. If your great calling in life is to be a *doktar*, you must master your hands. Let me show you something that has helped mine." Valerian took a small loop of string from his coat and wrapped it around his fingers. "I have done this for decades. Sharpens the tendons." Valerian's fingers moved like majik as a ballet of knots danced along the string. He made them join, dissolve, then move together in pairs. Then the string was just a loop again, and the knight handed it to Jack. "Here."

Jack took the string. Laced it between his fingers. Tied.

"Slower."

They sat together, man and boy, improving their one true gift.

As they did, Valerian told his tale of Falikos.

When the knight reached the top of the Black Rock, he found versläng pouring through the jaunt gate like a flood. Valerian plunged into them and set the doorway ablaze to stem the flow, but not before the dæmon had come through. He battled it there, between the burning trees, but the beast leaped from the top of Black Rock in pursuit of easier game. Valerian fought his way down the hill, but by the time he reached the training grounds, it was too late—the Watch was slaughtered, the beast was gone, and Abrahim Qin, his brother, was dead.

In the end, Valerian stood on the little island alone.

Jack stared. The Grey Knight had not escaped Falikos; he had survived it.

"It was Campion," said Jack. "He let them in."

Valerian's face was a dark mask of stone. He gestured to Jack's neck. "You're bleeding again."

Jack staunched the blood with the cloth.

Valerian set about cooking breakfast.

Neither of them said more about the Crimson Knight.

Warm meat filled Jack's belly. The air of the cave was thick with the lingering odor of pan-broiled venison. Jack felt his strength coming back little by little. As he leaned back against the rock, a sharp flare of pain raced across the claw marks on his chest. He winced, inhaling sharply.

"Is the pain returning?"

"A little." In his mind, Jack saw the blazing yellow eyes of the dæmon, and he shuddered. Quietly, he said to himself: "That thing is straight out of a nightmare."

"It is *ûzguk*," said Valerian.

Jack had heard the word before—the mere sound of it made him feel ill. Valerian stared at the fire, stoking it quietly, then spoke.

"You should understand something, Jack. At the Battle of Jaden Fields, we nearly killed the Necrórceror. He only saved himself by calling on the dark *wikk*—by summoning the Crownéd Dæmon. The Fell Prince made a deal with the devil. The beast saved his life, and serves him, for a time. In exchange, the dæmon took the healing power of the *wikk*. Listen"—

Valerian turned to him—"Chulurath *is* the Black Accord."

Jack imagined Valerian standing on the Bridge of Ahmen, facing down the great beast, alone.

"You said something to it, on the bridge." Jack's perfect memory recalled the sounds exactly: *"Keurk-äl v—"*

"Do not speak that here!" Valerian's voice was thunder as he stood, great and terrible. A fleeting shadow came quick as lightning as Nightingale shot one pale hand over Jack's mouth.

Both men looked terrified.

The elf's silver eyes stared at Jack. He raised a finger:
No.

Jack nodded. Slowly, Nightingale let him go.

Jack shrunk away, shocked. "I'm—I'm sorry," he stammered. "I thought I couldn't do majik—"

"That is *not* majik," Valerian said sharply. "That is the tongue of dæmons. Had you continued, the beast would have heard you—even from as far as the Broken Pass—and come for you." Valerian exhaled, dropping his hand away from his blade; his fury passed like a summer storm. "I'm sorry, Jack. You should not fear me. Ever."

Jack nodded; he hoped to go the rest of his life without seeing Valerian Tsai like that again.

The Grey Knight suddenly laughed. "You Toshans will be the death of me, I swear. So many questions." Valerian sighed. "Well. There's no harm in telling you, you will be gone soon."

Gone? What does th—

"Listen: When the Fell Prince summoned the beast to save his life, it came bound to a great rock, a stone called the Menhir Thrall, carved with Chulurath's true name. It is the beast's anchor to this sphere, a doorway. Do you understand?"

"Like a jaunt gate."

Valerian nodded. "A jaunt gate's dark twin. The words I spoke on the bridge (and the words you should not speak again) are a *command* in its own tongue, one it cannot deny, to return to the void. But the beast did not obey, which can only mean one thing: the Menhir Thrall is no longer *here.* The Fell Prince has moved it." Valerian rubbed the back of his neck. "Until I find the stone, the beast will continue to hunt."

"For what?"

It was Valerian's turn to be surprised. "How can you not know, Jack? It hunts for *you.*"

"Me?"

"It tracked you across the Irridin. It followed you into the Madrigal Verde. The only reason it did not haunt you to the citadel was the prince ordered it to Glyn Aker. It did not come for *me* on Falikos; it came for you."

Of *course*, it hunted him; Chulurath had virtually told him so. What was it the beast had called him? *The Prize.*

"Chulurath will not stop, Jack," Valerian continued. "It will keep coming. We have delayed it for a while, but it will never give up. Not until it has you."

Jack bit his lip. So the dæmon would be back. The running, the screaming, the fire; it would all happen again, and again, until he was back in the thing's claws. Jack's scars flared up and he shuddered. His hands balled into fists. "Then we have to kill it."

"Well said." Valerian smiled. "But even with three knightsblades and a host of men, we could not. An *ûzguk* crowned cannot die, Jack. Even I cannot kill it." The grey man shook his head. "Without the Menhir Thrall, we have no hope of stopping it."

So that's it, Jack thought. *I'm going to have to keep running—forever.* "But *why?*" he asked, his voice desperate. "What do I have that it wants?"

"*It* does not want you. It follows the will of its master: the Necrórceror." Valerian frowned. "Why *he* wants you, I cannot guess. I understand why he took Xiang-lo, but—"

"Xiang-lo." His patient again, the ever-present mystery. The man had confounded Jack since he first came to Keymark. And no one had ever given him a straight answer about why Xiang-lo was so important.

Jack looked Valerian dead in the eye. "I think it's time you told me about my patient."

Valerian Tsai set his jaw. He looked at Nightingale, but it was impossible for Jack to read the elf's face. Finally, the big man nodded. "Can you walk?"

"I think so." Jack suddenly felt the tingle of Nightingale's majik—the pain from his burns faded into a dull haze. But when he looked up, the elf was already gone.

Valerian slung the three knightsblades over his back. "Come."

Jack got to his feet, holding his chest. "Where are we going?"

"There is something you should see."

The boy, the knight, and the elf climbed the rocky steppe together.

As they traveled, Jack watched the thin man move through the green shadows. It was impossible to keep track of him; he disappeared in between bands of sunlight. His legs were shadows, his body was light, his bow was the trees. At one point, Jack lost track of the elf for a hundred yards while he was in plain sight.

"He's mute?"

"It's more complicated than that."

"How?"

Valerian smiled. "O, so many questions. Fine. The elves do not kill. That is an oath they hold very dear—they destroy nothing living. Do you understand?"

Jack nodded.

"Nightingale broke that oath. He had a friend—a woman— what you or I would call a wife. She was killed, and Nightingale sought revenge on her murderer. He killed. The elves forced him to leave the Elder Wood, into exile, into Keymark."

"Did they..." Jack swallowed. "Did they cut out his tongue?"

Valerian looked surprised. "You misunderstand, Jack. The elves could never be so cruel. Nightingale was *forbidden* to speak. And he has kept that oath for more lifetimes than you or I will ever see."

Jack couldn't imagine the will it would take to keep such a promise for so long—not being able to ask questions *alone* would drive him mad.

Trying to learn patience, he walked with Valerian silently, not quite watching the elf.

A multitude of waterfalls spilled down tiers of stone, splashing merrily into a series of pools in the rock, which, in turn, fed larger waterfalls. The flowing streams carved wormholes through the rock, and as Jack climbed, he found himself navigating a series of slides, chutes, and narrow caves. The air was thick with pixies.

Nightingale moved ahead, bounding over the rocks, much nimbler than either of the slow jaelin. Valerian picked up a branch, using it as a walking stick as he climbed the waterfalls. "It's beautiful, isn't it? They did a good job here."

"Who did?"

"The elves."

Jack wasn't really paying attention, focusing on moving his Chuck Taylors from rock to rock. "They made the waterfalls?"

"They made Keymark."

Jack stopped. *Made it?*

The big man continued climbing. Jack scrambled to keep up, listening to the story: "In the beginning," Valerian said, "Keymark was nothing but desert, a sphere of burning sand—no water, no life, not even air to breathe. The elves gave rise the Elaña, growing them out of nothingness, a doorway to God's infinite. And through the jaunt gates, the elves brought life. Air, light, heat, water, blooming green trees and plants and gardens. They blossomed here as the elves nourished the land acre by acre, and helped it flourish. The elves brought life to a place where there was only death and gave this sphere the living heartbeat of the *wikk.* They gave rise to Keymark as a mother births a child. Can you understand that?"

Jack eyed the green trees, the water spilling over the rocks beneath his feet, the pixies dancing in the currents of warm air above the waters. He glanced up the slope to Nightingale. The elf had been here, at the beginning. He had helped create all this. Nightingale leaped lightly over a rock, not listening to the story.

Jack rubbed the back of his neck, not quite able to believe it. "I've heard a lot of different things about the elves since I've been here," Jack said. "Not all of the stories match up."

"How so?"

Jack bit his lip. "Rooker Flynn says the elves are cowards."

Valerian stopped suddenly. "And who is Rooker Flynn?"

"A pirate."

"So he is a thief *and* a fool."

Jack smiled, thinking of the stories Rooker had told of the Border Knights. "He also said you are the greatest man in Keymark."

"I doubt he has met them all." The grey man disappeared up the rock. Jack followed, grinning to himself.

They climbed. Jack was getting winded; every step was up. But the big man never slowed his pace. The boy's body was exhausted, but his mind kept going. Curiosity tickled him with a thousand questions like it always had. But one kept coming back over and over: "The elves built the jaunt gates, right?"

"Grew them, yes."

"But the dæmon used the one on Falikos. Aren't the gates, well…good?"

"Elaña are not good or evil, Jack, no more than a rock is good or evil," Valerian said. "A rock can be used to build or to kill. The Elaña were used to grow a world from dust and ash, but they were also used by *men.* When the elves left Keymark, the gates fell to dark work—you saw that on Falikos."

Valerian finally stopped, leaning against a large stone near one of the pools. "The Border Knights tried to guard the Elaña, for a time. But in the end, they were too dangerous. We destroyed the ones we knew of, but many remained lost. It was impossible to find them all. At least, it *was, until*—"

"Xiang-lo," Jack guessed.

Valerian raised an eyebrow, impressed. "You *are* clever."

Jack glanced up and saw Nightingale perched on a rock above him, nodding. Jack rested against the rock next to Valerian, pleased he had figured out part of the puzzle.

"A month ago, Xiang-lo discovered a lost gate and was

nearly killed by the Necrórceror in the finding. Memphis found him, saved him, and brought him to Falikos." Valerian offered Jack a waterskin; the boy took it and drank. "We call him Xiang-lo (the Hero's Tongue for 'pathfinder') because he has a unique skill: he is drawn to the Elaña."

"A magician, like Memphis," Jack said.

"No, he has no skill with the *wikk,*" Valerian said. "But many men have a single bit of majik in them, and Xiang-lo's majik is finding what is lost. Once he sets himself on the trail of a jaunt gate, it is like watching a bloodhound track a rabbit. With his help, we found the lost gates, and destroyed them."

Jack cocked his head. "But not the one on Falikos."

"The Elaña are beautiful things. I thought I could protect one." Valerian let out a breath. "I failed. And now Xiang-lo is in the hands of the Necrórceror." Valerian lowered his head. "It would have been better if I had let him die."

"But why all the secrets? After the surgery, you wouldn't even let me see him," Jack said suddenly. "Valerian, all this time, I've been thinking I *killed* him."

"Jack—you must understand this: Xiang-lo has great majik, but he is *dangerous*, especially to you."

"But wh—"

"*Listen.* Just before he fell ill, Xiang-lo discovered the last Elaña. That jaunt gate"—Valerian extended one hand—"is here."

Jack turned. At first, he saw nothing. Then, he noticed the pixies. They were thicker here, daring in and among the rocks around the pool. As he looked more closely, Jack spotted the vines. Hidden among the white rock, they curled around the pool, blooming with leaves and white flowers shimmering faintly in the sunlight, a weaving of wood in a faint circle of light.

"The last of the Elaña," said Valerian. He watched Jack's face as realization hit the boy—

Home.

After all these days of hoping and praying, after all the terrors, all the fighting, all the blood, he was finally going home.

Jack's jaw moved up and down, unable to speak. "But…but you said you're not a wizard—you can't make it work…"

"I cannot," said Valerian. "But Nightingale can."

The elf closed his eyes.

The water in the pool rippled to life. Jack felt the tingle of the *wikk* surge through him, powerful but calm. Slowly, like the rising sun, the white vines began to glow with an unearthly luminescence. The blossoming light grew brilliant. The water fell still, then a single ripple radiated from the center of the pool as the beating of a heart.

"It is time for you to go home, Jack Swift."

Jack stood speechless.

Home.

Valerian sunk the walking stick into the earth. As he did, the tip caught fire, burning like a torch. Jack realized once he was gone, the Border Knight would burn the jaunt gate, and that would be the last of them.

Jack looked at Valerian. Sensing the boy's hesitation, the Grey Knight spoke with finality: "You have done what we asked of you, *doktar*, and suffered for it. You have my apologies, and my best and greatest thanks." Valerian Tsai smiled. "Go. And may the will of the *wikk* guide you."

Jack turned, staring into the light. He could feel the center of the pool pulling at him, calling to him, asking him to step inside. Inside were all the things he knew, all the things he wanted: his life, his bed…his *home.*

He took a step toward the pool.

Home.

The next step was harder than he thought.

Where he was going, there were no trols, no talking cats, no pirates, no tams, no pixies swimming in the light of double moons.

Home.

No walking dead, no roaches or sorcerers or demons that would follow him to the ends of the earth to kill him where he stood.

Home.

A world of logic and science and laws.

A world of policemen and firefighters, of judges, courts, and order. He would be *safe.*

Jack Swift's world was a safe world.

A world of seat belts, bike helmets, and kneepads. A world of safety locks, life vests, airbags, metal detectors, speed limits, and stop signs.

Home.

Filtered water, pasteurized milk, regular dental checkups, warning labels, childproof caps, immunization shots, life insurance, asset allocation, tax planning, strip malls, planned communities, sunscreen, diet pills, underarm deodorant, and hand sanitizer.

A world where every October, the six o'clock news came on to warn you that someone might put a razor blade in your Halloween candy.

A world where wild animals from around the globe were caged so they could be viewed from a safe distance behind the iron bars of a zoo.

A world of boundaries and borders and limits, a world sucked dry of exploration and mystery.

A world built by bureaucrats and lawyers.

A world where all the maps had been drawn.

Home.

A world without Border Knights.

A world without elves.

A world without *majik.*

Jack Swift stepped back from the jaunt gate.

"Jack," came Valerian's voice behind him. "What are you doing?"

The boy didn't answer. He couldn't.

"If you don't go now, you will not have another chance."

Jack Swift lowered his head. Let out a breath. Then picked up the torch.

He set fire to the gate.

Flames reflected in his eyes as the white vines crackled, burning hot and bright. They flared up once, then vanished into ash and were gone.

The boy and the Border Knight stood side by side. Neither spoke. Finally, Valerian Tsai put a strong hand over Jack's shoulder and led him away.

Jack cast one last look back.

Home.

He walked through the woods, staring at his Chuck Taylors.

Valerian and Nightingale were somewhere up ahead, leading a path through the forest, but the boy lingered behind, lost in thought. A pixie darted in front of his nose. Jack looked up and watched the shimmering light twinkle, then it flew away.

"You have changed, *doktar*," came the knight's voice. Jack raised his head and saw Valerian squatting on a tree stump at the edge of a large waterfall, whittling a long stick. "More than I realized." He did not look up. "I am not sure what you will become."

Nightingale stood nearby, watching Jack with those silver eyes. The boy dug his hands in his pockets and stared at his shoes, silent.

The knight continued to whittle. "Memphis told me you adopted another name during your travels."

Black Jack. Blond hair fell over Jack's eyes. He nodded, silent.

The knight glanced at Nightingale. The elf took a long look at the boy, then nodded agreement to an unspoken question. "It is the will of the *wikk,* then." Valerian stood, whittled one last stroke, blew the shavings off the tip, and held it out to Jack. "You will need this."

Jack eyed the stick; the point was as sharp as a spear. "For what?"

Valerian's face was unreadable. "There is another pool here that you might enter." The knight gestured to the waterfall behind him. Jack came to the edge and saw it fell down a long, hollow tunnel in the earth. It was deep; he could hear water striking water somewhere far below, but all he could see was blackness.

"What's down there?"

"Possibilities." Valerian's face was a blank mask.

Jack glanced down at the drop. "You want me to go down there."

"No," said the knight. "I do not want it. But I think you should."

The two men locked eyes. After a moment, Jack kicked off his sneakers and pulled off his tattered shirt. "Will you come with me?"

"You must go alone, Jack. I cannot help you." He held out the spear. Jack took it and turned to face the black hole.

He gripped the spear in his palm, felt the knife at his belt, touched the leather of the skidshield on his wrist.

And jumped.

A breath, then water. Freezing water. Currents buffeted him, and he was dragged down. Pushed backward, he cracked his ribs against a rock. It tore at his burns. Jack stopped himself from crying out, saving his breath. He tried to swim, but the water pushed him farther down. The current tried to rip the spear away from him, but Jack held it fast with both hands. Something tugged at his legs; he yanked them up, clutching them close to his chest. He was bounced around, colliding with more stones. His skin tore. Something smashed his forehead. His lungs shot out what little air they had left. And then somewhere there was a shimmer of light. Gripping the spear in his teeth, Jack pulled against the water with all his might, gripped the rock, and dragged himself through.

He broke the surface. Scrabbling for a handhold, he pulled himself up from the water, sucking whopping great lungfuls of air. He spat the water out of his throat, used the spear to prop himself up, and looked around.

There was nothing to see. The world was jet black. He was underground—he could hear his own breathing echoing off the rock around him—and there was no light. Taking another breath, Jack briefly considered going back the way he had come but knew the waters would tear him apart. There was no way but forward.

He felt his way blindly along the cave wall. For a long time, his useless eyes stared blankly as his hands scraped along the rock, skinning his knees and bumping his nose over and over again, and soon, he was utterly lost. The sound of water disappeared, and he was left with nothing but the echoes of his own breath. Now he found himself cornered, wedged in between the rock, with no way out. He panicked then, hearing his breath grow labored and fast in the endless night, reverberating all around him. Finally, his foot found free space beneath him, and he ducked down and crawled. Scraping himself along the rock on his belly like a worm, Jack pulled himself forward, feeling the stone grow closer and closer around him. He would be crushed by the rock here, crushed by the rock just like—

Claustrophobia set in, and he found himself lashing out at the rock, striking it with his fists, trying to push it away. Desperately, he scrabbled forward, knowing if he came to a dead end, it would be impossible to turn around. The cave closed in on him, inflexible fingers gripped at his body, fear clutched his heart.

Finally, he broke free and came out the other side. Now there was light—a single shaft spilling through a narrow fissure in the rock. Motes of dust spilled down like slow rain. There, in the center of the light, stood a single massive stone.

It did not belong here; Jack knew that instantly. It was alabaster white, polished smooth as water, a single pale finger thrusting up to the light. In the darkness, it seemed to glow. Fixated, he forgot his own fears, drawing closer to the obelisk.

It was then he heard the growl.

He turned. Two evil pinpricks of light blazed in the darkness—red, burning eyes. The twin flames grew larger, closer. The growl came again, and out of the blackness came the Wolf.

A massive black lupine head emerged from the shadows, mounted on shoulders tall as Jack's. Its eyes were blood; its claws were butcher's knives. And the teeth. Those glistening teeth.

Half naked, the boy took a step back, gripping Valerian's spear, fingers tight around the haft. The Wolf paced him, its huge body turning sideways, circling, those red eyes never leaving him.

A boy. The words came low in his ears, deep and dark, smooth and hard as ice. The Wolf's mouth did not move, but its words were clear. *Only a boy.*

He gritted his teeth. He didn't like the feeling of the voice in his head; it was cold and empty and cruel. "What are you?"

I am Nightmare, said the Wolf. *I am Guilt. I am Sorrow and Shame and Pain. I am Fear.* The Wolf continued to circle as the boy spun, keeping his spear at the ready. *I see you, man-child. I see what you are. I know you well.*

"And what am I?"

The Wolf licked its chops, its huge red tongue slavering. *You are Fear. You are Guilt and Sorrow and Shame. You are one of mine. You belong to me.*

Sharp teeth suddenly lashed out. The boy ducked away just in time, feeling the fur of the Wolf's chin rush over his shoulder. He recovered, backing up as fast as he could, but the Wolf had resumed its pacing.

You are Doubt. You are Regret. You are Despair.

It snapped again, but the boy was too quick to be caught.

You are Weak.

No, he thought at the Wolf. *No.*

I have dwelt in you long, boy. I see. I see. I am what you have become. I know what you are. The Wolf stopped, a growl rumbling deep in its throat. *You are Father-Killer.*

Silence. Jack could hear the beating of his own heart. The Wolf's breath rattled. A heavy weight pulled at the boy's soul, down, down into the blackness—the blackness he knew too often, too well.

You are mine, Father-Killer.

Nightmare ripped at his heart not with claws but with truth. In his mind, Jack saw his father go into the cave

(grave)

saw his own tiny hand, the hand of the little boy named Chief Raging Bull reach for the Indian weapons

Mine, his own small voice said.

Mine.

heard the rock crack. Heard the stone bark. Heard the cave collapse

(on me)

on his father, and bury him forever.

My fault.

Mine. Mine.

Nightmare was close now. He could smell its breath, hot and empty against his face. *Shame,* said the Wolf. *Fear. Guilt. Shame.*

No, his own thought came, but it had no strength.

Weak. Stupid. Useless. Shame.

Nightmare's chin stroked Jack's shoulder. The fur was warm against his bare skin. He closed his eyes, letting himself go, freeing himself to be taken in by the soft, warm pelt.

Yes, said the Wolf. *Come to me. There is comfort here. Rest.*

My coat is warm, and you wear it so well. So well.

"Dad—"came his own voice, far away and so small.

He could feel the muscles in the Wolf's jaws opening. Its pearly teeth slid softly over his cheek. He could not stop it. He didn't want to.

You are mine, Father-Killer. You have lived with me so long. I am part of you, boy. And you will be part of me. You have fed me so well. Feed me. Feed me with your whole heart.

My whole heart.

My whole heart.

No, came the voice inside.

I was a kid. A stupid kid.

Stupid. The Wolf's voice was louder now. *Stupid. Weak. Useless.*

No. The voice grew stronger.

Weak! The Wolf's bloody eyes flared. *Shame!*

It's not my fault.

Shame!

It's not my fault.

FEAR!

"*NO!*"

The boy drove his spear through the Wolf's mouth.

The point skewered through its chin, shattered its teeth, crushed the skull between its bloody eyes. As the spear snapped in half, the Wolf's roar became a yelp.

The Wolf fell to Jack's feet, dead.

Wind rushed through the cave. Jack threw up a hand to protect his eyes and watched the Wolf disintegrate. Its fur flew away like dandelion seeds. Its skin turned to dust and blew away into nothingness. Its teeth were ash, its claws were dust, its eyes were water and air.

When the last of the Wolf had blown away, all that was left in its place was a weak and harmless animal—a puppy—not a Wolf.

It whimpered in its sleep.

At the base of the white obelisk, something gleamed. Jack walked toward it. Cairn stones were piled up around the white pillar, each marked with a symbol. He could understand a few of them from his poor training with Rooker: *Peace,* one said. *Hero,* said another. *Heart, Bravery, Victory,* said the stones, *Warrior.* As Jack circled the tremendous pale obelisk, he saw another emblem he recognized, a single symbol carved deep into the white stone:

He stood on the grave of Black Jack.

Valerian knew. He knew.

Jack put one hand on the headstone. There, hidden in the rock, was a neatly folded packet of cloth, black as night.

He knew.

Jack reached out and picked the ebony scarf—the mask of the Black. Below it was an ebony tricorn hat, leather boots, and a suit of sable.

The will of the wikk.

Inlaid in the stone was a pale cylinder of wood. It hummed, high and bright. Nervously, Jack reached out and took hold of it. The jangling sensation of the wikk shot through him, and the piece came free in his hand.

He opened his palm. In it lay a thin, glimmering joint of a bamboo tree. It was a foot long and glowed with blue light. Symbols were etched in the bamboo, curved and lyrical, but he could not read them. The rod in his hand could only be one thing—

"Nepenthe."

Majik sang out like a choir. Crackling energy shot forth from his hand, filling the cave with blue light. The ground trembled beneath his feet. Stone cracked. Earth shook. Something smashed from the floor of the cave. A shaft of blue light shot out and darted straight for him. It collided with the piece he held—an identical twin. The two pieces snapped together end to end. *Tak!* A third piece burst from the rock, then a fourth, a fifth, shooting out of their graves. They came like blue thunderbolts, drawn to the majik in his hands. *Tak!* Another piece snapped into place. *Tak!* The chain grew larger. *Takatakatak!* Nepenthe came alive in his fist: seven feet of blazing blue light.

The sizzling heartbeat of the *wikk* surged through his blood.

The majik reached its climax, drawn into the living wood, then, with a thunderclap, the light died and the cave went black.

Valerian Tsai waited, hoping.

He sat on the rock, whittling with his knife, humming an old, old song. Nightingale hummed harmony.

As the light mellowed to the horizon, a silhouette appeared against the fading sun.

The Border Knight watched the shadow come, its walk steady and sure. Valerian looked on, silent. Soon enough, the figure came to a stop before him. The canvas shoes that had once clad a boy's feet were tossed to the ground, ragged and outgrown. The man wore boots.

The man in black set his long bamboo staff in the earth.

"Thank you," came the familiar voice from beneath the mask.

Valerian nodded. No more needed to be said.

When Jack Swift slept that night, his dreams were sweet; the only nightmare that came to him was the black-and-grey pup nestled next to his heart.

And, for now, he was the master of that.

HEAD ON A STICK

The best armor is to keep out of range.

Italian Proverb

P ixies fled through the trees. Panicked, they darted back and forth on silver wings, crying out to each other in terror. One—a beautiful young sprite—glanced behind her as the creature roared. Percussive waves blasted her tiny body; she fell, screaming. A single gigantic finger, black and burning, caught her. Flames leapt up; her wings dissolved to ash. The finger tossed her body upward into the great horned mouth that swallowed her whole.

Chulurath ate. Plucking another pixie from the air, the beast tossed it into its mouth. The tiny creatures gave the dæmon no nourishment—it did not need food—but the taste of the living *wikk* was satisfying to destroy.

It had lost the scent.

The beast had known something was wrong the moment it lost sight of the Prize. Suddenly, there were two trails of scent, two ribbons leading off in different directions. The dæmon had let itself become distracted, burning with desire to kill the grey man once and for all. The Paladine Knight had known vengeance was too powerful a call for the dæmon to ignore, and used it. Blinded by rage, Chulurath pursued the knight. But the old grey fox had tricked it, leading it a dozen leagues in the wrong direction. In the end, the false trail petered out, went cold, and died.

Chulurath consumed another handful of pixies, feeling them crunch between its teeth. Over the span of spheres and centuries, there had been many heroes who had stood against it, but few so successfully as the Paladine Captain. The grey man continued to stand in the beast's way, on the island, at the bridge…*and now it has taken the prey from my claws.*

The dæmon seethed, feeling the blackness build within. Its fury grew; the earth around its feet charred, burning. Trees suddenly leapt into flames; sap bubbled in their veins until they exploded, sending shards of wood flying. At the edge of the circle, plants wilted black, and animals died twitching, poisoned by its hate.

I will have the grey fox, thought the beast. *I will take the man-child from him. I will torture the boy. I will watch the fox writhe and wail in despair. I will gnaw the fox's bones, and feel his blood pour down my throat.*

Ash and cinders followed the beast as it strode back into the woods, enjoying the thought.

I will have them, man and boy—and soon.

Jack looked forward to seeing Leah; he had imagined several different possibilities for their reunion: a warm hug, awkward silence, or even a kiss, but nothing could have prepared him for the one word that came from her smiling lips:

"Daddy!"

Daddy?

Jack stared at her stupidly. Leah rushed past him, throwing herself into the arms of Valerian Tsai. He grabbed her up, swinging her around, grinning through his salt-and-pepper beard as she lavished the kind of affection on him that only a child could.

Before he could react, Jack found himself overwhelmed by Django and the others shouting welcome, pounding him on the back, relieved he was still alive. Memphis broke through, wrapped Jack up in his great brown arms, and hugged him tight, nearly choking the air out of him.

"He's her *father?*" Jack whispered in the trol's ear. "You said her last name was *Archer.*"

"I told you she could shoot your eye out from fifty paces." The trol grinned. "Archer is her vocation."

Jack scowled. "You could have been clearer."

Memphis shrugged his armored shoulders. "I told you she was off-limits."

Chance suddenly jumped on Jack, laughing. The cat's greeting was wildly enthusiastic, quick paws thumping Jack all over; by the time Chance was done, Jack was left with the feeling he had just been mugged.

Li-Bao was stoic as always, but when the croc clasped Jack's hand, a glimmer of relief shone in that one blue eye. "Welcome back."

Django Barón was last, but he did not look at Jack—the bull's eyes only saw Valerian Tsai—he dropped to one knee, bowing low. "The Grey Knight of the *Paladine*," said Django, awe in his voice. Li-Bao knelt quickly, grabbed Chance's neck, and dragged the cat down to a bow. The minotaur lowered his head. "It is an honor, *jai*."

Valerian looked at the bull, eyes sparkling. "You're Django Barón, aren't you?"

Django looked startled. "I…yes, sir."

"We've met," said Valerian. "You wouldn't remember; you were very small, no more than a calf. But I knew your father, Domingo, very well. An honorable man." It was impossible to tell, but Jack thought the bull actually blushed.

"And you have the look of the Cerulean Raja," said Valerian to Chance. The big cat smiled and nodded eagerly. "What number are you from the throne?"

"Twenty-fourth," said Chance, grinning.

"May your rule come quick and your reign be long," said the big man, knowing the proper greeting. Chance purred.

"And you." Valerian stepped forward, clasping Li-Bao's wrist, bringing the croc to his feet. "*Sakai*, warrior."

"*Sakai*, Valerian-*jai*," said Li-Bao.

Jack stared. "You know each other?"

"Li-Bao Sen is a samurai of the Tower Yongshi—a commander." Valerian smiled. "We've met many times." Jack marveled—the croc had never mentioned one word of his rank or his friendship with the knight—but then again, Li-Bao never mentioned anything.

"So," said Valerian to the Trio. "You follow Black Jack?"

Jack's breath caught in his throat.

Li-Bao and Chance hesitated, waiting for the bull's answer.

Django Barón said nothing. He eyed Jack up and down, noting the new outfit his master wore and, more to the point, his new staff. "That is Nepenthe."

"It is."

"And you are the Black."

Jack glanced at Valerian Tsai. The big man was silent. Jack paused, then said for the first time: "I am."

The minotaur nodded. "Then I follow you." A smile broke over the faces of the croc and the cat.

Jack came close to the bull. "I'm sorry I ever gave you reason to doubt me, Django."

"Doubt you? Never." The minotaur's eyes sharpened. "I knew who you were."

There was something in the minotaur's voice that suggested more than he let on. Jack suddenly realized Django had not just suspected him; he had *known.* Jack opened his mouth, but the minotaur beat him to it.

"Honor is a tricky thing, Black," Django stated, raising his horned head. "I have kept mine. And you have found yours."

A sudden growl came from an unexpected source—Fuji. The tam snarled at the black-and-grey pup that hid behind Jack's boots. A furious rage was locked on the gecko's face, a hatred Jack would have never dreamed it capable of. The tam snarled and lashed out at the dog, which yelped in fear. Jack snatched Fuji's arm.

What are you doing? Jack signed, angry.

Hound is wicked, Fuji signed, its eyes locked on the pup. *Tam smells it. Hound will hurt Apple Jack.*

The puppy whimpered, looking up at Jack for protection. He had not been able to leave the pup alone it in the woods—not because of any sympathy he felt for it—but because he knew it was better to keep Fear at his heel, where he could keep an eye on it.

It belongs to me, Jack signed. *I am responsible for it.*

It is dangerous.

Yes. It is.

Fuji scowled, not liking the dog, but a slow smile crept over its gentle face. *Fuji is glad you are not dead.*

Me too.

"I see you've found another pet." Leah stroked the pup's head. "It's cute. What's its name?"

"Shadow," Jack said before he knew why. The dog—the Wolf—was part of him, a shadow of himself, and the name fit.

Leah cocked her head. "You seem to collect every man and beast you meet, Jahk."

But not every woman. Fuji signed.

Leah raised an eyebrow. "*What* did it s—"

A white arrow *thunked* into the tree an inch from Jack's head. He spun and saw Nightingale waving his arm in a silent alarm.

"Who the devil is *that?*" asked Chance.

"Something is coming," said Valerian. "Let's be off the road when it gets here."

They moved, taking cover in a copse of juniper bushes. Memphis hunkered down next to the elf. "'Lo there, Nightingale." The elf winked in reply.

Crouching by Jack's arm, the tam gestured: *Fuji not hear.*

Me neither, signed Jack. Moments later, still far distant, he heard the drumming of horse hooves. The tam glanced curiously at Nightingale, signing to Jack: *Good ears.*

Hoofbeats, dozens of them, built to a roar, echoing from the surrounding rocks like an approaching army. "Stay hidden," whispered Valerian. Nightingale and Memphis crouched one either side of the knight, waiting to pounce. "We'll handle this."

The horses raced into view—a dozen animals led by a single masked rider.

At the grey man's signal, the trol and the elf leapt into the road. The knight raised a hand to stop the stampede. Cursing, the masked rider whipped the horses onward, but Memphis reached out his huge arms and caught the leading four stallions across the neck.

"Hold!" cried Valerian.

Swearing a blue streak, the masked man ripped his sword free—the blade rang loud and long. "First time in my life I actually *pay* for a horse," he spat, "and jes *look* where it gets me."

Jack knew the music of the sword and the curses of the rider. He sprang from his hiding spot: "Rooker!"

Rooker Flynn pulled the bandanna from his face, staring down at Jack with a grin. "Well, well. I'm bein' robbed by Black Jack hisself!"

The pirate swung one leg over the saddle and landed on his feet. Jack tackled him. Rooker pounded Jack on the back furiously, then pried himself away. "Good to see ya, boychick!" He eyed Jack over. "Nice *hat*."

"How did you find us?"

"*Ahh,*" the pirate grumbled. "Ya wasn't *too* tricky to find, kid—ya tore outta Glyn Aker with a flamin' beastie on yer heels. I jest followed the scorch marks."

"I thought you were going to stay locked up in the citadel forever!"

Rooker rubbed the back of his neck. "Yeh, well, mebbe ya were right about *one* thing, boychick. I dinnae figure a way to get the treasure outta there—so I started stashing it." He scowled. "I lost half the gold down that damned *pit* we came up, and *then* every Red Dwarf in the Bonespur came lookin' for me." Rooker sucked air between his teeth. "I gave 'em a good smacking, but I was all on my lonesome, wasn't I? Grabbed a few coins, thinkin' I could at least keep enough to get back the *Brigand,* but one of them little red devils took a hack at me, and I lost them too. Barely made it outta there with my *skin*." The pirate shot air through his nose. "Ever since ya left me, it's been one bad turn after another. So I figured mebbe I'd go lookin for m'lucky penny."

Luck. So that was it. Rooker Flynn was *still* convinced Jack Swift was better than a four-leaf clover and a rabbit's foot put together. Jack didn't care what he thought, or why. "I'm just glad to have you back."

Rooker smiled, less for Jack than for the benefit of the audience, announcing: "Good to see you too, Black Jack." He leaned in, whispering so the others could not hear: "They're still buyin' the whole *Black* thing, right?"

"Right." Jack smiled. No point in telling Rooker everything—not yet.

"Right." The pirate rubbed his hands together. "These three I know." He winked at the Trio. "Howya, boys?" Neither Django, Li-Bao, nor Chance responded; they had all hoped they were rid of the pirate for good. Rooker eyed Memphis. "The runty little trol I saw from the citadel, and—"His eyes fell on Leah. "*There* she is! The fair maid herself! We meet at last, darlin'." He slipped his hands over hers, gazing at her with silky eyes. "I'm Captain Rooker Flynn. I saved yer life."

Leah smiled politely, unsure what to make of the pirate. "If it hannae been for me, you and ol' Black here woulda been roasted to bacon." He looked her over. "Yer an eyeful, aright." He winked. "If ya ever get bored of the Boy in Black, darlin', ya can always take me for a tumble."

Rooker Flynn finally turned to meet Valerian Tsai—the man he respected more than any other in Keymark—face-to-face.

"So," Rooker said to Jack, "who's the old man?"

There were more than enough horses for everyone, including a towering Clydesdale for Django. There was no horse in Keymark that could carry Memphis, but the trol had no trouble keeping up. Valerian led the way up the road; Rooker Flynn trailed him, struggling to apologize, cramming his foot further and further into his big mouth.

Jack walked with the others. The conversation was held in hushed tones, and Jack could not figure out why until he realized they were staring at Nightingale. The elf remained separate from the group, just a shadow in the trees up ahead, but all eyes were drawn to him. Everyone had heard the stories of the Elven Exile, although few of the legends matched up—the man was a renegade killer, a forsaken lover, a butcher of thousands, a wandering pilgrim, a lone desperado hunted down by his own people. Whatever the tale they told, one truth remained constant: Nightingale was the only elf most of them had ever seen.

As they walked, Jack found himself drawing closer and closer to Leah, more interested in another story.

"Valerian Tsai's daughter?"

Leah smiled at the question; Jack got the feeling she'd been expecting it. "All my life."

"You could have told me, Leah."

"Does it matter?" She plucked a drifting dandelion seed from the air. "Being the daughter of a Border Knight is…tricky, Jahk. He's a great man, but everyone wants something great from him. There are more than a few people in Keymark who would take advantage if they knew. Campion did. That's why he kidnapped me—to use as a hostage." Leah's green eyes looked thoughtfully at the seed puff in her hand. "I never even told Benjamin. If he had asked for my hand, then…" She sighed. "Well. It would have been different." Leah blew, and the little seed went drifting into the breeze. "Sometimes it's not easy living in the Grey Knight's shadow."

Jack nodded, knowing exactly how she felt. His own father had left some big shoes to fill, not so big as Valerian Tsai's perhaps, but big enough. "So, who's your mother?"

Something dark passed over Leah's face, but she brushed her hair aside and it was gone. She smiled. "A lady keeps her secrets, Jahk. I don't know everything about *you*, do I?" She arched an eyebrow. "You tell me a secret, and I'll tell you mine."

"Valerian gave me a chance to go home."

Leah's head snapped up, staring at him. "To the Tosh? That's wonderful! But wh—"

"I burned the gate."

"*What?*"

"I decided to stay."

She stopped, dumbstruck. "But *why?* Ever since you got here, that's all you've wanted."

Jack shrugged, smiling to himself. He liked the idea of catching her off-balance. "Maybe now I want something different."

Leah stared at him; a curious grin broke over her face. "I may have to keep a closer eye on you, Toshan." She flicked the brim of his hat with a long finger. "There's more to you than I thought."

He walked on. As he heard her soft-booted feet hurrying behind, Jack decided he enjoyed the feeling Leah trying to catch *him* for a change.

Valerian raised a hand, and the group fell in behind him quietly. Jack peeked over Li-Bao's shoulder and saw—just beyond a break in the undergrowth—a crossroad. And like nearly every crossroad in Keymark, it was watched.

Rotting in the midday sun, the deadeye's flesh was falling off its skull. The pale snake-head stick that held up the severed head was covered in great globs of dripping black slime—it stunk of death. Hollow eye sockets twinkled tiny, unblinking eyes of green flame.

"Stay hidden," whispered Valerian Tsai. "There is no reason to reveal yourselves to him. And whatever happens, do *not* look into its eyes."

Memphis put a warning hand on the knight's arm. "Valerian. What are you doing?"

"Something I would rather not." The knight took a breath

and stepped directly into the gaze of the deadeye.

Green fire sizzled, blazing bright. Jack felt the shuddering cold of the dark *wikk* flow over him as the deadeye woke. Its decaying jaw creaked, bone grinding bone, and a horrific sound escaped its rotting lips:

Hhhhhhhhhhhhhhhhh.

Valerian planted his grey knightsblade tip down in the earth between his feet, standing firm. *Hhhhrah,* came the raspy scrape from the deadeye's severed throat. A wet swallowing noise gurgled from its lips. Jack suddenly was struck with horror as he realized it was laughing.

"Valerian," came the cold Voice of the Necrórceror.

"You see me clearly, Prince," said Valerian, unmoved by the terrifying voice. "As I see you."

"You ssee death, Border Knight." The Voice scraped like knives. Jack felt the strange pull of the *wikk*, dark and malevolent, and tore his eyes away. *"You ssee destruction and damnation and destiny. You ssee the future before you. You ssee your own doom."*

"I see a rotting husk upon a rotting pedestal," said the knight. "I see a son who has forgotten his fathers but yearns for their throne. I see a man who has cheated death but lives only to pay the price over and over again. Yes, I see death, Prince, but only for you."

"My blood is the blood of David King, sslave. I am his lasst heir. To me belongs the High King's chair, and I will have what is mine."

"That noble throne was toppled by the black blood your fathers shed upon it. Their butchery destroyed it. What you seek is a corpse, killed by a brood of vipers bearing your name. Your line ended a century ago on the Jaden Fields. All that remains is a hollow shell of despair, a raving corpse that will not die. But death will not wait forever." Valerian's words came strong. "How long, O Prince? How long before the deal you made is done? How long until the devil comes to claim its due?"

Furious hissing erupted from the deadeye's rotting teeth. Its voice burned wrath: *"Basstard son of a basstard race! You will feel the touch of death long before I!"*

Jack's head came up, and he found himself staring into the thing's flaming eyes. He was held fixed by its Voice.

"Tell me who the corpsse is, sslave. Your brotherss have felt my kisss—you will feel it lasst. And when you have gone, all that will be left of your kind will be the one you loved mosst; the one who betrayed you." The skull twisted into a hideous parody of a smile. *"How did it feel, Valerian Tsai? How did it feel to watch your brother turn against you? How did it feel when your beloved Campion used his one good hand to do my will?"*

Jack stared into the thing's eyes; he could not look away. He felt as if he were falling, falling into them, falling ever closer to the seductive power deep within, drawn to it. Far away, he heard Valerian's voice:

"Come out, O Prince! Come out and face me. You hide behind servants and slaves and masks." Jack took a single involuntary step toward the Voice, unable to pull himself away. "If you would be king," said Valerian, "come out and face me as one, and let your people see what you have become. I come for you, Prince." Valerian stood tall. "I am coming to Werrun *Fell!*"

The deadeye grinned delight as it cackled. *"Then you ssee it is true, Valerian—you ssee your own death."*

Jack took another step forward.

"Come!" commanded the Voice. *"You cannot sstand against me, knight! Come! You do not have your Armor. Come! You do not have your brotherss. Come! and let your blood be sspent at lasst!"*

Jack couldn't hear the Voice, couldn't understand the words. It didn't matter. All that mattered were those eyes. Those forever eyes—

Rooker's whisper came too late: "Jack! What are you—"

Jack walked into the clearing.

The gaze of the Necrórceror fell on him.

The deadeye shrieked. A wave of searing cold shot through Jack as if his blood were awash in chips of ice.

"The boy!" came the Voice. *"You have the boy!"* Jack's mind went numb; he watched as his foot took another step forward toward the skull. *"Come!"* commanded the Voice, loud, dominating. *"Come to me, boy!"*

"He will come, Prince." Valerian pulled his knightsblade from the earth. "And I am coming with him." Simmering silver light blazed from the blade as Valerian Tsai cut the skull in half.

A gibbering scream escaped the deadeye, trailed into the air for a lingering moment, then faded to nothingness and fell still.

Jack fell back as if a rope had been cut. He hit the ground hard, instantly dismayed the low pull of the dark *wikk* had gone. "It's…" he whispered, "it's so *beautiful.*"

Nightingale stood over him and placed one hand firmly on his chest. Suddenly, the insistent dark *wikk* was replaced by something else—something living. White. The need for the Necrórceror's flame ebbed and faded into a powerless memory. Jack looked up at the elf and blinked; Nightingale said nothing.

"He *told* you not to look," said Rooker Flynn.

Memphis hooked one thumb under Jack's arm and hoisted him to his feet. Leah came to him. "You okay?"

Jack nodded, trying to shake off the desire. They were an instant addiction, the eyes of the prince. They had seemed so perfect, like he could never be whole without them. Jack had a sick feeling in the pit of his stomach that he knew exactly what the heroin junkies on 103rd Street felt like.

Memphis cast a look at Valerian; the knight stood alone, silent.

"Valerian," said the trol. The grey man did not respond. "Valerian. We can stand at Highyon Garde." Jack heard a trace of desperation creeping into Memphis's voice. "We can hold it."

"David's Tower is besieged," said the knight. "I was there five days ago. The prince has it surrounded by a sea of versläng and kekubi. Highyon Garde will fall."

"But the Border Knights are there. Bantam and Stahl can—"

"Bantam and Stahl are dead. So is the Jade."

Shock struck Memphis dumb. A sharp cry cracked in Leah's throat.

"Dead?" shouted Chance. "That's impossible! Nobody can kill a Border Knight!"

"O, we can die as well as any man." Valerian's face was hard as stone. "Especially when the knife comes from a friend." He eyed the knightsblade in his hands. "Campion is earning his master's kiss."

Memphis's face twisted in anger. "You can't go to Werrun Fell. The Necrórceror will be waiting."

"Yes."

"He remembers who killed him, Valerian. He hates you."

"Yes."

"You can't stand against him. He'll summon the *ûzguk.*"

"Yes."

"He'll bring a whole army to stop you."

"Let's hope so."

The trol blinked. *"What?"*

Valerian smiled. "I wouldn't set foot in Werrun Fell; we'd be dead in seconds. But I hope the prince believed me as much as *you* do."

Rooker Flynn suddenly laughed. "It's a snipe hunt!" he exclaimed. "You *bamboozled* him!" The pirate grinned, slapping his hands together, rubbing them like he was starting a fire. "O, I *like* the way the old fox plays."

"Let's just hope he took the bait," Valerian said. "We need time." The Grey Knight slung his sword over his shoulder. "Keymark is finished. There are no more towers to defend. There is only one place left to stand."

"Where?" asked Memphis.

"The Paladine."

The Paladine Arch. Home of the Border Knights. Home of the *elves*. Jack felt his heart beat just a little faster.

Something clattered in the bushes. Branches snapped as something fled into the woods—something big. Chance was off like a shot after it, Nightingale close on his heels. There was a scramble and a few muffled shouts as the footrace broke into the trees.

"What was *that?*" said Rooker.

"A better question, pirate," said Leah, "is *who?*"

After a few minutes, the jinx and the elf returned empty-handed.

"Whoever it was, they were *fast*," growled Chance.

Nightingale glanced at Valerian. A dark look passed between them.

"How long was it there?" Leah frowned. "If it heard us, it could tell the Necr—"

"We have to move," said Valerian as he faced the group. "Leah, Memphis, Nightingale, and I are going into the Jutts—the mountains are the fastest way to the Paladine." He set his jaw. "If we are to part ways, it must be now."

All eyes fell on the man called Black Jack. He eyed them back and cocked his hat. "I'm always with you."

"And I," said Django.

"And I," said Chance.

"And I," said Li-Bao Sen.

"Hot damn." Rooker grinned. "Let's take a crack at 'er and see what breaks."

On a windswept rise above the Banpai Range, Campion Rei unbuckled his helmet, cradled it beneath his one good arm, and watched.

David's Tower was in flames.

Men screamed from behind the gates of Highyon Garde,

their cries empty against the waning sun. Rooftops blazed like gigantic torches. The palace was thick with smoke as the King's Keep choked out its final dying gasps. Thousands of the Necrórceror's kekubi hurled themselves against the cracking iron gates of the tower, many dressed in the armor of the samurai who once protected it. The last straggling defenders poured rocks, arrows, spears, and boiling oil down on the ghouls, but the dead only gave rise to more dead, coming again in wave after wave of relentless brute force. Versläng (some grown man-tall from eating their kin) scaled the stone ramparts like hungry spiders. At the peak of the battlements, the samurai garde fought them off, but for every dozen insects that fell, one made it over the wall. And then their venom flowed like wine.

It was strange, leading an army of monsters, not men. This was not the way Campion had imagined triumph when he had first become an apprentice under Valerian Tsai's mastery. The Border Knight captain had been kind, patient, and wise—but in the end, the grey man's ways were too slow.

Now the Crimson Knight had a new master, and his ways were quick.

He watched David's Tower burn and die. The Necrórceror would soon take the throne that had too long remained empty. And once the prince of Werrun Fell took his rightful place, at his right hand would stand Campion Rei.

The Crimson knightsblade grew brighter, burning in his armored fist, flames licking greedily against blood-red steel.

A rasping croak sounded beside him. Campion turned to find one of the kekubi standing by his side. A scowl crossed Campion's perfect face. "Get back to the line!" The zombies were useful, no doubt, but utterly unnerving. In the beginning, there had been dozens of them, meant only to be the eyes of the prince—now there were hundreds, perhaps thousands, of corpses under the command of the Necrórceror's death majik.

But every time Campion looked at one, he saw the face of his brother Farrior Han.

In response to Campion's order, the kekubi reached up, clutched its jaw with both skeletal hands, and ripped its head from its neck. The Crimson Knight took a step back as the dead thing held its severed skull aloft.

"Kneel," came the Voice.

Without hesitation, Campion fell to one knee and bowed. "Sire."

The prince's Voice spoke: *"Send three thousand to the Broken Pass. Do it now."*

"Sire, that will cut the Host in half!" As the words came out of his mouth, Campion immediately regretted them. An icy-cold vise suddenly gripped his chest, crushing his ribs.

"You will take the Seat of David without them."

Wincing, the traitor knight tried again. "Highyon Garde is nearly finished, sire. Give me one more da—"

Pain shot through Campion's chest, wracking his body in torment. He collapsed to the ground, gasping for air.

"Do not test me, Campion." The Voice grew darker. *"Or you will find our bargain forfeit."* The cold released him; Campion found his place on his knees. *"The Grey Knight moves on Werrun Fell now,"* continued his prince. *"And the boy comes with him."*

The doktar. Campion had known from the beginning the Fell Prince coveted the boy (even more than Xiang-lo), but what could be so important about a man half grown? Campion wondered but did not dare to ask. "The Grey Knight could never threaten you, sire. But I will do as you command."

"Yes," came the rattling Voice. *"You will."* A high, shrieking sound emanated from the kekubi's lips as the Necrórceror's power departed; the headless body collapsed to the ground with a meaty *thunk.*

Campion moved quickly, ordering one of the larger versläng to lead the hunting pack. The roaches were difficult to understand, their chittering speech incomprehensible to human ears, but they followed orders with unquestioning fervor like ants obeying their queen. In a few short hours, exactly three thousand versläng moved away to the northeast, making for the Broken Pass.

As he watched them go, the traitor knight glanced at the tower. The samurai on the walls watched as well. They would take courage from the retreat; hope gave heart to desperate men. It would take days to beat the fear back into them. Campion scowled. Valerian Tsai had taken away his moment of victory—again.

The Crimson Knight folded his arms over his breastplate and felt the powerful *wikk* of the Paladine Armor surge through him, granting solace to his uneasy mind.

But inside the hollow shell where his good right arm had had once been, Campion Rei felt nothing at all.

No kekubi were necessary to alert the dæmon. It was held firmly in the thrall of his master; their minds were one.

Fool.

Chulurath ripped a tree from the earth and cracked it in half. The grey fox had played his bait, and the little prince had swallowed it whole.

The Broken Pass? Ridiculous. The Paladine Captain had an oath to uphold—something the Fell Prince could never understand—the knight would die before he broke his word. He would defend the elves. He would make his last stand at the Paladine Arch.

The time to kill Valerian Tsai was now. Before he got there. Before he stood his ground. Before he donned his Armor.

But the fool prince would have his greatest weapon turn from its prey to guard a phantom trail—and under the thrall created by the Black Accord, Chulurath could refuse the prince no more than paper could refuse a pen.

The Crownéd Dæmon sniffed the air. Valerian Tsai was the last real threat left to it on this sphere. To destroy the grey fox now, when he was on the run and not yet at his full strength, was too tempting a call to resist.

And the boy. And the boy.

Chulurath licked its claws, tasting the youngling's burned flesh. The prince has ordered the beast to the Broken Pass—yes—but in his haste, the prince had not given further instructions.

He had not told his slave what to do *after*.

The dæmon moved quickly, setting a pace faster than the swiftest deer. It would fulfill the command of its prince and set one burning footstep in the Broken Pass. One.

And then it would head west, into the Jutts.

To hunt.

STEEPLECHASE

A mighty hunter, and his prey was man.

Alexander Pope

N epenthe felt good in Jack's hands.

The bamboo staff weighed nothing at all; the wood was smooth and invitingly warm to the touch. He swung again, bringing the staff around in a quick arc and thrust out sharply, listening to Abrahim's voice in his head. As the tingle rippled through his arm, Jack thought Nepenthe felt nothing like Rooker's singing saber—the feel of this *wikk* was not a jangling jolt; it was more like holding on to the side of a lion as it roared— and he liked it.

She was fast. Faster than he could ever be on his own. It was almost like she was guiding him, steering him. Jack let her—let her have the lead, let her come alive in his hands, let her dance. The carvings in the wood glowed as she blurred through the air with a soft purr, too fast to follow, humming contrails of vapor blue.

Fuji watched from one side of the clearing, Shadow from the other. Neither animal ever strayed far from its master, but the tam and the dog stayed apart like oil and water. Both watched him with curious eyes. Valerian and the others were somewhere up ahead, taking the first break of the journey. For now, Jack was happy to be left alone.

He spun again, listening to the bamboo staff purr against the air.

A hand suddenly shot out and held Nepenthe fast.

Nightingale.

Jack drew a sharp breath—he hadn't seen or heard him coming—the elf was as quiet as a falling leaf. Gripping Nepenthe, Nightingale eyed Jack. He held out his other palm: *Give it to me.*

Jack hesitated. Nepenthe felt good in his fist, it felt right— for the first time in his life, Jack felt *strong*. He knew the elf wasn't going to take it, but all the same, it was difficult to let her go.

Nightingale's silver eyes stared him down. Just *looking* at the man gave Jack the same sensation as the low tingle of the skidshield on his arm or standing too close to Memphis when he worked one of his spells. It was as if the elf was wrapped in the *wikk* or made of it.

Jack let go of Nepenthe.

Nightingale gripped her tight, brought her down over his knee, and cracked her in half.

Jack cried out in shock. Before he could react, Nightingale raised a hand. Jack felt a dull *thub* in his chest and found he could not move; he could only watch the elf through a warm haze.

Nightingale turned his attention to Nepenthe, running pale fingers over the elegant carvings in the wood. His hand shot out, snapping the bamboo at the joint, again and again, until the staff was broken into seven short sticks. He took the first stick and popped the round tip off with his thumb, revealing a secret compartment. Inside, were a set of slim tools that looked like lock picks. He flipped the short joint over, popped the opposite cap, and now something *different* was inside: a roll of parchment and a quill. He repeated the trick with the other sticks, revealing different tools (a tight roll of black cloth, a set of slim piton nails) contained within each. Fingers moving like a magician, Nightingale opened a cap, showed the bamboo joint was hollow, closed the cap, opened it again, and now the tube was solid wood. He flicked the stick and something *snapped* out of the top: a knife blade, silver and sharp—a bamboo dagger. Another flick, and a second blade joined the first, side by side like the tines of a fork. A *snap*, and they were gone.

Nightingale eyed Jack up and down, like a teacher assessing a student. He gripped one stick in his fist, tossed two others in the air, and the pieces snapped together end to end like magnets with a sharp *tak*. Nightingale flicked the other pieces up with his foot. They shot home—*takatakatak!*—and Nepenthe was whole again.

He popped the staff apart, but now the joints were connected by a gossamer-thin silver strand. *Tak!* Nepenthe snapped back together, and Nightingale spun her in a quick circle. Knives shot from either end now, forming a nine-foot double-bladed spear. Nepenthe blurred blue, gaining speed in the elf's hands. Her hum grew to a roar, and Nightingale drove her tip into the ground.

The rock split with a thunderous *crack.*

Nightingale glanced at Jack, raising an eyebrow. *Under-stand?*

Jack stared at him, dumbstruck. *A staff* and *a spear,* he thought. *The whomping stick.* Knives, spear tips, silver ropes, secret compartments—Nepenthe was more than just *fast.* And she packed a wallop.

The elf pulled out a bandolier—a long leather shoulder belt with two loops stitched into the thickest part. He cracked Nepenthe in half, sheathed her firmly in the loops, and presented the rig to Jack.

Jack found he could move. He bowed low, the way he had learned from Abrahim.

Nightingale bowed back.

Jack took the bandolier and looped the belt over his shoulder; the two staves hung across his back like Rooker's singing saber. Nightingale nodded, then handed over the final, seventh, piece.

It felt good to have her back in his hands. *Nepenthe.*

As he thought the word, the pieces suddenly shot from his back—*takatakatak!*—and she came together in his fist.

Nightingale nodded, satisfied, and walked up the hill.

Jack looked down at the staff and immediately started experimenting. He cracked it, snapped it back together, and fiddled with the gossamer strand (silky smooth, but *strong*). He popped open a hidden compartment, dropped in his surgical needle and thread, closed it, reopened it, and peered in—still there. He tried to get the knife blades to pop out, flicking his wrist as the elf had, but couldn't make it work.

How did he know how to do all this? It seemed like Night-ingale knew Nepenthe from before. And what about the bandolier? Did he already have it, or did he just make it? Jack realized he had little hope of getting an answer out of the mute elf.

"Jack!" came a voice from the hilltop. Rooker Flynn stood against the skyline. "Quit playing with yer little stick and get up here! We're going!"

Jack cracked the staff, sheathed it on his back, and hooked the seventh piece to his knife belt. He might not know how to make it work, but he liked the feel of Nepenthe on his hip.

He only hoped he wouldn't need her soon.

The Jutts were monstrous.

Jack had traveled the Appalachians, the Rockies, and even the South American Andes with his father, but the Jutts dwarfed them all. Rough grey stone rose up around the mounted riders until it encompassed and surrounded them like a giant's hand around a gnat. Even the cracked and fallen boulders that had broken away from the main bulk of the mountain were awesome in their sheer magnitude; single stones littered the narrowing path like discarded skyscrapers. When the riders came through a crack in the rocks, Jack looked up and realized they were barely at the knee of the mountain; the peaks rose into the clouds, disappearing into the wispy white of unimaginable heights. In fact, the pinnacle of the mountain towered above the fabled peak of Everest. No man or beast had ever summited the Jutts—its crown was beyond the reach of the living.

As they rode into the shadow of the mountain, Jack learned something new about himself: he was, without question, the World's Worst Horseman. In the beginning, he had liked the mare he was given, a powerful black beauty, and fed her carrots. But when he tried to control her, the nag immediately bucked and sent him flying into the dirt. Jack listened to every bit of Rooker's copious advice—grip the thing with his thighs, let the reins hang limp, relax in the saddle—but Jack found himself locked in a never-ending struggle for control, and soon longed for a piece of obedient Detroit-made automotive steel. By midmorning, the mean-spirited mare was walking under low branches, trying to brush Jack off by smacking him in the face with tree limbs. Jack was infuriated; his back was sore, his arms were tired, and his butt was numb. He swore constantly. By the end of the day, everyone was convinced he had named the nag Dammit.

Valerian Tsai pushed them onward into the Jutts until the last twinkling rays of the sun were lost in the gloaming and no light was left to guide their way. Even then, the knight moved forward, scouting the path ahead with Nightingale and Chance. Exhausted, Jack fell asleep by the fire, listening to Rooker's stories and the muted strains of Django's guitar. He never saw Valerian come back, but when Li-Bao woke him before the sunrise, the grey man was mounted and ready to ride. The Border Knight's tone had changed since they entered the mountains; he spoke rarely, and when he did, his voice was clipped and urgent.

Jack noticed that Valerian kept looking down the path behind them, watching for something. The young man suddenly got a bad feeling in his gut and kicked his horse a little faster.

At noon, they broke through the tree line—the invisible border above which green things cannot survive—and the land became a snow-covered desert. From below, the snow had looked majestic, even inviting, clean and radiantly white. But as the day wore on and the cold became harsh reality, a creeping chill crept over Jack's bones and settled in for a long stay. Huddling in the saddle, they moved upward across the exposed cliffs into a world of white.

When they made camp for the night in the lee of a huge rock, Valerian would not allow a fire. What little dinner they ate was hardtack and water, half-heartedly munched in silence. The wind whipped up to a howling screech. Jack found himself huddled together with Leah, Rooker, and Fuji for protection.

Although Black Jack's cloak was thick enough, he wished every minute for Polartec gloves, Vibram boots, and a jacket made of insulated Gore-Tex. But those things were far away, and there was nothing to do but hunker down and bear it out.

After a half night of half sleep, they moved on. Jack gave control over to the nag, letting her follow the others. He pulled his freezing hands tight to his chest and tried to sleep. He was still lost in a semiconscious doze when Valerian called an unexpected halt—the path ahead was blocked by a rockslide. Memphis went to work lifting the stones and chucking them over the edge while the others, too small to do much good, waited. Jack drifted off to sleep in the saddle, dreaming of a warm fire, the wood smell of a sauna, and

(rath)

His eyes flashed open.

Jack turned to see Valerian at the cliff edge, flat on his belly, looking down at the path behind them.

Jack joined him, but the grey man did not take his eyes off the path. His voice was grim. "You felt it?"

Jack nodded. None of the others seemed to have noticed, warming themselves near the rock pile. Side by side, the two men peered down at the route, watching, waiting.

Nothing. Not a whisper.

Jack turned to find Nightingale standing silently above him, his silver eyes staring deep. He stooped down, reached out one arm, and pointed. At first, Jack couldn't see anything. But then, miles and miles below, a shadow moved between the trees.

Valerian got to his feet. "Memphis. How long?"

The trol was at the rock pile, wrestling a large boulder. "'Bout another hour. But I d—"

"Let's give him a hand." Valerian moved to the pile and started hurling the smaller rocks over the side. The others joined him, puzzled, but went to work.

"Valerian-*jai*," Django began, "what is the—"

"We need to move."

The rock pile was cleared in twenty minutes. Valerian slung one leg over his saddle and rode out without saying a word. As the others followed, Jack cast one look back over his shoulder. He couldn't see the shadow, but it was back there, somewhere.

And it was coming for him.

The sun took its turn to torment them. This high up in the Jutts, there was no protection from the blazing radiation pouring down from a clear blue sky, and they were burned twice: once from above, and again as the sunlight reflected off the blinding snow at their feet. Even while his hair was frosting over, Jack found his skin parched and sunburned; the underside of his nose was lobster red. He wrapped the black mask around his face for the hundredth time and squinted his eyes, enduring the torture.

Memphis walked, keeping up with the horses, moving easily over his home terrain. Fuji rode with Jack, huddled inside his cloak. The conversation dwindled to nothing, in part because of the cold, but mainly because the group sensed the urgency coming from Valerian. As the sun began to fade into the east, they kept waiting for the grey man to call a halt, but the order never came.

Rooker finally piped up. "Gettin' cold, Cap'n." Valerian did not respond. Rooker glanced at Chance; the cat nodded, encouraging him. "How's about we get a fire going?" Valerian made no reply but kicked his horse on.

He did not call a halt that night. When the sun went down, they kept moving through the dark; Nightingale led the way when it became too black to see. They moved slowly in single file through the mountain pass, one horse nosing the tail of the next. By midnight, Jack couldn't feel his hands anymore. He dropped the reins, his nag too tired to try anything now, and held his arms tight around Fuji, combining their warmth. The freezing blackness went on forever, and Jack could not remember a longer, more miserable night.

No one discussed what was chasing them, but all of them knew. Over the course of the interminable night, the malevolent feel of the thing behind them grew stronger and more rank until it was impossible to ignore. Even the horses could feel it. Jack couldn't tell if the sensation was in his nose or in his head, but he kept catching the smell of burning flesh.

When the sun finally cracked the horizon, Valerian was behind them, sitting high on his saddle, staring down the path they had just traveled. Silently, everyone joined the Border Knight, hoping against hope that the trail would be clear.

Nightingale's eyes were not necessary this time. There, just above the tree line, a dark shape followed, dead on their path.

It was still miles back, just a hint of what was coming, but it had gained ground overnight.

Jack's shoulders fell. No rest, no stops, and still, they were too slow.

"We fight it," said Li-Bao, angry. "We pick a spot and make a stand."

"No." Valerian shook his head. "We have no chance that way. Our only hope is to move faster."

"Impossible!" said Rooker Flynn. "We cannae keep on like this."

"We can," stated the Grey Knight. "And we will." He dug his heels into his horse's sides and moved up the path at a gallop.

Rooker glared at Jack. He opened his mouth to complain and

(rath)

the stench of the beast suddenly hit them like a wave of rotting bile. Without another word, Rooker turned his horse and followed Valerian.

Black clouds rolled over the tops of the Jutts and hurtled down the mountain like a dark avalanche. Soon, they were surrounded by howling winds that threatened to rip them off the face of the mountain and send them plummeting to their deaths. Snow came in sideways sheets. The world went entirely white; no one could see more than a few feet ahead. The horses trudged through the blizzard, miserable. One of them, a chestnut mare,

the oldest of the mounts Rooker had purchased, stopped walking, fell to its fetlocks, and did not get back up again. Jack passed
the poor animal, knowing there was nothing he could do, and
the thing disappeared behind them, a white lump in the snow.

Jack shook off one of the blankets he had been using and
draped it over Dammit's neck.

The forced march continued. They moved higher, directly
into the heart of the storm. Howling winds cannoned down from
the cliffs, slashing against them, ripping between the rocks; the
sound became a caterwauling shriek that prevented any commu-
nication whatsoever, not that anyone had anything to say.

Shadow grew bigger. At first, Jack thought it was just a trick
of the light; the pup padded gamely alongside his horse, completely unaffected by the snow. But sometime after the storm
began, he realized Shadow was no longer a pup. It was now the
size of a fox terrier, dark and toothy. Jack gritted his teeth and
tried to get his panic under control. It was a losing battle—
Shadow grew stronger, feeding on his fear.

It was impossible to tell when day became night; most of
them were too tired to care. There was no rest. They just kept
moving through the white winds, cramming their eyes shut, the
horses slowly putting one foot in front of another. Jack dozed in
the saddle. He didn't dream but moved from snowstorm to
snowstorm in a white haze. At some point, he noticed Chance
was riding a different horse; his old one was gone. Jack drifted
back to sleep, feeling the storm winds rake against his body.

(rath)

He woke. The wind and the snow were gone. Jack blinked
and realized they were between two massive rocks, protected
from the open air. Valerian was off his horse, standing at a Y in
the path.

As the others dismounted, Jack got a good look at them, as
if for the first time. They were battered and beaten and bag-eyed
from the freezing cold and lack of sleep. Leah looked like ten

miles of bad road. Rooker had a permanent scowl frozen on his face. Django's woolly head and shoulders were caked with ice, and Chance's furry body had turned entirely white. Even Nightingale was a whiter shade of pale. But the worst of them, by far, was Li-Bao. The croc was made for warm, wet climates; the freezing temperature was murder on him. His salamander skin was cracked with ice and had an unhealthy-looking pallor. He had not uttered a single word of complaint, but he shivered uncontrollably, and Jack was startled to realize the croc looked close to death.

Only Memphis looked good—the trol was born for the cold of the Jutts. The rhino went to work heating the waterskins with his majik. Jack grabbed the first one, felt his numb fingers prickle from the warmth, and handed it over to Li-Bao. "Tuck this into your shirt," Jack instructed. "We need to get your core temperature up." The samurai nodded and took the hot-water bottle without comment. Under the best of circumstances, the croc was uncommunicative, but Jack was worried. Li-Bao couldn't take much more of this.

"We have a choice to make," said the knight.

All of them waited, miserable. Valerian eyed the two paths. "The right trail leads to the Narrows. It is the shortest path, but the trail is hard, and with the storm, it may be blocked." The big man turned. "The left trail will be open. But it leads to the home of the Juttlander trols. To the Horde."

Reaction to the name rippled through the group. Jack remembered Rooker's tale of the Horde attacking the Border Knights. If Memphis was the runt of the litter, Jack didn't want to imagine what the *bigger* ones looked like, much less a thousand, or ten thousand, of them. "They have no love of me there," continued Valerian. "But we may find allies against the beast."

"Great!" exclaimed Rooker Flynn. "Easy! Let's take it to the trols!" Several others nodded agreement. "Even if they dinnae help us, they'll do a helluva job slowing that black beastie down. Nothin' in the world can stand up to the Horde defendin' their young!"

"No." Jack was surprised to discover it was Memphis Kubiak who had spoken. The trol's voice was sharp. "We will not go there. I will not bring this kind of evil to the Horde."

"Why *not?*" protested Rooker. "To hear Jack tell it, yer no kin to them." Jack ducked his head, ashamed he had told Rooker Memphis's story. The pirate pointed an accusing finger at the trol. "Yer as much an exile as Nightingale."

Memphis's acorn eyes narrowed. "I will not lead that *thing* to my family."

"*Family?* Them brown-bellies left you out to *die!*"

"That doesn't matter. They're still my family."

Rooker scowled. "We lead that flamin' hunk of charcoal inta the Horde, and they'll go at it like bees on a bull. We buy us some time, slip our way through, and mebbe, what, a couple dozen damned trols get kilt in the bargain. I say that's a good deal all around."

Memphis's huge hand shot out, grabbed Rooker Flynn's chest, and yanked him into the air. The trol's face was twisted in a rage that Jack had never dreamed possible. Memphis snarled, clutching the pirate close before his sharp horn. His leathery fist gripped tighter; Rooker winced in pain as his ribs threatened to crack. *"You will not speak of my people again."*

"Memphis." Jack placed a hand on the trol's shoulder. He had never seen his friend this furious—it was frightening—but it needed to stop before Memphis did something he would regret. "Let him go." The trol's eye twitched, and for a moment, Jack thought he was going to rip the pirate in two. He let go. Rooker fell to the ground, gasping for air. When he regained his composure, he shot the trol a black look, but good sense overcame bravado; he held his tongue.

Valerian spoke: "The Narrows may be blocked." The grey man's expression was unreadable, but his flinty eyes were cold. "We may be forced to go to the Horde in the end and lose time in the bargain."

Memphis growled. "If worse comes to worst, we take Jaret's Cut."

"Jaret's Cut?" Valerian's voice became grim. "That crossing will go badly for us."

The Juttlander said nothing.

"Memphis," Valerian said softly, "I would not take us there willingly. If we go to the Horde, we *will* find help."

Memphis took a huge step forward and stood nose to nose with the knight. "I have followed you my whole life, Border-man." The trol's voice was low, laced with razors. "I have followed you without question, and I have asked nothing. I ask you now: Do *not* lead that thing to my family."

Memphis and Valerian stared each other down.

Other voices erupted, each man arguing his own opinion on which way to go. Soon, the bickering devolved into a full-scale fight as the trol and the Border Knight continued to face off in stony silence.

For the first time, Jack realized that they might never make it off the mountain. Memphis and Valerian had been his foundation, his rock—whatever happened, he knew he could depend on them. But that rock was crumbling beneath the weight of the dæmon.

And somewhere, far below, Chulurath grinned.

"Knock it off!"

A harsh, commanding voice suddenly stopped the fight cold.

Leah. Her eyes were fire. "Memphis! Remember who you are speaking to!" The rhino blinked and came out of his rage as if a spell had been broken. He ducked his head. "And *you!*" Leah turned to Valerian. "You said it was a *choice,* Father. So let us choose."

Abruptly, Leah turned to the group. "Who says we go to the Horde?"

Rooker's hand shot up. Chance nodded, raising a paw. Valerian brought up his hand. Silently, Nightingale followed the knight's lead.

"All those for the Narrows?" Memphis raised his palm; so did Leah. After a moment, Li-Bao Sen slowly raised a shivering hand and joined them.

"That's it!" Rooker slapped his hands together. "Four to three!"

"Not quite," Valerian spoke quietly. "There are still two more voices to be heard." The Border Knight turned to Jack. "What say you?"

Jack gritted his teeth. He had hoped to stay out of it, but here he was, right in the center. He glanced up at the minotaur, who had abstained from the vote as well. "Django?"

"I serve you, Black," said the bull. "Where you lead, I will follow."

Great. So it's up to me. Jack never thought he would find himself in the position of having to choose between Memphis and Valerian. He was left with two bad options—going to the trols seemed dangerous but had some scant appeal, if for no other reason than the safety of numbers; following the Narrows was faster but left them to fend for themselves. Somewhere in the back of his mind, Jack had the feeling that the dæmon was driving a wedge between them, and no matter which way he chose, it would drive them further apart.

But looking into Memphis's acorn eyes, Jack realized he had no choice at all.

"We go left," he said finally. "To the Narrows."

"So be it," said Valerian. He cast a look at Leah and kicked his horse up the narrow path to the left. Leah followed him, galloping to catch up.

Memphis smiled in relief. He put a hand on Jack's shoulder. "Thank you, boyo. Thank you." Jack nodded, and the trol followed the others up the trail.

Rooker Flynn lingered behind, sidling his horse next to Jack. "Dinnae worry about it, boychick," he said darkly. "Ya probably jest killed us all, but dinnae worry about it."

The Narrows were aptly named: towering walls of stone closed in on either side above them, looming like rocky vultures awaiting their death. Confined and cramped, the winds intensified to cruel speed that cut through the fissures like a blade. There was little room for the horses to move, and they were forced to pick their way through the channel with both eyes on the rocky crust in front of them. At some point, Jack realized the debris was not all rock; there were bones here. The skeletons of Juttlander trols, huge and white, littered the floor of the Narrows, stripped bare by years of cruel winds, their horns shredded away to nubs.

As they rose higher, the air grew thin. Oxygen came in short supply. Each breath became more and more of an effort. The horses labored, sucking air through freezing nostrils as their coats became covered in sweating foam that froze to ice.

Jack felt the eyes of his companions on him, and he regretted his decision to come here.

Shadow grew bigger. The dog was now the size of a large Labrador, speckled grey and black, pacing him on growing paws. Its tongue wagged as it watched Jack.

Guilt, came its dark voice. *Shame. Fear.*

No. Jack shook his head. *I made the choice, I live with it. Simple as that.*

But behind him, the stench of the beast grew stronger.

Sometime during their third night without sleep, they ran into the blockade. Memphis lit a torch, and in the flickering emerald flame, they saw a massive wall of stone and ice, piled a hundred feet high. Memphis could not hope to move the pile; it would take a hundred trols working a tenday without rest to make even a dent in the wall.

The Narrows were impassable.

"Trapped!" Rooker spat.

"Back!" shouted Valerian. "We must go back!"

"We can't!" yelled Chance. "*Can't you smell it?* It's right behind us!"

"We have to try," said Memphis. His voice was laced with fear. "We have to make for Jaret's Cut. *Now!*"

The Juttlander sprinted back down the path they had come, disappearing into the snow. Having no choice, the rest followed.

Backtracking, they recrossed what precious ground they had gained. The smell of the beast grew more dominant with every step; Jack gagged as the stench of burning flesh surrounded him. The horrifying tingle of the dark *wikk* burned into his skin. It felt like they were walking right into the dæmon's mouth. Every cell in his body screamed for him to run, to flee blindly away from the thing, back up to the wall, to scrabble and tear at the rocks and get away, away, away. But he forced his feet forward, moving toward the beast.

Memphis led them; the rest followed in the dark. Their hair was frozen, their skin chapped and raw. Leah fell from her horse. Jack was off his mount immediately, running. Valerian beat him to her side. Half frozen, the young woman regained her seat with their help, protesting that she was all right. As they rode on, Jack noticed Leah silently tying herself to the saddle.

They moved on, desperation pushing them. It was coming. It was close. Soon, it would take them.

When Memphis suddenly started shouting hysterical sounds at a blank ice wall, Jack was convinced the trol had finally been driven completely insane. But as the Juttlander's words disappeared in the howling winds, a crack appeared in the ice wall, revealing a hidden doorway. A tremendous rumble shook like stone. Yellow light split the ice; it rolled aside, revealing a passage as long and wide as the Lincoln Tunnel.

(rath)

A bellowing roar shook the mountain. Jack spun to find the path below blazing red flames, lit like a forest fire. It had them.

"Go! *Go!*" shouted the trol, and they drove their horses into the long dark hole. Valerian drew his sword, the knightsblade burning silver fire. As the scarlet flames of the beast grew more intense, Memphis shouted something, and the door began to rumble shut. Too slowly, it closed, shutting out the flames.

At the last possible moment, a dark clawed hand shot through the gap, reaching for them, then the door banged shut.

Jack reined up his horse and struggled to catch his breath, his heart pounding in his throat. Glancing sideways, he found the others were terrified—all except Li-Bao. The croc was sagging in his saddle, nearly dead.

"We cannot stay here," said Valerian. "It will not—"

Boom.

The door shuddered. Every eye snapped to it.

Boom, came the sound from behind the rock.

Silent, the group watched the walls shake from the blow. Snow and dust crumbled down from above. A crack appeared in the door.

Boom! Came the sound. *Boom!* It came again.

Boom! Outside, behind the rock wall, bellowed the savage roar of the dæmon.

They fled, terrified horses galloping.

Boom!

Stalactites of ice plummeted from the roof of the cave, hitting the ground around them like missiles, shattering frozen shards as the cave shuddered.

Boom!

Jack spun to see the mammoth ice-door splintering.

It split in broken chunks, every crack becoming bigger. As he watched, a piece fell away, and there, in the gap, was the burning yellow eye of the beast.

Boom!

They broke free from the far end of the tunnel, into the starlight. Far behind them, the door cracked and fell away, one edge clinging to the cave top like a broken arm. Chulurath roared.

They couldn't outrun it. Not now.

The dæmon came, its eldritch fire filling the cave with blazing light. Valerian dismounted, prepared to make his last stand. "Go! I will hold it back!"

Jack glanced up, seeing the piles of snow and rock mounted over the cave mouth. *Wait,* he said to himself, then yelled, "Rooker!"

The pirate reined in his mount. *"What?"*

"Give me Bessie!"

"What? Ya cannae fight that thing!" Jack spun his horse, snatched the blade from Rooker's scabbard, and tore it free. The singing saber screamed the shrilling sound of panic.

Gripping the thing in his fist, Jack leapt to the ground and hammered Bessie against the cave mouth like a berserker. Rooker shouted, running for him; Jack kept smashing. Bessie's screams intensified, doubling and redoubling in wave after wave of sonic fury until Jack was nearly deaf from the noise. The dæmon ran straight at him.

The sword's screams rose to a fever pitch, and then he heard it: the crack.

Above, the angled slope over the cave mouth shuddered as screaming sonics jolted it from its inertia, unable to remain still in the wake of such violent bedlam. It tore loose in a thundering avalanche of rock and snow. Jack tackled Valerian, driving the big man back as the wall came down. Twenty tons of snow and rock sloughed over the opening of the cave like a white waterfall.

Chulurath howled, then was lost, buried inside the cave.

As Jack and Valerian pried themselves from the drift, the others dragged them out. Jack was pulled free by Rooker; the pirate yanked the saber from Jack's frozen hands. "Why didn't ya jest *tell* me? I coulda…I woulda…" The pirate glanced back to see the size of the great white destruction Jack had created. "Damn, boychick."

Chance stared at the mass of snow. "How did you *do* that?"

Django pulled Jack to his feet; the minotaur's face shone with pride. "He is the Black."

"He is." Valerian smiled. The grey man sheathed his knightsblade, eyeing the collapsed cave mouth. "That won't hold it long. We have to keep going."

"Jaret's Cut isn't far," said Memphis. "We should be able to make it."

Weary to the bone, Jack dragged himself back onto his horse. As he rode on, Jack could hear, very faintly, the bellow of the beast.

Boom.

There was no rest.

A blizzard of white (not just snow but kicked-up whirlwinds of stale powder) surrounded them and blocked out everything there was to see. They rode through it, snow-blind, trusting the horses to keep their footing. Any thought of galloping was killed by the knowledge that one misstep would send them careening—rider and man alike—over the side of the cliff to their right.

Li-Bao was getting worse. The croc was unresponsive to anything they had to say, barely able to keep his eyes open. Jack tucked another hot-water bottle against the samurai's stomach, but he knew it wouldn't do much good. Li-Bao wasn't going to make it.

Surprisingly, it was Chance who stopped his horse and, with Django's help, pulled the croc into the saddle with him. The cat wrapped his furry arms around his blood enemy, doing his best to share his heat and keep Li-Bao alive.

Fuji slept cradled next to Jack's body. The tam had not stirred in hours.

Shadow had grown to the size of a Saint Bernard; its lupine head hung even with Dammit's belly. It grinned knives, its long tongue lolling over teeth white as its ice-crusted fur. It watched Jack, waiting. In his mind, Jack set up roadblocks against the panic creeping up on him, hoping he could hold it back long enough to get past Jaret's Cut. But when the dog had been fed enough fear, it would become the Wolf, and Jack knew he was not strong enough to fight it.

Chulurath was behind them. Jack could feel it—the *wikk* of the dæmon grew more powerful with each passing minute. It had broken free of the cave and continued its hunt.

Swaying back and forth in the frozen saddle, Jack pulled his hand out of his sleeve and found the tips of two of his fingers had gone black.

He stared at them blankly as if they belonged to someone else, then tucked them back inside his sleeve.

Time lost its meaning. Jack's body began to shut down. He dozed, his dreams fitful and disturbing, haunted with images of bloody murder. He tried to keep himself awake by citing medical journals: *Hypothermia: Body temperature falls below the levels required for homeostasis and operational metabolism. Stage one: Shivering, numb hands, shallow breathing.* Check. *Stage two: Weakness, slow movements, sluggish thinking. Lips, nose, and fingers become blue, or black when coupled with frostbite.* Check. *Stage three: Irrational behavior. Major organ failure. Death.*

Thum-da-dum.

Jack felt the horse moving underneath him, rhythmically swaying like his mother cradling him in her arms. *Thum-da-dum,* he sung, his eyes closed, lights swaying back and forth behind his eyelids.

Thum-da-dum.

Shadow's getting bigger. Fuji will have to bite him. Or maybe I'll put a stick in his mouth.

Thum-da-dum.

Valerian's got the bucket. There's pirates in the bucket, and they want their lizard-man back.

Thum-da-dum,
'cause here we come,
we've got a bucket of chewing gum.
I've got some,
you've got none,
let's go to the party and have some fun.
Thum-da-dum.
It's right behind you.

Jack snapped out of his daze and whipped his head around.

He could see nothing—the world was white. It wasn't just snow now; the air was *thick*. Maybe they had ridden into a fog-bank, or a cloud.

Maybe I'm still asleep.

He realized he was alone.

Jack's eyes darted through the white, but he couldn't see more than five feet in front of him. Everything—Valerian, Rooker, Leah, the horses, even the path—was gone. Only Fuji and Shadow were with him. Frightened, Jack called out, hoping for a response, but got none. He yelled louder, "Valerian! Memphis!" but was answered only by the shrieking of the wind.

Alone.

He grabbed the joint of wood at his belt and—*takatakatak!*—Nepenthe came together in his hand. It felt reassuring, but he spurred his horse faster, hoping he had simply fallen behind. After several minutes, there was no sign of anyone. Even his own hoofprints had been wiped away by the wind. He felt panic rising in his throat. He looked down and saw Shadow staring up at him, the hound's eyes hungry.

No. Stop it. Think.

If they weren't ahead, they were behind. Either way, he could find them; the path was narrow and there had been no breaks. *Or had there?* He glanced up and saw a patch of clear blue sky overhead. *If only there were some way I could get up th—*

Nepenthe flashed. A purr rippled through Jack's arm. The top joint of the staff went *thwonk* and shot up like a mortar shell. Jack watched the gossamer-thin line trail up behind it. Twin knives snapped out and sunk into the rock ledge above.

"Oh, n—"

Jack was ripped into the air. Gripping Nepenthe in white knuckles, he shot upward, flew over the lip of rock, and landed awkwardly on the peak. Twin blades retracted with a *snak*, and the joint fell free from the rock. It darted back to Nepenthe with a sharp blue *tak.*

Woah.

Nightingale didn't show me that. *I wonder if—*

His thought cut off sharply as he spotted Valerian's horse below. The knight was not far ahead, less than a quarter of a mile. As the cloud cleared, Jack realized the group was moving toward the edge of a huge precipice. Memphis and Rooker were arguing, both pointing back along the trail. Valerian and Nightingale were already retracing their steps, Django and Leah at their heels.

Jack heard the wind stop. The air grew eerily still. The scars on his chest suddenly burned hot.

(RATH)

Jack spun to find a massive black claw reaching over the edge of his rock. Snow sizzled, turning to steam beneath the burning talons. One curled horn crested the ridge, then another. And then, those wicked, gleaming yellow eyes.

(Chu-lu-Rath)

Chulurath roared. The sound buffeted against Jack, only feet away from the beast's gaping maw. As one claw came for him, Jack threw himself over the ledge.

The snow saved his life. Without it, he would have bounced down the rock like a bag of meat. As it was, he slid. He rebounded off a rock, got spun around, slipped on his backside, and shot out over the path. At the last instant, his hand caught the foot of the trail—he held on to the edge with three fingers, hanging over a bottomless nothing. Jack dragged himself over the cliff, ran to his horse—and *rode.*

He galloped past Valerian, shouting a warning. The others reared their mounts to follow his escape. Heedless of the danger, Jack pushed the terrified nag to its limit; when he reached Memphis, he barely pulled her up in time to stop her from going over the precipice.

"It's here!"

"Come on!" shouted Memphis.

They ran. They rounded a rock face and found themselves at a ledge—the end of the trail.

"This is it! This is Jaret's Cut!"

The drop went down forever. Far below, Jack could see clouds drifting by, giving a false bottom to the abyss; beneath them were miles of open air. Across the chasm, nearly fifty yards away, was a ledge with a wide, clear path that ran parallel to the one on which they stood. A thin, rickety wooden rope bridge had once connected the two sides of the gap but now hung limply against the stone face on the far side, cut away from the posts on the near edge.

Jaret's Cut was a dead end.

"*No!*" The trol's eyes went wide.

Jack had led them here. He had led them to this.

Somewhere behind, too close, Chulurath roared victory.

Rooker Flynn came, then the Trio. Shock hit them as they saw the trap—they could not go forward; they could not go back. A sudden growl sounded in Django's throat.

"We have to—"Leah began.

"Have to *what?*" shouted Rooker. "We're *cooked!*" He drew the singing saber and turned to face the beast with a wild daredevil look in his eyes.

Django unslung his battle-axe. "This is as good a place to die as any." He eyed Jack. "And with good people."

Jack gripped Nepenthe, but the purr of her *wikk* gave him little hope.

Valerian and Nightingale arrived last; they immediately realized the hopelessness of their situation. Nightingale was off his horse in a heartbeat. He strode to the ledge and stared across the gap. Valerian unsheathed his knightsblade, his face dark.

"Get ready."

Jack felt Nightingale's cloak brush up against him, and he turned. The elf stood at the very edge of the precipice, eyeing the far side with an intense stare. With one quick motion, he drew the longbow from his back, nocked an arrow, and let it fly.

As the shaft sped from the bow, something caught the butt: a silvery strand identical to Nepenthe's. The arrow arced away; the line sped out, attached to the bow. The peacock-feathered shaft flew straight, then fell down, down, down into the clouds and disappeared. Far away, Jack heard a quiet *thok.*

Nightingale grinned. He gripped the silver strand and pulled. Hand over hand, he drew the line taut, reeling it in. And as it came, Jack saw what Nightingale had hit: the arrow was sunk fast into the frayed rope that had once connected the bridge to the near side. As Jack stared, the rope-bridge rose from the clouds like a miracle.

"Django! Help us!" Jack leapt to Nightingale's side and pulled. With the bull's help, the bridge came, foot by foot, until it arrived at the ledge. Quickly, the elf lashed the rope to the bridge posts, and Jaret's Cut was open.

Chulurath roared, sensing hope. Its flames grew brighter, nearer, closer. It would not be denied.

Together, Jack and Valerian pushed Leah onto the bridge. She took one look back, then ran on light feet across the abyss. Nightingale followed her, then Django, the big bull carefully picking his way over the rotten wood. Chance slung Li-Bao's arm over his shoulder and led him across. Rooker gripped his saber, still spoiling for a fight, then bolted after them.

"I'm last," said the knight, standing his ground. "Go."

"Come on, Memphis," urged Jack. The trol's body suddenly shrank as he took on his lizard shape—the rope bridge would never hold his real weight—Jack threw him over his shoulder, grabbed Fuji under one arm, and ran across, Shadow hot on his heels.

Jack ran, suspended over infinity. He watched his feet, stepping over the gaps in the rotten wood. Between them, he saw nothing but white. Racing as fast as he dared, he made his way across and his feet finally found stone.

He spun to find Valerian standing at the far end. The knight checked to make sure Jack had made it across, then moved out onto the bridge. The grey man only made it a few feet before his body was silhouetted from behind by the blaze of the beast.

Screaming, Chulurath burst through the snow. It lunged for the bridge. The dæmon would have reached it had it not been for the horses. Terrified, the trapped animals bucked and whinnied at the feet of the beast, looking for a way to escape, blocking its path. Enraged, Chulurath grabbed one of the horses—Django's big Clydesdale—and hurled it, screaming, off the cliff. The other animals went mad with fear. They charged past the dæmon, bucking like bulls, galloping like fury, and disappeared down the trail.

Valerian sprinted off the bridge. Leah and Rooker hacked at the bridge rope with savage blows. Across the great divide, Chulurath howled.

Everyone hacked. Shimmering steel fell. Ropes, wood, and posts splintered under the slashing fusillade, and suddenly the bridge fell free.

"*Ha!*" Jack heard himself shout. The others gave a cheer of triumph as Jaret's Cut fell into the clouds and disappeared.

Trapped on the other side, Chulurath bellowed rage. It paced back and forth, eyeing them like a rabid dog in a cage, looking for a way to attack. But there was no way it could reach them.

Jack fell back against a rock, clapping a hand to his chest, never so glad to see fifty yards of thin air.

"It can't get across!" yelled Memphis. "You see? We made it!"

Chulurath burned. Flames crackled from its black carapace, building to a thunderous crescendo.

"It'll never catch us now!" Rooker laughed. "It'll have to go back the way it ca—"

(rath)

Chulurath unleashed a savage scream

(Rath)

lunged forward

(RATH)

and jumped.

The leap was impossible.

Impossible.

It hurled itself from the side of the cliff, launching its flaming body into the chasm, burning and shrieking like a living meteor. Whatever strength it held, whatever evil compelled it, it came in suicidal rage. The beast made it halfway across the gap before it fell. Then it dropped away, below the edge of the chasm, down into the mist, and disappeared in the clouds.

Jack heard it disappear, fading down, down, down into the great deep—

Boom.

Too soon.

Boom.

The bottom was miles down. Miles.

Boom.

Jack felt the rock at his feet tremble. He looked down over the edge.

Shrouded in mist, it came up the wall.

Claws punched deep in the rock, sending showers of stone flying. *Boom.* It clawed upward. *Boom.* It came. *Boom.* It came.

Boom.

Nightingale unleashed his longbow, nocking and firing faster than Jack could see. Leah joined him, her own bolts chasing Nightingale's. They bounced off the dæmon's horns, burning to ash. Memphis shouted something incomprehensible; emerald jets of flame smashed down on the beast. It never slowed. Rooker and Django muscled a huge boulder toward the edge. Chance and Li-Bao lent their strength. Jack joined them, pushing with all his might. The boulder toppled over the edge like an anvil, falling directly at the beast's head. One claw lashed out and shattered the stone to powder.

It came.

Only Valerian Tsai did not move. He stood at the edge, his eyes closed. In one hand, he gripped the Jade knightsblade, in the other, his Grey.

The beast's head rose over the edge and *roared*.

Valerian struck. The knightsblades burned like twin stars. As they smashed into the beast's horns, one clawed hand shot out, grabbed the Jade, ripped it from Valerian's grip, and flung it into the abyss.

A burning talon shot out at Chance. The cat froze, paralyzed in fear. Li-Bao cannoned into the feral tom, knocking the cat out of the way. Talons hit the croc. A scream. Blood sprayed the air.

Li-Bao Sen fell back, his belly ripped open, his shoulder a bloody stump, his right arm gone.

Memphis charged, howling. His huge brown hands grabbed the beast's flaming arm, trying to force it from the wall. Chulurath grunted, flung one arm into the sky, and brought his fist down on Memphis like a hammer. A crunching sound split the rock; the trol's thick bones shattered like glass.

The fist withdrew. Memphis Kubiak lay still, crumpled, deformed, and broken.

Time slowed.

Jack saw it all at once: Nightingale and Leah firing madly; Rooker screaming and bashing madly with his sword; Fuji, cowering under a rock, hands clutching its head; Valerian, bloody, cradling his left arm; Chance struggling to pull Li-Bao away; and Memphis...*Memphis.*

Shadow grinned the bladed teeth of a Wolf named Fear.

…with your whole heart.

Jack charged the beast.

Chulurath struck. Jack shot out his arm. He felt the flaming claws ricochet off the skidshield. He leapt for the dæmon. His feet landed on the beast's chest. He gripped Chulurath by the horn. Fiery pain shot through his hand. The scars on his chest sizzled. He ignored it. Nepenthe flashed bright blue; twin knives snapped out, a spear tip.

Now.

He struck the beast in the one part that frightened him most—

—its eye.

Chulurath screamed.

Black jelly burst as its burning yellow eye went out like a shattered lamp. As it clapped one hand to its face in agony, it let go of the cliff—and suddenly, it was holding on to nothing at all.

They tilted backward into the white together.

Jack heard Leah scream. Standing on the dæmon's chest, his spear buried in its eye, they fell.

Into the abyss, they plummeted. Air rushed past Jack's face, ripping his hair back, burning his eyes. The dæmon's flames whickered around him. Chulurath stared at him with one blazing eye, grinning wicked teeth.

"Mine."

No.

Something punched into Jack's back like a fist. The strap around his chest suddenly jerked *hard* against his ribs. Air shot out of his lungs as he was ripped backward, away from the beast. Chulurath grabbed for him—its claws caught nothing but air. Its face twisted in a gruesome rictus of rage, screaming, the flaming devil plummeted into the clouds and was gone.

Suspended in midair, Jack grabbed the bandolier around his chest, twisted, and saw a peacock-feathered arrow buried in the leather between his shoulder blades. Another inch, and it would have severed his spine.

Above, Nightingale pulled the silver strand and brought Jack back to the world of the living.

As Jack set foot on solid ground, he found Li-Bao screaming. The croc's guts were exposed; he could see the small intestine. Chance knelt, cradling Li-Bao's head. Not stopping to think, Jack grabbed the torn flesh, forced the gash closed, shook the needle and thread from Nepenthe's hollow joint, and stitched. He shut the wound and went to work on the truncated stump of what had once been Li-Bao's right arm, cutting off the hemorrhaging blood. As he did, he heard Leah murmuring soft words, and the samurai passed out.

Memphis.

Broken and bleeding, the rhino lay like a mutilated toy. The long horn at the end of his nose was crushed to splinters. No muscle moved; no breath came. His heart was silent.

Jack bent to the trol's lips, formed a seal with his own, and gave him the kiss of life. *"Django!"* The minotaur came, jolted from his shock. "Push on his chest! Like this! Hands like *this!*" As Django began pumping, Jack exhaled into Memphis's huge lungs. *Breathe…*

Nothing.

One minute.

Nothing.

Two.

No heartbeat. Nothing.

Leah placed a hand on his shoulder. "Jack…"

He flung her arm away and kept going.

Breathe. Breathe!

Django kept pumping. The others watched, silent.

Please, dammit. Please.

Oh, God, please…

A gasp shot from Memphis's lungs. Rank air exhaled from his mouth; Jack Swift thought he'd never smelled anything so sweet.

Coughing, the rhino looked around in a daze, straining to speak. Something gurgled out of his mouth. *"Va-Valerian…"*

The Border Knight was at his side, gripping the trol's giant hand tight.

Memphis's eyes closed. "I'm…I'm sorry." Tears began to fall. "I did this."

"It's all right. Shh. Be still."

In sudden pain, Memphis gripped the knight's hand like a vice. *"Ahh!"* His eyes flashed open, a look of panic shooting across his face. "Is my dad okay? Is he all right?"

Valerian glanced at Jack, worried. "He's fine, Memphis. He's safe."

"I can…*hhh*…I can't feel my legs." Jack looked down. The tree-trunk-size bones beneath Memphis's spine were shattered, destroyed.

"Valerian," the rhino gasped, his breathing thin. "Make sure my dad's okay. I need…I want…" Memphis's voice cracked. "I want my *dad.*"

Then, Memphis Kubiak drifted away.

And the cold wind of the Jutts rose up and howled.

CALM BEFORE THE STORM

*All great things are simple,
and many can be expressed in single words:
freedom, justice, honor, duty, mercy, hope.*

Winston Churchill

Albino bats wheeled through the dawn sky in pale swirling clouds, escaping the coming sun. They disappeared by the thousands into the cave-peppered walls of the Kern. As the last creature beat an uneven retreat on one broken wing, a shriek split the wind. A kestrel plummeted down from the rising sun and hit the flying rodent with a meaty thump, talons gutting its prey. A short, terrified sound escaped the bat as it was borne off to be killed, devoured, and destroyed.

Bantam Pham knew how it felt.

Unmoving, silent, he stood his lonely post, hour after endless hour.

The morning grew hotter. Sweat rolled into his eyes, but there was no way to stop the sting, so he endured it. Spring was nearly over; the blazing heat of summer would soon roll in. But then again, it was doubtful he would live that long.

For sixty-six days, he had stood vigil, day and night, never sitting, never moving, never sleeping. In the old days, the watch would have lasted only ten hours, but the old days were over; there was no one left to relieve him. Legend had it Abrahim Qin, that crusty old badger, had once stood vigil for five months straight, back when the Nomads first took the Deuce.

If need be, Bantam could stay in this position for a year, a decade, a century—the Armor would never let him sleep—it lent him its power, keeping him alert and keen. The thought unnerved Bantam; he could stand here forever, still as the statues that lined the wall behind him, and as alone.

Nightmares plagued him.

Even awake, specters flitted before his eyes. The Armor showed him visions. He had been forced, again and again, to watch the Azure Knight die, cut down by the Crimson's blade. He saw the Amber murdered over and over. And the Titian. And the Jade. Helpless, locked in his place, Bantam Pham watched his brothers fall, one by one, over and over. It was too much to bear, but the Armor showed him more: David's Tower was ablaze.

Black-shelled creatures swarmed over dead bodies, bodies that rose up and walked. The Crimson, his brother, commanded the Fell Prince's Host, and would lead them here, to him.

Standing before the Paladine Arch, Bantam Pham, the youngest of the Border Knights, the seventh, the Indigo, waited for his time to die.

Sweat dripped into his eye. He let it sting.

Now the visor of the Indigo Armor showed him something new. There, far away, coming down from the snowy reaches of the Jutts—a small group of travelers.

As Bantam looked closer, he saw one man he knew very well.

His captain—the Grey.

And for the first time in days, Bantam Pham allowed himself to hope.

Hope is a dangerous thing.

It can keep a man going when all seems lost, can keep him standing, keep him fighting. But when nothing is left but despair, nothing but blackness and panic and the promise of death, the tiniest sliver of hope—the narrowest thread—can seem as solid as a steel cable. That thread bears the illusion of stability, of substance, of strength, but it is only a fool's fantasy. Hope is delicate. Hope is fragile. And a man can grip it too tightly.

Bantam seized it like a drowning man.

He had long ago abandoned himself to death, forgotten what it was like to even hope for survival. The strange prospect of *living* grew vital in his heart; the idea built, relentlessly, from dream to demand. A sense of reprieve washed over him like a condemned man pulled from beneath the executioner's axe.

He would never go back to that.

Never.

Bantam Pham took hold of hope, and it took hold of him.

He would live.

No matter what it took.

They carried Memphis down the mountain. Jack rigged a *travois*, a kind of triangular stretcher, to drag the trol's massive weight. They took turns hauling him down, step by step, but the brunt of the work always fell on Django's big shoulders. Li-Bao insisted on walking (he refused to let anyone carry him), and Jack was forced to repair the popped stitches in the croc's gut every few hours. Chance never left the samurai's side, hooked under Li-Bao's one remaining arm like a furry crutch.

They came around a rock, spied the Kern, and for the first time, Jack understood how powerful the elves were. A massive ring of white volcanoes circled the valley below, extending away to the north and west. It was impossible to tell how big the Kern was—even from this height, Jack could not see the far end of the ring. Masked by the wisps of pale smoke that eddied up from the volcanoes, the Elder Wood was completely hidden from view.

Jack immediately realized two things: one, the volcanoes were the natural result of the elven majik; the entire Kern was (in geological terms) brand-spanking new, still cooling a hundred years after the sheer power of its creation. The second: it was a perfect defense.

There was only one entrance—the Paladine Arch.

It was beautiful. Thirty feet high, the marble-white wall formed a semicircle around the base of the Kern, but it was more than a barricade—it was a monument. Intricate patterns laced the stonework: marble vines, lilting bas-relief, and leafy stone palms decorated its entire length. As they drew closer, Jack could not tell where one stone ended and the next began—it seemed as if the Paladine were carved out of one tremendous block of white stone. Half a dozen statues of men, tall and proud, stood recessed in the stone on either side of the entrance—the Arch itself.

It curved high above the rest of the wall, narrow and majestic, the white crown of the Paladine. There were no gates, no doors, no barriers. The Paladine Arch stood open, as it always had.

The Indigo Knight stood vigil before the entrance, his knightsblade buried into the ground between his feet, a perfect replica of the statues lining the wall behind him.

"Hold," came the booming voice from within the Indigo helm. "What is your intent?"

Valerian Tsai stepped forward. "To defend the Fair Folk from all who would do them harm."

"Then welcome home, my captain." The knight pulled the helmet off, revealing the smiling, sweaty face of a young man not much older than Jack. "Valerian." The Indigo Knight embraced the grey man tight.

"Brother." A smile crossed Valerian's tired face.

"Brother."

The Grey Knight turned to his daughter. "Leah, get the rest inside."

She led them under the Arch. The compound inside was not large; the stone buildings within were simple and unadorned, save for a single statue of a man in the middle of the courtyard. The place was absolutely empty; Jack got the feeling no one had been here for a long time—then he remembered the Border Watch should have been the ones to occupy this place.

Django pulled Memphis inside one of the bunkhouses, moved two large mats together, and deposited the trol on top of them. Chance led the croc to a bed.

Had it not been for Xiang-lo's surgery, Li-Bao would have died. But Memphis's satchel still contained the leftover medicines from the appendectomy. The Betadine and hydrogen peroxide had kept Li-Bao's wounds from going rancid during the arduous trip down from the Jutts. The only thing that would help the samurai now was rest. His arm was gone forever, but he would live.

Memphis was a different story.

He had never regained consciousness. The major bones in the rhino's legs were completely shattered. No splint or cast would fix him; even the best medical facility in the United States of America would have difficulty saving his legs.

Memphis's reconstruction would take a dozen specialists working day and night—Jack did not possess a fraction of the skill necessary to perform that kind of surgery.

The trol would never walk again.

But being a cripple was the least of his worries. Septicemia, blood poisoning, had taken over his body. The Juttlander's heart rate was all over the place, sometimes galloping, sometimes barely evident; his breathing was shallow and rapid, his skin feverish to the touch—the thermometer from the trol's satchel read 115 degrees. That alone was more than enough to kill a man, but the rhino's physiology was a complete mystery—Jack had no idea what Memphis's temperature *should* be, even in the best of circumstances.

Only one thing was clear: Memphis Kubiak was dying.

So far, Jack had been able to hold the infection back with antibiotics; the lincomycin injections seemed to work best on the trol's strange immune system, but he absorbed them at an alarming rate, and the infection was progressing. Soon, the dwindling supply of injections would be gone, and then, it would be just a matter of time.

Jack fingered the glass ampules of antibiotic in his hand like precious diamonds. He placed his other hand on Memphis's sweating forehead. It was impossible to believe this colossus who had once seemed so terrifyingly strong, so invincible, could be made so fragile.

"Stay with me, Memphis. You fight this."

The trol did not respond.

When Jack came outside, he found two Border Knights arguing.

"I don't understand you," said the Grey. "Why wouldn't you let them in?"

"I didn't think it was right," replied the Indigo. "I don't know what they're planning. They could be spies for *him*."

The knights were talking about a small group of people camped outside the Arch. Jack hadn't seen them on the way in—they were huddled at the far end of the wall. A disparate group, mismatched travelers, the people looked like they had been there for a while. They came out of their tents now, watching.

"It is not our occupation to deny pilgrims," said Valerian sharply. "We protect the elves from invasion, not guests."

"I don't thi—"

"Let them in."

The man named Bantam Pham hesitated. Valerian stepped forward. "You have not been relieved, Border Knight. You still stand vigil." His voice was hard. "Let them *in*."

Nervously, one by one, the pilgrims came forward. From behind his armored helm, the Indigo Knight asked each: "What is your intent?" The answers varied; some sought knowledge, others majik, some were simply curious, but each reply amounted to the same thing: *to see the elves.* As Bantam allowed them to pass, each traveler walked under the Arch, through the courtyard, to the wall of the Kern. There, between the rocks, was a narrow cave, little more than a crack in the rock—the only passage into the Elder Wood. The pilgrims disappeared into the cave and were gone.

Leah, Rooker, and Django came out to watch the silent procession. As the last of the men vanished into the Elder, Jack found himself wanting to follow them inside.

When the final pilgrim had gone, the Indigo Knight turned to Valerian. "Relieve me."

The grey man sighed. "Bantam, I am weary to the bone. You can s—"

"Relieve me." The Indigo Knight's voice was quiet.

Valerian's steely eyes stared at him. Slowly, he drew the Grey knightsblade and drove it into the ground next to the Indigo with an authoritative *thump.* "You are relieved."

Bantam Pham unbuckled his helmet and tucked it under his arm. His youthful face was tarnished by an uneasy look. His voice quavered: "They're all dead, aren't they?"

The grey man exhaled a breath and nodded. "All save Campion."

"He betrayed us."

"Yes."

"He commands the Fell Host."

"Yes."

"He brings them here."

"Yes."

"Valerian." The young knight's eyes grew desperate. "Valerian, we cannot possibly survive. Not against an army. Not without the Watch. Not without the other *knights.*"

"Bantam." The big man placed one steady hand on the Indigo Knight's shoulder. "We will defend the Paladine as we always have."

"*How?* Just you and I, alone, standing against the assembled might of the Necrórceror?"

"If need be."

"It's impossible!"

"We have done impossible things before."

"Valerian. We cannot stand."

The Grey Knight eyed the younger man. "We took an oath, Bantam. Remember that."

"An oath to each other! Not to *them!*" Bantam thrust one arm at the entrance to the Elder. "They *never* asked us to defend them. Never! And they have never given us help, not *once.*"

"You forget yourself, Border Knight." Valerian's voice took on an edge. "The elves gave us our blades. They gave us our Armor." Valerian stepped closer, his eyes stern. "And they gave us all much more than that, long before you and I were born."

Bantam lowered his head.

Valerian stared the Indigo Knight down. "We will stand."

"They will kill us."

"They will try."

"We will die here."

"Bantam." The knight smiled. "Are you so afraid to die that you would live a coward?"

Bantam suddenly threw his helmet to the ground. "Better to live a coward than die a hero." He stepped away from the Grey Knight, his face hard. "You have relieved me of the vigil."

Valerian grew still, his face lined with remorse. After a moment of silence, a quiet voice came from his lips. "I have."

The Indigo Knight unbuckled his breastplate and let it drop to the ground. "It is finished." He tore off his vambraces. "The men I swore allegiance to are dead." He discarded his gauntlets. "I renounce my oath." The Indigo Armor fell to pieces around his feet.

Jack stared, unable to believe what he was seeing.

"Don't do this, Bantam." Valerian's voice was low. "It will haunt you."

"Come *with* me, Valerian," the Indigo Knight pleaded. "Come with me back home. We have centuries left to us, even without the Armor. We can be happy. We can be *free*." Bantam opened his palm. "Come home."

Valerian stared at the ground. "My place is here. *Your* place is here."

"Not anymore." The young man plucked the Indigo knightsblade from the ground. The grey man did not look up, nor did he try to stop him.

"Goodbye, Captain." Bantam Pham gripped the pommel of his sword and walked away into the wilderness, away from the Paladine Arch.

Valerian Tsai stood alone.

As the Grey Knight picked up the pieces of the scattered Armor, Leah came to him. Her expression was worried, but after a few quiet words, she went back inside the Arch. The grey man silently carried the Armor out along the wall.

Jack followed.

"Can I come with you?"

The grey man looked tired, beaten. "I would like that."

Along the wall, six statues stood like frozen sentries, each one nestled within its own smaller version of the Arch. No birds nested there; no spiders crafted webs to catch their prey; the statues were pristine. Man-high, crafted with meticulous skill, the stone warriors looked almost real. Each figure was adorned in its Border Armor, smooth and polished, untouched by the elements. Valerian stopped before one. Jack looked up.

Abrahim Qin. Cast in stone, the old walnut stood big as life, dressed in shining cobalt-blue Armor. Wizened eyes peered out from stone brows, a glistening helmet clasped at his hip. It was a perfect likeness: even now, the statue looked ready to bark instructions to its students. Valerian drew the Azure knightsblade from its sheath at his back, presenting it flat in both hands. "I have returned what is yours, Border Knight."

Abrahim moved. Stone grated against stone as the statue lifted one heavy foot and stepped down off the pedestal. Jack took a step back as the thing came. It reached out, silently took the Azure knightsblade from Valerian's hands, and bowed low. Valerian's quiet voice came: "I will miss you, Abrahim. You were my rock. Rest easy, my friend." Abrahim's statue resumed its perch. It planted the sword tip between its feet and placed the helmet over its head, obscuring the face forever.

Valerian moved down the wall. Jack saw the other knights of the Paladine: the Jade, the Titian, and the Amber, each statue suited in shining plate armor, etched in their individual color. All wore their helmets. All were missing their swords. Valerian had carried the Jade knightsblade since Glyn Aker, but it had fallen from Jaret's Cut and now lay somewhere at the base of the Jutts, lost.

Valerian stopped at the statue of the Indigo Knight. "Kneel," he said. A perfect replica of Bantam Pham obeyed his command. Valerian adorned the statue with the Indigo Armor, strapping on the gauntlets, gorget, breastplate, and greaves. Finally, he presented the Indigo helm. The statue took it. "Cover your face," said the grey man as he turned away. The statue did, and then resumed its post, silent.

Last came Campion Rei. His handsome countenance looked out over the plains, hair swept back over his brow, eyes sharp and alert: the model of what a hero should look like. Of all the statues, only the Crimson was without Armor—the man wore it now. As Valerian stared at that perfect face, Jack suddenly realized the grey man looked old: hard lines were etched in his face, deep shadows darkened his brow, his eyes were careworn and tired. "You were my brother, Campion," came the old man's cracking voice. "I loved you as my own. But you have no place here now. Begone." At Valerian's word, the statue disintegrated. Campion's hair became ash and dust; his handsome face melted away. His chest and legs crumbled, falling in a powdered cloud of sand that scattered into the wind until nothing remained on the dais but dust, and then that, too, was gone.

Valerian sat down against the pedestal. Jack joined him. They sat like that for a long time.

"The statues can't help you," said Jack. "Right?"

Valerian shook his head. "They are not men."

"And none of us can wear the Armor."

"No."

"Can we at least close the gates?"

"There are no gates, Jack. The Paladine cannot be shut. The way to the elves has always stood open, and always will."

Jack hesitated. He dreaded the next question. "So why defend them? They're more powerful than any of us, Valerian. They can build mountains; they can build whole *worlds.* Why fight their battle for them?"

Valerian nodded. "They could hold, for a while. Their majik could confuse the enemy, trap him. But they will not kill. And eventually, they would be overrun. They would fall."

"But I don't understand. I know you took an oath, but…why do you defend them?"

Valerian sighed. "The elves gave birth to Keymark, Jack. They are the wellspring of our lives. Would you allow someone to destroy your mother? Or your father?"

Jack thought of the moment he had attacked Rooker Flynn when the pirate insulted his father. Of Memphis, slowly dying because he would not lead the beast to his family. Of the way his own little hands had torn at the rocks that buried his dad.

"No. I wouldn't."

"Then you understand."

Inside the Arch, at the center of the courtyard, stood one last statue: Valerian Tsai. A perfect replica of the grey man, the statue was clad in stark grey Armor etched with thin, intricate lines of shining silver filigree. Like all the others, the Armor was a heroic blend of a European plate and feudal Japanese, but the Grey was—Jack thought—the most magnificent.

"I am Valerian Tsai, first of the Border Knights," said the grey man. "I have returned to uphold my oath." The statue knelt before him. Slowly, reverently, Valerian Tsai adorned himself in steel, encasing his body in the raiment of the knight. Leah and Nightingale watched. Rooker and the Trio were silent. Even Fuji and the dog looked on.

Armored, Valerian held his helmet at his hip and turned to face them. His voice seemed different—more powerful, deeper. "None of you are bound to this place by duty or honor. You may go, back to your homes, or past the Kern into the Elder. I urge you now: escape the battle that comes."

No one moved. Not one of them.

Leah watched her father, pride shining out of her like a beacon.

Wordlessly, the Grey Knight donned his helmet and moved to the sword waiting for him before the Paladine Arch.

The last of the Border Knights stood vigil.

Jack woke up with his head lying on Memphis's arm. He shook the cobwebs from his brain; his limbs felt wooden and slow. He yawned, checking on Memphis. The trol was still unconscious, unchanged. Jack snapped an ampule, injected the antibiotic, and stepped outside, stretching.

It was well past noon. Jack flicked his arms, trying to get his body to wake up. As he walked, he saw Rooker Flynn standing on the parapet behind the wall. The pirate had a satchel full of spears and was sharpening their tips against a whetstone. Rooker spied Jack and grinned. "Morning. You look like a kekubi, walking around like that." He handed over a steaming tin pot of coffee. "Have a cuppa."

"Mmph." The stuff was hot, thick as lava, and tasted horrible. Jack took a look around. Nightingale and Chance stood together above the Arch, keeping one eye on the open plains beyond. The rest of the compound was deserted. He took another sip of the coffee.

"Get yer eyes open, boychick. Ya been asleep a day anna half."

Jack blinked. "What?"

"Jutts musta taken it outta you. Django too. Leah's up, though. Girl's tough as rocks."

A day and a half. Jack shook his head; he still felt exhausted. "You want some help?"

"Nar, jest puttin' an edge on." He finished sharpening the spear tip, placed it against the wall, and moved on to the next. "Figure we'll need more than one."

"I'm kind of surprised you're sticking around."

Rooker stopped. His silky eyes narrowed. "Now, why's that?"

Jack shrugged. "For one, you don't think much of the elves."

"*Ehh.*" Rooker shrugged. "Never really met one before. Nightingale's alright."

"Rooker. There's nothing in it for you."

"O *really?*" Rooker grinned. "Nothing? Boychick: When this is over, they're gonna make songs about us. Long ones. Loud ones. Live or die, they're gonna *remember* us. Good stories are the only way men can hope to live forever. And I aim to make sure I get my own verse." He flicked the spear tip. "Besides. I'm sticking with my lucky penny. And yer still here, ain't ya?"

Jack was forced to grin. "I guess I am."

"Good." The pirate went back to work. "Now go wake up somewhere else. Yer breathin' my air."

Jack looked around for something to occupy himself. The battlements were already well stocked with food and water, provisions intended for the much larger Watch; it would take a year for them to exhaust all the supplies. Spears, swords, and shields were waiting at every turn, an extensive armory within easy reach of every conceivable defensive point. Jack soon realized there simply wasn't anything to do but wait.

He found himself circling back toward the entrance to the Elder Wood, drawn like a moth to a flame. The cave was smooth and narrow, just big enough for a horse. At the end of the passage stood a simple wooden gate, only hip high and partly open. Beyond it, he could make out nothing but a warm golden-green light: a soft, inviting glow that hinted at a whole new world beyond.

"You can go inside." Jack turned to find Leah standing by his side. The glimmering light from within the Elder caught her features. Her eyes sparkled. "I've been there once. When I was a child. It's…it's beautiful."

The longing in her eyes struck him. He turned to watch the glowing light, humming with a green *wikk* all its own. Jack felt the Elder Wood calling to him, beckoning him to come, promising sweetness and wonder and delight like he had never known, not since he was a child and all was right with the world.

"No." Jack turned away. "No. If I went there…I have a feeling I might not come back."

Leah smiled faintly, nodding. "I know what you mean."

They walked on together, leaving the small gate behind.

They passed beyond the compound into the thick woods contained within the Paladine. The wall was bigger than it looked; they were soon lost in the green. Jack stared up at the mountainous Kern. It was so strange to see *white* volcanoes; they were usually black, the color of hardened lava, and never grew so close together. The thick veins of sulfur, too, were white, and emitted none of the usual hellish smell. Even the fumes were odorless. The Kern should have been evil and forbidding, a dark tower of lava; the elves had somehow made it good.

Jack and Leah walked alone, silent in each other's company. Both of them knew this might be their last time alone together—or together at all. As they walked, Leah took his arm, holding him close. He said nothing; neither did she.

They walked that way, listening to the breeze and the birds, watching the glorious setting sun, and for a time, everything was perfect.

Jack fought the urge to speak, knowing he would ruin it, but in the end, he couldn't resist. "Leah"—he cleared his throat—"if we make it out of this, maybe you and I could—"

Leah suddenly laughed. Jack stopped short. "What?"

"Oh, Jahk." Leah smiled, still laughing. "What in the *world* makes you think we're going to make it out of this?"

She said it simply, without regret, without fear. And it was in that moment that he finally knew for certain: they had no chance.

She brushed the hair away from his face, her eyes shining. "If you're going to say something to me, you'd better do it soon."

"I—"

Bats—an army of bats—leaped from a nearby cave, woken by the setting sun. Like the volcanoes, they were alabaster white, and burst from the cave as smoke from a gun. Screeching, they whirled away into the Jutts, hunting for their nightly meal.

The idea hit Jack all at once, like jumping into freezing water. His eyes lit up, brilliant, watching the white cloud circle off into the sunset. "Bats—"

"Bats?" Confused, Leah stared at him. "*That's* what you want to say to me?"

But Jack Swift did not hear her; he was far away, buried in books, flipping through countless pages, lost in a lifetime of learning. "I've got to find that cave." He plunged up the hill, leaving Leah behind.

"Jahk! What the devil are you—"

He ignored her. The idea gripped him: a crazy, stupid, impossible idea.

A shrieking yowl suddenly sounded from the Paladine—Chance calling the alarm. Jack and Leah stopped short, staring in the direction of the cry.

They ran for the Arch.

Jack sprinted up the battlements.

Django was already there, standing alongside Chance and Nightingale. Even Li-Bao had come, gripping a scimitar in his one remaining hand. As Jack took his place beside Rooker Flynn, the emotion that hit him was not fear but confusion. He didn't have elf eyes, or even Chance's sight, but from here, the Fell Host looked tiny, almost insignificant. The invading army that threatened to massacre them all couldn't have consisted of more than a few hundred men.

They didn't seem to be monsters, just a ragged assortment of figures moving purposefully across the open fields toward the Arch. Maybe it was a scouting party. Or better yet (Jack thought crazily) this was all that was left of the Necrórceror's army.

Django Barón pulled back on the gigantic longbow he had found in the armory; the weapon was twice as long and twice as thick as a pool cue. The arrow was the size of a sapling—an arrow made for a giant. The bull's mighty muscles flexed, pulling the bowstring back as far as he could; the weapon quivered from the strain. Nightingale was by far the best archer of the bunch, but the minotaur had range.

"Hold!" came Valerian's sharp voice from below.

Nightingale suddenly lowered his bow. Chance and Django did the same. "Well," came the cat's curious voice. "*This* is interesting."

The approaching group was not versläng, not zombies, not dark monsters. They were men. Jaelin men, jinx-cats, llystra crocs, hammer-dwarves, long-legged runners, even Red Dwarves, accompanied by a ragged assortment of wagons, carts, horses, mules, dogs, and tams. As they approached the Paladine, Jack saw the travelers were divided into two separate groups that never quite came together as one.

The Grey Knight's voice rang out. "What is your intent?"

The two groups stopped and looked to each other, unsure who should speak first. From the smaller group, a man came forward: a huge barrel-chested dark man, a hammer slung over one shoulder, his head bald as a bowling ball.

Hatch the Smith.

"We come to lend our arms." The leader of the Tucumcaris placed the hammer between his feet with a *thud.* "We come to aid the Border Knights." Hatch glanced up to see the man in black standing above. "We come"—he looked Jack right in the eye—"for Black Jack."

A bellow of voices erupted from the crowd; Hatch must have brought every man in Tucumcari. "He saved our village from the great wyrm," the smith continued. "He gave us wealth beyond imagining and asked nothing in return." Another cry rang out from the Tucumcaris. Hatch's eyes found Jack again, and a rare smile crossed his face. "We are here to return the honor."

"We come for the Black as well," came a voice from the second group. A stunning blonde woman limped forward, dressed in flowing garments of silk. Jack recognized her face but had never known her name. The last time he had seen her, the fine clothes had been singed and burned, her hair caked with blood, her leg torn open by claws, screaming pain in a crowded, dirty carpenter's shop. "I am Karen Jase, regent of Rimmy's Cull." Her voice was powerful and bold. "The Black healed my people from the venom of the versläng. He healed me." She glanced up at Jack; a proud expression came over her face. "We are here for *him.*"

Last, a lone man stepped forward from the crowd. He removed his hat, balling it up in his hands nervously. "I...I come for Black Jack. And I come for Valerian Grey. And…and I come for all of you. My name is Andy Ibis and—"The thin tailor from Glyn Aker finally stood straight, his voice brimming with emotion: "You saved my wife and my *son*." He swallowed back tears, nodding. "I'm here to do what I can."

Silence from the crowd; then, suddenly, together, they were cheering. Hands slapped Andy Ibis on the back, thumping him merrily.

As the shouting died down, Valerian's thunderous voice split the air. "How did you know we were here?"

"Ah," came a high tenor voice. "I'm afraid *I'm* responsible for that." The long-legged runner named Finnegan rose above the crowd. He looked exhausted; the fur on his legs was dirty and matted with a thousand miles of mud. "I, ah, I followed you. From Tucumcari to Glyn Aker, to the base of the Jutts. I was hiding when you spoke to the Necrórceror, when you tricked him."

The deadeye, Jack thought. So the shadow in the woods who had escaped had been Finnegan—no wonder Nightingale or Chance couldn't catch him. "I told Hatch," the runner said. "He got the village together and we moved out to find you. We ran into the Regent's people along the way, who were headed for Highyon Garde and, well…" Finnegan shrugged, apologetic. "Here we are."

"Go home." Valerian's voice came quietly. "I see farmers and artisans, bankers and tradesmen. Your intentions are noble, but you are not warriors. I cannot defend you all. Go home, or pass the Kern into the Elder and take what safety the elves can offer. There is nothing you can do here but die."

Hatch stepped toward the knight. "We will have no homes to go to, Valerian-*jai*. They will be burnt, razed, and destroyed. If the Fell Prince takes the Elder, and the *wikk* of the elves, there will be nothing left at all. You are the final chance for our wives, our husbands, and our children." Hatch gripped his hammer. "We will make our last stand with *you*."

Cheers broke out from the crowd, the loudest yes.

It was impossible to see beneath Valerian's helmet, but Jack swore he could feel the big man smile.

"You mean no harm to the elves, and so I cannot hinder you. Welcome, friends."

As they came through the Paladine Arch, every last one of the volunteers touched the legendary Border Knight; their hands ran over his Armor, drawing strength from the steel, and the man.

Hatch came with gifts.

Blades made from the jabberwok's teeth and bones, carved without flourish, but razor sharp; suits of chain mail linked from the great wyrm's smaller scales, breastplates made from the larger ones; bracers built from its conical toes—the smith passed them out to the men as they came. Rooker Flynn quickly took the finest breastplate for himself. Chance merrily greeted the small contingent of jinx-cats from Rimmy's Cull; Li-Bao was met with silent bows from his people. Tams and horses and dogs were everywhere, and the fort became a bustling village.

As greetings were exchanged, Hatch came to Jack. They shook hands, and Jack drew him close, whispering in his ear. "You know who I am, Hatch. And you still came."

"I told you, Black. The people need hope." Hatch eyed Nepenthe. "And from the look of it, there may be good reason to believe." The smith held up a stunning vest of wyrmscale. "I made this for you," he said. The armor was well crafted and light, custom-built for Jack's frame. "And this." He presented a shield, a flat disc of spiraling scales, massive and beautiful, virtually impenetrable. "I was thinking you might have use for it."

"I do." Jack took the shield, knowing no matter how spectacular it was, he would never abandon Valerian's skidshield. "Django!" The big bull, never far away, appeared at his side.

"Yes, Black."

"Hatch, with your permission, I would like to present your gift to my lieutenant."

"As you please."

Django Barón stood dumbstruck. "Me?" The bull fell to one knee. "The Black's shield? It is an honor I do not deserve."

"Stop that." Jack smiled. "You deserve it more than anyone." Jack took the bull's arm, hauled him to his feet, and gave him the shield. The minotaur bowed his head and quickly rejoined the mustering men, a proud grin locked on his face, carrying the shield like a priceless treasure.

"You inspire more than your fair share of loyalty, boy." Hatch put his hands on his hips, watching the men assemble. "Now comes the time when you earn it."

Leah took command. Ordering men with quick, sharp direction, she had them armed and armored in half an hour, then assigned captains to take charge. Karen Jase (one of the few accustomed to combat and leadership) was one; Hatch Smith was another. Rooker Flynn was given a group of men and quickly began barking orders, delighted to have command of a real crew.

Leah called a conference to assign positions. She crafted a defense quickly, putting the majority of men on the wall with longbows, spears, and pikes, assembling fighting units for skirmishes, and a group of volunteers to stand inside the Arch behind Valerian. Her decisions came fast and final, and there was no debate. As Leah commanded the men, she reminded Jack of her father.

"I need forty men," Jack said abruptly.

All eyes fell on Black Jack. Several hands shot into the air, volunteering. Only Leah frowned. "For what?"

"Majik," he replied. He couldn't tell her the real reason (the Toshan reason) in front of everyone else. But the revelation that had struck him during their walk together might be their only hope—if only he could make it work.

"That's a quarter of our force, Jahk." A desperate look came into her eyes, silently pleading with him. She would not contradict him in front of the others, not directly, but she had few fighters and little time to prepare them. Losing so many would be devastating to her defenses. But still, she could not openly defy Black Jack.

As the silence lingered, the men grew nervous, feeling the tension between the two. Jack knew if he asked again, Leah would have to give in. He glanced down and saw Fuji, the little gecko licking his fingers, unaware of the conversation around him.

"Tams," Jack found himself saying. "Give me tams."

"Tams?" came the response from several surprised voices. Someone laughed.

"Take all you want!"

"Take the *dogs* while you're at it!"

"They're worthless!"

Rooker Flynn eyed Jack, scratching his chin. "O, I dunno. Ya might be surprised what ol' Jack can do with *worthless.*"

At the entrance to the cave, the tams gathered. Dozens of them, crawling over the rocks, a moving mass of color. Jack could see why the people of Keymark had written them off—they moved without purpose, skittering to and fro, eating bugs and licking themselves. When he tried to gather them together, not even half obeyed, and the ones that did were quickly distracted and went back to playing.

Fuji arrived with the last of the bunch; Jack quickly began signing: *Get them together. They all need to hear this, and understand. They need to listen. Can you do that?*

In response, Fuji chirruped loudly, and every gecko head shot up. They came quickly, gathering together in a rainbow-colored pile of pebbled bodies. Fuji glanced up at Jack. *Ready.*

Tell them we're going to build a kiln…an oven. We need rocks and lots of wood to burn. We're going to boil off the vein from the side of this hill. We're going to need all the charcoal from the camp piled up over here, and buckets, and shovels for the guano, and—

Wait-wait-wait, signed the tam. It was too much all at once. *What is guano?*

Bat droppings. Their…their feces.

Fuji gave Jack a strange look. *Bat feces?*

Jack sighed. It was too much to explain, and he had no time. *Will they do what I tell them?*

Of course. They are tam.

Can they count?

Fuji smiled proudly. *Tam count good. All the way up to sixteen—fingers and toes.*

Good enough. This is what we're making.

Jack picked up a rock and scratched this onto the cave wall:

Tell them to get rocks and wood. We'll go from there.

Fuji relayed the orders; the tams instantly launched themselves to the task, scurrying into the forest. As they went, Jack leaned against the cave wall.

It won't work. It can't. I've never done this before—never built something from scratch. My lab partners are amphibians. They can't understand me or count to seventeen. And I have no time, no time.

It won't work. It can't.

Shadow padded over the ground nearby, eyeing him. Waiting.

But damned if I'm not going to try.

The kiln was built in two hours, fired up and burning.

Tams worked in frenzy, scuttling from one task to the next without pause. They ran like greased lightning, sometimes alone, sometimes in teams, gathering everything together in the blink of an eye and going back for more. They never stopped moving, single-minded in their purpose, following every command to the last detail with ruthless efficiency.

When night came, they did not stop. When they were told to go into the cave, into the dark, and dig through ten-foot piles of bat crap, they never hesitated. When, at midnight, the sulfur finally started bubbling out of the rock in white-hot pools and three of them were badly burned, they never quit. When the sun came up and Jack finally fell asleep, exhausted, they kept working. The tams simply would not stop.

Within the Paladine Arch, the men nervously watched the firelight flickering from the caves. They had come here for Black Jack, but their hero's legend grew stranger with each passing moment. Scuttlebutt passed from one man to the next as rumor gave way to wild speculation. He was preparing majik, one man claimed, to immolate the Fell Host. Another confirmed the Black was creating some kind of huge golem, a monster to crush the Crimson Traitor. He was bringing the elves to fight. He was summoning the Border Knights back from the dead. He was calling upon the White Lady herself. And with each new tall tale, their hopes grew to something like courage.

At noon the second day, Jack gathered his created components, crushed them down with mortar and pestle, measured them out according to the formula, and combined them together. As he prepared the final mixture, he heard Shadow in his head, the Wolf's voice mixed with his own:

It won't work. It can't work. The sulfur here isn't even yellow—maybe it's not even sulfur. The ammonia in the bat crap won't work. The measurements will be off. You remembered it wrong. It won't work. It won't work.

But it worked.

By God, it *worked.*

Jack Swift stood over Memphis's limp body, wishing.

Wishing the trol would come back. Wishing he would smile again, laugh again. Wishing he would just wake up. But the trol's pulse had dwindled to virtually nothing—there were six seconds between every heartbeat—six agonizing seconds that Jack was sure Memphis was dead. Then the low, deep *tha-thump* came from his dying football-size heart, and another eternity would begin.

Jack had left the tams to their work. They were not smart, they were not clever, but they were obedient. He had shown them how to mix the formula, and after the fifth batch, they had not varied from his instructions once. And so he left them, to come here, for this.

In his hand was a small glass ampoule: the last of the antibiotics. He had searched the upturned contents of the trol's satchel several times, but there simply were no more. After this, it would be over.

He stroked Memphis's head. It was surprisingly soft—the brown leather skin felt good to his fingers. The trol breathed in, out. *Tha-thump.*

"Please," whispered Jack. "Please come back." He kissed Memphis's forehead. He snapped the ampoule, injected it into the vein, and dropped it to the ground. It was over. There was nothing more he could do.

Li-Bao Sen found him there, lying on the trol's chest. Watching silently, the croc felt the stump where his good right arm had once been. "Jack." His voice was low. "You should come and see this."

Wordlessly, Jack followed the croc. Up the steps to the top of the wall where men were gathered, silent. Nightingale's long blond hair flew in the wind, blue eyes staring; Leah, Django, and Chance stood beside him. Rooker Flynn leaned against the parapet, one foot up on the wall, a longbow slung over his shoulder.

Jack looked.

The grasslands beyond the Paladine Arch were covered black in an endless throng of marching horrors.

The Fell Host had come.

Battle of the Paladine Arch

*And how can man die better
Than facing fearful odds
For the ashes of his fathers
And the temples of his gods?*

Horatius

They had no hope—Jack saw that from the beginning.

Kekubi covered the grasslands, marching shoulder to shoulder in lines a hundred deep. Their steps fell in unison, tromping forward like a slow-beating drum. It was not just a march; the zombies moved as thousands of marionettes tied to the same string. Some were ragged and shabby, decomposing as they came, but many, too many, were fresh dead, the bodies of defeated defenders still wearing the red-and-gold uniforms of David's Tower.

They were dead men now, and served the Necrórceror.

Versläng came with them, moving freely among the zombies in tight hunting packs, roving gangs of gnashing teeth and claws. Black rotting ichor dripped from their fingertips, poisoning the grass beneath their feet. The roaches had fed well on their own dead, growing larger with each cannibalized morsel. When Jack had last seen versläng in Glyn Aker, they were still small, most only the size of dogs. These had grown to the size of men, walking upright and grinning bladed teeth. Some were bigger than Memphis. But there were three who had turned the Necrórceror's campaign into a moveable feast, devouring half an army of dead roaches along the way. They were giants; taller than the walls of the Paladine itself, towering over the army like whales among minnows. The whickering tendrils on their forearms looked like half-buried schools of octopi, whickering, flailing, and hungry; their chitinous armor heavy, thick, and impenetrable.

And there, at the head of the Host, surrounded by a sea of sin, rode a solitary man mounted on a bloody black charger, wearing the dark Armor of the Crimson Knight—the Traitor Campion Rei.

Just out of bow range, the crimson commander raised one gauntleted fist and called the Fell Host to a halt. His mount whickered furiously.

"*Valerian Tsai!*" he announced, his voice amplified by the helmet, loud and vain. "By the order of the One True King of

Keymark, you will abandon your post, revoke your oath to the Elder Wood, and cast off your Armor, or the King's Army will slaughter you where you stand!"

Standing alone before the Host, the Grey Knight did not reply.

Campion removed his helmet, revealing his perfect, beautiful face. His blond hair ruffled in the wind; his eyes were lit with victory. "I have returned home, Captain!" he shouted in his own voice. "With more warriors that even you can defend. Not alone. Not without the other knights by your side. Not without our brothers." Campion threw back his head. "Cast down your Armor, Valerian! Cast it down!"

Valerian Tsai stood, silent.

Campion's eyes flared. "Will you not answer me, Valerian? Will you not recognize your brother? Answer me!"

The Grey Knight said nothing.

Campion snarled. "If you will not answer to me, then perhaps there is one whose authority you *will* recognize!"

A hundred kekubi stepped forward. As a man, they reached up, gripped their heads, and lifted. Sinew popped, flesh ripped, and bone cracked as each severed skull was raised aloft. They spoke with a single chilling sound that Jack remembered all too well: the Voice of the Necrórceror.

"Submit," came the Voice from a hundred dead mouths.

"Submit to the will of your king. Submit to the Fell Host. Submit to the returning glory of the Blood of David. Kneel, Valerian Tsai. Kneel, and your death will be merciful."

"You are not my king." Valerian's voice came suddenly, sharp. "You are master of nothing. You rule living mud and dead men. The elves are not your servants, and the men of Keymark are not your slaves. You are no king—you are a ravening, covetous ignorant *child*. And you shall not pass these gates."

A low sound began from a hundred dead throats, a warbling, wailing, gobbling howl that rose to a bone-shivering shriek of rage. It tore through the men of the Paladine like a knife; many covered their ears in terror. The scream built to a pinnacle until a single word spat from a hundred lips: *"Kill."*

They came running.

As the mouthpieces of the Fell Prince collapsed, the myriad kekubi and versläng rushed in a headlong charge for the Paladine Arch.

Nightingale, Leah, and Django unleashed their bows at the same moment, felling three of the leading runners, and the battle had begun.

The Fell Host did not come in battalions, squadrons, or companies—they came as a swarm. Like a single beast with a million arms, they ran, howling and screeching in a bombardment of war horns and bloodlust.

The men of the Paladine paled in horror. Several broke ranks and fled, flying from the wall. They raced across the courtyard, abandoned their weapons, escaped through the low tunnel of the Kern, and disappeared into the bright-green glow of the Elder.

Shocked, Jack watched them run. Around him, several more eyes darted toward the elven gate, torn between fight and flight, losing their nerve.

"Good!" came Rooker Flynn's loud voice. "Now we're rid of the cowards, we can put up a real fight!" The captain grinned, lifting his bow. "Let's show em the way to hell, boys!" He loosed an arrow at the throng, bull's-eyeing a versläng through the head.

Jack led the cheer rallying behind the pirate; the remaining men, emboldened, opened fire. Jack loosed his arrow, moved close to Rooker, and whispered: "Thanks."

The pirate grinned fiercely. "When death comes to smile atchya, boychick, best ya can do is smile *back*." Rooker nocked another arrow, pulling it back to his ear. "But I'd say we're all about to die young."

Arrows flooded down from the wall, skewering the advancing creatures like steel-tipped rain. Nightingale's arm alone was worth twenty men. His hand flickered from the bowstring to the clutch of arrows before him faster than the eye could follow, unleashing a stream of darts into the Fell Host with unerring accuracy. With him were the best archers from Rimmy's Cull and Tucumcari, and though they could not match his prowess, they took heart from the silent elf's skill and redoubled their efforts. Leah came closest to matching his speed, each shot perfect. Django's javelin-like arrows fell less rapidly, but with devastating effect, pinning two and three attackers at once. But no matter how many of the Host fell, still more came, and every moment drove them closer to the Arch.

Quick versläng charged forward and hurled spears with deadly force. Men toppled from the battlements in a cascade of screaming humanity. Jack saw the man beside him hit square in the chest, his mouth a wide O of shock as he fell wide-eyed into the courtyard.

Karen Jase ducked through the barrage, leading a small group of Cullans low along the wall above the Arch. She shouted a command, and the men rose up, shot out their hands, and blazed majik. The wizards—her own personal bodyguard—attacked.

A blistering torrent of concentrated *wikk* hammered down on the advancing kekubi: emerald fire, crimson darts, and indigo rockets. The leading edge of the Host was immolated in the blast, crushed beneath the might of their combined majik.

And still, they came.

Jack glanced down at Valerian Tsai. The last Border Knight had not moved. He stood his vigil, fifteen feet beyond the Arch, the knightsblade buried in the earth at his feet, motionless as the statues of his fallen brothers. Masked in Armor, his face shielded from view, the grey man stood waiting.

Arrows and spears flew, felling opponents on both sides. Leah shouted orders to the men, drawing them to the center of the wall as the Fell Host closed in on the Arch. Rooker stood next to Jack, one leg cocked up on the wall, firing into the Host with a wicked grin on his face. Jack fired again and, for the first time, hit his target. He was a terrible bowman, but at this range, it simply didn't matter; the Fell Host was so thick, it was impossible to miss.

Impossible.

The Falikos ambush was nothing compared to this throng—it was the difference between a lake and an ocean. Versläng and kekubi covered the field like black water, a never-ending juggernaut of teeth and claws. Fighting them back was like battling a tidal wave; they might succeed for a moment, but in the end, they would drown.

Jack saw Leah; her eyes widened as the monsters charged at the Grey Knight. She unleashed her arrows in a blind frenzy, trying to hold them back, trying to defend her father.

But in the end, there was nothing she could do.

As they reached the Last Knight of the Paladine, the leading edge of the Host hesitated, fearing the man's stillness. They gathered mere feet from him, bunching together even as arrows fell, slaying them. The Grey Knight did not move.

Kekubi lowered their heads, drool dripping from cracked teeth. Versläng hunkered on their hind legs, the tendrils on their arms flickering. All of them—all at once—leaped.

Valerian moved.

The knightsblade sprung from the earth and cut an arc through the first row, splitting them in half; he lunged, skewering three feet of monsters on his steel, turned, killed another six with the backhand stroke, and whipped the blade forward to destroy four more. Two dozen monsters fell.

A grey armored foot took one step forward.

Kekubi fell headless to the ground; versläng shattered like black glass; dozens were decimated with each thunderbolt strike. The knightsblade blazed silver fire in Valerian's grey-gauntleted fist, laying his enemy to waste.

Jack finally understood the power of the knight—the young man felt Valerian's strength pounding through the air in waves.

Anywhere in the world, Valerian Tsai was the finest swordsman alive—but here, standing in defense of the Paladine Arch, clad in the Armor of the Grey, he was more than that—he was their Defender.

Valerian waded into the midst of the Fell Host, decimating the enemy. As they surrounded him, the Grey Knight did even more damage, cutting them down in swaths like a scythe through wheat. Everything, living and dead, fell before his steel.

But still they got through. Some of the smaller versläng got under his guard, attacking his legs. As he crushed them underfoot, more fell on him, pouncing on his sword arm, tearing at his Armor with their claws. Kekubi gripped his body, throwing all their weight on him, bearing him down. A huge roach leaped on his shoulders, slashing at his head. It gripped his helmet, trying to tear it free.

Valerian disappeared beneath the tide. Leah screamed. Jack's eyes flew wide. And then—

A stroke of thunder without sound.
A violent thump of wind. Time slows.
The air falls silent, as if all sound has been sucked into the cen-
ter of the fray. Dust hangs in the air, frozen. Jack has felt this
once before, in Rimmy's Cull, but here, at the Paladine, it is—
The shock wave hits like God's fist.
It crushes out, breaking the enemy, smashing them away, away,
away… A thunderclap. An earthquake.
The ground shakes; the air ripples.
Versläng and kekubi are torn apart, thrown from the epicenter
of the concussion like peas on a drumhead. The shock wave is
huge; an acre of land shudders beneath its might.
At the center stands Valerian Tsai, covered from head to toe in
ichor and filth. The Grey Armor sizzles, hating the grime, and
burns itself clean.
Heat shimmers from Valerian's shoulders, wreathing his head
in a crown of steam—
his Armor shines bright.

Valerian drove the knightsblade into the ground at his feet. Waiting.

Cries erupted from the Arch. Men thumped the wall with their fists, shouting and hollering. They had heard the legends of the Border Knights all their lives, from the time they were little children, but none of them had ever dreamed this.

The Fell Host halted.

Versläng and kekubi screeched at Valerian Tsai from just outside the crater of bodies surrounding the Arch. Campion raised his fist; the war horns sounded, joining their noise until the air was full to bursting with an earsplitting bloodthirsty cacophony.

And they came again.

As the battle was rejoined, Jack felt a tug at his sleeve. Fuji stared up at him, two other tams at his side.

Rooker Flynn watched as Jack's little blue-and-gold tam make those weird gestures with its fingers; the boy responded in kind and the tams scurried away with a purpose, ducking under a hail of arrows.

The pirate squinted after them. "Little lizards gonna save our damned skins, eh?"

Jack forced a grin. "Better believe it."

Monsters fell by the hundreds, men by the dozens. But now the Fell Host was not just attacking the Arch—they came at the wall itself. Kekubi died in bunches at the base; versläng leapt over their remains to claw their way up the stone. Arrows and spears picked them off, but still, they came, skittering over the blank faces of the silent statues, leaving a trail of slime over the fallen knights of the Paladine.

Silent thunder rolled as Valerian defended the gate, destroying twenty, thirty, forty, monsters at a time. The Grey Knight held the Arch.

But the men on the wall were losing the battle.

Twitching bodies grew into great mounds; each new wave of the Host began its ascent of the wall from a higher point, crawling over the bodies of their slain comrades. Nightingale stopped protecting Valerian and switched to picking off the rising versläng, mowing them down before they climbed too high. Karen Jase's magicians blazed fire, blasting the Host back. But in the end, there were too many.

Too many.

Nightingale's clutch of arrows went dry. The silent elf fired his last shot, impaling a crawling versläng through the chest, and drew his sword. There were no more arrows to fire, no spears left to throw. All the men of the Paladine could do now was wait—wait for the Host to come over the wall.

Leah shouted orders, gathering pikemen to the front, preparing for hand-to-hand combat. Jack and Rooker stood side by side, waiting. Jack gripped Nepenthe in sweaty palms, watching the Host crawl ever closer. He glanced at Rooker; the pirate looked uneasy.

Jack leaned in. "Still believe my good luck?"

That dangerous war-grin spilled over Rooker's face—his bravado was untouchable. "Boychick, I seen ya fly. I seen ya go toe-to-toe with an *ûzguk*. I seen people cross the world jest to join ya. I seen ya pretend to be a man, then *become* him. I believe." He nodded. "Jest don't pick today to prove me wrong."

The Host came over the wall.

Jack struck first; Nepenthe purred blue, crushing the nearest versläng like a black watermelon. Cheers bellowed from the wall as men joined the attack. Long pikes stabbed down into the heart of the Host, impaling versläng, decapitating kekubi. Steel punched into the rising tide, holding it back, sending bodies tumbling.

And the mound grew.

Ten, fifteen, twenty, feet of bodies lined the wall. Some were still alive, unable to escape, trapped under the sheer weight of the dead on top of them. Versläng paused at the base to devour their trapped brothers—their cannibal growth was immediate; the roaches grew larger, more armored, taking on the power of their dead. As the tide rose, the piles overbalanced, toppled, and fell, burying the Host under an avalanche of dead roaches. More came, climbing again, dying again; each time they were struck down, the Host gained ground. No matter how many the men of the Paladine killed, there were more.

There were always more.

The Host reached the top. Nepenthe blazed in Jack's hands, swatting them back, cracking versläng shells. Rooker drew the singing saber and hacked kekubi down; Bessie screamed her battle song. Django's axe hacked them in half; Nightingale's blades struck faster and faster in a whirlwind of steel.

And Leah. Leah led them all, red hair flying wild, leaping from stone to stone, striking down attackers left and right, commanding new men to take the place of the fallen, always strengthening their defense, always bringing the fight to the enemy. Leah led the men of the Paladine: led them in strength, led them in passion, led them in courage, a defending commander locked in a hopeless fight.

She fought them to a standstill. The climbing Host could advance no further against the shimmering steel of her men.

Valerian Tsai would not let the Fell Host pass under the Arch; his daughter would not let them over it.

Astride his bloody black charger, Campion watched from afar. He had held back his three behemoths—the giant versläng towered above him, claws grasping the air in murderous anticipation.

Now he set them loose.

Massive strides crossed the flatlands; giant talons threw up hunks of turf at their heels. Horrible shrieks bellowed from their armored mouths as they charged, ravenous for blood.

Men fled. Terrified, they abandoned the wall, fleeing for the Kern. Leah shouted at the ones who stayed behind, calling for their courage, calling for their steel. Jack joined her, hollering at the top of his lungs for the men to hold, to stand, to fight.

The behemoths came, giant feet crushing their tiny brothers in a lethal rush. One went right, one went left, and one went straight for the Arch.

They hit.

Jack ducked just in time. The men who did not went flying from the wall screaming. The wall of the Paladine Arch could not be broken, not by man or majik, but under the combined might of the behemoths, it buckled. Awestruck, Jack watched as the behemoth in front of him crunched one foot into the pile of bodies outside the wall, rose up, and struck. Jack dodged to the side; he felt the sickening tickle of its forearm tentacles brush his cheek; the impact of the fist blew him sideways, and his head cracked against the stone.

Dazed, Jack could not think. Something hit the wall again; he watched a man gripped in giant claws, then disappear. Jack heard himself shouting, shouting for Rooker, shouting for Leah, shouting for anyone.

I am here.

Fuji appeared at his side. The tams were with him. Each had a small water barrel strapped to his back, marked with the emblem of Black Jack. They cowered as another giant fist struck the wall, but the tams did not run.

Jack grabbed the barrel from the tam. "Rooker!" he shouted over the thundering blows. *"Rooker, I need you!"*

Rooker Flynn scrabbled along the wall and threw himself down beside Jack. His eyes were wide. *"Yeah?"*

"You see this?" Jack pointed at a spiraling string coming from a tiny hole in the barrel.

"Yeah!"

"Light it!"

Rooker shot him an insane look. "*This* is yer great plan?" he shouted. *"A barrel with a pig-tail?"*

"Just light it!"

Rooker frowned, and as another giant fist hit the wall, he snapped his fingers and lit the pig tail.

The bats were the key.

They had hung from the caves of the Kern for three hundred years, dropping their waste onto the stone in a centuries-high pile of excrement. But beneath that guano, Jack knew—brewing in the mix of ammonia, uric, phosphoric, and oxalic acids—was a nitrate called saltpeter.

And *that* was majik.

The Chinese discovered the extraordinary blend of chemicals in the ninth century, back in a time when Jack's sphere was no more evolved than Keymark. They had used the astounding formula for ceremonies and celebrations, and for the delight and wonder of their children. And it was this formula, this *majik*, that Jack Swift had written on a cave wall with a rock.

Boiling the sulfur out of the hill had been the most difficult part; the charcoal was readily available from the Border Knights' supplies, and there was an infinite supply of batshit. And once you crush eight parts charcoal with three parts sulfur and ten parts saltpeter, you get real majik:

Gunpowder.

The pig-tail fuse crackled, hissing like an angry snake.

Black Jack stood tall before the behemoth. He whipped his arm forward, hurling the powder keg like a football straight into the giant's mouth. Turning, he grabbed Rooker and threw him to the ground, covering his head. For a half second, nothing happened, and—

The bomb detonated. Exploding fire rocked the air. Iron nails the tams had packed into the barrel shot out in every direction. Percussive force rattled Jack's bones in a thundering roar.

Jack never saw what happened to the behemoth's head, but when he mustered the courage to peek over the battlement, it was gone above the neck. The decapitated giant stood for a moment, as if confused what to do next, then fell to the ground in a lifeless heap.

Stunned silence overwhelmed men and monsters alike, struck dumb by the explosion.

Then the men of the Paladine roared like trumpets.

Jack grabbed another barrel and sprinted with Rooker for the other side of the Arch. Leah and Django were pinned down by the second behemoth. Jack saw the thing's claws lash out against the bull's wyrmscale shield; sparks flew as Django defended Leah. Rooker lit the fuse, Jack tossed the bomb, shouting for everyone to get down. It exploded magnificently—but this time, the metal shrapnel was deflected against the giant versläng's thick, chitinous armor.

More men grabbed bombs from the tams, lit them, and threw. Explosions detonated against the thing, pounding it back, but the shrapnel bounced off like rain, and it struck back. A dozen men were swept from the wall in a single stroke, many falling into the throng of versläng waiting below. Jack tried for another shot into the mouth, but the giant reared its head aside at the last instant. The explosion took half its face off. Furious, the thing struck the wall with terrible force, bashing the men that remained until only Django and Leah stood against it.

Jack spied a dozen tams struggling with the big barrel—the one they had packed first, before they knew how powerful and heavy the things were. Ducking under a swing, Jack grabbed Leah. "Come on!" They raced down the stairs together, the minotaur close behind.

The behemoth brought up one massive leg and stepped over the wall.

Jack grabbed the barrel, trying to lift it. "Django!" he yelled. The big bull grabbed the two-hundred-pound barrel in his muscled arms and hefted it aloft. Above them, the behemoth roared. Rooker snapped the fuse alight, and with all his might, the minotaur heaved the barrel into the air.

The blast blew them back; fire lit the sky. Django hooked his arm around the three of them and threw up his shield, protecting them from flying shrapnel. Shards of chitin and quivering tentacles showered them in a chunky spray as the giant cockroach was blasted to stew.

As Django Barón lowered his dripping shield, Jack saw the minotaur had painted something on its wyrmscale face—the sigil of his master, the emblem of Black Jack.

The eyes of man and master met as cries of "*Black Jack! Black Jack!*" came from the remaining men. The bull smiled proudly. "Now they know. Now they see. You are legend."

Only Valerian Tsai stood against the last giant. By the time the first bomb went off, he had defended a dozen blows from the thing's tremendous claws, each one raking against his Armor in a sizzling shower of sparks. By the time the second bomb exploded, the Grey Knight had absorbed enough damage to destroy an Abrams tank. Finally, he found his opening: the knightsblade chopped off the behemoth's leg at the knee. Howling, the crippled giant fell to its hands. Valerian hacked off its arm at the elbow, then drove his blade through its skull and pinned it to the ground like the insect it was.

Instantly, the Host was on him, their attack relentless, merciless, unstoppable.

In the entire time he defended the Arch, the Grey Knight had stood his ground, never giving an inch—an unshakable pillar of strength.

Now, he took one step back.

Astride his black charger, Campion smiled.

The behemoths had served their purpose. He watched his former Captain closely: the way his left arm took just a bit longer to come up, the way the grey man's strikes come just a bit slower. *Patience,* he thought as Valerian was forced back another step. *You taught me that, old man.*

Another step back.

Another.

Sensing the change, versläng and kekubi abandoned the wall and joined the blitzkrieg on the knight. They hurled themselves at him, senseless of their own deaths, each slaughtered creature gaining a fraction on an inch. And in that way, little by little, Valerian Tsai was driven into the shadow of the Paladine Arch.

There, Li-Bao Sen stood waiting—with one good eye and one good arm.

Leah had placed him in charge of the reserves to ensure that her father had fresh blades if the monsters reached the Arch. The serpent samurai wore a jade commander's flag high on his back, rippling in the breeze. Surrounding his banner were a handful of volunteers, including Andy Ibis, Hatch Smith, and one last figure no one had ever expected to follow the croc: Chance.

The feral tom hated his blood enemy from the beginning. But ever since Li-Bao saved his life in the battle with the dæmon, Chance had never once left the croc's side. The cat tended his wounds, carried his equipment, acting as nurse, attendant, and servant. He had convinced several other jinx-cats to do the same, and all stood waiting at Li-Bao's command. The croc had saved Chance's life—the big cat meant to repay the debt.

Watching the oncoming Host, Chance stood beside his partner, gripping the new weapons he had borrowed from a brother jinx: steel-tipped razor gloves, fit tight to his paws. He eyed the croc.

"Not too crippled to put up a good fight, samurai?"

Li-Bao's blue eye stared at the cat's new weapons. "You need eight blades, little kitten." He hefted his scimitar. "I need only *one.*"

They grinned at each other once and leapt to the charge.

Even handicapped, Li-Bao was a master, each thrust a kill; his missing right arm replaced by his muscled tail, undercutting the Host and sending them to the ground where his men could finish them off. Chance was a blur of fur, jinx claws shredding the enemy like paper. The cat and the croc fought shoulder to shoulder, Chance on the llystra's right, making three good arms between them.

Andy, Hatch, and the others joined in, forming a human wall beneath the stone of the Arch. Hatch's hammer fell, crushing versläng like bugs. Andy was no swordsman, but his fury made up for his lack of skill; he fought as if his precious newborn son were right behind him.

The battle found its home in the choke point beneath the Paladine Arch; the Fell Host were slaughtered by the hundreds. And still, they came.

Valerian did not summon the shock wave now—either he was too exhausted or feared wounding his own men. He fought valiantly, each stroke perfection, but after killing hundreds, thousands, even the Border Knight grew tired.

"The Grey needs a breather," said Chance.

"Then we should shoulder the burden for him," said Li-Bao, killing another kekubi.

"This is too tight a spot anyway."

"We need some space."

"Then we're agreed." Chance grinned as both of them shouted: *"Django!"*

The bull's axe sliced over their heads, decapitating three kekubi at once. The cat and the croc ran to him, leaped up, and grabbed a hold of the minotaur's big horns, placing their feet on his massive head.

"Catapult!" yelled Chance, and the minotaur jerked his horns. Li-Bao and Chance shot into the sky like missiles, arms spinning. They arced up over the top of the Paladine Arch and landed smack-dab in the thick of the Host.

Shouting like madmen, they fought, felling the shocked creatures by the fistful. They battled back-to-back, a roundhouse of steel. When the throng grew too close, Li-Bao's tail lashed out, the nimble cat jumped over it, and a semicircle of attackers fell like tenpins. Together, they formed a two-man front. Li-Bao lost the tip of his tail. Chance lost his ear. And still, they fought, roaring together against a sea of black.

Valerian Tsai had one moment to catch his breath. He gripped his left arm—the one the dæmon had injured in the Jutts—cradling it as if it were broken. He straightened, gripped the knightsblade, and attacked.

Jack Swift stood, watching, and found his feet were made of stone.

The Fell Host kept coming. Jack saw the claws of the versläng, the teeth of the kekubi, and the blood they shed. So much blood. To plunge forward into that fray was to dive headlong into death. Maybe he wouldn't die fast, maybe he would stand for a while, but then something would cut his arm, then his leg, then his face; he would lose his footing, and sooner or later, he would fail, fall, and die. Jack's fingers clasped his little stick in sweaty fists, afraid for his life.

A growl rumbled behind him.

Shadow's red eyes glowed.

During its time at the Paladine, the dog had settled into something the size of a German shepherd, but the dog was gone. It smelled the fear now—the Wolf.

Yes, it said. *Run.*

Run away. Prove what you really are, boy. Flee.

Flee and live.

Fear gripped Jack's heart like cold iron. *No. Not now. Not ever.* Gritting his teeth, he stared Shadow down, raised one fist, and pointed at the Host.

"Sic 'em."

Obeying the man who was still its master, the Wolf snarled and tore into the Host with savage teeth.

Nepenthe came alive in Black Jack's hands. He smashed the first versläng back five yards, the next ten. Shimmering blue fire lit the stone inside the Arch. He smashed them away from Rooker, away from Leah, away from Django. The majik purring through his arms was almost unbearable, filling him with a sense of power electrifying and terrible. When they struck at him, the skidshield flashed, shielding him from the blows. Ahead, the Host swarmed around Li-Bao and Chance; Jack gripped the staff like a baseball bat and swung for the fences. Seven feet of blue blazing light ripped through the air, destroying everything in its path. Versläng shattered from his touch; kekubi dropped like stones. Somewhere in the back of his mind, he heard men shouting *"Black Jack! Black Jack!"* and he drove forward, pushing his way to the very tip of the battle. And then he stood shoulder to shoulder with the Grey Knight.

Nepenthe and the knightsblade blazed side by side.

The Crimson Knight waited. The versläng did not matter. The kekubi did not matter. The jaelin on the wall did not matter, nor did jinx or llystra or dwarves or the Toshan fire the young *doktar* summoned. No. All that mattered was his old master.

All that mattered was Valerian Tsai.

Campion had trained under the grey sensei for years before he was deemed worthy to take the Armor. He had fought alongside his master in a thousand battles in a thousand different places. He knew the grey man, knew how powerful he was, how far his strength and faith could take him. But even the Grey had his limits. Campion had seen him falter, seen him fail. But in those times, the other Border Knights had been by his side, the Azure, the Jade, the Indigo.

The Crimson.

The empty Armor of Campion's right hand twitched.

He could still feel it, that phantom fist, just as he had felt his flesh-and-blood hand before it was taken at the Battle of the Jaden Fields. The Fell Prince had given him that ghostly gift, that phantom hand, on the day of the Black Accord—the day the Last Prince should have died. Campion had been able to ignore the ghost for the first few years, to pretend he felt nothing at all. But over the decades, it tickled at his mind, an itch he could never scratch, pestering him until it finally drove him mad.

And then, when his mind was ripe for the taking, the Crimson Knight heard the prince's Voice:

I will give you your right hand…if you will become mine.

At first, Campion had laughed. The idea was ridiculous. To betray his brothers, to join with the enemy—unthinkable. But the Voice lingered in his mind for a long, long time, and every year, it grew louder. And every year, he hated Valerian Tsai just a little bit more. Hated the grey man for making him a knight, hated him for leading them to the Jaden Fields, hated him for the Crimson. Without the Armor, Campion could not even wield his sword—he had no hand to bear it. He was dependent on the Armor to make him a whole man. But Valerian Tsai could take the Armor away. Valerian, the Voice in his mind told him, *would* take it away. And so the idea tickled at him in the same way his missing hand tickled him, little by little, until, finally, Campion Rei broke.

He had not known, truly, if he were capable of the act until the moment he skewered Abrahim Qin on the tip of his knightsblade.

After that, it was easy.

Campion murdered the Border Knights, his brothers, one by one, all for *this* moment.

All so Valerian Tsai would stand alone.

Finally, the moment came. One of the faceless Host scored a blow on the Grey Knight, and the old man fell to one knee. Valerian's few remaining allies jumped to defend him; his daughter and the young Toshan in black struck down the creature, but it was too late—seeing the grey man on his knees was all Campion needed.

The Grey Knight was tired.

Fresh and young, the Crimson Knight kicked his bloody steed and charged for his old master.

The horse came like a black cannonball with a red devil on its back.

The Crimson Knight charged over the Fell Host, trampling them underfoot in his headlong stampede. Campion's flaming knightsblade came high and struck down on Valerian's helm.

Never in the history of the Paladine had one Border Knight struck a blow against another.

The impact was a red-hot explosion of pure *wikk*. Men were blown aside from the blast; versläng and kekubi were crushed to dust. The impenetrable walls of the Paladine cracked and splintered at the sound of the blow.

Valerian Tsai fell to the ground, his helm cloven in two.

Leah screamed.

She attacked the Crimson in rage, her sword hammering at the blood-red Armor. Her blade shattered from the impact.

Campion's fist smashed Leah to the ground, crushing her jawbone to splinters.

Jack's mouth gaped wide in horror. He ran to her side, shouting her name, but Leah was senseless, broken, her beautiful face crushed.

Rooker Flynn give a shout; the singing saber screamed bloody murder, clanging against the Armor. Nightingale's blade joined him, the silent elf as grim and determined as death. The Trio leapt to their aid, crying vengeance. But Jack could barely hear them. All he could see was Leah.

Fury burned his blood like fire. Jack got to his feet. He threw himself at the Crimson Knight. Nepenthe blazed electric blue. He struck a blow hard enough to shatter rock, but against the Armor, it meant nothing.

Nothing.

In Rimmy's Cull, they had managed to do Campion Rei harm. But here, under the Paladine Arch, where the Armor of the knights was born to be, the Crimson Knight was untouchable.

The blazing knightsblade struck at Jack. His arm shot up to block the blow; the skidshield flashed bright as the sword struck. The red blade glanced aside, and Jack was smashed back into the dirt. He heard something in his wrist snap. Stars swimming before his eyes, Jack saw one steel foot crush down before him. He looked up; the Crimson Knight towered over him, blade poised to skewer him through.

Terrified, Jack raised his hands to defend the blow, knowing it was over.

The flaming blade fell. Something huge blurred in front of Jack's eyes.

Django Barón.

The great bull threw himself between Jack and the Traitor, bringing up the tremendous shield that bore the name of the man he called master.

Hatch Smith had forged the shield well; the jabberwok's scales were bound fast, hard as diamonds.

The knightsblade punched through it like glass and buried deep into Django's mighty heart.

The minotaur fell at the Crimson Knight's feet.

Jack scrabbled forward, shouting something. Django's big eyes looked up at Jack. The bull smiled. Then he was dead.

Tears streamed down Jack's face. Above him, the Crimson Knight raised his sword to strike again.

"Enough!" came a thunderous voice.

Everything stopped. The Crimson Knight turned, his Armor creaking, and found the source of the command.

Valerian Tsai stood.

A deep, angry furrow cut down the center of his face. Blood crusted his salt-and-pepper hair; sweat poured down his brow; deep lines etched dark circles under his eyes. Each breath was labored and too quick, as if he could not get enough air. He slung the useless helmet to the ground and gripped the Grey knightsblade in his fists. "Face *me*, Campion."

The Crimson Knight straightened, bringing himself to his full height, and walked slowly toward the grey man.

No one moved. No one breathed. The few remaining volunteers stood, watching. Even the tattered remains of the Fell Host stood silent.

Jack glanced at Rooker, and together, the two men started toward Campion.

"Get *back!*" shouted Valerian, his voice sharp. "You cannot survive this."

"Nor can you," said Campion. He took off his helmet, revealing his handsome face, fresh and eager. He grinned. "Yield, Valerian-*jai*. Yield, sensei. And I will be quick."

Valerian's blade came up. "Come, brother."

A breath, and their swords clashed like thunderstorms. Jack was blown backward from the impact of their combined power. The few versläng and kekubi who had dared to get close were destroyed instantly. The Grey and the Crimson battled, skill against skill. The walls of the Paladine shuddered and cracked, smashed to rubble with each blow. The earth at the feet of the two knights blistered. Red fire smashed against silver light, and to Jack, it seemed as if all the *wikk* in the world was gathered here to take part in the fight.

It was a great and terrible thing to witness.

Campion hammered his master without mercy. Each stroke would have killed a normal man ten times over; the Grey Knight was driven back, smashed, crushed. Not one of Valerian's blows touched the Crimson—the grey man's strength was spent—each strike was batted aside as if it came from a child. Against the Fell Host, Valerian Tsai had seemed nigh invincible; against another Border Knight, the grey man's weakness was unmistakable.

Soon, Valerian's sword arm failed. The Crimson smashed the Grey like a lightning bolt. Valerian's Armor splintered.

Another strike, a crack of thunder, and the Grey gauntlet surrounding Valerian's left hand shattered. Campion did not slow—his attack was barbaric. The Crimson knightsblade fell again and again, shattering Valerian's shoulder plates, his greaves, his vambraces, until the Grey Armor was torn asunder and fell to the ground, a smoking, charred wreck.

Campion kicked out, sending the grey man sprawling against the pedestal that bore his statue. Bloody and beaten, Valerian Tsai gripped the stone, barely able to hold his own weight.

"You are no master, old man." Campion grinned victoriously. His Crimson Armor was shining, untouched. "I am the better knight."

With a last effort, Valerian rose to his feet. "You are no *knight.*"

He unbuckled the scarred breastplate, the last of his Armor, and let it fall to the ground. The grey man straightened, his voice thin and raspy. "I still stand, Campion."

"You stand alone."

"No." Valerian's steely eyes rimmed with light. "I have a *host* of men with me, Campion. A hundred thousand men, free men who stand with me—for courage, for faith, for honor. You stand alone, Campion. You stand for *nothing.*"

Campion sneered. "Die, old man."

The Crimson Knight raised his flaming sword for the final blow.

Valerian Tsai did not need Armor to be a whole man.

Without it, he was quicker.

His blade flashed first, cut the Crimson sword aside and took Campion's head.

A moment, and the Crimson Knight fell.

Before his corpse touched the ground, Valerian spoke one single word and the Crimson Armor fell to blazing dust.

Campion Rei lay dead in the dwindling cinders, his right arm finally quiet.

Valerian Tsai thrust his sword tip into the earth at his feet.

Jack stood awestruck. A shout rose up from somewhere. Others joined it. Soon, the shattered walls of the Paladine were rocked with the cries of triumphant men. The Fell Host, the few dregs that remained of the once indomitable multitude, fled through the Arch, away into the fields, fleeing before the resounding cries of victory.

It was finished.

Valerian Tsai walked to his daughter, knelt, and held her head in his strong arms. "Leah?"

"M'aright," she murmured through her broken jaw. "M'okay. Ah luv yu, Dad."

The grey man held her close.

The few men who had survived the Paladine, only twenty-three of them, found themselves wrapped in the strange turmoil of after-battle—the uncanny adrenaline-sapped sensation that vacillated wildly between exultation and exhaustion. Many shouted victory, amazed, incredulous, thrilled. Still more simply sunk to the ground and wept.

Jack Swift ignored them all. He knelt beside the body of Django Barón, stroking the bull's black hair. The minotaur had stuck by him through lies and truth, never questioning his honor, and, in the end, had saved his life. Jack kept finding himself thinking that Django was going to get up, going to talk to him, going to pick up his big guitar and play a long, sad song. But the big bull was still.

A hand clasped Jack's shoulder. Rooker Flynn stood over him. So did Li-Bao and Chance, the remains of the Trio. Their eyes were cast down, silent.

Finally, Li-Bao spoke: "We should hang his shield over the Arch"—his voice croaked—"so no one ever forgets."

Jack nodded slowly. "I should do it." He picked up the big shield, still solid save for the single hole punched in its center, and made his way alone up the steps of the Arch. The wall of the Paladine was shattered, lying in crumbled ruins around him, but the center, the Arch itself, remained.

Nightingale stood atop the Arch. The lean man stepped aside. Jack mounted Django's shield over the keystone, facing it out toward the plains.

As Jack turned, Nightingale's thin fingers came up and made a single sign the elf had learned from watching Jack and his tam:

Thank you.

The silent elf disappeared down the steps.

Jack stared out over the plains, alone, looking over the carnage of the battlefield. The bodies of the Fell Host were splayed out over a quarter mile of wasted grassland.

He took a deep breath and let it go, unable to believe it was finally over.

He heard people shouting his name. He turned and saw Andy Ibis, Hatch Smith, Karen Jase, and many more gathered in the courtyard, shouting *"Black Jack! Black Jack!"*

Jack's heart grew warm. He grinned, looking down at Rooker, Chance, and Li-Bao as they cheered him on.

Even the tams chirruped, Fuji leading the pack, a huge smile on the tam's little face.

Something stung Jack's chest like poison.

His scars burned hot.

A sound split his skull

(rath)

Thwack!

The Crownéd Dæmon Chulurath hit the boy like a hawk hits a mouse. From its grave at the bottom of the Jutts, its missing eye had been traded for black bat-like wings, wings it now used to lift its prey into the sky.

Nepenthe spilled from Jack's numb hands. The staff tumbled to the courtyard below and struck the stones, breaking into seven pieces with a hollow clatter.

In a rush of black wings, the dæmon and its Prize disappeared into the clouds, and were gone.

Chapter 19

FELL

Abandon hope all ye who enter here.

**Inscription on the
Entrance to Hell**

He is flying.

He does not know how, he never wakes enough to understand, but usually in his dreams, flying is a freeing sensation. Now he is trapped, gripped, pinned, his arms clamped against his chest—a chest burning with fire.

Stones are below him, giant stones, mountains, high and jagged and pointed and sharp, and when he falls (he knows he will fall), they will pierce his heart, his lungs, his eyes. The stones will eat him, and if they do not, the black cloud above him (he can never quite see it but hears the beating of its leathery wings) will finish the job.

The black cloud has teeth; it smells like burning flesh, like hatred, like death.

Something else is coming now—he sees it through the pain, sees it during the times when he is not blacking out (there is no rest when he sleeps, just more pain and fire and claws and teeth), and the thing is coming closer, somewhere down there in the black clouds, coming up at him, coming faster and faster.

It is a mountain, a fortress, a tower.

Black stone, dull and dark, shrouded in mist and fog and fumes. It is pointed like the stones, old like the mountains, black like the cloud.

He fears it.

Suddenly, the tower comes for him, rising up, growing bigger and darker until the sky is gone and there is nothing but black dying stone. Tattered flags whip in the high, cold wind above— he has seen the emblem on the flags before, three edges of a circle, drawn to the center, drawn toward an unformed conclusion, but he cannot remember where and something is wrong with that because he *always* remembers, remembers everything, remembers Leah telling him

(Leah is dead, she must be dead, that's why I can't remember)

something about the markings, something about falling, fell, fell, *Fell.*

He falls.

Air rushes past him. His hair flies back. Black stone cracks his cheek, his jaw, his nose. His left arm sings pain from where the Crimson Knight broke it (he's dead and gone, like me), and he rolls over screaming.

Something slithers over his ankle, his broken arm, his face.

His eyes open to find the pink eyes of a white snake.

Snakes. Three, five, a dozen of them, white, milky albino snakes all over his body, coiling around him, smooth and cold and horrible. He throws one off. They bite him, needles piercing his arms, his legs, his face.

Then the big ones are coming, white snakes like tree trunks, slithering from the dark, milky scales scritching over the stone. They hiss softly, searching the air with their tongues, pink eyes blind, and they find him. Looping coils of muscle wrap around him, bearing him down, wrapping him in scaly white until he cannot move at all. The little ones are wiggling across his face. He sees the jaws of a big one open, fangs reaching out to touch him; a long pink tongue licks his face. The fangs touch his scalp and bear down. They sink into his skull and he screams.

"Enough," comes the smooth voice.

The snakes withdraw instantly, scritching back to their dark corners.

He is trembling—from fear, from cold, but mostly from the repulsive touch of the dark *wikk* that has come alive in his head, worse than a thousand snakes and roaches and worms. The *wikk* is not simply dark; it is perverted, corrupt, grotesque.

Its owner steps forward into the light; a coal-black shape spills out over the stone like oil, manifesting as a solidified shadow. Behind him, the great dæmon descends to one knee, bowing low before its master. As the shadow shape comes closer, Jack is hit with a wave of revulsion, the *wikk* wiggling inside his skin diseased and rancid.

"My dearest Prize," comes the silky voice beneath the cowl, "you are finally mine." He throws back the cowl, revealing the face of the Necrórceror.

Valerian was right; the Fell Prince is a child.

Fifteen years old when he died at the Battle of the Jaden Fields, the prince has not aged a single day since. His face is young and smooth, untouched by time, his blue eyes bright and sharp, his thin lips cruel. Blond locks spill like golden wheat over the thin silver crown on his brow. The odor of the foul *wikk* clings to him like death.

"You should not be so surprised, boy," the young man's voice comes like black ice, and Jack realizes the prince is reading his mind. "Yes," says the Necrórceror, "I can hear you. And I warn you: I am no child. But you are right—the *wikk* within me is perverted. Corrupt. And grotesque." A crooked smile splits his thin lips. "But you will fix that, won't you, Jack?"

Black smoke surrounds them both, snaking down Jack's nose, his mouth, his throat, choking him. His eyes squeeze tight, burning, and when he opens them, he is somewhere else.

The Great Hall of Werrun Fell is black as onyx, high and thick and sharp. Dim light trickles through windows thin as arrow ports. Birds and bats and flying things skitter in its rafters. Empty tables line the walls; abandoned chairs are piled high with dust. Only one great seat is clean, dominant in the empty room, raised high over the vasty nothingness: the throne of the Fell Prince.

Jack's eyes stream tears from the smoke. As he coughs black chunks from his lungs, he sees three things that seem out of place in the Great Hall. The first is a huge white sheet covering a shapeless lump. Suddenly he knows that the Necrórceror will pull back that sheet, will show him what is hidden beneath. Some part of him already knows this, and he does not want to see.

The second is the giant black rock resting near the throne. It is huge, squat, and breathing steam. The stone is alive. On its face is carved a crooked, unreadable symbol: ugly, cruel, and evil. The rock does not belong here—he can feel that in his bones.

Last is the chunk of ice. It is twisted and jagged as if a rainstorm were flash frozen into place. Within the ice, concealed beneath the frosty face, is a dark shadow, a shape buried within. It reaches out as if trying to break free of its icy coffin. It is nothing but a faceless form, a frozen ghost.

But Jack fears the shadow.

More than death, he fears it.

The Necrórceror waves a dismissive hand at the great dæmon kneeling by his side. "Back to your hole, *ûzguk*," says the prince. "Back to your cage."

The Crownéd Dæmon Chulurath, the great beast Jack has feared like no other terror in Keymark, obeys its master, backing away like a dog, bowing like a slave. Submissive, it retreats to the black stone. The *ûzguk* raises its fists. Black chains lash out from the wicked symbol, binding the dæmon's wrists and feet and waist until its tremendous body is pulled backward, arched painfully against the stone, agonized, like a victim on a medieval rack. It does this willingly for its master, and only now does Jack realize the might of the dæmon means nothing before the power of the prince.

"The *ûzguk* is useful," says the prince. "It has brought you to me at last. But its deep *wikk* comes at a heavy price, Jack. I made a bargain with the beast, nearly fivescore years ago now, the day the Tsai struck me down at the Jaden Fields."

The Black Accord.

"Yes. Some have called it that, but none more so than I. The beast took the white *wikk* to fulfill its part of the bargain, to keep me alive. But the terms of a dæmon's covenant are never to be trusted, Jack. My life came with a price."

The Fell Prince opens his robes and lets them fall to the floor; Jack stares in horror. Beneath the Necrórceror's youthful face lies a cadaverous wreck of what once was a body. His hands are bony claws; his arms burned and blackened; his legs strips of dried, muscled jerky, bone dry and ravaged; and from his stomach hang limp strings of desiccated entrails. But his chest is the worst. The rib cage is snapped and torn, open wide, a black mouth revealing a gutted wreck of necrotic lungs and a dead, lifeless heart.

"The wound Valerian Tsai left behind," says the dead boy. "Grown large these hundred years. The beast will not let me die, but neither will it close my wounds and make me whole." The Fell Prince leans in, grinning white teeth. "It *hurts*, Jack. It hurts every month, every day, every minute, since he killed me."

A hundred years of agony, Jack thinks. *Death would be better.*

"No! Not better!" shouts the Necrórceror, his voice shrieking against the stone. "I am the last of my line, boy! Do you not understand *yet?* I am the last of the blood of the High King David. If I pass, so does my father, and his fathers before him. No. It is better to live in anguish than let that noble thread be severed. I am *noble,* boy. And I will be *king.*" The prince takes up his cloak and wreathes himself in its folds once again; the crown shines dully upon his brow.

"One hundred years and one day," he says. "That is the term of the Black Accord, the term of the dæmon's service. Now that time draws nigh. When it is done, the beast will take back what it has given, and I will fall to dust." The prince turns, his long, cadaverous fingers caressing Jack's cheek. "But now, I have *you*, boy. My last, greatest victory."

The Necrórceror turns to the white sheet that covers the lump. Jack already knows what lies beneath. The Necrórceror rips the sheet aside like a magician revealing a trick, and Jack's worst fears are realized.

Scalpels, clamps, forceps, syringes, needles, and a legion of surgical equipment. A stainless-steel operating table, heart-rate monitors, defibrillator paddles, operating theater lights, a gasoline-powered generator. And there is more. Medical coolers, each bearing the logo of different hospitals from all over Jack's earth, each labeled according to their contents: liver, kidney, small intestine, lungs, heart.

Jack stares at the equipment, sick to his stomach. He knows what the prince intends. "You want me to heal you."

The prince smiles. "Just as you healed Xiang-lo. Just as you healed the Cullans." The prince taps the operating table, the exposed bone of his fingertip ringing against surgical steel. "I spent decades trying to find a solution, Jack, trying to discover a way to make myself whole. But without the Great Bells…*well*. Then, Campion told me what you had done, how you had healed Xiang-lo, the miracle you performed. And then I realized the solution lay not in majik but in *science*."

The way the prince says the word makes it feel dirty in Jack's ears.

"Xiang-lo was the first key," the prince says. "I needed his skill, his power, to find the Elaña of Werrun Fell—the jaunt gate my father lost. And I nearly had him until the grey man's runt snatched him away. So I took him from Falikos, where Campion and the *ûzguk* should have captured you both, but after the attack, they sent only the Pathfinder. In the beginning, Xiang-lo resisted. But I lent him a portion of my pain, and in the end, he found the gate. And while you have fled across Keymark from me, I have gathered the tools you need to work a second miracle. *My* miracle."

His cold fingers brush the hair from Jack's brow. "You will be my savior, Jack. You will be my *doktar*."

Cold creeps into Jack's skin; the icy hand is dead. He cannot stop shivering.

"I can't do it," he says, defying the chill. "It won't work. Surgery isn't majik. I can't just…piece you together like a jigsaw puzzle. And even if I could, you would never survive."

The Necrórceror laughs. High and wild, a laugh like the sound of smashing glass, rising to an insane shriek. "*Still*, you do not understand, boy! Let me instruct you. Let me share my pain." Cold hands grip Jack's neck; agony shoots through him like a dagger: His ribs break, smashing to splinters. His arms die, cracking and black. His lungs fold in on themselves, shrinking to raisins. Jack Swift feels his heart stop.

He lies on the ground, staring, unable to breathe, the blood quiet in his veins. He is dying. He is dying. He is dying.

The Necrórceror touches him now, and his heart leaps back to life. His lungs drag in a raspy breath, sensation tingles back into his fingers, and Jack discovers he is sobbing.

"I have felt that pain for a century," says the prince. "Take it from me now. Take my hands, take my lungs, take my heart. I cannot die, Jack Swift," comes the cold voice behind the cowl. "But you can make me *live*."

Jack pushes himself up from the floor. *I could do it,* he thinks. *He's breathing without lungs. He's moving without a heartbeat. I could tear him apart like an old car and he would still be alive—if you can call that alive. I could do it.* His mind races, exploring the possibilities, the challenge of it, of putting a man back together without the fear of death.

I could do it.

Jack gets to his feet and stands before the Necrórceror. He thinks of Valerian, of Memphis, of Leah. And the answer is clear.

"No."

The prince's eyes flash. The cold in Jack's bones suddenly deepens; the pain comes back in waves. He ignores it. "You killed good people on Falikos," he says. "You killed them in Rimmy's Cull, at Glyn Aker, at the Paladine Arch. You killed Abrahim. You killed Benjamin. You killed Django. You killed my *friends*. And the ones who are still alive would die to stop you." Jack stands as straight as his body can manage. "You can torture me. You can burn me, freeze me, cut me, and kill me. But I will *never* help you. And if I'm still alive to see it, I'll be glad to watch you *die*."

He expects pain, crippling, staggering, unbearable pain. But the Necrórceror does not give it to him. Instead, the boy-king smiles. "But I have something far more precious than your *friends*, Jack." The Necrórceror grins white teeth. "Come. See what I have."

His black robes flutter against the floor, and now he stands before the massive chunk of flash-frozen ice. Unable to stop himself, Jack is drawn forward. An unbearable sense of foreboding rises in his throat, and he feels a chill deeper than any he has known in his entire life. But the dread comes not from the Necrórceror—it comes from the ice.

"Xiang-lo." The Fell Prince smiles. "The Pathfinder. Your patient. Your miracle. The man you snatched away from death."

Jack can barely see the shadow beneath the frost. The ice is jagged and misshapen as if the man were still fighting for his life when the Necrórceror worked his dark majik, his hands grasping in frozen fight, fingers still reaching beyond the ice.

"He is precious to you," comes the Necrórceror's smooth voice.

"No," Jack says quickly. "I never met him."

"O, but you *have*, Jack." The Necrórceror smiles. "You know him so very well."

The Necrórceror slides his palm across the ice, wipes the frost away, and Jack sees. Sees the incision he made. Sees the stitches. Sees the brown freckle on the man's belly. Sees

(Xiang-lo is not one of us)

his chest

(he has no skill with the wikk*)*

his arms

(we called him Pathfinder)

his neck

(his majik is finding what is lost)

his nose

(like an invisible map only he can see)

his eyes

His eyes.

Eyes Jack knows so well—eyes he has known since before memory began.

That shock of red hair.

And the scar.

The scar above his left eye. The scar he got when he fell into the tree on Mount Katahdin.

Jack barely hears his own voice.

"...Dad?"

Alex Swift rubs his rough digger's fingers through his seven-year-old son's long blond hair. He is proud of his boy. He always has been.

But Jack is not his son, not today. Today, his boy is Chief Raging Bull, and Alex is content to be his Indian scout.

It comes as a surprise when his son finds the hole leading underground.

Usually, it's Alex who does the finding.

He has a knack for discovery—always has. It's not even really a skill, more of a talent that was stuck in his head from the time he was a kid, like Jack's memory—his one true gift. He knows where someone would go to build something, to create something, to hide something.

It's the reason he knows there is something behind this wall.

Breaking the rock, he finds the passage, just where he knew it would be. He drops down on his haunches, looks his boy in the eyes, and tells him to stay here—not knowing this will be the last time he looks into those seven-year-old eyes he loves so much—and disappears into the cave.

The Indian tribe (*were* they Indian? Alex isn't so sure now) buried something here—something they wanted to keep hidden. Usually, that would mean gold, or some religious artifact too sacred to bear revelation. But this...this feels different. There is something more here. He can feel it tingling beneath his skin, in his blood.

He steps over the albino bull snake without giving it a second thought; he has no fear of snakes, and an albino in a sealed-off cave isn't unusual.

Then he sees the second one, and the third, the fourth, the tenth.

He pops the Maglite between his teeth, squeezes around a tight corner where a boulder has fallen, and sees two things at once:

The first is a ring.

A huge fifteen-foot ring of vines and leaves, growing in a place where no plant should be able to grow. The vines form a perfect circle, intertwined in shades of white. Small dancing lights, living things much larger than fireflies, circle the air around its leaves.

The second is a man, shrouded in black robes.

White snakes curl about the man as if born from his body. He is taking something, a small white box, from the Indian artifacts hidden here. The man turns abruptly, surprised by Alex's sudden appearance. He hisses.

His hands—long, cadaverous fingers lined with rotting, dead flesh—lash out; strange syllables issue from his hidden tongue. The tingling sensation beneath Alex Swift's skin suddenly turns dark; invisible fingers clutch at his heart, and he knows he is going to die.

"Jack!" he shouts with a painful breath. *"Get out!"* He drops to his knees, stars swimming before his eyes, the air sucked from his lungs.

Bright flashes scorch the room; Alex thinks his brain is dying from asphyxiation, then he realizes the light is coming from the ring. An explosion of sound splits the air, the sound of rushing water, loud as Niagara; the air bubbles and something horrible steps from within the vines.

It is a beast, huge and monstrous.

Leathery skin, like a brown rhinoceros, covers its muscled body. Its acorn eyes flash, startled at the sudden scene.

Its thick fingers dart up and flash emerald fire.

The man in black is blown backward, screeching.

The brown colossus grabs Alex Swift by his waist and runs for the ring.

Something blasts behind them.

The rocks of the cave crack like thunder and fall.

Alex is shouting for his son to get out, get out, as the beast hits the ring.

There is a flash of white, and everything is gone.

Later, when he helps them, when he helps the Border Knight Valerian Tsai find the lost jaunt gates of Keymark, promised that he will see his son again, they give him a name.

The Pathfinder. Xiang-lo.

Jack is sobbing at his father's feet.

His hands clutch at the ice, clawing at it as he clawed at the Badlands rock that buried him, trying to touch his dad, to reach him, but his father's body remains locked behind the ice and the boy's fingers feel nothing but cold.

The Necrórceror stands over the boy.

"Valerian used your father," comes the cold voice. "Used him to find the lost gates, to destroy them. But I had another use for him. And for his son."

"*Let him go!*" shouts Jack, tears streaming down his face. "*Let him go! Give me back my* dad!"

"No, little *doktar.* You will do as *I* say. You will give me life."

"I can't!" Jack cries, bellowing anguish. "It's *impossible!*"

"You will work your miracle on me, boy," says the prince, his voice cold and distant. "Or your father will suffer for it."

The dead hands of the Fell Prince lovingly caress the ice that binds Jack's father. They find Dad's frozen hand, five fingers thrust past the block of ice.

The Necrórceror grips the smallest of the fingers and snaps it off.

"*No!*"

The Necrórceror flings Alex Swift's finger into the fire where it melts, crackles, and burns to ash.

Jack is screaming. He cannot stop screaming.

"Nine left, boy. Then his arms below the elbow, then his legs below the knee. After that, I will melt the ice and let you hear your father weep." The Necrórceror leans in, a finger touching Jack's chin. "But you can stop that, Jack. All you have to do is *make me live.*"

Jack's eyes are crammed shut, hot tears spilling out onto the cold stone. He has no choice. None at all.

He stands, wiping tears from his face. "I'll *try.*"

"Well done," whispers the Necrórceror. He hooks one cold arm over the boy's shoulder, leading him toward the operating table. "Let us begin."

Rooker Flynn cinches the saddle tight.

The chestnut stallion is the fastest horse he can find from the men of the Paladine, and he has paid every penny in his purse for it. He packs his kit bag swiftly, jamming food and supplies into the pouch, his hand constantly checking for Bessie, making sure she is strapped tight to his back.

Leah Archer is the one who finds him. Her arm is in a linen sling; her broken jaw is colored purple and black. Even so, her words are clear: "Where are you going?"

"To find him," the pirate says, closing his bag tight.

Leah's eyes drop. "He's dead, Rooker. You saw it. The dæmon took him. He's gone."

"Mebbe. Gonna find out."

"You'll never find him. How can you even hope to track him?"

"The dog." Rooker jerks his head at Shadow. The big grey animal is tied to a post, the rope bound tight around his straining neck. "He's been tryin' to run ever since the dæmon came. Tough to tie up too—damned thing keeps getting bigger. S'got some kinda connection with the kid. I'm gonna follow it."

"I'm coming with you," Leah says.

"Yer not," Rooker says. "Ya can't ride with that arm, and I don't need ya slowin' me down."

"Then take Chance," she protests. "Or Nightingale."

"No." Rooker crosses to Shadow; the wolf is biting furiously at its leash.

"You're going to get yourself killed, Rooker."

"Mebbe." Rooker hunkers down by the dog and grips its furry neck. "But I owe it to him to try." He slips loose the knot. Shadow, free, sprints under the Arch like a bullet heading east.

Rooker swings one leg over the saddle and looks down at the girl.

"He's my friend."

The pirate spurs the horse, galloping through the remains of the Paladine Arch following the dog into Wastelands.

Jack is coated to his elbows in blood.

It is not his blood, nor is it the blood of the patient who lies on the operating table. It is the blood of dead men, innocent men, who tried to do the right thing by putting an orange sticker on their driver's license that says: ORGAN DONOR. If they had known who, or what, they were giving their organs to, they would have decided differently.

It is a morbid mess. He is building a living body from scratch, and it is gruesome. In the beginning, everything he tries fails miserably; if his patient were a living man, he would have died a hundred times over. But the Necrórceror is not alive, nor is he dead, and he is right—Jack cannot kill him.

In the beginning, he tries. He slits the Necrórceror's throat with the scalpel, slashing the jugular on both sides. The cut would kill any living thing, but the Fell Prince simply stares at him, the gash in his neck lifeless, bloodless. The Fell Prince smiles and invites him to continue.

Jack keeps his eyes locked on his patient. He never once looks at his father.

With every mistake, Jack learns. What he does not know already, he discovers in the stacks of medical books piled high around the table. There is no shortage of books, nor of equipment—the Fell Prince has collected the resources of a dozen hospitals; his tools are legion.

He starts with the heart—an artificial biventricular polyurethane device designed to pump 9.5 liters of blood per minute through the human body, manufactured by SynCardia Systems in Tucson, Arizona. The artificial heart costs a fortune; Jack has five of them. After several failed attempts to connect the SynCardia to the Necrórceror's rotting veins and arteries, Jack gives up and begins using the thin rubber tubing to replace the dead vascular system. He threads new veins through the Necrórceror's body, cutting channels in the prince's skin until the man lying before him is flayed open in strips, his entire body exposed like a medical student's cadaver.

And still, the prince watches him.

Every time Jack grows weary, every time he rests his eyes or begins to nod off to sleep, the Necrórceror shares his pain.

Jack screams, blazing pain jarring his eyes wide. The prince's pain is worse now; he feels the new cuts in his body, feels his exposed nerves, feels it all, and he shares that pain with his *doktar.*

Each time, Jack forces himself back to work, reading and cutting and stitching, and each time, he knows the pain will come again and soon. He is exhausted to the point that he cannot remember how many days he has been awake now—he thinks the sun has set three times but remembers it rising five.

Then, a moment of success.

He connects the kidney to the SynCardia heart for what must be the twentieth attempt, but this time, the first time, blood courses its way through the organ. Jack stands back, watching the thing move, borrowed blood circulating through the kidney, alive.

On the table, the Fell Prince smiles.

Hands trembling, Jack goes back to work.

Hours pass, then days. Each organ has its own difficulties, each group of problems piles high on the backs of its brothers, and each time, Jack finds a solution. As he works, as the strange living machine begins to grow and takes shape, Jack realizes what he is building, and what he is doing to himself in the process.

He is not just performing surgery on a patient. He is resurrecting a creature from the flesh of dead men, bringing life to a creature, and in the process, turning himself into a horrifying monster, the living equivalent of Victor Frankenstein.

At some point, unsure whether it is day or night, he finds himself shouting hysterically at the gasoline-powered generator, and he does not recognize the shrieking sound of his own voice.

Slowly, the monster comes to life. Kidneys, pancreas, liver, small and large intestines, all moving, all working. As the Syn-Cardia pumps blood through them, some of the original veins and arteries in the Necrórceror's body come back to life. The ones that do not, Jack replaces. There is majik at work here, sure enough; the Fell Prince's head itself requires no work at all—it has never died—and when Jack reconnects his manufactured veins to the prince's severed jugular, warm blood begins pumping through his monster's brain.

The lungs are the penultimate thing Jack installs; they are just as difficult as he expects them to be, but in the end, when he steps back from the body, the blue-veined sacs expand and retract, rising and falling, and for the first time in a century, the Fell Prince breathes.

Jack's mind is a confused babble of voices; some his own, others he does not know. He has no idea how long he has been awake—seven days is enough to be declared legally insane, and it has been much, much longer than that. His head jitters back and forth on his neck, eyes darting from side to side, checking and rechecking the familiar territory of the Necrórceror's body. Now the heart, he thinks, now the heart

(do it with your whole heart)

because his patient

(always the patient, never the name)

cannot depend on the SynCardia forever—the machine was only designed as a short-term solution for a complete heart transplant. The skin he can graft later; he can gauze everything that is still exposed, wrap him like a mummy, and the Fell Prince can deal with that pain. And the muscles, the Necrórceror doesn't even *need* muscles; he can move his limbs with majik, he can do anything, his patient can do anything, anything, anything.

Blood-dried hair sticking out madly in all directions, Jack goes to work on the heart.

It is a good heart, strong and healthy, the heart of a thirty-five-year-old donor from Bloomington, Indiana. A Hoosier heart.

Jack tears away the SynCardia, ripping the plugs from the generator; the Fell Prince dies for the thousandth time. Jack lowers the heart into the open chest cavity (past the wound Valerian Tsai made) and works his last bit of scientific carpentry. The pulmonary artery is first, connecting the muscle to the lungs, where it will reoxygenate the blood; then the pulmonary vein, bringing it back into the heart; then the aortic semilunar valve; then the big, fat aorta; and then the stitching is done, the tubing is done, the carpentry is done.

It is finished.

Breathing rapidly, Jack grabs the defibrillator machine, plugs it into the genny, and hears the familiar electric whine charging up within the box. He feels the air crackle in anticipation.

He lowers the paddles to the prince's chest and hits the triggers.

Nothing.

He warms it up again, takes the settings higher. Hits him.

Nothing.

He turns up the dials, then realizes he doesn't need to be careful. *My patient cannot die, my patient can take anything, my patient is perfect.* He cranks the juice all the way up. Sparks fly from the genny. Jack lowers the paddles and hits him one last time.

Smoke billows up from the prince's body. The defibrillator goes dead; the generator shudders and dies. The surgical lights shatter and go black. Jack throws down the paddles, cursing. By the light of the fire, he finds the box containing the pacemaker, knowing that if he can't beat the heart one way, he'll beat it another. He grabs the box, sending everything else clattering to the floor, and—

Tha-thump.

He stops cold.

Tha-thump.

Jack turns, part of his mind screams, *Yes;* another part screams, *No, no, no!*

Tha-thump.

The Necrórceror sits up.

His cold eyes watch his own beating heart.

Both men stare.

For a moment, there is silence.

Then the Fell Prince begins to laugh. A high, wild laugh that rises to the black rooftops of Werrun Fell. And Jack finds he is laughing with him.

"Alive!" the Necrórceror cries. *"Alive!"*

Jack is crying and laughing and clutching his chest, his exhausted brain unable to process anything. He finds himself looking at his father for the first time in so many days, mouthing words in a combination of triumph and horror, "I did it, Dad. I did it."

Rising to his feet, the Necrórceror takes one last look at his heart and wraps himself in his robes. For the first time in a century, he is whole, alive, a complete man, and it feels magnificent.

"Thank you, *doktar.* Thank you."

Jack hears a deep sound—a roaring laugh that rises like lava.

At first, he thinks it is the prince, but it is not.

Then he thinks he himself is laughing and he has finally gone completely insane, but he is not.

It is the dæmon.

Chained fast to the rock, Chulurath is laughing.

A dark, hollow, wicked laugh, bubbling over with malicious delight. The Fell Prince freezes, staring up at the great beast.

Its one remaining yellow eye flashes. "One hundred years," its malevolent voice cackles. "One hundred years and one day, Prince. *That* was the term of our Accord. But now you live—too soon. You have broken our bargain."

The Fell Prince takes a step back.

"The Crownéd Dæmon is no longer your slave."

Flames leap from its massive shoulders; its great arms come forward and shatter the chains binding it to the rock. The great dæmon is free.

"I have broken nothing!" screams the young prince. "Get back to your cage!"

"Your life is mine to give, little prince, mine to take." Chulurath shoots his great clawed hand forward; the Necrórceror dives aside, smoke trailing from his cloak, and attacks.

The black stone of the Great Hall cracks. Windows shatter; the floor buckles. Debris falls from the ceiling as the two great royals clash. In the end, the crown of the *ûzguk* is mightier.

One flaming claw drags the Fell Prince screaming into the air.

The dæmon grips the Necrórceror in both great fists and rips him in half.

The living body of the Fell Prince is torn asunder. His fresh blood, minutes old, bathes the Great Hall. The death the young prince escaped a century ago finally comes for him, and the line of the High King David comes at last to a bitter, bloody end.

With his last breath, the dark majik of the Necrórceror is shattered. The towers of Werrun Fell topple and fall.

The Crownéd Dæmon Chulurath roars.

The sound is deafening. Flames rise up all around Jack; he drops to his knees, choking for breath. A terrible footstep approaches.

The beast towers above him.

"You," comes the dark voice of Chulurath. Jack stands no chance before the power of the dæmon unleashed; all he can do is pray his death will be quick.

His eyes fall on the chained rock behind Chulurath, and on the strange inscription burned into its surface. The rock. The symbol.

"Now you die, little Toshan."

Jack is staring at the stone.

"Why kill me?" he hears his own crazy voice come. "Your master is dead."

"Master?" comes the beast's voice. "No man is master of the *ûzguk*, much less a Dæmon Crownéd. I abided the little prince for a short time, a passing moment, to gain entry to this sphere. Now it will be mine."

Something brushes at Jack's mind, but his exhausted brain cannot remember why.

"Why kill me?" his crazy voice says again. "I mean nothing to you."

"You mean nothing, boy. And you caused me pain." Its fingers touch its horned face. "You took my *eye*."

It steps forward. Jack isn't looking. He's looking at the stone. Valerian Tsai's voice comes.

The Sapir Menhir.

An anchor, a doorway.

Chulurath raises his flaming fist to crush him.

I can't do majik.

The words are not majik, says Valerian's quiet voice. *They are a command—one it cannot deny.*

The strange memory of Jack Swift comes to his aid for the last time as he repeats the words Valerian Tsai spoke on the Bridge of Ahmen with reckless perfection:

Keurk-äl ve gredd ûzguk Chulurath kharat!

The Sapir Menhir breathes deep. The strange sigil burned within its surface leaps to life. The *ûzguk* screams. Its body burns, high and bright. Jack shields his eyes from the inferno. Blazing, Chulurath is pulled back, back toward the Sapir Menhir. The beast's body cracks from the heat. It folds in on itself, disintegrating, flaming chunks of flesh torn through the doorway, back into the flaming hell of its home. It is ripped apart until only the horned head remains, staring at Jack with one blazing yellow eye—and then the Crownéd Dæmon Chulurath is gone.

The Sapir Menhir blazes hot as the sun; the stone shatters to oblivion.

Jack is running for his father.

The prison of ice has melted from the heat. Alex Swift lies on the wet stone. He is still. Jack drops to his knees.

His father is not breathing.

"Dad? *Dad?*"

He presses his lips to his father's mouth and gives him the kiss of life. All alone, he breathes into his dad's lungs

(please)

pumps his chest

(please)

again

(my fault)

again

(my whole heart)

again

(please, God, please…)

And Alex Swift breathes.

He wakes.

Jack is sobbing.

The man stares into his boy's eyes.

"…Son?"

Jack Swift clutches his father close.

When Rooker Flynn rides over the ridge following the dog, he already knows something has changed. He has seen the bodies of the versläng, melted back to mud and shell, the corpses of the kekubi, lifeless and still. The black tower of Werrun Fell is cracked and shattered; huge chunks of stone have crumbled to the earth. There is nothing left.

He expects, at best, to find Jack Swift dead—if he finds him at all.

There, amid the wreckage of the tower, on a large stone, surrounded by the pale shoots of young green trees, sit two men.

Their heads are close together; both are smiling. The pirate had thought to find monsters, dark creatures, black majik, and unnatural beasts.

But instead, he finds the simplest thing in the world—a father talking with his son.

FOR THE LAST TIME

> *Life is a voyage that's homeward bound.*
>
> **Herman Melville**

T rumpets blasted a fanfare of triumph, a joyful strain of celebration heard all across the little island of Falikos.

Thousands of men gathered here; their numbers had increased night and day, the revelers feasting and drinking and growing by the hundreds until the island was virtually overrun, and even the Great Hall Barrelmount was filled to bursting.

Wellam the cook, red-cheeked and irritable as ever, shouted at his sous-chefs, trying to keep up with the constant demand for food. The fat cook had never left the island—he survived the massacre by hiding in a vat of pickle brine for almost a tenday until even Valerian Tsai had left. Now Wellam commanded an army of cooks once again, overjoyed he had plenty of men to feed.

And how they ate. It was a celebration, the ending of an age, and so it was time for dessert: iced creams, piping-hot fruit pies, many-tiered cakes, whipped trifles, spiced puddings, apple crumbles, caramel swirls, toffee crunches, chocolate mousse, flaming sugared cherries, and still, they begged for more.

Men and women danced together in the green fields that had seen too much death; the women threw cherry blossoms over their head as they spun, and whichever man the petals fell upon, they kissed passionately with red lips.

Trumpets sounded again and the revelers began to listen, gathering toward the western side of the island, toward the cliffs. There, they began to cheer in loud voices, making their own trumpeting sounds in a thunderous outpouring of hurrahs for the man who had brought an end to the Fell Prince, the hero named Black Jack.

Atop the rock, Jack Swift stood watching them, a tremendous grin on his young face. To his left stood Valerian Tsai. To his right stood Xiang-lo—Alex Swift—his father.

"Now?" Jack asked the grey man as the cheers below doubled and redoubled.

Valerian smiled. "As you like."

Jack drew back on the mighty wooden hammer as far as he could, then lunged forward with all his might and struck the Agrat-ban-Nakane.

The Great Bell sounded for the first time in a century, deep and loud and long. Instantly, the tingle of the white *wikk* that had been missing for too many years reverberated over the entire island. All across Keymark, in Rimmy's Cull, in Glyn Aker, in Highyon Garde, at the Paladine Arch, and even in Werrun Fell, the Great Bells rang.

The tingle of the white *wikk* flooded over them—the healing majik of Keymark was unleashed. Jack felt it run through him like warm water, bright as music.

He spun quickly to see what he wanted most.

Light came back to Memphis Kubiak's eyes, and they shone. Color returned to his leather-brown skin as he woke from his hibernation, hale and hearty. As his splintered horn grew back, the smiling rhino rose from his palate, wrapped his arms around Jack's body, and hugged him tight.

Li-Bao Sen's severed shoulder grew bone, then muscle, then sinew and flesh, until the croc's arm returned, strong as ever. His missing eye would never grow back (for that wound was old—too old for even the Great Bell to mend) but the tip of tail he lost at the Paladine Arch grew long and green.

Leah's jaw healed swiftly, her face pink and beautiful once again. Chance's missing ear blossomed, then flipped up like a soldier standing at attention. The cuts and scrapes of Rooker Flynn's handsome face faded, but the pirate was too distracted to notice, kissing one of the lusty women at his side like a thirsty man.

The wounds on Jack Swift's chest grew pink, fading to thin white slashes. The scars of the dæmon's claws would never completely heal, so deep and dark was the majik behind them, and Jack lived with their pale remains the rest of his days.

When he hugged his father, Jack felt all ten fingers of his dad's strong hands against his back.

A new energy took hold of the crowd; those who were struck with sickness, disease, or wounds suddenly found themselves in the pink of health, and those who were not ill at all were filled with more energy and vitality than they had known since the time they were children.

And so they danced and shouted and celebrated with wild abandon, all cheering the name of Black Jack.

Jack yelled and hollered gamely along with the rest of them until a gentle hand touched his arm. It was Andy Ibis; the tailor from Glyn Aker. He held a large folded piece of cloth in his hands, and presented it to Jack.

"For you," he said, a shy smile on his lips. "My wife and I made it. A…a kind of banner for your victory. It shows Nepenthe and depicts two of your great battles: the moment you flew from the heights of Akkadian, and your victory over the white serpents of Werrun Fell." Andy's face grew flushed. "I hope you like it."

Jack unfurled the banner. Stitched in white against a black background was the emblem Andy Ibis had made for him:

Jack stood in shock, staring at the familiar symbol, but when he turned to thank the tailor, the man was gone.

"Come," said Valerian Tsai, throwing one arm over Jack's shoulder. "I have something to show you."

They walked together through the scorched trees atop the Black Rock. "The Great Bells have the power to heal all living things," said Valerian. "Not just flesh and bone. As you see." He pointed upward.

Jack looked and saw life returning to the trees.

Charred bark turned from black to a healthy brown; limbs that had burned away blossomed, bursting forth with life, green leaves unfolding like tiny flags, rippling in the branches above their heads.

A white vine emerged from the blossoms, growing, reaching through the branches. More vines sprung from it, twisting and intertwining around themselves until a great ring appeared in the boughs above, a perfect circle of living vines, blooming with white flowers.

The Elaña came back to life.

"I owe you an apology, Jack," said Valerian. "I tried to keep you from your father all this time, and I must tell you why. I made a promise to Xiang-lo—to *Alex*—that I would return him to the day he left, to the Badlands, to his son."

"And then," Dad said, "I got sick."

"And the will of the *wikk* brought you here, Jack. And I simply had no choice. If the two of you met, if you saw each other, there would be *no* chance to set things back the way they were. For you, Jack, it has been seven years since your father left. But for Xiang-lo, it has been only a tenday."

It was true—Alex Swift had not aged at all since that day in the desert. Jack glanced at his dad, unable to stop this grin.

Valerian spread his hands. "I can take you back home, but not to the time when you left each other. I'm sorry, Jack. I took your childhood from you, and from your father. I can never repay that debt, and I only hope you can find forgiveness for me."

Jack looked at his dad, then to the grey man. "You didn't take my father from me, Valerian. You brought him back."

The grey man smiled. Jack Swift took Valerian Tsai in his arms and hugged him tight.

"Now"—the grey man cleared his throat—"I think you are ready to go home."

Jack nodded.

"Home?" said the pirate. "That'll take *forever.* He's from all the way out on the Hyperion Mesa—some little hole called Chi-ga-go."

Jack laughed. "Rooker, do you want to come *see* my hometown?"

"Ahh, ya seen one little jerkwater village, ya seen 'em all." There were three young women vying for Rooker's attention, and the pirate was doing his best to be generous. "Here," he said to Jack. "Ya might need this when ya get there."

The pirate reached into his coat and pulled out seven sticks of bamboo: Nepenthe. He tossed her to Jack.

"I get around a bit myself, kid. Next time I'm out that way, bet yer boots I'll drop in." The pirate flicked the brim of his hat and walked away. "See ya, boychick." As he strode down the hill, Rooker Flynn grabbed the nearest beauty around her hips and whispered something in her ear that made her giggle.

Li-Bao and Chance said their goodbyes and walked away together, arms slung over each other's shoulders. Nightingale disappeared into the trees. Shadow took one last look at the young man and padded away.

Something tugged at Jack's sleeve. He looked down and saw Fuji. The blue-and-gold tam held out something in his tree-frog fingers.

Apple.

Jack took the fruit. The little tam chirruped, scurried away into the blossoming leaves, and was gone.

Jack turned to find Leah. She cocked her head, green eyes sparkling. "I think I'll miss you more than I expected, *doktar.*" She smiled and kissed him square on the lips.

It was a long kiss. Valerian *harrumphed*, and she drew away.

"Be well," she said. And for the rest of his life, whenever he smelled cherry blossoms in the springtime, Jack Swift thought of

Leah Archer.

Had they known they would see each other again, in another land at another time, perhaps they would have said more. But for now, that was how they parted, each quietly longing for the other.

"All *right*, boyo," said Memphis, clapping his great hands together. "Let's take a jump and see where we land."

Above them, the jaunt gate glowed white for the last time.

Dawn rises over Chicago. A group of cardinals cluster on the Stearns Bridge, pecking hungrily at a discarded hunk of bread. A bright flash startles them into the air. When they have scattered, three men stand in their place.

Memphis sniffs the air. "Not bad," he says. "Four, maybe five, hours off."

"From what?" asks Jack.

"From the time you left."

Jack's eyes widen. "Five *hours?*"

"Will o' the *wikk*, boyo. You're back in time for breakfast. Now"—Memphis smiles—"if you don't mind, I'd like to get going. I really don't know how you people take that *smell*. I need to get these boots off and feel some grass between my toes."

"Wait," says Jack and wraps his arms around the trol, hugging the great rhinoceros with all his strength. "Thank you."

A warm grin spreads over Memphis's broad face. "You're welcome, Jack. Goodbye."

Memphis winks and falls backward over the bridge.

As Jack runs to the guardrail, he sees the trol is gone—a small brown-speckled lizard falls through the air and hits the water with a tiny splash. Something underneath the water rumbles, Jack feels the tingle of the *wikk* for the last time, and then it is gone.

They eat a lot of pizza. Neither of them can stop talking. Jack tells his adventures of pirate ships and fighting beasts; Dad tells his of finding gates and kidnapper knights. Everything is new. Everything from the first word to the last to the way it sounds when they say it. They can't stop touching each other, in hugs, squeezes, and grabs.

Jack has other adventures to tell from *before* Keymark.

A sharp rap sounds on a dirty door, and it opens.

"Ms. Rose Haig?"

"Yeah?"

"I'm Jack Swift's father, he won't be requiring your services any longer, you won't see him again." He slams the door in her face.

They eat more pizza.

They go to the Field Museum. They grab a Bears game at Soldier Field. The Shedd Aquarium. The Museum of Science and Industry. They're just places to go while they keep talking. They have no plans whatsoever, Valerian's sack of platinum coins paving the way to anywhere.

Finally, they wind up at the Bean. The proper name for the thing is the *Cloud Gate*, but in Chicago, you call it the Bean because it's a giant mirror in the shape of, well, a bean. People pose for pictures in front of it, underneath it, holding it up; there are a million different photos that have been taken there. At the center of the Bean is a place where all the reflections come together. Jack realizes for the first time this place feels very much like a jaunt gate, a circle that pulls at your soul.

He and Dad reach up and touch the surface, marveling at the reflections.

Jack looks into the mirror and sees himself standing side by side with his father, both of them reaching out to each other.

And that, of all the amazing things before or since, was the best magic Jack Swift ever saw.

Note from the Author

You can call me Andy. We're friends now.

You have listened to me tell Jack's tale through the magical connection a book provides, a psychic conduit directly from me to you. You honor me with your time, and I humbly thank you for your kind attention.

If you enjoyed *The Legend of Black Jack* please review it and share the book with your friends. I would love to continue Jack's story and only your enthusiasm can make that happen.

I want to thank Ryan Wing, James Turner Mohan, Simona Molino, Diana Weir, Andrew Straatman, Brian Snyder, Kate Jarosinski, Mom, Dad, Will, and my wife Gloria. I love you more.

I hope we have the opportunity to talk again; I have more to tell you.

—A. R. Witham

About the Author

A. R. Witham is a three-time Emmy-winning writer-producer and a great lover of adventure. He is the world's foremost expert on the history of Keymark. He loves to talk with young people and adults who remember what young people know. He has written for film and television, canoed to the Arctic Circle, hiked the Appalachian Trail and been inside his house while it burned down. He lives in Indianapolis.

If you would like a sneak peek at his upcoming stories, please reach out to him:

arwitham.com